NIGHTHAWK

By Kathryn Le Veque

Print Edition

Text by Kathryn Le Veque
Cover by Kim Killion

KATHRYN LE VEQUE NOVELS

Medieval Romance:

The de Russe Legacy:
The White Lord of Wellesbourne
The Dark One: Dark Knight
Beast
Lord of War: Black Angel
The Falls of Erith
The Iron Knight

The de Lohr Dynasty:
While Angels Slept (Lords of East Anglia)
Rise of the Defender
Steelheart
Spectre of the Sword
Archangel
Unending Love
Shadowmoor
Silversword

Great Lords of le Bec:
Great Protector
To the Lady Born (House of de Royans)
Lord of Winter (Lords of de Royans)

Lords of Eire:
The Darkland (Master Knights of Connaught)
Black Sword
Echoes of Ancient Dreams (time travel)

De Wolfe Pack Series:
The Wolfe
Serpent
Scorpion (Saxon Lords of Hage – Also related to The Questing)
The Lion of the North
Walls of Babylon
Dark Destroyer
Nighthawk

Ancient Kings of Anglecynn:
The Whispering Night
Netherworld

Battle Lords of de Velt:
The Dark Lord
Devil's Dominion

Reign of the House of de Winter:
Lespada
Swords and Shields (also related to The Questing, While Angels Slept)

De Reyne Domination:
Guardian of Darkness
The Fallen One (part of Dragonblade Series)

Unrelated characters or family groups:
The Gorgon (Also related to Lords of Thunder)
The Warrior Poet (St. John and de Gare)
Tender is the Knight (House of d'Vant)
Lord of Light
The Questing (related to The Dark Lord, Scorpion)
The Legend (House of Summerlin)

The Dragonblade Series: (Great Marcher Lords of de Lara)
Dragonblade
Island of Glass (House of St. Hever)
The Savage Curtain (Lords of Pembury)
The Fallen One (De Reyne Domination)
Fragments of Grace (House of St. Hever)

Lord of the Shadows
Queen of Lost Stars (House of St. Hever)

Lords of Thunder: The de Shera Brotherhood Trilogy
The Thunder Lord
The Thunder Warrior
The Thunder Knight

Highland Warriors of Munro
The Red Lion

Time Travel Romance: (Saxon Lords of Hage)
The Crusader
Kingdom Come

Contemporary Romance:

Kathlyn Trent/Marcus Burton Series:
Valley of the Shadow
The Eden Factor
Canyon of the Sphinx

The American Heroes Series:
The Lucius Robe
Fires of Autumn
Evenshade
Sea of Dreams
Purgatory

Other Contemporary Romance:
Lady of Heaven
Darkling, I Listen
In the Dreaming Hour

Multi-author Collections/Anthologies:
With Dreams Only of You (USA Today bestseller)
Sirens of the Northern Seas (Viking romance)
Ever My Love (sequel to With Dreams Only Of You) July 2016

Note: All Kathryn's novels are designed to be read as stand-alones, although many have cross-over characters or cross-over family groups. Novels that are grouped together have related characters or family groups.

Series are clearly marked. All series contain the same characters or family groups except the American Heroes Series, which is an anthology with unrelated characters.

There is NO particular chronological order for any of the novels because they can all be read as stand-alones, even the series.

For more information, find it in **A Reader's Guide to the Medieval World of Le Veque**.

Table of Contents

The Next Generation Wolfe Pack

The Wolfe

William and Jordan Scott de Wolfe

Scott (Wife #1 Lady Athena de Norville, issue. Wife #2, Lady Avrielle Huntley du Rennic, issue.)

Troy (Wife #1 Lady Helene de Norville, has issue. Wife #2 Lady Rhoswyn Johnstone, issue.)

Patrick (married to Lady Brighton de Favereux, has issue)

James – Killed in Wales June 1282 (married to Lady Rose Hage, has issue)

Katheryn (James' twin) Married Sir Alec Hage, has issue

Evelyn (married to Sir Hector de Norville, has issue)

Baby de Wolfe – died same day. Christened Madeleine.

Edward (married to Lady Cassiopeia de Norville, has issue)

Thomas

Penelope (married to Bhrodi de Shera, hereditary King of Anglesey and Earl of Coventry, has issue)

Kieran and Jemma Scott Hage

Mary Alys (adopted) married, with issue

Baby Hage, died same day. Christened Bridget.

Alec (married to Lady Katheryn de Wolfe, has issue)

Christian (died Holy Land 1269 A.D.) no issue

Moira (married to Sir Apollo de Norville, has issue)

Kevin (married to Lady Annavieve de Ferrers, has issue)

Rose (widow of Sir James de Wolfe, has issue)

Nathaniel

Paris and Caladora Scott de Norville

Hector (married to Lady Evelyn de Wolfe, has issue)

Apollo (married to Lady Moira Hage, has issue)

Helene (married to Sir Troy de Wolfe, has issue)

Athena (married to Sir Scott de Wolfe, has issue)

Adonis

Cassiopeia (married to Sir Edward de Wolfe, has issue)

Author's Note

Welcome to Patrick's story!

This one has been a long time in coming (because I wrote *The Wolfe* twenty years ago), but I think it's well worth the wait. We essentially get to see the next generation of the de Wolfe Pack, right about thirty years after *The Wolfe* takes place and about fifteen years before *Serpent*. So this is a peek into the world directly after Jordan and William's story.

Patrick is a big man destined for greatness. We also get the sense that he is his father's favorite son. The family clearly loves him and he loves them. It was great fun giving Patrick a journey that took him from a serious knight to a man who had fallen in love and learned a thing or two about life (and women). I hope you think so, too.

Things to note: Berwick Castle features in this story and at this point in history, it was at the transition point between the end of Henry III's reign and the beginning of Edward I. Edward made major improvements to the castle and to the city's defenses, but I've taken artistic license in moving up those improvements and having Henry start them. I'm about ten or so years off from Berwick really having been a massively built-out bastion, but there is little history about the castle prior to 1296, so I've taken the liberty of having the stone rebuilding of the castle starting a little early.

Castle Questing doesn't exist – it is a creation of my imagination although I can tell you exactly where it sits on the topography of England. More fun things to note: the knights bearing names you will recognize – Hector and Apollo de Norville are the sons of Paris and Caladora de Norville, while Alec and Kevin Hage are the sons of Kieran and Jemma Hage (*The Wolfe*). Kevin has his own story in *SCORPION*, set when he's about fifteen years older. Anson du Bonne is the son of

Stephen and Genisa du Bonne (*The Gorgon*), Damien d'Vant is a son of Dennis and Ryan d'Vant (*Tender is the Knight*), and Colm de Lara is a grandson of Sean de Lara and Sheridan St. James (*Lord of the Shadows*).

Patrick has several brothers and we get to meet two of them in this book. Scott and Troy de Wolfe have also appeared in *SERPENT* and they will eventually have their own books. And as a final note – look for a new character, Kerk le Sander, in this book. He has quite a story behind him, coming out in my 2017 novella duet with NYT Bestselling author Sharon Hamilton entitled *The Trident Legacy*. It would seem that Patrick's friend, Kerk, has an immortal soul. Fun stuff for great reading!

More characters of note: Daniel de Lohr makes a brief appearance in this book. His novel is *SHADOWMOOR* and Chad de Lohr is mentioned as well as the de Shera brothers (*SILVERSWORD* and *THE THUNDER LORD*, respectively), so if you haven't read any of those books yet, they are must reads. In my world, everything is tied in!

In all, this is a great adventure with a good deal of passion in it because Patrick and Brighton have an incredibly strong bond, as you will see. As always, I truly hope you enjoy the book!

Love, Kathryn

PROLOGUE

In the heady days of Yore,
There upon a moonlit shore,
Came the knight known one to all,
A warrior to heed the nightbird's call.
Son of The Wolfe, a legacy born,
A knight of skill, yet his heart was torn.
A heart so bold, demanded by kings,
Yet a lady claimed it, an angel without wings.
A nightbird with a warrior's soul,
This is now the story told.

~ 13th c. chronicles

July, Year of our Lord 1269
Westminster Palace, London

"NO ONE ENTERS a room like a de Wolfe." An elderly man with a head of gray hair and one droopy eye spoke. "Even from afar, the moment the doors open and you enter, it is as if all of the air in the room is sucked out by your mere presence. Your father has the same gift, by the way. Think not that you are special in that regard, Patrick de

Wolfe."

An enormous knight with eyes the color of jade and hair as dark as a raven's wing was halfway into the great hall, heading towards the dais at the far end where the king sat. Great Henry, he was called, an elderly man who had ruled England for over sixty years. But the king was in poor health these days and his voice was barely above a whisper, which meant that one of the king's advisors had to repeat what the man had said so that Patrick could properly respond.

All was formality and pomp within the great hall of Westminster Palace. A mere knight was expected to respond to a kingly statement.

"You have accused my father of such things before, my lord, or so I have heard," Patrick responded loudly, as the king's hearing was also very poor these days. "In fact, he told me that you have refused to allow him to enter a room before you for that very reason."

He was drawing nearer to the king now, his heavy leather boots clapping against the wooden floor in loud succession; *boom, boom, boom....* Such a big man made very big sounds. He closed the gap quickly for he'd come with a purpose. An audience with the ailing king was something quite rare these days, even for the man who had been appointed to serve as the monarch's personal Lord Protector. He had only just reached London and had sought audience with the king, which was granted as soon as the king was feeling better. Now, Patrick had arrived and the king could not be more pleased about it.

But the one person in the room who wasn't pleased with Patrick's arrival was, in fact, Patrick himself. He wasn't one to be nervous or jumpy as a rule. But as he came to a halt before Henry, he realized that he was just that – *nervous.* God help him, he was here with a purpose in mind and if the king didn't grant his request, he wasn't entirely sure what he was going to do. It all came down to the case he would lay out for the king and how convincing he would be. He'd done nothing but pray about it, fervently.

Sweet Christ, let Henry be in a generous mood today!

From the way Henry was staring at him, however, it was difficult to tell just how generous Henry intended to be. The man had been ill for quite some time now and his skin was yellowish, his eyes sunken. The silks swathing his body hung on the man's thin frame. He was staring at Patrick as if the man's most recent remark had offended him and, in truth, Patrick was coming to wonder if it had. He and Henry had an easy repartee, as easy as one could have with the king, because Henry owed much to Patrick's father, William de Wolfe. It was on that basis that Patrick had established his own relationship with the monarch and answering the man as he had was something that usually gave Henry a grin. But, at the moment, that grin wasn't forthcoming.

Patrick waited.

The grin finally came.

"Cheeky devil," Henry muttered after a moment. Then, he lifted a finger in Patrick's direction. "Now, you will tell me why you seek audience with me. You are my Lord Protector, Patrick. I have been waiting for you to arrive and assume your duties."

"I know, my lord."

Henry's eyebrows lifted when there was no more of a reply than that. "Have you nothing more to say?" he asked. "You have never before sought an audience and I will admit that it has me concerned. Speak, now. Tell me what is of importance to you."

Patrick looked at his monarch. Now, the moment had come. Swallowing away his nerves, he brought forth the speech he had planned for weeks. Now, the time was upon him to speak it. He could not delay.

"This is a formal request, my lord," he began quietly. "It seemed best served to follow protocol and request an audience."

"So you did. What do you want?"

Patrick took a deep breath, eyeing the advisors that stood around the king, knowing he was about to bare his soul for all to hear. It was an embarrassing event, to be sure, but the needs of his heart were stronger than his pride. The damnable, stubborn de Wolfe pride. But he hardly cared; if the seasoned men surrounding Henry thought him weak for it, then so be it.

"My lord, it has been the pinnacle of my career as a knight to personally serve you as my father once did," he said in his rich, melodious baritone. "As a warrior and as a subject, I could ask for no higher honor. But several weeks ago, I had an experience with a raiding band of Scots that has changed my outlook on life. It happened at nearly the same time I received word that I was to come to London to attend you, in fact."

"Is that so?"

"It is, my lord."

"And how did this encounter with the Scots change your outlook?"

Patrick cleared his throat softly again; his nerves were still there. "Because there was a woman with them," he said quietly. "She was a captive, you see, so I brought her back to Castle Questing for my mother to tend. My lord, it is because of this woman that I wish to return home."

The king may have been ill and hard of hearing, but he wasn't daft. He could see something reflected in Patrick's eyes, something he'd once seen in the eyes of Patrick's father. *It is because of this woman that I wish to return home.* Long ago, Henry remembered William de Wolfe in a seemingly similar predicament with the woman who turned out to be Patrick's mother. A man so in love that nothing else in the world mattered, not even the prestige of serving a king. He sighed faintly.

"You want to marry this woman, I take it?" he asked.

"I already have."

Henry was intrigued. "You have?" he said, astonished. "I did not know this. Who is she?"

"Her name is Brighton de Favereux. Her mother is the sister to Gilbert de la Haye of Clan Haye."

"I know of him. But who is her father?"

Patrick seemed to falter. "Magnus, my lord."

"Magnus de Favereux? I do not know him."

Patrick shook his head. "Nay, my lord," he said. "Magnus of Norway. He is the Norse king."

That seemed of great interest to Henry as well as his advisors. The great Earl of Canterbury, Daniel de Lohr, happened to be in London at this time and had been visiting with Henry at Westminster. Patrick had known the man since childhood and he liked him a great deal. The House of de Lohr and the House of de Wolfe went back generations and were great allies. It was Daniel, standing on Henry's right, who spoke.

"Who told you this, Patrick?" Daniel asked calmly.

Patrick turned his attention to the big, blonde earl, still powerful and agile in his sixth decade. "Her nurse, my lord," he replied. "An old nun was also captured by the raiding party and she told me of Bridey's true identity. It has been kept secret for many years."

Daniel's eyebrows furrowed. "The lass has been raised by nuns?"

"Aye, my lord."

"A daughter of the king of the Northmen?"

"Aye, my lord."

Daniel looked at Henry, greatly perplexed by the story that was coming forth from one of the most reasonable young knights he had ever known. It sounded like madness to his ears but he knew there had to be a complex reason in there, somewhere. Henry, equally perplexed, held up his hand to silence both Daniel's questions and Patrick's replies. He was only growing more confused by the moment.

"Patrick," he said with quiet insistence. "I think you had better start from the beginning, my son. You have married a woman who is the daughter of the king of the Northmen and a Scottish mother?"

Patrick nodded, feeling some of the nervousness drain out of him as he realized that Henry was truly interested in what he had to say. So was Canterbury. These were two men he greatly respected. There was so much to tell he hardly knew where to start. With a sigh, he focused on the beginning of his tale, going back to that night that changed the course of his life. He hadn't known it then, of course, but he certainly knew it now. And he wanted nothing more than to head back north to Northumberland, to the borders between Scotland and England, where his family ruled.

Where Brighton was.

Fixing the king in the eye, he began his complicated tale. "I have, my lord. And I did not have permission to do it."

"I see. And now there is trouble?"

"Possibly, my lord."

"Then start this story from the beginning. And leave nothing out."

Patrick complied. "It was a dark and stormy night…."

CHAPTER ONE

⌖ The Tale Begins ⌖

Five weeks earlier
Whiteadder Water, near Foulden
England/Scotland Border

THEY HAD BEEN waiting for them.

Hidden by a grove of black, shadowed trees beneath a crystal-cold night sky following a violent rain storm, the *reivers* from Scotland never had a chance. The English overlords from Berwick Castle had been alerted by their patrols that a raiding party of Scots was heading away from the coast after having ransacked an English settlement.

The English patrols had kept track of the *reivers* as they'd headed inland, sending word to their lords at Berwick because they knew that the castle, held by the House of de Wolfe and a garrison for the English king, would send a highly-trained squad of men to intercept the Scots. Rumor had it that they had a woman with them. Based on the accounts of the village that had been raided, the woman had been a spoil of war.

Fearing it was an Englishwoman that had been abducted fed the bloodlust of the English from Berwick. By anticipating the movements of the *reivers*, the English had been waiting for them as they'd passed through a lesser-traveled road heading south. Once the group passed into England, those in the trees swooped on them.

The Nighthawk had found his prey.

The fight had been chaotic. Somewhere along the line, the *reivers* had picked up more men. So by the time they hit the trees where the Nighthawk and his men were waiting, they had nearly doubled in number.

But it was of little matter; the men waiting in the darkened trees were English knights of the highest order, men born and bred for battle. Sons of de Wolfe, de Norville, Hage, and a few others rushed to the road to engage the Scots, who had been startled by the confrontation. Mostly, the *reivers* were men who raided and ran. They didn't necessarily go looking for a fight.

But the English did.

The *reivers* were well-armed and, quickly, the English found themselves in a heavy battle. But they, too, were prepared for the fight with a myriad of weapons. Beneath the three-quarter moon, maces struck, swords chopped, and flails swung. Men were grunting with effort, groaning in pain. Because the *reivers* wore cloaks covering their dirty bodies, the English were aiming for the cloaks as sort of a broad target-practice. Hitting a cloak meant hitting a Scotsman and, soon enough, the Scots began to go down. Some of them were even running off, heading north from whence they came. But most were scattering as the English gave chase.

The Nighthawk wanted no man left alive. He wasn't known for his mercy in a fight. Sir Patrick de Wolfe was the man known as the bird of prey, mostly because he was cunning, swift, and merciless, all glowing attributes as far as the English were concerned. But as far as the Scots were concerned, the man was a vicious predator and someone to be avoided at all costs. Unfortunately, on this night, there had been no avoiding him.

He was out for blood.

One man's blood in particular. Patrick had led the charge from the trees into the group of raiders and he had singled out the man in the lead, the one that seemed to be driving the rest of the group. That was the man he wanted to subdue because he was sure if he eliminated the leader, the *reivers* would fall apart. But the man he'd singled out had proved wily. He'd kept himself buried back in the roiling mass of men during the battle but Patrick hadn't lost sight of him. It had been something of an effort to kill others in order to get to him, but like a dog with a bone, Patrick hadn't let go. He'd gone right for him and when the man realized he was being pursued, he'd broken off from the group and headed back the way he'd come.

Patrick's heavy-boned war horse was fast because the animal had enormous strides so he could cover a good deal of ground in a charge or in a chase. He put that talent to work as he closed the gap between him and the man he was pursuing, which made his target panic. Things began flying off the horse to lighten the load on his strained horse, including a large burden that went flying off, landing somewhere along the side of the road. Patrick wouldn't have thought anything of it except he swore he saw a pair of legs as it went flying. *A man*, he thought, although they'd been slim legs. *Mayhap a woman*. In any case, he couldn't think about it now. He had a target to catch.

It hadn't taken him long to catch his victim because the man's horse simply wasn't faster than Patrick's. He caught up to the man, grabbing him by the arm and dragging him off of his horse. As the man struggled and kicked, Patrick dragged him back to the outskirts of the skirmish where two of his knights waited. He tossed the man to the knights, massive men with powerful bodies and powerful weapons. The last he saw, Kevin Hage and Apollo de Norville had made short work of the prisoner, acting upon Patrick's standard order in a situation like this.

Leave no man alive.

With the leader evidently killed, the fighting had died down a great deal with dead *reivers* on the road and only a few others showing futile resistance. Patrick could see one of his knights, Sir Hector de Norville, in a fairly nasty fight with a big Scotsman. Patrick kept an eye on the fight, not wanting to help Hector because the man would undoubtedly view any assistance as an insult. The de Norvilles were arrogant that way. So he backed off, looking around to see if there was any other clean-up he could help with.

And then, he saw it.

Back down the road where his target had thrown the body off his horse, Patrick could see something moving in the moonlight. The man who had been thrown was staying close to the ground, crawling away from the road. Patrick spurred his war horse towards him. He didn't want the man to get away so he was fully prepared to take a second hostage. Reaching the edge of the road, he could see that the figure had entered the tree line. It was quite dark in the trees at this time of night and, frustrated, Patrick didn't want to lose his quarry. Dismounting his steed, he charged off into the bramble.

The trail wasn't difficult to follow, mostly because of the sounds. He could easily follow simply based on the sounds, which were decidedly female. Intrigued, he plowed through a hedge, across a creek, and through a bramble of trees on the other side. There was quite a bit of foliage, making it difficult to see in the three-quarters moon, but he happened to catch a glimpse of something moving off to his left, along the ground, and he grabbed it. The object turned out to be a foot. He yanked hard.

With a scream, a woman was pulled from the bushes she had been trying to hide beneath. Patrick couldn't really see her, but he knew it was a woman because men didn't make that kind of sound, – high-pitched and breathy. Once he'd yanked the woman free of the concealing leaves, he grabbed her arms and hauled her to her feet.

"Name, woman!" he boomed.

The woman was very light in his grasp, small, with fragile bones. He could feel it in his grip. She was gasping with fright.

"Bri-Bri-!"

He shook her, hard. "Speak!"

"P-please do not hurt me!"

A Scots accent, he thought with disgust. It was faint, but detectable. He'd heard stronger. Surely she was complicit to whatever the *reivers* had been up to. Although merciless in battle, he wasn't one to kill a woman, no matter if she was the enemy. Therefore, without another word, he bent over and threw the woman upon his shoulder easily, marching back the way he had come.

The battle on the road had died down considerably by the time he returned. There were at least two dead men along the side of the road that he could see. Still more men, wounded or dead, were lying on the actual road itself. He could see his knights milling around, making sure their enemies wouldn't rise up again to attack them. The wounded were being put out of their misery. They were still feeling the rush of battle, their movements edgy and their voices sharp. When men on the road tried to move, they were kicked back down.

Patrick made his way across the road and over to his knights, dumping his load onto the ground next to the dead. She landed with a grunt.

"Secure this one," he told the knights. "She will return with us."

It was a surprising command given the fact that they didn't normally take prisoners. As the knights moved in to do his bidding, the young woman held up her hands.

"W-wait!" she cried. "P-please, m'lord – I am not with them! T-they took me from Coldingham!"

That terrified plea gave Patrick pause. Having heard there were captives among the *reivers*, he was coming to wonder if there wasn't some truth to that rumor.

"Coldingham," he repeated. "The priory?"

"Aye, m'lord."

"What is your name?"

"B-Brighton de Favereux, m'lord."

Patrick's gaze lingered on her. He couldn't see much in the moonlight, but one of the things he could see was an enormous pair of eyes gazing back at him. He could make out the shape of a delicate face, but little more.

"These men abducted you from the priory?"

"T-they did, m'lord."

She had a bit of a stammer in her speech, but it was hardly noticeable. She had a rather sweet voice, somewhat husky. The more she spoke, the more he realized that the Scots accent wasn't too terribly strong, either, at least not enough to offend him. It was just a hint of a lilt.

"Can you prove this?"

The woman faltered. She looked down at herself as if searching for some proof upon her person. Then, she lifted her arms.

"Y-you can see that I am wearing the garb of a postulate, m'lord," she said. "If it is proof you seek, it is all I have to offer."

Patrick snapped his fingers to his knights, pointing to the young woman, and they swarmed on her, checking out what she was wearing beneath the dirty, smelly cloak. They pulled at it and sniffed, inspecting the fabric. When Kevin lifted his head to Patrick and nodded shortly, that was all Patrick needed as confirmation.

"She will return with me," he commanded quietly. "Make sure there is no one left alive and then gather the men. We must return."

The knights were on the move, one of them physically lifting the lady off of the ground and carrying her away while the second knight went forth to carry out the remainder of Patrick's order. Seeing that the battle was finished for the most part, Patrick followed the knight carrying the lady. When the man set her to her feet, Patrick was standing right next to her, waiting.

"So the Scots violated the sanctity of the priory," he said quietly. "That is not their usual target. What was their purpose?"

The woman was flustered and unsteady on her feet. "I-I do not know. They did not say."

"Then how did they manage to wrest you from the place? It is fairly fortified, as I recall."

The woman shook her head. "I-I do not know, to be truthful," she said. "I-it was at Matins that they came. We were moving from the church to the cloister when they swept through. I could hear shouting, with men on horses racing through the garden. Sister Acha was running towards me and calling my name. Before I could go to her, men took me from the abbey. I believe they took Sister Acha, as well, because I saw a man on horseback claim her. Y-you must make sure she is safe, m'lord. Please."

Patrick turned in the direction of the road where there were several bodies on the ground. He had a rather ominous feeling that a nun might be among them. Word of a dead nun spreading among the English would put every Scotsman on the borders at risk for the priests of the north would rally the vengeance cry. English lords would take up that cry and send out men whose sole job would be to exact revenge on behalf of the church. Patrick had seen that before. Now, the circumstances surrounding the raiding Scots was taking an ominous turn.

"You will remain here," he told her. "Do not move. My men, who do not know you, might mistake you for an enemy. Stand here and wait for me to return."

The woman simply nodded her head, nervously, pulling the smelly cloak more tightly about her as Patrick headed off to the road.

Still muddy from the storm they'd had only a few hours earlier, Patrick began to move through the dead on the ground. He counted at least twelve of them and there were probably more who had fled and were cut down by his men. In fact, none of his men were on the road any longer, either lingering on the edges of the road or missing altogether. He knew those men must have gone after *reivers* who had fled so he wasn't concerned about them. But the litter of bodies on the road *did* concern him; he was concerned there was a wounded or dead nun among them.

His concern was well-founded. Bunched up between two dead Scots was a tiny body. He thought it had been just a cloak at first, perhaps something that had fallen off of one of the men in the heat of battle, for it sincerely looked to be just a piece of clothing. But he poked it with his boot on a hunch and heard it groan. Bending over, he rolled the body onto its back.

A small face, covered in mud, was the first thing he saw. Then, two eyes became evident, although it was difficult to see because of the darkness of the night. He could see eyeballs glittering and that was the only way he knew the eyes were open. In fact, he might have thought the person to be one of the *reivers* except for the fact that he or she was truly tiny. That seemed odd to him somehow. He couldn't help the sense of foreboding in his heart that continued to grow.

"Speak," Patrick said quietly. "Who are you?"

The person, sunken cheeks heaving in and out, took a few gasping breaths. "Bridey? Is she injured?"

It was a woman. His heart sank. That was when Patrick received confirmation that he had, indeed, happened upon the other woman in this equation. It was clear that she had been badly injured in the fight that had gone on, a helpless victim torn between the *reivers* and the English knights.

"Are you from Coldingham also?" he asked.

The woman tried to move her head but she couldn't quite manage it. "Aye," she muttered. "I am. Is Bridey well?"

"You mean the other woman? She is well."

That seemed to ease the old woman a great deal. In fact, she let out a hissing sigh that was long and unsteady. Then it seemed as if she didn't draw another breath for a very long time after that. Patrick thought she might have passed away, in fact. But she resumed breathing after a time, reaching up a weak hand to grasp at him. She ended up grabbing the hem of his wet, muddy tunic.

"Time is growing short, my lord," she breathed. "Thou must listen to me. It is important, for the sake of Bridey."

Patrick shifted so he was kneeling beside the woman, one mailed knee in the mud. He wasn't particularly interested in a deathbed confession, for he had a good deal to attend to already and listening to a nun's final words was not among those tasks. But something in the woman's glimmering eyes caused him to take pause. For in spite of his deadly reputation, Patrick was a man with a heart. It was close to the surface, unlike others, which was something of a dangerous trait. He wasn't as hardened as most when he probably should have been.

Therefore, a dying old woman had his attention. He tried not to feel foolish for it.

"Quickly, now," he said with quiet firmness. "Tell me what you must."

The woman didn't let go of his tunic. "Brighton de Favereux is the woman in your possession."

"She gave that name."

The old woman tugged on his tunic. "That is only what others must know of her," she whispered. "They must never know the truth. To know the truth about her would cause strife and war as thou cannot comprehend. I have been with her since her mother brought her to Coldingham, and it 'tis I who have tended her every need. Bridey is as a daughter to me, my own child."

Patrick was torn between curiosity and impatience. "You are her nurse," he said. "I understand. What is this truth you speak of?"

The old nun gasped as if suddenly in pain. For a few long moments, she didn't say anything and Patrick wondered if this was, indeed, her end. But she eventually took another breath, steeling herself. Her grip on Patrick's tunic tightened.

"Thou art English," she murmured. "It is now thy duty to protect her. The child that was given unto me was the daughter of Lady Juliana de la Haye and Magnus Haakonsson, King of the Northmen. Her real name is Kristiana Magnusdotter but she was given the name Brighton de Favereux to conceal her identity. Lady Juliana, a daughter of the House of de la Haye, was given over to the Northmen as a hostage, to cement a peace between the kings of the North and Clan Haye. Lady Juliana was meant for a Northman king but she lay with Magnus, then a prince, and beget his child. She was sent home in shame because of it. When the child was born, Lady Juliana was forced to her to bring the child to Coldingham in order to protect her. No one must know of the child's existence for it can only bring the Northmen down upon us. If they know she is here, they will want her back. She must never go back."

Patrick had to admit that he was quite astonished at what he was hearing. In fact, it was too incredible to believe. His brow furrowed. "Sister, I am not a fool," he said steadily. "I do not believe in these wild tales and rumors. But the lady will be protected until she can be returned to her family. You have my promise."

His response seemed to seize the old woman up. Her other hand came up to grip his tunic, pulling at him, as her eyes widened, her muddy face taut with panic.

"Nay!" she gasped. "Thou must not return her to her family! They wish to forget of her existence! And thou must not permit Clan Swinton to take her, for they shall only ransom her and barter her as one would cattle. Please… thou must protect her, good knight. Deliver her to Jedburgh or Kelso. The church is the only safe place for her."

The woman was starting to make an impact on him. Her sense of urgency, of fear, was palpable and as much as he didn't want to admit it, the sense was infecting. He could feel it. He tried to shake it off.

"The church is *not* safe for her if the raiders could get to her," he pointed out. "Are the Scots who abducted you part of Clan Swinton, then?"

"Aye. Somehow, they have discovered her true identity."

"And they came to take her?"

"Aye."

Patrick was increasingly confused about the situation. A Northern princess hiding amongst the postulates at Coldingham Priory? And a rival clan to Clan Haye coming to abduct her, to ransom her? It made absolutely no sense to him but. somehow, he believed it. As wild as the tale was, he believed it. He doubted a dying nun would lie to him but, still, it was a fantastic tale.

"Then I promise you that she will not come to harm as long as she is within my custody," he said quietly. "She will be safe."

"Swear it upon thy oath, sir knight."

"I swear it."

The old woman's grip abruptly loosened and she sank back into the mud as if all of her strength had suddenly left her. She lay there, her eyes gazing up into the dark sky as if seeing her heavenly reward above, waiting for her. Her features, so recently tight with fear, eased tremendously.

"Then I am content," she murmured, although he barely heard her. "God will reward thee, sir knight. Bridey is a sweet and lovely soul. Pray thee be kind to her."

With that, she took her last breath and was gone. Patrick found himself looking down at the woman, wondering what on earth he'd gotten himself in to this night. If what the old nun said was true, the *reivers* this night were far more than a simple raiding party – this had been an organized band of Scots looking for a prize. That being the case, it was also fairly likely that if they knew of the girl's identity, as the nun suggested, then he could take her to any of the priories along the border but, sooner or later, someone would try to come for her again. *Clan Swinton*, the old nun had said. Ancient rivals of Clan Haye. Nay, they wouldn't give up if they wanted the girl badly enough.

So he found himself in an unwanted quandary. He didn't want to be responsible for a prize between clans but his sense of duty, and now a promise to a dying woman, had put him in that position. This wasn't what he needed, not now. He was due to leave Berwick soon, to go to London to assume a post as part of the king's personal guard. It was a prestigious post and one he very much wanted, one that brought great honor to his family. It wasn't every knight that was asked by Prince Edward to assume the post as a personal Guard of the Body to King Henry, a position coveted by many but offered to few.

He had been the lucky one.

Wealth, admiration, and distinction would be his. His mind and ego had blown up around what was to come. But now… now, Patrick felt as if he was at the precipice of something that might keep him rooted to the north. He couldn't simply dump the woman on his father and then run for London. Nay, that would be cowardly of him. But he didn't want to remain in the north and defend the prize he'd taken from the *reivers*, either, as if it were his responsibility to do so. In truth, now it was.

God's Bones, why had he agreed?

Damn that old woman!

Using the old, muddy cloak worn by the nun, Patrick wrapped the small form up tightly in it and carried her over to the nearest knight. Sir Hector de Norville was directing some of the men-at-arms as they rifled through the bodies, turning to see Patrick approach. Tall, muscular, and sinewy, Hector was a congenial and intelligent man, married to Patrick's younger sister, Evelyn. He pointed to the bundle in Patrick's arms.

"What have you found?" he asked. "Were there valuables with this group?"

Patrick shook his head. "Nay," he said. Then, he nodded his head in a motion that suggested Hector follow him. Hector did and, a few feet away from the men-at-arms, Patrick came to a halt and faced Hector. "These men raided Coldingham Priory and came away with two women from what I've been able to deduce," he said quietly. "There is a young woman, who seems uninjured, and then this old nun, who was mortally wounded in the fighting. The nun needs to be taken to the nearest church so they can dispose of the corpse."

Hector pulled back the muddy cloak to see the old woman's dirty, white face. He covered it back up. "God's Bones," he hissed. "A dead nun is never a good thing. The English around here will frown greatly upon her death, Atty."

Atty was what the knights called Patrick, who had been a quiet child with a speech impediment. Unable to say his own name, it had come out as "Atty", which was now a term of endearment among the family. Patrick no longer had the speech impediment. The little boy who'd had it had grown into a mountain of a man, but the nickname had never gone away. Now, it was part of him. Hearing that affectionate name come from Hector along with the very same thoughts he'd had about the dead nun and the displeased English somehow hammered home the seriousness of the situation, in more ways than one. With a heavy sigh, he nodded.

"I know," he said. "Where is the nearest church?"

Hector cocked his head thoughtfully. "St. Cuthbert in Berwick is the nearest one I can think of."

"Then have one of the men take the body there. Tell them… tell them we simply found her dead along the road. Tell them no more than that. If we do, we may have more trouble than we can handle."

Hector understood. "I will do it myself."

Patrick nodded. "Good," he said. "I cannot tell you the rest of what the old nun told me, not here, but I will when we return to Berwick. An interesting tale to say the least."

Hector cocked an eyebrow, interested, but said nothing. That time would come. Obediently, he took the dead woman from Patrick's arms and headed off in the direction of his steed.

Patrick watched the man walk away, trying to push aside what the old nun had told him, but he couldn't quite manage it. His thoughts turned towards Lady Brighton. *Bridey*, the nun had called her. Perhaps Lady Brighton could shed some light on the situation, but not here. Not now. They had to clear out and return to the safety of Berwick Castle before they found themselves set upon by more Swintons or any of the other clans in the area. The southern part of the Scots border was full of men eager to slit an English throat. Even though Patrick was half-Scots through his mother's side of the family, he was all English in training and mentality, and he had no desire to engage in any more battle this night.

"Patrick!"

The shout came from off to his left, over where several English were piling together the Scots dead. He could see one of his knights heading in his direction and, even though the night didn't illuminate the man's features, he knew who it was simply by the shape and size of him.

Sir Alec Hage, the eldest of the Hage brothers under his command, was broad-shouldered but he was also quite tall, which made him a rather intimidating character. With his father's dark blonde hair and his mother's amber-colored eyes, he possessed none of the Hage characteristic cool and all of his mother's fire. He, too, was half-Scots through his mother, who happened to be a cousin of Patrick's mother.

In fact, Patrick was related to all of the Hage and de Norville knights because their mothers were all cousins. Alec also happened to be married to Patrick's younger sister, Katheryn. It made for a rather big family and there was little delineation between cousins and brothers. As far as Patrick was concerned, they were all his brothers.

"Swinton bastards," Alec said as he drew near. "Every one of them."

Patrick nodded. "I know," he said. "Who told you?"

Alec pointed off to the group of dead. "They did before I slit their throats," he said. "Did you know they raided Coldingham Priory?"

"I did."

"They would not tell me why."

Patrick waved him off. "I think I know," he said. "Pile the dead and return to Berwick. Once we arrive, gather the knights. I have a need to speak with them."

Alec couldn't help but sense something serious behind that request. "What is it?"

Patrick shook his head, his expression guarded as he glanced around at the dead and wounded. "Not now," he said, slapping Alec on the arm. "Return to Berwick in a hurry. Do as I ask."

Alec didn't question him again. There was something mysterious afoot but he didn't press; he knew that he would be told soon enough. Therefore, he went about his duties as Patrick continued on to the spot where he left the abducted postulate. He could see the young woman in the darkness, sitting on the cold ground. The more his gaze lingered on her, the more he thought about what the old nun had said.

A Northman princess....

He could still hardly believe it even as he looked at her. Was this woman truly the daughter of Magnus, King of the Northmen? Being this far north in England and situated along the coast, he'd dealt with a few threats from Northmen, but very few. They mostly traveled far to the north, along the coast of Scotland and into the outlying islands. A few of those islands were still ruled by Northern kings and they battled the Scots for control constantly. Nay, there wasn't much of a threat at Berwick. Their threat came from the Scots. But having a king's daughter in their midst might change their luck.

"D-did you find Sister Acha?" the young woman asked anxiously when he drew within earshot.

Her question jolted him from his ominous thoughts. "I found her," he said. "She was mortally wounded and has since passed on. One of my men is taking her to St. Cuthbert in Berwick so they can attend to her."

He probably should have couched the news more tactfully because the woman's face screwed up in grief as she struggled to bite off her tears. "S-sweet Jesus," she breathed, crossing herself reverently. "I-I had hoped not to hear that news. I had prayed so dearly for her safety. S-so… dearly…."

Patrick realized he should have been kinder in telling her that the woman who had raised her since birth was dead. "I am sorry," he said, feeling a stab of remorse. "But I have ensured that she will be tended to. And I promised her that I would look after you and I intend to do just that. We must return to my home."

The young woman wiped her face furiously, wiping at the tears from her eyes and the mucus from her nose. "W-why can I not return to Coldingham?" she asked. "That is *my* home."

Patrick reached down and grasped an arm, pulling the woman to her feet. "No longer."

She looked at him with great concern. "W-why not? Why can I not return?"

He began to walk her in the direction of his charger, pulling her with him although she wasn't moving very well. She seemed to be resisting. "Because it would be foolish to take you back there," he said. "The Scots found you there once. They will find you again. We are, therefore, going to Berwick Castle."

That seemed to cause the woman to dig her heels in even more. "B-but I do not wish to go there," she insisted. "P-please, Sir Knight… I simply want to return to Coldingham."

Patrick paused, turning to the woman in the darkness. It seemed to be growing colder, he thought, for their breaths were hanging heavy in the air. More than that, the mood was cold between them as well. She was no longer grateful he had saved her from the Scots, now wanting to go back where she came from. He wondered if she would be foolish enough to fight him on it.

"Lady, I will *not* return you to Coldingham, so you will kindly stop asking," he said flatly. "I promised your nurse that I would ensure your safety and that means you will not return to the priory."

She was puzzled. "B-but I do not understand *why… w*hy would the Scots return for me? Why do they want me?"

She was asking the question as if she truly had no idea of what was really happening. Patrick was coming to think that the young woman didn't realize she had been the target of the raid. Based on what Alec had told him, that the Clan Swinton men had admitted to raiding Coldingham, and also based on what the dying nun had told him about the lady's identity, he was more convinced than ever that the old woman hadn't been lying to him. There were strange forces at work here, all of them directed to this rather confused young woman, and he was fairly certain this wasn't the place to tell her. He needed to get her to safety and then he would seek his father's advice on what to do with her. It was truly the best solution he could come up with at the moment.

"You must trust me, my lady," he said, his voice quiet. "I cannot return you to Coldingham and arguing with me will not make it so. Know your place, be obedient, and do as I say for now. To go against my wishes would not be in your best interest."

There was a threat in that statement and, fortunately, the young woman seemed to understand that. She simply lowered her head and shut her mouth, wiping at her eyes now and again and he knew she was still weeping for her nurse, for the situation in general. Truth be told, he didn't blame her. The entire circumstance had been somewhat shocking for them all.

With an enormous hand on her arm, Patrick pulled her over towards his war horse, an animal amongst many war horses that the knights were now mounting. The contingent of knights escorted their commander and the lady hostage back to Berwick Castle, for on this night, the battle was over for the moment as the *reivers* were quelled and their prize wrested from them.

But as Patrick headed back towards Berwick with the lady seated behind him on his horse, he was seriously coming to wonder about the events of this night and how they might affect his plans for the future.

He was about to find out.

CHAPTER TWO

Berwick Castle

BERWICK CASTLE WAS a bastion that had changed hands many times over the years. Originally built by the Scots at an important location over the River Tweed, it was a very strategic location that had originally been a timber outpost. The English managed to capture it several years ago and turned it into a stone fortress with a massive set of walls that surrounded it, the city, and even went all the way down to the river.

After the recapture from the Scots those years ago, the fortress was immediately turned over to the House of de Wolfe to manage. Patrick had been a boy when the rebuilding of Berwick had started. His father, along with his close ally, the Earl of Teviot, both had armies stationed there to ensure the Scots wouldn't try to reclaim it and, for twenty years, no one had really tried. There had been a few threats, but nothing the English couldn't repel.

And the building continued. The stone walls had gone up, as had a massive keep, a hall, towers, kitchens, stables, and even a chapel. To reinforce the city, walls had been built around the village of Berwick using the citizens as labor. Now, the city walls and a very proud castle kept the populace of Berwick safe from harm. Ever since Patrick had taken command of the castle four years earlier, the Scots had been unwilling to test The Wolfe's brightest and best son. No one wanted to tangle with the Nighthawk and that was the way Patrick liked it.

Riding in from the north, Patrick and his men had passed through one of the several fortified gates into the city. Lit up with torches and staffed with heavily armed de Wolfe men, this gate was the one that faced north, towards the borders, so the dozens of men that staffed it waved Patrick through. His party then continued on down the road that paralleled Berwick Castle somewhat until they came to the entry gate of the castle, known as the Douglas Tower, which led to a wooden bridge that spanned a fairly deep gully with a stream carving through the bottom of it. They called it "the chasm". That bridge dumped into the main gatehouse of Berwick, an enormous structure known as the donjon.

The castle was lit up with torches against the dark night as men patrolled the grounds with both dogs and weapons at their side. Berwick was so large that, at any given time, there were more than a thousand men stationed there and the command structure was strictly regimented. Even the lowliest soldier had assignments and duties, as Patrick ran the castle in a stringent military fashion. This close to the Scots border, there could be nothing less than strict discipline on the part of the English.

This was the last line of defense between England and the threat from the north.

It was into the bailey of this massive structure that Patrick took the postulate from Coldingham. The men that had ridden in with them knew their duties so Patrick didn't bother to say anything to them as he dismounted his steed and pulled the woman off behind him. The keep was directly in front of them, the largest structure in the entire fortress.

Four stories in height, the uniquely-shaped keep soared over the countryside, a beacon that could be seen for miles. Forming an odd "U" shape, it had many chambers in it as well as storage vaults on the lower floor. As Patrick approached, he could see two small figures standing in the doorway. He knew the shapes were his sisters, Katheryn and Evelyn, before he ever saw their faces. They were the chatelaines of his keep, married to his knights as they were, and they were very astute. They would know when their husbands and brother would be returning. As soon as his boot hit the bottom step of the flight that led up to the second floor entry, the women came down to greet him.

"Well?" Katheryn said. "Was anyone hurt? Where is my husband?"

Patrick glanced up at the woman who looked a good deal like his mother; lovely, with honey-colored hair and big green eyes. "No one was hurt," he said. "Your husband is back with the men, somewhere. He will be here shortly."

While Katheryn was satisfied, Evelyn still had questions. "Where is Hector?" she asked, but she was mostly focused on the lady in her brother's grip. Interest in her husband's location faded for the moment as she inspected the disheveled woman. "Atty, who is this?"

Patrick stopped to look at the source of his sister's interest and when he did, he was in for a surprise. He'd not seen the lady in the light. When his gaze fell on her, he felt a bolt of shock run through him – illuminated in the torches was a woman of unearthly beauty. She had brown hair, but it wasn't just any shade of brown; he could see highlights of red and gold reflected in the torchlight. Her face was sweetly oval, as he'd noticed in the darkness, and she had the biggest eyes he'd ever seen in a shade of blue that was reflecting pale in the weak light. Her nose was pert, her skin like cream, and her rosy lips shaped like Cupid's bow.

He'd never seen anything like her in his entire life.

"This… this is Lady Brighton de Favereux," he told his sisters, sounding like an idiot because he was so caught off guard by the woman's beauty. "We saved her from a raiding party."

"Is she a prisoner?"

"Nay. But…."

Before he could continue his sentence, his sisters rushed forward and pushed him out of the way, taking hold of the disheveled, frightened lady. Patrick found himself overwhelmed by small women, trying to keep hold of the postulate but being summarily removed.

"My goodness," Katheryn said with concern as she put her arm around Brighton's shoulders. "What a harrowing experience, my lady. But you are safe now. Come with us and we shall tend to you."

Another thing about Katheryn that reminded Patrick of their mother was the fact that she could be rather pushy. "Not now, Kate," he said sternly. "I have many questions for the lady. I must ask now while the situation is fresh in her mind."

Both Katheryn and Evelyn scowled at him. "Look at her," Katheryn said, sounding like she was scolding him. "Are you so cruel that you cannot see how exhausted and terrified she is? She needs food and a bath. We shall tend to her and when she is fed and rested, then you may question her. Are you truly so heartless, Patrick, that you would think of your own demands over her comfort?"

He frowned. "This has nothing to do with being heartless," he said. "I have many pressing questions for the lady and…."

"They can wait," Katheryn said firmly, pulling Brighton up the stairs with the help of her sister. They were boxed in around her, preventing Patrick from retaking her. It was a rather smart tactical move against him. "Let us feed the woman and make her comfortable. Then you can go on with your tasteless military interrogation."

Patrick knew he was licked. He shook his head in frustration, watching his sisters escort Brighton up the stairs and into the keep, being most attentive and kind to her. It would be futile to argue with them, he knew, stubborn women that they were. As he stood there with his hands on his hips, greatly annoyed, he felt someone come up beside him.

"Was that my wife?" Alec asked. "What is she doing with your captive?"

Patrick's eyes narrowed at the man. "She stole her from me," he declared. He jabbed a finger at the keep entry. "That bold, unreasonable woman that you married stole my captive. Hell, she isn't really my captive. I do not know what she is, but whatever she is, I have need of her before the women have their way with her. Go and summon fifty men, heavily arm them, and bring them to the keep. I will need just that many men to fight off my sisters so I can have my captive returned."

Alec fought off a grin. "You could just ask them to return her, you know."

Patrick's scowl grew. "I *did* ask them, you dolt," he snapped. "And you see how they answered me – they pushed me away and took the lady into the keep. Christ, these women are going to be the death of me. When you married Katheryn and asked if she could come with you to Berwick, I should have denied you!"

Alec couldn't help but laugh now. "I have astonishing news for you, Atty," he said. "You are three times their size. You could easily overwhelm them both and take back your captive. Did you not realize that?"

He sighed heavily and turned for the keep entry, wearily dragging himself up the stairs. "They would only tell my mother and then she would beat me," he said. "I realize that I am a grown man, Alec, but you of all people should understand the fear of a mother. In fact, I fear your mother more than my own. She might actually try to gouge my eyes out."

Alec's laughter grew. "But she would do it lovingly."

"Aye, Aunt Jemma would lovingly gouge my eyes out and then lovingly tend me as I am blind for the rest of my life. God, what a prospect."

He could hear Alec's snorting behind him. "It is the lot we lead in life, having strong and stubborn mothers," he said. "Do you still want me to gather the men or are you going to go crawl into a corner and cry now?"

"Gather the men. I shall cry later."

Snickering, Alec turned and headed back to the gatehouse where the knights would be gathered. There were several men in the command structure of Berwick that needed to be part of Patrick's meeting and Alec went about to spread the word. As he headed off into the bailey, Patrick continued up the stairs and into the vast keep.

The entry to the keep was cool and dark, lit only by a pair of sconces on the wall with fatted torches, burning hot into the dimness. The foyer was two-storied, the height of it cutting into the third floor above. An unusual mural staircase that was built into one wall, led to the floor above. From the third to the fourth floor was a spiral stair built into the width of the north wall. The keep was a glorious piece of architecture, most fitting for the de Wolfe knights and ladies who lived inside it.

But Patrick wasn't concerned about the stunning architecture of the keep. He was lingering on the woman his sisters had stolen away from him. Straight ahead was a small hall, one used by the family for meals or for meetings. He headed into it, seeing that there was a fire blazing in the hearth, stoked by thoughtful servants. He caught sight of one of the house servants, an older man whose sole duty it was to make sure every room had peat and wood and kindling, and he sent the man to the kitchens for wine.

He needed it.

As the man fled, Patrick yanked off his helm and set the thing on the table. He began pulling off his gloves, gloves made for hands that, when fisted, were the size of a man's head. There was nothing about Patrick de Wolfe that was small, in any fashion, and his father liked to take credit for his size when his mother knew full well it was the Scots in him that gave her son his great strength and size.

The gloves came off and Patrick tossed them onto the table as well, his mind shifting from the captive woman to the old nun and what he'd been told. He began to remove his weapons, unstrapping his broadsword and laying it, and the sheath it was lodged in, upon the tabletop as well. Soon, the sword was joined by a host of smaller daggers he kept on his body. He was just removing the last one when he caught movement out of the corner of his eye, turning to the chamber entry to see both of his sisters with Lady Brighton between them.

Surprised, his brow furrowed as he gazed upon them. "Why are you here?" he asked, annoyance in his tone. "You made it clear that I was not to be part of anything you were planning."

Katheryn twisted her lips wryly. "It seems that Lady Brighton insists on speaking to you first," she said, clearly unhappy. "She will not let us help her until she does."

Patrick's gaze was on Brighton although he nearly smiled at his sister's tone; she had been thwarted in her maneuvers against her brother and was displeased. He felt somewhat victorious. He pointed to the bench seat against the table.

"Then sit, Lady Brighton," he said politely. "Kate, this does not involve you and Evie. You will leave us, please. I will send for you when I am finished with the lady."

"Do not be too unkind to her, Patrick. She is very weary and frightened."

"I will not be too unkind."

Frowning, Katheryn and Evelyn quit the room under protest. They would push Patrick around to a certain extent but when it came to his command, they knew better than to argue or question him. As his sisters wandered away, dejected and unable to help their visitor, Patrick waited until he heard them mount the stairs to the third floor before speaking.

"My sisters mean well," he said. "Did they introduce themselves?"

Brighton nodded. "T-they did, my lord."

His gaze lingered on her. Here, in the light of the chamber, she was even more beautiful than he had initially observed. He liked the way the corners of her mouth tilted upward when she spoke and her eyes, he was coming to note, were the color of the ocean. It was a great and mysterious blue. He tore his gaze from her long enough to push his weaponry away, far down the table, so there was nothing between them. Heavily, he sat opposite her across the table and was preparing to speak when Brighton interrupted him.

"I-I must know why you feel it would be unsafe to return me to Coldingham, my lord," she said nervously. "I-I know you told me not to ask you again and to be obedient, and I swear that I am trying to be obedient, but I simply do not understand any of this. I was taken from

Coldingham by despicable raiders and I will be ever grateful to you for saving me from them. I-it never occurred to me that I would not be returning to my home and you will not tell me why."

She was verging on tears by the time she was finished. Her bravery was only holding out so long and Patrick could feel a tug of sympathy towards the lady and her plight. He was coming to think, perhaps, he had been too hard in his response to her, shutting her down and expecting her not to react to it. Or it could be the fact that he was being sucked into those big eyes, now filled with frightened tears. Those eyes were having an effect on him, like nothing he'd ever experienced before. He struggled to ignore his attraction to them as he considered his answer.

"When the Scots broke into the priory, did they say anything to you?" he asked, avoiding her statement for the most part. He had questions of his own that he needed answers to. "Did they ask you any questions at all?"

Brighton blinked, quickly wiping away the tears, as she was genuinely trying not to weep. Sister Acha had always told her that crying was a weakness and she did not want to appear weak to this enormous knight. He frightened her, too, but she didn't want him to know. She was trying very hard to be brave in the face of a most unsettling day.

"T-they did not ask any questions, my lord," she said, trying to think back to the chaos of the morning. "It all happened so quickly. But… but I think I heard them asking for me by name."

"What did they say?"

"I-I think they asked for de Favereux. At least, I thought I heard them ask some of the nuns."

"What happened when they asked?"

Brighton chewed her lip, pondering the question. "I-I saw them strike a nun who did not answer them," she said. "A-another nun finally pointed to me as Sister Acha tried to take me away. It was quite chaotic, you understand. Everyone was fearful for their lives."

Patrick nodded. "As well they should be," he said. "But did you not find it strange that they asked for you by name?"

Brighton nodded hesitantly. "T-to be truthful, I had not thought on it at the time," she said. "B-but I am thinking of it now. All I know is that the Scots swept into Coldingham and came away with me and Sister Acha. I do not even know why they would want someone like me. I am no one."

So she must not know her true heritage, Patrick thought. *Either that, or she does not think that I know and does not want to give herself away.* He regarded her carefully for a moment, considering what he would say next.

"Are you certain?" he asked, watching her reaction. "What is your lineage?"

She shrugged. "I-I was brought to Coldingham as an infant," she said. "Sister Acha raised me. She is the only mother I have ever known."

He could see her tearing up again at the thought of the old nun who had perished that night. "What did she tell you about your lineage?" he asked.

She sniffled delicately, wiping at her eyes. "T-that I was a bastard," she said quietly. "We prayed on it often."

"But nothing else?"

He was probing her and she sensed it. His line of questioning indicated that he was searching for a specific answer. Cocking her head curiously, she gazed at him with that wide-open look that told him that she more than likely had no idea what he was talking about. There was something in her expression that suggested utter innocence.

"W-what else could there be, my lord?" she asked.

He hoped to God she wasn't playing him for a fool. Either she was genuinely naïve or she was extremely manipulative. Given the fact that she had been raised in a convent, he couldn't imagine she was the latter. Overall, he didn't get that sense from her. He opened his mouth to reply but the servant he'd sent for wine returned, bringing a pitcher and a single cup. The man looked stricken when he saw the lady at the table also, but Patrick simply took the pitcher and cup from him and sent the man away.

Putting the cup in front of Brighton, Patrick poured her a measure of wine before drinking directly out of the pitcher himself. After two large gulps, he set the pitcher down and wiped his mouth with the back of his hand.

"How old are you?" he asked her.

Brighton took a timid sip from her cup. "I-I have seen nineteen summers, my lord."

"And in all that time, no one has told you the story of your birth or your lineage?"

She was appearing increasingly curious. "N-nay, my lord. There is no story."

"Is that what you were told?"

"I-I told you all that I know." She lowered her gaze a moment, her curiosity turning into puzzlement. "I-is it important?"

Patrick felt as if he had no choice but to tell her. For her own sake, she needed to know. Or, at least he had to tell her what he'd been told. If she was truly being hunted, then she had a right to know it.

"Before your nurse passed on, she told me of your heritage," he said quietly. "While I have no reason to disbelieve what I was told, I cannot confirm it, of course. Your nurse told me that you are to be protected at all costs, my lady. She also told me that your real name is not Brighton de Favereux."

Brighton gazed at him for a moment, her eyes widening in surprise as his words sank in. "W-what do you mean, my lord?" she asked, puzzlement overwhelming her. "I-I do not understand."

Patrick found himself studying that utterly exquisite face, fixating on that for a moment before he realized she had asked him a question. Feeling foolish for being distracted, he turned back to his wine.

"Your Sister Acha told me that you were brought to her as an infant," he said. "That much you know. But what you apparently have not been told is that your mother was from Clan Haye and that she was given over as a hostage to the Northman to secure an alliance. Your mother lay with a Northman prince and you are the result. That Northman prince is now king of the Northmen and, somehow, the *reivers* that came to Coldingham had discovered your true identity. It was you they had come for, my lady, and you they managed to capture. I had received word from our patrols that there was a raiding party riding south, close to Berwick, and rumor had it that there were captive women among them. When I set out to subdue the raiders and rescue their captives, I had no idea what I was really getting myself in to but your Sister Acha managed to wrest a promise from me that I would keep you safe. And that, my lady, is why you cannot return to Coldingham. You are a valuable commodity and your identity has been revealed. Men want you and they will keep coming for you until they have you."

Brighton listened to his speech with increasing astonishment. By the time he was finished, her eyes were so wide that they threatened to pop from her skull. She stumbled up from the bench, a hand over her mouth in shock as she faced him.

"N-nay," she finally breathed. "That cannot be true."

"Your nurse told me it was true."

Brighton wanted very much to deny it but being that Sister Acha had told him such things, she couldn't, in good conscience, refute him. Sister Acha had never lied to her, not ever. But it didn't make any sense to her and confusion such as she had never known filled her mind.

"S-she must have been mistaken," she gasped. "Mayhap… mayhap her wounds had polluted her mind because what she told you is pure madness!"

"She did not seem mad, my lady."

"I-it is! It is madness! I am not… I am not who she said I am!"

"How do you know if you know nothing of your lineage?"

He had a point but Brighton wasn't really listening to him. Her mind was muddled with shock and the room began to rock unsteadily. All she could think of was a wild story from a dying woman's lips. It simply wasn't true, any of it! There was no way she could be the daughter of a Northman… *a king.*

She didn't have a drop of royal blood in her!

"I-I am a bastard," she said, sounding very much like she was pleading with him. "What you have said… you must have misunderstood. Sister Acha would not have told you such things!"

"That was exactly what she told me."

"You are lying!"

Patrick thought she looked rather unsteady. He stood up, hoping that he might calm her building hysteria. "I do not lie, lady," he said, his baritone turning gentle but stern. "I understand that it has been a difficult day for you so I will forgive you your slander. But the information I give is the reason I cannot return you to Coldingham. If what your nurse said was true, then your life is at risk, more than you know."

Brighton shook her head, turning away from him and putting her dirty hands over her ears. She was stumbling blindly for the door.

"I-I will not hear you," she gasped, feeling increasingly lightheaded. "I-I must return to Coldingham. I… must…"

She went down, fainting dead away in the doorway. Patrick rushed to her side, turning her over onto her back to make sure she hadn't hurt herself when she fell to the floor. She was out cold, now with what looked like the beginnings of a bruise on her forehead. Feeling rather guilty that he had somehow contributed to this state, he scooped her into his arms and headed for the stairs that led to the upper floors where Katheryn and Evelyn were lurking. He knew his sisters would take good care of the overwrought woman.

But even as he held her in his arms, he couldn't get past the fact that she was rather sweet and soft against him. She was average in height for a woman but long-limbed from what he could see, and that face… God's Bones, that face was fairly close to his as he cradled her against his chest. He found himself looking at her when he should have been looking at the stairs; the shape of her lips had his attention more than anything.

Curvy, perfectly formed, and lush… a woman of this kind of beauty didn't belong in a convent. In fact, it was a crime as far as he was concerned. Based on her perfection alone, he was willing to believe she was of royal blood because only a royal lineage would create something so flawless.

But as he looked at her, he was also aware of something else… that his desire to protect the woman was building. He'd only promised an old woman he'd do it because he'd had no other choice. And even as he'd ridden to Berwick with the lady behind him, he was regretting that he'd given his vow to protect her. He didn't need the complication. But now, looking into her pale face, he couldn't help the sense of protectiveness that swept him. It may have been foolish and misplaced, but he felt it nonetheless.

Perhaps there was a reason he'd ridden out with his patrol this night to stop the *reivers*. Normally, he didn't ride with war parties like that. But for some reason, tonight he had. Something had compelled him to go and now he was starting to see why. Perhaps God had wanted him in that place, at that time, because one of His most precious creations needed protecting.

Foolish thoughts, to be certain. But thoughts he couldn't seem to shake.

"WHAT IS SO important this night, Atty?" Hector asked as he leaned over to collect a cup of wine. "Our intercept of the raiding party was a success and we managed to recover one of the women. Why are you not happy?"

Patrick eyed the man. "I think we received more than we bargained for this night."

"What do you mean?"

Back in the small dining hall, Patrick was now surrounded by his men. When he'd taken Lady Brighton up for his sisters to attend to, his men had filtered in, including Hector, recently returned from his trip to St. Cuthbert's. Now, the small hall was full with de Wolfe, de Norville,

Hage, and three more knights that Patrick had left behind when he'd ridden off to intercept the *reivers.*

Sir Anson du Bonne, son of Baron Lulworth of Chaldon Castle, was a strapping man with reddish-gold hair and an easy demeanor. He was a well-liked man within the ranks and usually in command when Patrick was not at Berwick. The two other knights who were not related to de Wolfe, de Norville, or Hage were Sir Colm de Lara and Sir Damien d'Vant, men from very fine families, powerful and skilled warriors in their own right. Patrick particularly liked Damien, who had a wicked sense of humor and much the same personality that Patrick did. Big, blonde, and easy-going, Patrick considered Damien a friend.

Those three, along with the de Norville brothers, Hector and Apollo, and the Hage brothers, Alec and Kevin, rounded out the men in the room. The servants had brought forth more wine and cakes of oats and honey, something to feed big appetites, but Patrick wasn't eating. He was into his fourth cup of wine, feeling his head swim a bit, hoping it would ease these odd and unfamiliar thoughts he'd been entertaining.

A dead nun, a terrible secret, and Patrick was increasingly troubled by it all. So he stood by the hearth, trying to avoid the smoke that was spitting out into the low-ceilinged room as he gathered his turbulent thoughts.

What to tell the men….

"What I mean is that the raiders we subdued were not random outlaws looking for a convenient target," he answered Hector's question belatedly. "I mean that I was told they were looking for a specific victim. We interrupted their plans."

Hector frowned as he stood back from the table, nearer to the hearth because his bones were cold. "Be plain, man."

Patrick sighed heavily. "That woman I brought back to Berwick," he said. "Did any of you get a look at her?"

Hector and Alec looked at each other before shaking their heads. "I did not," Hector replied, looking to his brother, Apollo. "You were guarding her. Did you get a good look at her?"

Apollo, one of the youngest knights in Patrick's corps, nodded hesitantly. "Somewhat," he said, looking at Kevin, who was even younger than he was. "Did you?"

Kevin lifted his big shoulders. "A little," he said, looking back at Patrick. "I did not notice anything out of the ordinary with her. Why do you ask?"

It was a loaded question. "Before she died, the nun you took over to St. Cuthbert told me something about her," Patrick said, his gaze moving between Kevin, Apollo, Hector, and Alec. "I will tell you exactly what she told me – that the young woman we rescued this night, a woman who goes by the name of Brighton de Favereux, is really a bastard daughter of Magnus, King of the Northmen. Her mother is from Clan Haye who had been delivered to the Northmen many years ago as a hostage to ensure an alliance, only she became pregnant by Magnus when he was still a prince. The woman was sent home in shame and the child, when she was born, was taken to Coldingham Priory under an assumed identity. Apparently, no one but the old nun knew who the young woman really is and, as she lay dying, she asked me to promise to protect her. I did because I felt I had no choice, but now that I have had time to think on it, I fear I have assumed a massive burden for the House of de Wolfe. The *reivers* we intercepted, men from Clan Swinton, had gone to Coldingham with a purpose – to abduct this woman and we have taken their prize."

It was quite an unexpected tale and, by the time he was finished, all of the men in the room were looking at him with various degrees of disbelief. No one said anything right away, instead, glancing at each other as if trying to determine just how mad Patrick had evidently become. Alec finally spoke.

"She's a… a princess?" he asked for clarification. "Magnus… isn't he the Dane king they call the Law-Mender?"

"Aye."

"He is a fearsome warrior, Atty."

Patrick nodded. "So I have heard," he said, seeing the astonishment on their faces. "Be that as it may, that is what I was told about the girl."

Alec frowned. "Are you sure you did not misunderstand?" he asked. "Is it possible the old woman had lost her mind in her final moments?"

Patrick shook his head. "I did not misunderstand and it did not seem to me as if she had lost her mind," he said. "She seemed quite serious, in fact. I do not think a woman of the cloth, especially in her dying hour, would lie to me."

That made sense to the men in the chamber, lending credit to the tale. A nun most certainly wouldn't lie about something so terribly serious. Now, it was even more shocking if the news was actually true. Given the evidence presented, it seemed to be. Alec scratched his head, baffled, unsure what more to say.

"But how did Clan Swinton know of this?" he asked. "How could they possibly know?"

Patrick shrugged. "The old woman did not say," he said. "But it is clear that someone, somewhere, knew of her identity other than the old nun and the mother of the child. And that information has made its way to Clan Swinton."

"How old is the young woman?"

"Nineteen years, she tells me."

"And Clan Swinton is only seeking to claim her *now*? If all of this is true, how long have they been sitting on such information? And why make a move for her now?"

Patrick was just as puzzled as the rest of them. "I cannot answer that," he said. "What I do know, however, is that they will soon know that we have her. I would be willing to assume they will not be happy about it. They will want her back."

That was more than likely an understatement. Now, a simple encounter with *reivers* was taking a puzzling and serious turn. Hector actually shook his head as if trying to shake some sense into it. It was all quite overwhelming.

"You are telling us that the woman we rescued tonight is a Dane princess?" he asked. "And no one knew about her until now?"

Patrick cocked a dark eyebrow. "It seems that way," he said. "But the old nun said something rather ominous – that if the Northmen knew of her existence, they would come for her. She said that if word of her true identity got out, it would bring war and strife. It seems that something like that has already started, at least with Clan Swinton. Already, the struggle for her has begun."

Hector puffed his cheeks out, a gesture that suggested that statement was quite true. "She is Dane and Scots," he said. "That makes her quite rare. What a peace offering she could be with the clans to the north who fight the Danes on a continual basis."

Patrick lifted a finger. "Think about it," he said, as if something suddenly occurred to him. "Clan Swinton could ransom her to her father or sell her to the highest bidder in the highlands for the same purpose. Either way, they become wealthy. That could have been their purpose for abducting her."

"You are not going to want to hear what I have to say, Atty," Anson du Bonne spoke. Calm and reasonable, he made even the worst news sound as if they could not all live through it. "I have not seen this woman and I was not part of the skirmish earlier this evening, but in listening to you speak… holding this woman, and if she is who you say she is, could bring not only the Scots down upon us, but the Northmen as well. What if… what if Clan Swinton, outraged that they have lost their hostage, sends word to Magnus and tells the man that his bastard daughter is now being held by the English? The king will bring his longships onto the shores of Northumberland and we will have a nasty feud on our hands. With that in mind, remember that this woman is nothing to you. She is nothing to any of us. If you want my advice, I say give her back over to Clan Swinton and wash your hands of the entire thing. It is either that or you draw your family into a war that will tear the north apart."

Ominous words from the level-headed young knight, but it was advice that Patrick badly needed. He'd been thinking the very same thing, in fact, but had been reluctant to admit it. With another heavy sigh, he planted himself at the table, his features pensive as he mulled over the situation. Wearily, he rubbed at his chin.

"I cannot," he finally said. "I gave my word that I would protect her."

"Is your word worth more than the lives that will be lost if you keep her here at Berwick?"

Patrick's gaze flicked up to Anson. "My word is my bond," he said. "So is yours. Could you so easily cast off a vow, Anson? I think not."

"So your honor is more important than a coming war?"

Patrick was increasingly torn, knowing that Anson was simply trying to help him think clearly. But all he was doing was making him feel foolish and confused.

"I do not know," he muttered. "Mayhap, it would be best if I took the girl to Castle Questing and had my father decide what is to be done. I gave my word to protect the girl and I will not go back on it. But my father may have other ideas on what is to be done. I find that I cannot think clearly about it tonight."

Hector put his hand on Patrick's shoulder. "I think that is a fine choice," he said. "Take her to your father and let him decide. This should not be your decision, anyway. This is too big for one man to make."

There was truth to that. Patrick simply nodded. "Then I will leave for Castle Questing tomorrow and take the woman with me," he said. "Meanwhile, we should be vigilant for any armies moving in from the north, coming to reclaim their hostage. Patrols should be vigilant, as well. I do not want any of our men falling into the hands of Clan Swinton to be used as a hostage against the return of the girl."

Hector slapped him affectionately on the shoulder before moving to pour himself more wine. "Agreed," he said. "I will ride to Castle Questing with you, in fact. I will bring my wife, as she has not seen her mother in a month. She will want to go."

Patrick started to shake his head as Alec spoke. "If you take Evie, then Kate will want to come," he said. "You cannot take Evie to see her mother and not bring her sister. Furthermore, they will both want to bring the children. You know that."

Patrick held up a hand, annoyed that his simple trip to Castle Questing was now turning into a family event. "Fine," he snapped, "but make sure the women and children are ready by dawn. I will want to leave early if we are to make it to Castle Questing while it is still light. And set up a contingent of at least one hundred men as an escort. If we have women with us, I want them well-protected."

Hector nodded, settling himself at the table by Alec as they turned the subject to other things and began to drink heavily. Across the table, Anson and Colm and Damien were still looking at Patrick, still lingering on the subject of the Dane princess. It was a serious dilemma they found themselves in and no one felt that more keenly than Patrick. It was tearing him in all directions.

"Shall I ride with you to Questing, Patrick?" Damien asked. "Alec will be riding escort for his wife, and Hector for his, but you may need help with the lady."

Patrick shook his head wearily. "Nay," he said. "I will leave you in charge with Anson and Colm. Seal up this place and be vigilant until I return."

Anson nodded. "The Swinton Clan cannot muster great numbers to move against us, at least not by tomorrow or even next week," he said. "But they are allied with Dunbar and Black Douglas. I would be concerned that they would draw on that alliance if they tried to summon numbers against us."

Patrick knew that. He gazed into his empty wine cup, studying the dregs at the bottom as if to divine his future. "The truth is that they do not know we have the girl," he said. "We left no man alive from the raiding party and we brought those left with us back to Berwick. It will, therefore, take some time for the Swinton Clan to realize we were the force that met their raiding party and, in truth, they can only assume we took their prize. They will not know that for certain. That is what I need to speak with my father about. And, God's Bones, I do not need this complication right now, not when I am due to leave for my new assignment in London soon. This is not something I had anticipated nor do I want, but it seems that I am involved just the same."

Anson's gaze was steady from across the table. "I was wondering how long it would be before you brought that up," he said. "You do not want anything interfering with your new post with Henry."

"Nay, I do not. Especially not something like this."

The subject died down after that, mostly because no one knew what more they could say about it. There was much unknown revolving around the woman and the situation in general. There wasn't one man at the table that wasn't secretly glad that Patrick was taking the girl to his father at the mighty bastion of Castle Questing to, perhaps, make her William de Wolfe's problem. Not that Patrick was a coward by any means, because he wasn't, but the situation that had fallen into his lap was too big for one man to handle.

Even a lap as capable as Patrick's.

Unbeknownst to his men, Patrick's thoughts were revolving around the lady as well, but in a different fashion. After his fifth cup of wine, he finally left the small hall, heading to the staircase that led to the upper floors. He was fairly tipsy at that point but something was urging him to see to Lady Brighton's health after her fainting spell. He was quite certain she was fine, with his sisters to tend her, but there was something pulling at him that demanded he see for himself. He would never admit that to his men, of course, especially after the conversation they'd just had about the woman. So he felt a bit deceptive and sneaky as he lied about seeking his bed but, instead, headed to see to the lady.

A Norse princess. Clan war. Northman war.

All of those things were spinning around in his head, made worse by the drink, but above it all, he could only think of the fact that the lady intrigued him so. It was purely her beauty and he knew that. He was hoping it was something that would pass, but he couldn't shake the sense of attraction. He was coming to realize that he didn't want to.

As torn as he was at the moment, he did know one thing – as much as he professed not to let anything interfere with his new post with Henry, something told him that breaking his vow to the old nun would be more difficult than he imagined. And not all of it had to do with his honor.

Much of it had to do with his intrigue in the beautiful young woman who had quite easily captured his attention.

He was a man in trouble.

CHAPTER THREE

"WHAT DID YOU say to the woman to upset her so?" Katheryn demanded, though not unkindly. Her voice was full of concern. "She was hysterical, Atty. What nonsense did you tell her?"

It was dark and quiet at this hour. Standing on the landing of the third floor living quarters, which was more of a corridor than it was actually a landing, Patrick tried not to look too guilty or too defensive in the face of his sister's question. The amount of wine he had in his veins, however, was making it difficult. As a man who tended to ride on his emotions, wine only made it worse.

"It is no nonsense, I assure you," he said quietly. "What did she tell you that I said?"

Katheryn gazed up at her older brother, rather perplexed by the entire situation. "Something about Dane kings and royal blood," she said softly. "What *did* you tell her?"

Patrick didn't want to answer the question although, strangely enough, it wasn't because he didn't want to tell her personally. He knew he could trust her; Katheryn wasn't a gossip. But he found he simply didn't want to go through the entire explanation again. Perhaps when he was less tipsy, he would.

"I will tell you later," he said, peering over her head and into the darkened chamber beyond in an attempt to locate the lady. "Alec should be heading up to bed shortly. We must move the lady to another chamber. Has she calmed sufficiently?"

Katheryn nodded. "She has. She is resting now."

"Where do you intend to put her for the night?"

"I have sent Evelyn to prepare the smaller chamber at the end of the corridor, the one with the beautiful view of the river. That way, I will be close by if she needs anything."

Patrick turned to look down the corridor, seeing an open door at the end and a faint light moving around. "The chamber next to mine?"

"Aye."

Somehow, he drew an odd satisfaction out of knowing the lady would be so close to him. He wondered if his sister could see it in his expression so he tried to appear unnaturally detached.

"Thank you for your kindness in tending her," he said, "but this will not be a permanent arrangement. I am taking her to Questing tomorrow and you and Alec shall be going also because Alec thought you would like to see Mother. Since the lady has nothing but the clothes on her back, I was hoping that you could prepare a few things for her, things that a lady might need on a journey. I am not entirely sure how long she will be at Questing, so anything you can loan her to wear or to use will be appreciated, I am sure."

Katheryn simply nodded, eyeing her brother in the weak light. Her gaze was somewhat probing. "There is something strange in the air, Atty," she said after a moment. "What is it about this lady that has you so rattled? What is really going on?"

He looked at his sister, realizing he hadn't appeared as detached as he'd hoped. "I do not know what you mean," he said. "I am not rattled. And there is nothing strange about her or the situation."

That wasn't the truth but he was trying to deflect Katheryn's questions. She was very intuitive and he didn't want her knowing his mind or his thoughts, especially not when he didn't even know them. As far as the truth behind Lady Brighton, his sister would know soon enough. He just didn't feel like talking about it.

Katheryn must have sensed his reluctance because she didn't press him. She simply waved him off and stepped back into her chamber.

"You needn't worry about the lady tonight," she told him. "I will take good care of her. She will be ready to leave in the morning. Are you going to sleep now?"

Patrick realized his sister wasn't going to let him see the lady because she was keeping him out of the room, guarding the door like a dog. So he simply nodded his head.

"Aye," he muttered. "I should try to catch a few hours of sleep."

"Still having trouble sleeping these days?"

"Still."

Katheryn wasn't unsympathetic. Patrick was known to be a terrible sleeper, made worse when he was worried or troubled. She wondered if he didn't look terribly worried or troubled right now, although he didn't seem willing to admit or elaborate on it. He was a man who tended to tell her his thoughts and feelings based upon the close relationship they shared, but tonight, that didn't seem to be the case. She could sense that there was much more he wasn't telling her.

"How much have you had to drink tonight?" she asked.

"Enough."

"Enough to help you sleep?"

"Probably not."

"I will bring you a tonic. It will help you sleep."

He made a face. "None of those tonics. They taste terrible and do nothing."

Katheryn cocked a well-shaped eyebrow. "I have a hammer that will do much better than the tonics will but you never let me try it."

He fought off a grin as he turned in the direction of his chamber. "Get away from me, you brute."

He could hear her giggling as he walked away.

Wearily, Patrick made his way down to the end of the corridor where his large chamber faced over the bailey and the donjon. It was a corner room so he had a view of the southeast and east exposures. It was a comfortable chamber for the garrison commander and he had a good many possessions stashed inside – a large table with maps, chairs, cushions, a wardrobe with a good amount of clothing, gifts and trinkets given to him over the years, and an enormous bed that was quite messy. It was comfortable enough but the problem with the chamber was that he could hear everything going on in the bailey below, and he was very attuned to any sounds or movements by his men. It was a terrible chamber for sleeping in.

Still, he tried. It was his chamber, his bed, and he was happy here. Head muddled with drink and his thoughts whirling, he stripped off his clothing and fell into bed, hoping to shut out the world for a few hours. Given what had happened that night and what he was potentially facing, he suspected shutting the world out was an unrealistic expectation. He knew he wouldn't be able to shut his mind off long enough to sleep.

He was right.

"I HOPE YOU will be comfortable in this chamber, my lady," Katheryn said. "I have sent for hot water because I am sure you would like to bathe before retiring. It has been a trying day for you."

Brighton stood just inside the doorway, still wrapped up in her smelly cloak and coarse woolen clothing. She was exhausted and not feeling particularly well after fainting earlier. All she really wanted to do was sleep but it was difficult to refute Lady Katheryn, who had been quite kind to her. The woman was grimly determined to be of service and Brighton didn't want to insult her. But, given the day she'd had, her manners weren't at their best. Her patience was brittle.

"I-it has, my lady," she said. "To be truthful, all I want is a little food and sleep. That is all I require."

"Nonsense." Evelyn came in behind her, her arms full of garments. She went over to the bed, throwing everything down. "A bath will do you a world of good. Kate, this is everything I believe will fit her."

Katheryn went over to the bed to inspect what had been brought. "I recognize these," she said as she pulled forth a dark green wool. "This was yours, was it not?"

Evelyn nodded. "I could wear these before I gave birth," she said. "But since my last child, they no longer fit around my breasts or even around my hips. Although Mother has suggested I simply alter them, Hector has had new clothing made for me so I really do not need them. Our guest is welcome to whatever will fit."

It was extremely generous and Katheryn held up the dark green surcoat, looking at it in the light of the blazing hearth. Her gaze moved between the garment and Brighton, still standing near the door, watching everything around her with suspicion and some fear. The woman appeared grossly uncomfortable.

"As I explained, Lady Brighton, my brother will be taking you to Castle Questing in the morning," Katheryn said, trying to make their guest feel more relaxed. "You will need clothing to travel with and I believe these garments will fit you. Mayhap after you have bathed, you would like to try these on?"

Brighton looked at the clothing on the bed and in Katheryn's grip. Her composure, her patience, was slipping further and further.

"P-please," she sighed. "I… I simply wish to be left alone. A little food and sleep is all I require. I do not wish to try on clothing and I am completely opposed to leaving for anywhere other than Coldingham Priory. Will you please… *please* go away and leave me alone?"

She wasn't being snappish, rather begging to be left in peace. She sounded on the verge of tears. Katheryn placed the garment onto the bed again.

"I realize this has been a difficult day, my lady," she said patiently. "You must understand we are only trying to help you."

Brighton sighed sharply. "I-I do realize that," she said, "and I am grateful. But I do not need your assistance. I can do for myself. Please, leave me in peace."

Katheryn wasn't going to push the woman, who was clearly still very upset about her situation. It was with great reluctance that she tugged on Evelyn's sleeve, motioning the woman out of the chamber.

"As you wish," she said, backing away towards the door. She gestured towards the table near the bed. "There is a comb and soap on the table if you wish to use it. Hot water will still be sent up… are you sure you do not wish for any help bathing?"

Brighton shook her head firmly, her brown hair wagging in her face. "I-I do not require your help," she said. "Please do not think me rude, but I simply need to be left alone."

Katheryn was somewhat dejected but tried not to show it. She felt a good deal of pity for their distressed guest. Still, she obeyed her request as a good hostess would.

"As you wish," she said quietly, hand on the door latch as she began to pull the door shut behind her. "But if you should change your mind, you know where my chamber is. Please do not hesitate to send for me."

Brighton simply nodded, watching as the woman left the chamber and shut the door. She remained unmoving, standing there, for several moments afterward as if waiting for Lady Katheryn and her sister to come charging back in. They seemed to want to hover around her. But the seconds ticked by and the door remained shut. Brighton finally let out a massive sigh and tossed off the smelly cloak. Immediately, she ran for the window.

Freedom!

Her first thought was that of escape, which was foolish considering she had seen the layout of Berwick Castle when she'd been brought in and escape was more than likely impossible. That was only confirmed when she stuck her head from the lancet window, looking over the monstrous castle as men patrolled their stations with torches and dogs barked from the walls. She'd never seen anything so enormous and the view from her window showed the river with the moonlight reflecting from it. But it also showed the castle walls which were very tall, indeed. There would be no way to escape over those even if she was able to lower herself from the window.

There was no way out, indeed.

Dejected, Brighton came away from the window. Perhaps it would have been better had the Scots taken her. At least she might have had the chance to escape their encampment. She was certain they wouldn't have taken her anywhere like this massive stone prison. For the first time since being taken from Coldingham earlier that day, she truly began to feel like she was a prisoner, now trapped by people who had supposedly helped her.

Reality began to sink in. Tears came to her eyes as she sank back against the wall, sliding down until she ended up on the floor on her buttocks. This had been the worst day of her life; not only losing her freedom, but losing Sister Acha as well. The old woman who had raised her from infancy, who had been both mother and father to her, was gone, killed by the English. She knew the Scots hadn't killed the woman because she had been alive until the English attacked; at least, that's what she presumed. The big knight who had taken her back to Berwick had told her he'd found the woman alive on the road but she soon passed away.

But not before telling the knight a fantastic story.

Sweet Mary, how she hated the English right now! They were lying to her, keeping her captive, trying to cram some foolish story down her throat and force her to accept it and digest it. Well, she wasn't going to do it. She wasn't going to accept their lies and the captivity they'd imposed on her. Perhaps she couldn't jump from the window or even escape the walls of her prison. But if what Lady Katheryn said was true and the English planned to move her tomorrow, then she'd be out of the walls and at least have a fighting chance to escape.

She wanted to go home.

A knock on the chamber door startled her from her mutinous thoughts. She didn't answer and, a few moments later, the knock came again. Cautiously and angrily, she stood up.

"W-who is it?" she barked.

"Water, m'lady," a timid servant said as she cracked open the door to peer inside the room. "I've brought ye a bath."

Brighton simply stood there as the door opened wider and the small female servant slipped in, followed by two men bearing a copper tub between them. Behind those men came several more servants bearing large buckets of steaming water, pouring them into the copper tub once it was set on the floor near the hearth. The female servant who had led the water brigade into the chamber had linens in her arms, towels, and she set them down on the bed.

Brighton stood in tense silence as buckets of water splashed into the tub, eyeing the English servants with hatred. She wanted to tell them all how she loathed them, but she bit her tongue. She didn't even know why she did, but she did. When the tub was finally filled and the male servants vanished, the female servant remained. But a sharp word from Brighton sent the woman scurrying out. Before Brighton shut the door, she saw Lady Katheryn standing down the corridor, perhaps to see if the visitor had changed her mind about needing her. Brighton simply shut the door in her face.

With the room quiet and the tub steaming, Brighton eyed the bathwater. She now reconsidered her stance about food and sleep only. It had been weeks since she'd had a bath, as the postulants at Coldingham were told that bathing was impure for the body and soul, and that it brought about wicked thoughts. Therefore, they would wash their face and hands regularly but bathing their entire body was quite rare.

The more Brighton looked at the hot water, the more alluring it became, something naughty and wonderful at the same time. Wonderful won over. She wanted to feel clean and warm again, even if it was a comfort provided by the hated English.

The clothes began to come off.

Beneath the smelly cloak, she wore a sheath-like garment of heavy, scratchy wool and a woolen shift underneath it that wasn't much softer. She had simple shoes on her feet, just two pieces of leather sewn together, really, and they didn't do much for comfort or warmth or anything else. She pulled them off. The outside garment came off first, then the shift beneath. She grabbed the bar of soap on the table before plunging into the hot water, sending it splashing out all over the floor. Steam rose as the water splashed onto the heated stones of the hearth.

A bath!

It had been such a terribly long time since she'd known such luxury that Brighton submerged herself completely in the water, saturating her hair and body. But, God, it felt delightful and she began to lather up the soap furiously, smelling it, only to realize that it smelled of roses. It was sweet and heady, and the lather wasn't really more than a slick foam, but she slathered her entire body with it, rubbing the soap in her hair and scrubbing until her skin was red and tingling. It was heavenly. And it was enough to make her grateful to the English for providing her with this rare opportunity.

But that's where her gratitude ended.

Brighton eventually rinsed the soap off, leaving the water white and murky, but it was still warm and lovely and she huddled in the tub, simply enjoying the enveloping heat. She hugged her knees against her bare chest, her thoughts wandering back to the trials of the day, back to the horror that she'd lived through.

Back to thoughts of Sister Acha.

Thoughts of the dead nun swept over her and tears filled her eyes. Brighton wept softly for the woman, truly devastated for the loss. But she comforted herself with the thought that Sister Acha was with the Heavenly Father. The old woman with the heavy Scots accent had been blessed with very strong faith so she had no doubt the old woman was where she belonged. Still, Brighton would miss her. She would miss that stubborn, strict, and honest woman.

... honest?

A woman who, according to the enormous English knight, had been harboring a deep and disturbing secret about her young charge. The knight's words rolled through her mind – *you are the daughter of the King of the Northman and your mother is Scots. I promised the old nun I would protect you.* In hindsight, she'd never known Sister Acha to lie and the truth was that the English knight had no reason to lie to her, either. He told her a greatly puzzling and complex story. The man had no earthly reason to make it up simply to confuse her. It would have been an elaborate hoax with no purpose.

Therefore, it stood to reason that Sister Acha may have told him exactly what he said she did – a story of a bastard infant who had been placed in her care those many years ago.

The daughter of a king.

The more Brighton pondered that, the more it began to make sense. She was a bastard, a child committed to a convent, someone with no past. But one thing had been certain – her future had been set. She had always known she would take the veil. She didn't want to be someone else, someone she didn't know and someone she was afraid of. A future that was uncertain now. She simply wanted to return to Coldingham and take her vows as she'd always planned. She wanted no part of this disturbing new world.

Lost in despondent and frightening thoughts, the water in the tub finally cooled to the point where she had to climb out and dry off. The female servant had left drying linens on the bed and she used one of them to vigorously dry her skin. Her first instinct was to put on the smelly, scratchy woolen robes she was so accustomed to, but her gaze seemed to drift to the clothing on the bed.

… new, lovely clothing.

Did she even dare? It was clean and it was beautiful. Brighton could see several garments piled up so she went to the bed and began to go through them. A green wool, a red silk, and a blue damask were all very beautiful and elaborate. She'd had never seen such pretty things. But they were very intimidating for a woman who had only worn simple wool her entire life. When she came to the bottom of the pile, however, there was a shift of lamb's wool, unbleached, and very soft. It was enough to cause her to toss the linen towel aside.

The lamb's wool shift went over her head, soft and warm. For the first time in her life, she experienced something against her skin that wasn't poking or scratching it. It was pure heaven, like wearing clouds, but she knew Sister Acha would have frowned upon it because wearing scratchy clothing meant to suffer, or so the woman would preach. Brighton had been content to accept that until she tried on the lamb's wool.

Now, she wasn't so sure.

Smooth and flowing, it tied beneath her breasts for some form against her body and the sleeves were very long, flowing past her hands and warming them. Delighted at the feel of the fabric, it was enough to cause her to forget her misery, at least for the moment. For once in her life, she was experiencing comfort as she'd never known. It was a small bit of brightness in an otherwise horrendous day and she collected the comb from the table that Lady Katheryn had left behind, sitting on the warm stones next to the hearth and running the comb through her hair to dry it in the warmth of the room.

For all of the hell she'd been through that day, at least this moment was moderately comforting. She may not have been happy or even content with anything about her circumstances, but at least this small sliver of time was peaceful. She was alone without the hovering English women. She'd bathed alone and she'd dressed alone. It was what she was familiar and comfortable with. She murmured a prayer of thanks, which included a plea for strength for what was to come. For what she must do. She was certain God was listening.

She had to go home.

A soft knock on the door roused her from her prayers. Thinking it was the servants returned for the tub, she bade them to enter.

But what came through the doorway was not what she had expected.

The peaceful moment, achieved with such difficulty, was gone.

CHAPTER FOUR

PATRICK HAD HEARD the entire thing.

Unable to sleep, he'd been listening at his door when his sister had escorted Brighton to the chamber next to his and he'd heard the ensuing conversation. His sisters wanted to be helpful but Brighton wanted nothing to do with them. She hadn't been rude but she hadn't exactly been kind. He could hear the apprehension in her voice, the confusion and sorrow of a day that had changed her entire life.

Not that he blamed her.

His sister had been surprisingly obedient to Brighton's wishes and the voices had eventually fallen silent. He'd remained at his door, however, listening, wondering if he shouldn't try to speak with Brighton and apologize for his role in her traumatic day. Every contact he'd had with the woman had been volatile and upsetting, and being a man of feeling, he didn't like that. He hadn't meant to upset her with what the old nun had told him, but he still felt strongly that it had been the right thing to do. The woman had to understand her station in life and the threats against her, now that she was out of the confines of the priory. He wouldn't always be around to protect her, especially in light of his appointment for Henry. So perhaps if she understood how unique her bloodlines were, she would understand the need for caution.

Servants arrived at her door a few minutes later. He could hear them banging about. Water splashed. But the door shut again and he didn't hear anything more after that, not for quite some time. In fact, he began to worry about the silence, his mind concocting a few terrible scenarios. What if the woman had taken that bathwater and drowned herself in it? What if she had fashioned a noose with the bed linens and was, even now, hanging from the rafters? Being as distressed as she was, he couldn't be certain she hadn't done one or the other.

It wasn't that Patrick was a worrier; he was simply one of those people who tried to think of all angles of a situation. That damnable emotion he was so capable of saw to the stress part of his personality and, in a situation like this, he couldn't help but think the worst. He didn't want the woman killing herself because of what had happened on this day. That would have made him very remorseful, indeed.

Patrick was vastly intelligent and flawless in his decision-making skills, but there were times when his concern for a situation – or people – gave him pains in his belly. The physic told him he needed to relax more, to pursue something that would calm his naturally strong character, but so far he hadn't found anything to keep his attention long enough to actually relax him. Heading to London as he was to assume his prestigious post, he was fairly certain he never would.

He was going to be on edge the rest of his life.

It was, therefore, his strong personality and sense of curiosity that kept him by the door, listening, letting his imagination run away with him until he finally heard movement. He congratulated himself on the fact that she hadn't killed herself. But he was still inclined to believe that he needed to have at least one calm, civil conversation with the woman to ensure she understood what her life would be like from now on. More than that, he hadn't even told her that he would be taking her to Castle Questing on the morrow.

It would probably be the polite thing to do.

Summoning his courage, he opened the door to his chamber and stepped into the dark corridor. Lifting his hand, he rapped softly on her chamber door. When she bade the caller to enter, he opened the door and timidly stuck his head inside the chamber.

"Lady Brighton?"

His gaze fell on the bed but she wasn't there. Soon enough, he caught movement out of the corner of his eye and saw her sitting in front of the hearth on the warm stone. He almost didn't see her because of the angle of the entry and when their gazes locked, her head came up and her eyes widened. Patrick could see fear in her eyes and he lifted a hand to ease her.

"I mean you no harm, my lady, I swear it," he said quickly. "I came to see if you require anything."

Brighton shook her head, pulling her knees up against her chest in a move that was clearly defensive. "N-nay," she said with apprehension in her voice. "I do not require anything."

Patrick almost bowed out, simply because she looked so frightened, but the cold tub caught his eye. "Let me have the bath removed," he said, turning his attention out into the cold corridor and snapping his fingers at one of the servants lurking down by Katheryn's chamber. "Send for men to take the bath away."

The servant fled down the stairs and Patrick stood by the door of Brighton's chamber, awkwardly, as he waited for the servants to return to fetch the cold bath. The silence between them was tense but Patrick pretended not to notice. He kept his attention out to the corridor, not daring to look at Brighton for fear she would erupt in terror and chase him away. He didn't want to go away, not yet. He was still determined to speak with her. Therefore, he refused to look at her until a contingent of servants finally clamored up the steps and into the lady's chamber, removing the cold bathwater with buckets before finally removing the copper tub itself.

Brighton, meanwhile, had moved to the other side of the room, far away from the English who were invading her chamber. Her hair was nearly dry now, with a slight curl to it as it hung to her buttocks, and the lamb's wool garment was heavy and concealing. Still, she felt threatened by a knight in her chamber, who was by far the largest man she'd ever seen. Standing before him, she'd barely come to his sternum.

His hands were big enough to crush her skull.

As the servants came in and out of the chamber performing their task, Brighton had taken the opportunity to study the big Englishman from a safe distance. He had very dark hair, nearly black, and his eyes were a pale shade of green. With his square jaw and straight nose, she had to admit he was easy on the eyes. In fact, he was quite handsome in her opinion. But since she had no use for men, that opinion was for naught.

Still, he had her interest, purely out of curiosity. He was out of his mail and dressed in a simple tunic and breeches, with boots rising on legs that were as big in circumference as her entire torso. He lingered in the doorway as the servants moved in and out, turning sideways in it because his shoulders were nearly as broad as the doorway itself. Surely it wasn't easy to move around with size like that, but he seemed fairly agile. Aye, he was a fine example of a man, a rather surprising bit of perfection, if she were to admit it, but those thoughts didn't matter. He was English and he was hated.

That was all that mattered to her.

The servants eventually cleared out, taking their buckets with them and leaving the chamber quiet with only the fire snapping in the hearth to fill the still air. As Brighton literally stood in the far corner of the room, as far away from the activity as she could go, Patrick finally turned to her.

"I hope you are warm and comfortable now, my lady," he said in that deep, rich baritone of a voice. "If there is anything else we can do to make your stay more pleasant, I hope you will let us know."

Brighton regarded him a moment. "T-there is something you can do."

"You need only name it."

"Y-you can let me go back to Coldingham."

He wasn't surprised to hear that request. "Alas, I cannot," he said. When he saw her features tighten, even from across the room, he sighed faintly. "My lady, I have come to offer my apologies for the role I have played in your turmoil today. I have contributed to the chaos and distress, but it has been unintentional, I assure you. Much of what has happened, or what has been said, is as much a surprise to me as it is to you. Please believe me when I say that I did not wake up this morning with the sole intention of upsetting you into hysteria. Quite the opposite. I hope you will consider that before judging me too harshly."

It was a very kind apology, in fact, and Brighton was rather surprised by it. He sounded humble and sincere. It was difficult not to believe him and as she mulled over his words, her stiff stance eased, just a bit.

"I-I am willing to believe that is the truth, my lord," she said. "I do not even know your name."

He smiled faintly, perhaps with some chagrin, and the deep dimples that carved into both cheeks set Brighton's naïve heart to racing. "For that, I am terribly sorry," he said. "Please do not tell my sisters. I would never hear the end of it."

"T-then who are you?"

"Sir Patrick de Wolfe at your service, my lady," he said without hesitation. "I am the garrison commander of Berwick Castle."

She nodded faintly, absorbing his name. *Sir Patrick de Wolfe.* "D-De Wolfe?" she repeated. "I have heard that name, I think."

Patrick nodded. "I have a rather large and extended family all over Northumberland," he said. "My mother is Scots, in fact, and we are related to Clan Scott. English father, Scots mother. I am born of two countries."

Brighton was inevitably relaxing with the calm conversation. Considering his easy manner, it wasn't difficult. "Y-yet you fight for the English."

He shrugged. "My father is an English baron and a much-decorated knight," he said. "I was born in England, so that means I am English."

She nodded in understanding, but it was done in a manner that suggested she might not have agreed with his decision. "T-then you had no choice?"

"Probably not."

He meant it in a jesting way, which was surprising. Brighton hadn't considered that the big English knight might actually have a sense of humor. She did, too. But she wasn't quite ready to jest with him in return.

Not yet, anyway.

"I-I am sorry for you, then."

He shook his head. "Don't be," he said. "I am fulfilling my destiny and I am content. In fact, it is good that we are on the subject. The last time I tried to speak with you about your destiny, or at least tell you what your nurse told me, you had a rather violent reaction. Although I am not unsympathetic to your response, you must look at it from a different point of view – destiny is nothing to fear, my lady. It is what we are born to be. It is to be embraced, as people like us are destined to make a difference in the world."

"D-do you truly believe that?"

"I do."

Brighton's first reaction was to resist what he was telling her as she had resisted before, but his words made a good deal of sense. With the air calm between them and the news of Sister Acha's story having been something Brighton had already heard, it was easier for her to hear it a second time. But the fear, the disbelief, was still close to the surface. She simply couldn't help it.

"I-I was not there when you spoke to Sister Acha," she said. "I do not know what, exactly, was said, but I simply cannot believe she would tell you such a thing. I have spent my entire life with her and she never even hinted about knowing something of my past. Surely, she would have told me."

Patrick shrugged. "Mayhap she never saw the need," he said. "She carried the secret alone and when she realized she was dying, she was unwilling to take the secret to her grave."

Brighton thoughts lingered on Sister Acha and the great secret. The more she thought on it, the more puzzled she became. "B-but I cannot believe Mother Prioress would not know," she said. "No one does anything without her blessing. Moreover, it was she who would have taken me in to the convent as an infant and she who would have asked Sister Acha to tend me. Therefore, the mother prioress would have known, too. Why did *she* never tell me?"

Patrick didn't have an answer to that. But it made him think of what he had discussed with his knights earlier with regard to the lady's secret; *it is clear that someone, somewhere, knew of her identity other than the old nun and the mother of the child. And that information has made its way to Clan Swinton.*

Was it possible the mother prioress allowed the information to leak to the Swinton?

Or perhaps she told someone who did?

Patrick couldn't honestly imagine that was the case. But it did spell out the fact that more than Sister Acha knew of Brighton's true identity.

If there was one, there had to be more.

"I cannot say, my lady," he said, trying to be of some comfort. "But I swear to you on my oath as a knight that your Sister Acha told me of your true lineage. I am not entirely sure she wanted me to tell you, but I believe it is your right to know. It is not my privilege to withhold that information from you."

Brighton pondered his statement for a few moments. She was feeling comfortable enough with Patrick's presence to come away from the wall, meandering in the direction of the hearth. With that comfort, her stammer, which usually happened only when she was nervous or stressed, faded away.

"It is not something I am prepared to hear or even accept," she said, coming into the light. "I would very much like to speak to Mother Prioress about this. If only she could tell me what she knows, mayhap she can confirm what Sister Acha told you. At least then I would have no cause for doubt."

Patrick didn't really hear much after her first few words. Once she came into the light, he was stricken by the ethereal vision of a stunning beauty draped in white and illuminated by the flames. Her hair, long and silky, tumbled down her back. But that sweet, delicate face was lined with strife. He found himself watching her lips as she spoke, watching the way the corners of her mouth curled upward. He could have watched her speak forever, for certainly, she was an enchanting creature.

And she was more enchanting by the moment.

But he realized she was expecting a response to whatever she said and he had to think hard on the words she'd spoken, struggling to remember just a few. He didn't want to ask her to repeat herself; that would have been humiliating. But, then again, he could watch her lips as she spoke again.

Those luscious, curvy lips….

"Although I promised your nurse that I would protect you, the truth is that I gave my word before realizing the full impact of the situation," he said. "I am to leave for London and a royal appointment in a fortnight and it will make it difficult for me to keep my vow. I am, therefore, taking you to my father upon the morrow. He is a great warrior and a very wise man. I believe it would be wise to seek his counsel. You will be safe at Castle Questing until he can decide what is to be done. Until then, I hope you will enjoy the hospitality of the House of de Wolfe."

She regarded him, half of her face illuminated by the firelight. "Then you will not take me back to Coldingham?"

So they were back to that subject again. He cocked his head. "My lady, do you really wish to return only to be abducted again?"

"There is no certainty that I will."

"Are you willing to take that chance?"

She sighed, frustrated. The stammer began to return. "B-but you do not know that for certain," she said. "Mayhap these men who seek me will forget about me entirely. I am willing to take the chance that they will."

Patrick took a few steps into the room, closing the door enough so that it was cracked and their voices wouldn't carry so much. There were several people asleep on this level and he didn't want raised voices waking them. For what he was about to say, it was quite possible that the next raised voice would be Brighton's.

"Let us assume you are wrong," he said. "Let us say that I return you to Coldingham and deliver you back to the mother prioress, as you have asked. Now you are home but the priory you have known all your life is no longer safe for anyone, least of all you. Clan Swinton broke the sanctity of a priory to get to you and I would be willing to believe that one or more nuns lost their lives in the process. They do not care who they harm in their quest to abduct you. So by taking you back to Coldingham, not only is your life in danger, but so is everyone else's. Are you truly so determined to return there now that you know that? I cannot believe that you would be so selfish."

She was both surprised and hurt by his words. "I-I am *not* being selfish," she insisted. "I simply want to go home. You cannot fault me for wanting to go home."

He lifted a dark eyebrow. "Nay, I cannot fault you for wanting to go home, but I have repeatedly explained to you why it would not be a good idea," he said. "Let me take it a step further. Let me tell you what will happen once Clan Swinton is able to return you to their stronghold. They will more than likely throw you in the vault or lock you in a chamber. You will be fortunate if you have a food or fire. They will treat you like a commodity, a bargaining piece, because that is all you will mean to them. I can only imagine they will try to ransom you but while they wait, each man in the clan will more than likely violate you in ways I will not describe. I think you understand what I mean. They have no such restraint and no reason to keep you pure and untouched while they await their ransom demand. Then, depending on who pays your ransom, you could be given over to another clan you do not know and those men might very well do the same thing to you. Are you understanding any of what I am telling you, my lady?"

Brighton was looking up at him, her eyes swimming in tears. "T-that is a despicable thing to say."

"It is the truth."

"Y-you could be wrong."

"Then I will ask you this one last time – are you willing to take that chance? If you are, then I will return you to Coldingham tomorrow and you can take your chances. But know this; I will not return to save you again. If I leave you at Coldingham, I wash my hands of you and of my vow, because you clearly have no grasp of what I am trying to do – I am trying to help you. If you are too foolish to take that help, then I have nothing more to say."

She maintained her focus on him, staring him down just as he was staring her down. It was will against will at this point and, to tell the truth, Patrick had no intention of returning her to Coldingham even if she asked it of him. He was willing to bank on the fact that somehow, someway, he was getting through to her so she understood what, exactly, her desire to return home entailed. It wasn't a simple thing in the least.

He was hoping to scare her into staying. He could only pray she was smart enough to realize it.

After an eternity of staring at each other, Brighton finally broke away. Patrick watched as she quickly wiped at her eyes, flicking away any tears that might be bold enough to escape.

"T-then what will happen to me if I do not return?" she asked, looking into the fire. "I have no family and nowhere to go. What will become of me?"

He eased up his serious stance, relieved that she was at least considering what he was saying. In fact, he was vastly relieved and trying not to show it.

"I do not know," he said honestly. "That is why I want to take you to Castle Questing and to my father. He will know what to do. Mayhap you will end up as a lady-in-waiting in a fine house or, mayhap, you will become a nurse to a family of children. There are many things for you, I think. You must not despair. My father will help you."

He was trying to sound positive, as if there was hope for her future. It seemed to work because her tears eased. Whatever turmoil was roiling in her heart, he seemed to soothe the pain. It was actually quite kind of him to do it; giving comfort to a woman he didn't even know. A woman who had fought him at every turn.

She dared to look at him again.

"T-then I suppose I should thank you for making me your burden, Sir Patrick," she said. "It was a great presumption for Sister Acha to extract a promise from you to watch over me and you were kind to agree. I suppose a lesser man would not have."

Patrick sensed that, finally, the hostile barrier was down between them. He hadn't honestly been sure that would ever happen. Feeling the least bit more personable towards her, he took a step in her direction.

"I realize you do not know me," he said quietly. "I do not know you and all we have really known of each other has been violent and sorrowful. But please be assured that I am an honorable man and I will protect you until it is no longer my duty to do so. You will be safe, Lady Brighton, I swear it."

It was a chivalrous declaration. As Brighton gazed up into his pale green eyes, she began to feel something she'd never felt before. It was like a burning in her belly, a slow burn that spread throughout her limbs and caused her knees to shake. Looking into Patrick's handsome face also caused her to feel a bit lightheaded and she had no idea why. Perhaps it was because she was upset and exhausted. Or perhaps she was simply being ridiculous. All she knew was that looking at the man made her want to collapse right into him. Quickly averting her gaze, she took a step away from him.

"I-I believe you," she said, struggling against the giddiness. "I-I suppose I have little choice but to trust you. I do not mean it the way it sounds, but it is the truth."

Patrick felt the warmth between them as well, something that sparked the moment he came near her and looked deeply into her eyes. In fact, even as she moved away from him, he couldn't take his eyes from her, his gaze moving down that beautiful hair and noting her luscious womanly figure beneath the wool. He'd never seen finer and, more and more, his appreciation for her beauty was turning in to something else. He wasn't quite sure yet, but something was changing for him.

And it scared him to death.

"Then please enjoy the rest of your evening," he said, moving back to the door, realizing that his cheeks were actually flushed. *God's Bones, am I giddy?* "We shall leave at dawn on the morrow and my sisters are preparing a traveling bag for you. If you need anything this night, there is a servant in the hall at all times or my… my sister's doorway is down by the top of the steps."

He had almost said that his chamber was right next to hers, suggesting that she could come to him if she needed anything. But that wouldn't be proper nor would it be safe. *Whatever you think you're feeling for the girl, kill it!* He told himself as he put his hand on the latch and opened her chamber door wide. He wasn't even waiting for an answer to his statement but before he could get clear of the chamber, he could hear Brighton's soft voice behind him.

"Y-you have my thanks, my lord," she said. "You have been most kind amidst trying circumstances and if I have appeared ungrateful, then I apologize. I know you are only doing what you believe to be right."

Patrick paused and, against his better judgment, turned to look at her. Softly lit by the glowing fire, he swore he was looking at an angel.

"You have not appeared ungrateful," he said. "And it is my pleasure to be of service, my lady."

He turned again, quickly, to leave, but she stopped him. "T-that is something else I must mention," she said. "You need not address me as 'my lady'. I am a mere postulate, after all, and not bred from nobility. 'Mistress' or even 'sister' will do."

His gaze lingered on her even as he reached out to pull the door shut behind him. "Given that I believe what Sister Acha said, it would appear that you are far more than a mere postulate," he said quietly. "And I will continue to address you with a term of respect and nobility. Get used to it."

With that, he pulled the door shut behind him, simply to cut short his view of her. He wasn't entirely sure he would be strong enough to leave had he gazed upon her much longer.

God's Bones, what is in your head? He scolded himself silently, making haste for his own chamber and shutting the door softly behind him. He even bolted it for good measure, as if that would stop him from wandering out to the lady's door again. And what a lady she was.

Giddy? Indeed, he was.

Foolish?

... more than he wanted to admit.

He didn't sleep the rest of the night.

CHAPTER FIVE

TO FLEE OR not to flee... that is the question....

Aye, Brighton wanted to flee. At least, she thought she did. Now was her opportunity, out in the wide open spaces of the road.

But something was holding her back.

It could have been the fact that there were several big knights riding escort to their traveling party, men on fast horses that could easily catch her if she decided to run. Or it could be because Lady Katheryn and Lady Evelyn had been as kind as possible to her that morning, helping her to dress in traveling clothes, making her feel as if she was honored and special. It could also be because she had been introduced to Lady Katheryn and Lady Evelyn's children that morning, delightful boys and girls who were quite enchanting and happy. They reminded her that there was joy still left in the world. Or, it could be because Patrick had made an impact with her the night before.

She was scared to return home.

There was also something about Patrick himself.

The day, in early June, was clear and mild, and Brighton found herself in a carriage with Lady Katheryn and Lady Evelyn, and Lady Evelyn's baby. The child was not quite a year old, a red-cheeked cherub named Adele. The baby looked a good deal like her father, the tall red-haired knight, Hector, and she had been smiling at Brighton since nearly the moment they'd left Berwick. Brighton couldn't help but smile back.

The other de Norville and Hage children were riding in another carriage, at least the younger ones were. But three of the boys – Lady Katheryn's two eldest, Edward and Axel, and Lady Evelyn's eldest boy, Atreus, were riding ponies near the carriage, shepherded by their fathers.

Lady Katheryn and her husband had three boys, the youngest one, Christoph, riding in the wagon, and Lady Evelyn had two boys and two girls, with one son, Hermes, and her other daughter, Lisbet, also riding in the wagon. Four big dogs rounded out the passengers and were companions as well as protectors to the offspring.

It was quite a tribe of children and pets that had come along in the escort heading for Castle Questing. Because there were so many women and children, Patrick and the other knights had doubled the number of men-at-arms and, even now, heavily-armed men on horseback rode in concentration around the wagons and carriage. Lady Katheryn had noticed them from the start of their journey and, even now as they bumped down the road, she kept glancing up from her sewing, peering from the cab window.

"There are so many armed men out there, it looks as if they are escorting the pope," she muttered. "Does Patrick truly believe we are going to be set upon? We are flying de Wolfe banners, for Heaven's sake. Anyone would have to be daft to attack us."

Evelyn shifted the baby, looking out of the window. "We would make a very large target," she said. Then, she caught sight of something in the distance and smiled. "Look at Atreus. He is so happy to be riding his new pony. I have never seen Hector so proud."

Katheryn grinned as she stabbed at her sewing. "So is Alec," she said. "He spent an hour instructing Eddie and Axel this morning before he ever let them on the ponies. I do believe this is the first time we have ever traveled and allowed the boys to ride on their own."

Evelyn nodded, looking from the window a moment longer before pulling her head inside. "Mother will be so thrilled to see them," she said. "They have grown in even the past few months when she last saw them."

Katheryn agreed. "She will," she said. Then, she cast a sidelong glance at her sister. "Was it difficult to convince Hector not to stop at Northwood Castle to visit his parents? We passed close to them a while back, I think. I heard Alec say something about it."

Evelyn shook her head. "We see his father all of the time. You know that Paris comes to Berwick whenever he can because he has two sons there. It was not difficult to pass Northwood this time."

Small talk bounced between the sisters; talk of children and of their mother and father, and of family at Northwood Castle, which evidently wasn't far away. Tucked in the corner of the carriage, Brighton listened to it all. The sisters weren't deliberately being rude but Brighton was rather glad they'd left her out of the conversation; she didn't feel much like talking. She found her thoughts drifting to the countryside, to Coldingham, and to her uncertain future.

Here she was, traveling with unfamiliar people – people she considered the enemy – but they had all been very kind to her. No one had treated her as an enemy and, perhaps, that was part of the reason she was increasingly reluctant to flee. These English were kind and welcoming people. It was all quite confusing, but there were things about this new world that weren't so bad.

She might even come to like it someday.

"I am very sorry, my lady." Katheryn's soft voice cut into her thoughts. "We have not meant to exclude you from the conversation. We would be very pleased to speak on any subject you choose."

Brighton tore her gaze away from the carriage window, turning to the women who were smiling politely at her. She forced a smile in return.

"Y-you were not excluding me," she said. "I was content with my own thoughts."

Katheryn smiled. "That is sweet of you to forgive us our insult," she said. "We did not have much chance for pleasant conversation last night or this morning, really. I have not even had the chance to ask you if your clothing fits adequately."

Brighton looked down at herself. She was wearing a dark blue woolen traveling dress, lightweight, with layers of shifts beneath it. The garment was cinched tightly in the waist, giving her a rather exquisite appearance. She was full-breasted, something she'd never really paid any attention to because she'd spent her entire life in ill-fitting woolen robes. This morning when the ladies had put the traveling dress on her was the first time she'd ever noticed she actually had a figure and it was a stunning one. She thought she might have seen the English knights, including Patrick, give her second glances when she'd climbed into the carriage that morning, attention that embarrassed her. She'd never known anything like it before.

"I-it is beautiful," she said simply, lifting her head to look at her traveling companions once again. "I…I have never worn anything like this before."

"It suits you," Evelyn said confidently. "It used to be mine but I can no longer fit into it. I am more than happy to give you my clothing that no longer fits. I am pleased you can use it."

Brighton nodded, a hesitant gesture. "Y-you have been most kind, my lady," she said. Then, she looked between the two of them. "You have both been most kind. As I told you last night, I do not mean to appear ungrateful for anything you do for me, but this is all quite… overwhelming."

Katheryn and Evelyn were understanding. "I cannot imagine what you are feeling," Katheryn said quietly. "But we will do everything we can to make you feel comfortable."

Brighton wasn't sure what to say to that. She'd never known such genuinely nice people. She simply nodded and returned her attention to the open window, which happened to face north, into Scotland. Her home. Katheryn and Evelyn exchanged sympathetic glances.

"Will you tell us about your home, my lady?" Evelyn asked, simply to keep the conversation flowing. "Have you lived in a convent your entire life?"

Brighton sensed they were simply trying to include her in conversation so she wouldn't feel left out. She wished they didn't feel that way, for she truly didn't have any desire to chat the journey away, but she responded to them nonetheless.

"I-I have," she said. "Coldingham is… well, it is my home. I love it there."

"Did you receive an education?" Evelyn asked. "Did you have regular duties?"

Brighton nodded. "I-I learned to read and write," she replied. "Sister Acha was insistent that I learn. I can speak Latin and Italian because one of our sisters, Sister Andria, only spoke Italian and a little Latin. She was in charge of the kitchens so if you wanted to eat, you had to learn to communicate with her."

Katheryn and Evelyn were fascinated with an Italian nun. "That is wonderful," Katheryn said sincerely. "I have never actually met someone who lived in a convent. Did you have times of leisure or did you pray all day and all night?"

Brighton grinned at their naïve questions. They acted as if she had lived on the moon for the past nineteen years. "W-we prayed at appointed times, just as you do," she said. "When we were not praying, we were working. I worked in the kitchens and in the garden. Some nuns worked with the animals, as we had many sheep and goats, and some nuns did the sewing, the scrubbing, and things of that nature. We also had a small infirmary where nuns would tend the sick, but we are not a healing order so the infirmary was very small."

Katheryn and Evelyn were very interested in life in the convent. "Was it a big garden?" Evelyn asked. "The one you tended, I mean. Our mother has a large garden at Castle Questing, where we grew up, but Patrick would not let us have a flower garden at Berwick. He says that military installations do not have flower gardens, so all he allows us to grow are vegetables for the table."

Brighton's thoughts shifted from Coldingham to the enormous

knight with the pale green eyes. Even the mere thought of him caused her heart to flutter, just a bit. It was an unfamiliar feeling, indeed. *The man must have put a devil's curse on me to make me jump every time I so much as think of him!*

"W-we did grow some flowers, but we mostly grew herbs and vegetables," Brighton said. "We grow a great deal of lavender and roses, for even roses can be eaten or used in medicines. Roses are my favorite."

"Mine, too!" Evelyn piped up, shifting the baby on her lap. "When Hector and I were courting, he would bring me roses all of the time. He still brings them to me on occasion. He is thoughtful that way."

Courting was such an alien concept to Brighton that she hadn't much to say to that. These women lived in a world of husbands and children, and she did not. Still, she was having her first glimpse into a world other than that of a convent and she wasn't hard pressed to admit it was intriguing. A world where husbands and wives and children made life happy and content. Inevitably, her attention moved to the baby, who was grinning at her again. When Evelyn saw where Brighton's attention was, she lifted the baby in her direction.

"Would you like to hold her, my lady?" she asked. "Adele is a very good baby. She would be no trouble."

Although Brighton hadn't spent any time around children, she had a strong maternal instinct. She liked to nurture things, both plants and animals, and she was very fond of children as a rule. With a timid smile, she reached out for little Adele.

"S-she is very beautiful," she said as Adele slid into her hands. "How old is she?"

Evelyn's affectionate gaze was on her daughter. "She will have seen one year in September," she said. "She is such a happy girl. She has been a joy, unlike my other three, who were holy terrors at this age. The screaming they went through!"

Katheryn chuckled. "At least you have had two girls to balance out the males in the family," she said. "I am outnumbered."

As the two sisters giggled and chatted about their children, Brighton settled the baby on her lap and cuddled her. She was sweet and soft and warm, grinning her big four-toothed grin. Brighton was very content with the baby in her arms. Adele eventually fell asleep against her. As Brighton sat back against the seat, cradling the sleeping child, she was coming to think that there was nothing so sweet in this world as a child in her arms. Having never experienced such a thing, her first experience was one of joy.

Something more in this strange new world that pleased her.

The party bumped along the road for another hour or two, with the men outside the carriage talking, issuing commands, and the children on ponies running about under their father's supervision. At one point, Brighton caught sight of one of the knights – and it was difficult to tell who it was with all of the armor the man was wearing – with a very small boy on the saddle in front of him. The child was having a marvelous time.

In all, it had been a relaxed journey in spite of all of the heavily-armed men. Somewhere around the nooning hour, the party came to a halt and the knights moved the carriage and wagons off the road, into a field that had a brook running through it. The children were released from their ponies and from the wagon, as were the dogs, and soon there was a gaggle of children running around, screaming and laughing, playing in the warm weather. Dogs barked and chased the children as the adults brought forth food for the nooning meal.

Brighton climbed from the carriage, helped out by one of the knights she remembered from the night before, the one who had been at Patrick's command when he'd carried her away from the fighting. She didn't know his name but he looked rather like Katheryn's husband with big shoulders and green eyes. Since she didn't know him and he made her rather nervous, she quickly walked away from the carriage, moving clear of the commotion between the ladies and the children and the dogs. She'd handed the baby back over to Evelyn long ago and, now with her arms free, she looked around at their surroundings as she rubbed at her arms, somewhat numb from having held them in the same position for so long.

A light breeze blew through the trees, fluttering the grass, and no one seemed to pay her much attention as she stood there. The men-at-arms on horseback had spread out, undoubtedly to watch for any threats to the party, and the knights seemed to be lingering with the women and children. The knight who had helped her from the carriage was now on the ground with two small boys jumping on him, while off to the left, Katheryn was in the embrace of her tall, red-haired husband. It was a delightful family scene, to tell the truth, and Brighton could tell that these people were all quite close to one another. There seemed to be a good deal of love and camaraderie going on, something she found very sweet.

In truth, it wasn't something she had seen much of in her life, this kind of love and camaraderie. The nuns of Coldingham could be rather severe and harsh, at times. There wasn't a good deal of affection at the priory. Even Sister Acha had been a strict woman, not given to fits of emotion, so Brighton was rather awed by the sight of people who were open with their affection.

She was also saddened by it.

Saddened in that she had never known such tenderness. She found herself wondering what it would be like to be embraced the way Katheryn's husband was embracing her, or hugged the way that Evelyn hugged her children. Such sweetness to it all, something she'd been denied her entire life. She began to feel a longing in the pit of her stomach that she couldn't begin to describe, a longing to be shown affection and treated tenderly. She hadn't really known what she was missing until now. And now that she realized how much more there was to life, she felt both confused and deprived.

Soon enough, she couldn't watch the tender scene any longer. It hurt her heart to witness such care and love, and she had no idea why. Swiftly, she turned for the nearby brook as it disappeared into a copse of trees. Trudging through the long grass with her skirts held up, she disappeared into the trees as well.

Anything to be free of witnessing things she would never know.

It was cool in the trees as the sunlight filtered in overhead, birds singing in the branches. Lost in thought, Brighton wandered deeper into the grove. Alone in the trees, the urge to flee washed over her again but she fought it. She's already decided against it. She was, therefore, a woman without a home, without a family, and without any place to go.

She was lost.

Feelings of depression swept her. It was difficult not to feel sorry for herself. Her hands brushed the traveling dress she was wearing and she looked down at it, thinking on the English who had given it to her. It was lovely to have people be so kind to her but it couldn't go on like that forever. At some point, she would have to settle somewhere and find a life of her own, which wouldn't include Katheryn and Evelyn and their charming children. It wouldn't even include Patrick, the big knight who made her heart flutter strangely. She didn't like feeling that her future was nothing but fog, unable to see through it yet knowing something was there just the same.

It was the unknown she feared.

"Lady Brighton?"

A soft, deep voice startled her and she turned to see Patrick coming through the foliage. She took a step back, away from him, intimidated by the sight of him. Even after their calm conversation last night, she still wasn't completely comfortable in his presence.

"I-I… I just needed a moment of privacy, my lord," she said, her stammer strong because she had been startled. "I should have told you, I suppose. I am sorry."

Patrick shook his head. "You need not apologize," he said. "If anyone should apologize, it should be me for invading your quiet moment. I came to make sure you were well. My sisters were concerned."

Brighton smiled faintly. "I-I am well," she said. "They worry over me as if I am one of their children."

Patrick gave her a lopsided grin, the dimples running deep. "They are very motherly," he agreed. "You'll not escape that, no matter if you are a grown woman. They will still be concerned for you."

He said it somewhat humorously and she dared to smile in return. "I-it is very kind of them," she said. "I do not mind. They were quite motherly this morning as they helped me to dress."

She looked down at herself which made Patrick look down at her as well. He'd spent the entire morning thinking of her even though he couldn't see her, tucked back in the carriage with his sisters as she had been. But the vision of her before she'd entered the carriage back at Berwick stuck with him.

Dressed in a deep blue wool that clung indecently to her figure, he'd been struck by her womanly curves just as the other knights had been. Alec and Hector, the married men, pretended not to notice but the unmarried men, Kevin and Apollo, noticed without trying to seem as if they weren't. That had infuriated Patrick, who had sent the young knights to ride point at the head of the column, far up ahead of the lady they'd briefly lusted after.

Not that he'd blamed them for their reaction, but he wanted their minds on their duties and not on the lovely young woman in the carriage. At least, that's what Patrick told himself. The truth was that he wanted to be the only one thinking about her. The curvy figure encased in dark blue and her beautiful brown hair plaited in an elaborate braid was something for his eyes alone.

He was sworn to protect her, after all. In some odd way, that meant she belonged to him.

... didn't she?

But she had been saying something to him just now, hadn't she? Something about his sisters smothering her...? He realized that he hadn't really heard her and, again, not wanting to embarrass himself by asking her to repeat what she'd said, he pulled on the few words he'd managed to hear in order to concoct an answer. But he was coming to think that the woman could suck every thought from his head without even trying, for she'd done it before with him.

He looked at her and his mind seemed to go to mush.

"My sisters try their best to be helpful," he said belatedly. "They have been my chatelaines at Berwick for a few years and I find them indispensable."

Brighton couldn't help but noticed he seemed detached. It had taken him forever to answer her even though he was looking right at her. She was coming to think that he didn't have much interest in what she had to say, which embarrassed her greatly. Clearing her throat softly, she put her head down and gathered her skirts, preparing to move past him.

"A-again, my apologies for wandering away," she said. "I will return with you now if that is your wish."

He reached out, a massive hand grasping her arm before she could walk away. "That is not why I came," he said. Then, he lifted his other hand, which she hadn't really noticed because it had been partially concealed behind his back. He had a bundle in it, a kerchief that was wrapped around some items. "My sisters said you'd not eaten so I brought you some food. Would you sit and eat now? We only have a few minutes before we must continue on our way."

The food bundle in his hand enticed her, for she was hungry. She nodded her head, watching him as he moved to a big rock next to the creek. He set the bundle down and untied it, revealing a good deal of food within. He smiled weakly.

"If you please, my lady?" he said, pointing to the feast.

Hesitantly, Brighton made her way to the rock and sank to her knees beside it. Beneath the cool shade of the trees, she timidly picked up a piece of hard white cheese, biting into it. It was very good. Quite famished, she collected a piece of bread as well. Mouth full, she looked up at Patrick.

"I-I will gladly share if you've not eaten, my lord," she said.

Patrick had been waiting for the invitation because he'd brought enough food for two people. It had been rather clever of him, he thought. Casually, he planted his big body on the edge of the rock, taking a piece of cold beef and popping it into his mouth. All the while, he kept eyeing Brighton as she ate ravenously.

"How has your journey been so far?" he asked, simply to make conversation.

She nodded her head, swallowing the bite in her mouth. "P-pleasant," she said. "I held the baby for some of the journey. She is very sweet."

"Adele?" he said. "Aye, she is. She is adorable and looks just like her father, much to my own father's displeasure. He had hoped she would look like a de Wolfe."

Brighton put more cheese in her mouth. "I-I am coming to understand that everyone in your command is related," she said. "It has not been explained to me, but I see there are relations around you, at least with your sisters. Do you have more?"

He nodded. "I have a rather large family," he said. "In addition to Katheryn and Evelyn, who are with me at Berwick, I have five brothers and another little sister who are not. You see, it all started many years ago when my father married my mother. I have already told you she is from Clan Scott. My mother came with two cousins who married two of my father's knights. Aunt Jemma married Uncle Kieran and Aunt Caladora married Uncle Paris. When those three couples had children, they all ended up marrying each other, so Katheryn and Evelyn are married to a son of Jemma and Kieran, and Paris and Caladora, respectively. Our three families are deeply intertwined."

Brighton was listening with interest. "I-I see," she said. "Do you have a wife I've not met, then?"

He shook his head. "Nay," he replied, giving her a rather embarrassed grin. "Oh, it was not for lack of trying on Uncle Paris and Uncle Kieran's part. They had a daughter or two they tried to saddle me with… I mean, marry me to… but I felt strongly that there was much I want to accomplish in life and it would be difficult for a wife to have a husband with great ambitions. I could not condemn her to such a life."

Brighton chewed on a small green apple. "D-do you mean this appointment for Henry, the one you spoke of last night?"

"Aye."

"W-what will your duties be for the king?"

Patrick swallowed the food in his mouth, reaching for a piece of cheese. "To simplify the explanation, the king is an elderly man and he has not been well," he said. "The king has several men who are his personal guard, called the Lord Protectors, and I have been given the honor of being the captain of that group. I am to leave for London in a fortnight to assume my post by September."

Brighton was vastly impressed. But she realized that she was also somewhat disappointed. She wasn't sure why, but she was. Perhaps it had something to do with him leaving in a couple of weeks and her never seeing him again. Other than the priests, Patrick was the only man she had truly had any contact with outside of the walls of Coldingham. Hated English or not, they had established a strange bond. Right now, they were having a lovely conversation, something she'd never done before, at least not like this.

Never before with a man who made her heart flutter strangely....

"Y-your family must be very proud," she finally said. "I am sure you will be very successful."

He shrugged. "A position like this is very powerful and highly coveted," he said. Then, he lowered his voice. "Can you keep a secret?"

She nodded, curious, indeed. "I-I can."

"Not even if a thousand *reivers* sudden charge these trees and try to beat it out of you?"

She grinned at his jest. "N-not even then, I promise."

He lifted a dark eyebrow to emphasize how serious this was. "Only my father knows this, my lady," he said. "If my mother found out you knew before she did, she would beat the both of us."

Brighton held up a hand as if to take her oath. "I-I swear it will never leave my lips, ever."

He nodded firmly. "I believe you," he said. "Then I shall tell you. Along with my appointment to the Lord Protectors, I have been bequeathed lands and title to go with it. Once I assume my post, Penton

Castle will become mine as well as the title Lord Westdale. Henry offered me larger properties to the south, but my heart and my family are here in the north. Penton Castle guards a major road from Scotland that leads into Carlisle. It is a very big place, built upon the ruins of a Roman fort, and it has seen more than its share of action from the Scots."

Brighton was duly impressed. "W-who is there now? I mean, whose army?"

"Henry's."

It all seemed quite prestigious to her. "T-then I will congratulate you," she said sincerely. "You are to become quite important."

He shrugged, a cross between a modest and an arrogant gesture. "Lands and title will thrust me into the heart of London's politics, but I am confident I shall execute my duties flawlessly," he said. "Truthfully, I have no idea when I will actually see my property, as I will probably be in London for a very long time. Edward, the king's son, has given me as much freedom as I need to protect the king and control who has access to him. I think it will be a very interesting position, at any rate. Not many men will go against the word of the Nighthawk."

Brighton cocked her head curiously. "N-Nighthawk?"

He nodded, swallowing his cheese and then picking up a small apple. "My father is known as the Wolfe of the Border," he said, taking up most of the apple in one bite. "He is also Warden of the Northern Borders. Have you never heard of him? Well, you will if you spend any time in the north. Because they call him The Wolfe, I have earned the name of Nighthawk for my prowess in battle. I am the only one of my brothers to have earned such a moniker."

Brighton rather liked that name. "N-Nighthawk," she repeated. "They are great hunters."

"As am I."

She grinned at his boastful statement. "I-I would believe that," she said. "You had no difficultly hunting down the *reivers* last night."

He tossed the apple core aside. "That was nothing," he said. "They left an easy trail to follow."

Her smile faded as thoughts of Sister Acha returned and the terrible cost of the skirmish the night before. Averting her gaze from Patrick, she reached for another apple. "I-I suppose that you could easily track me as well even if I tried to flee for home, then."

He regarded her a moment. "I could. Do you intend to run? I thought we had settled that last night."

She put the apple in her hand down, brushing her hands off on her skirt. "I-I will be honest with you, my lord," she said. "I still had thoughts of running for home this morning, even after our conversation last night. Coldingham is all I know, you see, and for me to simply forget about it so easily… I cannot do that. When I wandered into these trees just now, I even thought it would be very easy to slip away but I remembered what you said last night about my being selfish. If I run to Coldingham, and if men are truly after me, then trouble will follow. I do not wish to bring trouble to my home."

He watched her as she stood up gracefully. "That is wise."

She sighed, gazing out over the creek, having no idea he was watching her profile as she did. "B-but if you take me to your father, will I not be bringing trouble to him, too?"

Patrick was not only watching her profile, he was watching the curve of her lips again when she spoke. It was mesmerizing. "You will," he said, "but my father is a great knight. He can handle all of the trouble that the Swinton Clan wants to throw at him. Do not worry about him."

She turned to him, her sweet face in earnest. "B-but I do," she said. "If I will bring as much trouble as you say, then there is nowhere I can go that will not bring trouble. I do not wish to cause trouble for those who have been kind to me."

He was starting not to hear her words again, daydreaming about that angelic face. But he forced himself to listen. He stood up, towering over her.

"I would not worry about that if I were you," he said. "You are my ward now and as long as you are, no harm will come to you. Do you not believe me?"

She nodded, her heart beginning to pound against her ribs as his powerful form loomed before her. "I-I do," she said. Then, she paused. "I am calmer now, my lord. Will you please tell me again what Sister Acha told you about my… my lineage? I promise I will not become hysterical. I honestly do not remember everything you told me, only that my real father is a Northman king. I would be grateful if you would tell me, once more, so that I remember all of it."

Patrick knew they should be heading back to the others now that their meal was over but he couldn't quite seem to do it. He was rather enjoying talking to her, just the two of them. He didn't want to disrupt that, at least not until he had to.

"Are you sure?" he asked quietly.

"P-please."

He sighed faintly. "She told me that your mother is Lady Juliana de la Haye and your father is Magnus Haakonsson, King of the Northmen. Your real name is Kristiana Magnusdotter. But you were given the name of Brighton de Favereux to conceal your identity. Shall I tell you more?"

Brighton nodded shortly, as if she didn't want to hear it all but knew she had to, and he continued. "Your mother is a daughter of the House of de la Haye and she was given over to the Northmen as a hostage, to cement a peace between the kings of the North and Clan Haye. When she became pregnant, she was sent home in shame. When you were born, your mother was forced to bring you to Coldingham in order to protect you." He paused, looking her in the eye. "Sister Acha said that no one must know of your existence for it can only bring the Northmen down upon us. Those were her words, exactly."

Brighton's features were lined with distress but she was trying very hard to show courage. "Juliana de la Haye," she murmured. "W-where does the Clan Haye live?"

"Further to the north, I believe," he said. "Like most Scots along the coast, I am sure they have had their share of encounters with Northmen. Making an alliance with a hostage makes perfect sense."

Brighton didn't really know much about alliances. Truthfully, she didn't know much about anything right now. Her senses, her mind, were very muddled. She was trying to process the information when a shout came from outside of the trees and Patrick shouted in return, a confirmation that they were soon to return to the group. He turned to Brighton.

"We should be departing shortly," he said, somewhat gently. "Did you have enough to eat? You can take the rest of the food with you in the carriage if you wish."

She nodded absently, still lost in thought, and he moved to collect the food. She put her hand on his arm before he could move out of her reach. Patrick came to a pause, looking down at that distressed, heavenly face as she turned her attention upward to him.

"D-do you think… do you think your father could write to Mother Prioress and ask her if she knows anything about my true lineage?" she asked hesitantly. "If I could only have her confirmation, mayhap I could find peace with all of this. As I told you last night, I cannot believe that she would not know the truth. If it is too much trouble for your father, I would be happy to write the missive if he would only be kind enough to supply a messenger."

Patrick could feel her hand on his arm like a searing brand. Such a small hand, a delicate touch, but it was burning a hole through him.

"It will not be too much trouble for him to do that," he said, wondering if the quivering he felt in his chest at her touch could be heard in his voice. "In fact, I think it is a very good idea. I will suggest it to him."

Brighton was visibly relieved. "Thank you, my lord. I am very grateful."

He gave her a brief smile before continuing on his quest to gather their meal. As he wrapped it back up in the kerchief, he spoke.

"You do not need to continue addressing me formally," he told her. "I do not mind for you to address me as Patrick."

Brighton looked at him with surprise. "Patrick?"

He nodded, looking up from the bundle of food in his hand. "May I call you Brighton?"

Brighton was rather startled with the request. Pleased, but startled. "O-of course," she said. "But no one calls me Brighton except Mother Prioress. To everyone else, I am known as Bridey."

He grinned. "I know," he said. "Sister Acha addressed you by that name. I had no idea who she was talking about at first. I will also call you Bridey if it does not displease you."

"I-I would be honored, my – I mean, Patrick."

He chuckled and reached out to take her elbow, politely escorting her out of the copse of trees and into the green field beyond.

CHAPTER SIX

That Evening
Castle Questing
Near Mindrumill, the Borders

ARRIVING AT CASTLE Questing had been somewhat surreal.

Against the backdrop of a pale blue sky, the castle sat on the top of a crag, perched like a crouched lion that was waiting to pounce. Built of Torridonian sandstone, the building blocks were pale, almost a cream color that turned golden when sunrise or sunset hit it just right. Locals called it *oir caisteal*, or the golden castle, for just that reason. It was a magnificent and imposing sight.

Because the castle sat so high, it could literally be seen for miles. The party from Berwick had spotted it several miles out and, as they approached, the sun was setting so that as they were about a half-mile away, the sun hit the stones just right and that golden castle appeared for them all to see. For those who had been born and raised at Questing, it was a welcome sight, indeed.

As the group from Berwick drew closer, a welcome party soon emerged from Questing, moving swiftly along the road that led down the side of the crag and racing for the Berwick group at breakneck speed. Young men on powerful horses met with the incoming party and as Brighton watched with great curiosity. Patrick cuffed one of the young men on the head affectionately. Two other young men on horseback swarmed the other knights and made their way back to the wagon where the children were riding, now bundled up as the sun began to set. In the carriage, the women could hear the children screaming in delight.

"It must be Thomas and Nathaniel," Katheryn said, sticking her head from the carriage window to see what was going on behind them. "Oh – I see Adonis, too. Wait, Adonis! Put him down! Put Christoph down, I say!"

Evelyn was trying to see as well. "He never listens," she said unhappily. "Adonis de Norville! Do you hear us? Put Christoph down. And… nay! Do not pick up Hermes! Put him *down*!"

Brighton had no idea what was going on; all she knew was that the children were laughing and screaming, and their mothers weren't happy about it. The situation must have resolved itself because Katheryn and Evelyn came back into the cab, a little ruffled but seemingly satisfied, at least for the moment.

"I am going to box his ears when we reach the castle," Evelyn muttered. Then, she saw the look of concern on Brighton's face and she smiled sheepishly. "I am sorry, my lady. We are speaking of young uncles who like to take the boys for a ride on their excitable horses. The last thing we need is for someone to fall off and break an arm."

Truthfully, Brighton thought it was rather amusing the way the children were so thrilled to see their uncles. "W-whom are you speaking of?"

Katheryn answered her. "Thomas de Wolfe, who is our younger brother," she said with disapproval in her tone. "He is to be knighted in a few years but right now, he is just a troublemaker and a rascal. There is also Nathaniel Hage, my husband's youngest brother, and Adonis de Norville, who is Hector's youngest brother. They all serve at Questing and they are naughty young men full of spit and vinegar. They need daily beatings!"

Brighton fought off a grin. "D-do they not get them?"

Katheryn remained stern a moment longer before bursting into soft laughter. "Not nearly enough, although I am sure my mother tries," she said. "I am so happy you are going to meet our mother. You will like her a great deal."

Brighton had to admit that she was rather curious to see Castle Questing and meet the occupants. Having spent her entire life sequestered at Coldingham, with a very rare trip to Eyemouth on occasion, two trips to two castles in as many days was a great anomaly for her. It was rather disorienting, but also exciting. She was, therefore, quite curious about the big castle where the mighty Wolfe of the Border lived, the great knight she'd heard Patrick speak of.

The man who would determine her destiny.

With that in mind, she felt more than a little apprehension as the group made its way through the substantial village that was gathered up around the base of the castle and began to make the trek up the hill. Looking from the window of the carriage, she had to crane her neck back to look up the side of the crag to the massive castle on top of it. She'd never seen anything so big, like an entire city unto itself. The carriage and wagons seemed to have a little trouble going up the hill because the horses were exhausted and the angle was steep, but eventually they made it to the top.

And that was when the entire world opened up.

The great gatehouse of Castle Questing was open wide as more people rode out to escort the party inside. Brighton couldn't really see the gatehouse, just a corner of the massive thing, but she could see the entire eastern and part of the northern side of the walls, which were enormous. She counted four massive, powerfully-built towers, including part of the gatehouse, that were all constructed in the same fashion – the towers flared at the bottom to prevent men from easily mounting them. It was clear that Questing had all sorts of design details that would prevent an attacking army from gaining easy access.

But that wasn't the structure's only defensive feature – a great moat had been dug out upon the rise, looking more like a small lake. Additionally, the enormous walls flared out at the top, extending the battlements outward, which was another design element to prevent an attacking army from easily mounting them. One would have to be a spider to climb up the walls and then scale the underside of the battlements that jutted outward. The entire place was built to withstand a massive siege and then some, a fitting home for the great Wolfe.

It was impressive and awe-inspiring, this mighty castle at the top of the hill, and Brighton drank it all in. Soon enough, the carriage passed through the gatehouse, which was as big as a keep. They passed through two enormous gates and across a ditch dug inside the gatehouse. The ditch was spanned by an internal drawbridge. Over the ditch, she could see murder holes in the roof of the gatehouse. If some fool army was lucky enough to breach the steel gates, then they had a very large ditch and murder holes inside of the gatehouse to deal with. It was ingenious.

Once through the treacherous gatehouse, the party spilled into the vast outer bailey. Men swarmed around both the carriage and the wagon behind it. When the door opened, Evelyn was sucked out by a young man who hugged her so hard that she grunted. When he released the woman so she could catch her breath, he reached for Katheryn but she balked.

"You will not squeeze me so tightly, Thomas de Wolfe," she scolded. "Try it and I'll throw a fist into your throat."

Thomas laughed. Dark-haired like his brother, Brighton could see some of the family resemblance. But in her opinion, Patrick was much more handsome. Thomas didn't have nearly his brother's size, either, but he was nonetheless a handsome male specimen. He was also quite young, perhaps no more than fourteen. He took his sister by the arm as she climbed from the carriage.

"My lady," he said, bowing with great exaggeration. "I will treat you like the fragile princess you are. Am I holding you too tightly? Is my voice too loud? Shall it shatter your precious ears?"

Katheryn sighed heavily, eyeing her brother. "Shut your yap," she grumbled. But she soon softened, fighting off a grin. "As much as you annoy me, it is still good to see you."

Thomas grinned brightly. "May I hug you?"

Katheryn cocked an eyebrow. "You may, but if you crack bones, I will beat you within an inch of your life."

Thomas laughed and took his sister in his arms, giving her a warm hug. He was about to turn away when he caught sight of Brighton, still in the cab. Curiosity – and great interest – suddenly filled his expression. He took on the appearance of a hunter, in this case, for lady flesh. All of those young man urges flowing through his veins lit a fire under him at the sight of a lovely woman.

"You have brought someone with you," he said, swiftly moving for the cab. "I did not mean to be rude but I did not see you, my lady. Thomas de Wolfe at your service."

He was addressing Brighton and she hesitantly moved for his outstretched hand. But the moment she moved to take it, a mountain of a man was between her and Thomas. She really didn't even have to see the man's face to know it was Patrick and her heart began to flutter again. It was as if her heart knew it was him without benefit of sight.

Patrick growled at his brother. "Back away, whelp," he said. Quickly, that tone changed when he turned to Brighton and reached out to take her hand. "My lady, permit me to assist you. Welcome to Castle Questing."

Brighton climbed out of the cab with Patrick steadying her as her feet touched the dirt of the bailey. Now, she could see the place in its entirety – Questing had both inner and outer wards, both of them surrounded by soaring walls. The shape of the castle, in general, looked something like an "H". The gatehouse to the inner bailey was open, a much smaller structure than the main gatehouse, and through the opening she could see buildings in the inner ward. Oddly enough, she didn't see a central keep, but many buildings all strung together, built against the inner wall. Her observations were cut short, however, when she heard Patrick address her.

"I am sure you are weary," he said somewhat quietly, as joyful chaos went on around them with families reuniting. "I will introduce you to my father and mother and then you may rest until the evening meal."

Brighton was a bit anxious at the thought of being left alone in a strange, new castle. "B-but where will you go?" she said. Quickly realizing that sounded as if she had personal interest in his plans and very much as if she didn't want him to leave her, she amended her words. "T-that is to say, will you not speak with your father right away? I should like to be part of that conversation if you will permit it. It is about me, after all. I feel I should be present."

Patrick took her hand and tucked it into the crook of his elbow. He hadn't missed that wistful tone in her voice, the one she'd tried to quickly cover up. "You will be part of that conversation," he assured her. "And I intend to tell my father why I have come as soon as possible. Besides… when he sees that I have brought you to Questing, a stranger, he will understand that this is not entirely a social visit."

"Atty?" Thomas had been standing at his brother's side nearly the entire time, realizing his brother had no intention of introducing him to the beautiful young woman. "Who is your guest? Will you not introduce us?"

Patrick turned impatiently to his young brother. "If I had any choice in the matter, I would not," he said flatly. "But, seeing as you and the lady may run into each other during the course of her visit here, permit me to introduce you to Lady Brighton de Favereux. Lady Brighton, my brother, Thomas."

Brighton nodded to the young man, who dramatically bowed before her. "T-Thomas and I have met," she said. "He did, in fact, introduce himself."

Patrick's eyes narrowed. "He did?" he said, frowning at his brother in a threatening manner. "That was bold of him. And impertinent. Say the word and I shall punish him."

Thomas grinned impishly and dashed away. "You'll not lay a hand on me!" he declared. "Mother will have something to say about that!"

"Say about what?"

A woman's voice with a heavy Scots accent came from behind.

Patrick turned quickly to see his mother approaching with their father, but his father headed directly for the grandchildren who were starting to squeal at the sight of him. As Patrick's father growled like a bear and scooped up wriggling, giggling grandchildren, Patrick greeted his mother with a kiss.

"You are looking well, Mother," he said. "How have you been?"

"Well enough," she said, her gaze finding the woman standing next to Patrick. "And I see ye've brought me a guest. Why did ye not send word ahead?"

Patrick turned to Brighton. "Mother, this is Lady Brighton de Favereux," he said. "Lady Brighton, this is my mother, Lady Jordan Scott de Wolfe."

Brighton had never really been taught how to properly greet nobility, with a curtsy and averted eyes, so she simply stood there and smiled timidly at the beautiful woman with Patrick's pale green eyes.

Lady Jordan de Wolfe was rather petite. Her honey-blonde hair was wrapped up in a braid that was secured in a coil at the base of her skull. Though she was in her fifth decade, there were very few lines on her face. In fact, she looked quite ageless, serene and lovely, and far too small a woman to have birthed such an enormous man as Patrick. But she clearly had, for Patrick had some look of her about him, and Brighton automatically had a good feeling about the woman. There was something in the glow of Lady Jordan's eyes that foretold of warmth and kindness.

"'T-tis an honor, my lady," she said.

Jordan cocked her head curiously. "Do I hear Scots?"

Brighton's smile grew, although it was modestly. "Aye, my lady," she replied. "I have spent my life at Coldingham Priory."

Jordan was quite interested in the beautiful young woman with the Scots accent. "Coldingham," she repeated thoughtfully. "I've heard of it. North, near Edinburgh, I believe."

"Aye, my lady."

"But ye dunna have much of the brogue, lass. Where were ye born?"

Patrick intervened at that moment; he had to. His mother was already leading into the very reason for his presence at Questing and he didn't want to discuss it out here in the open.

"Later, Mother," he said, putting himself between Brighton and his mother. "The lady is the reason why we have come. Would you be so kind as to take her inside and show her where she may rest? I must speak with Father."

Jordan had the curse of curiosity in all things. She was obedient to her son in action but her mind was still very curious about the girl, even more curious after Patrick had said what he had. She took Brighton by the hand.

"Come along, my lady," she said. "Come and rest after yer long journey."

Brighton was willing to go with the gentle Lady Jordan. But the moment she took a step, she heard a loud and seemingly unhappy Scottish brogue among them.

"Alec?" a woman said. "Did ye think not tae come inside tae greet yer own mother? I had tae come out here tae find ye!"

There were so many people in the bailey greeting the incoming party that it was difficult to see where the voice was coming from. It was a loud voice, indeed. Brighton found herself being pulled away from Patrick, into the group of people, until they came upon Alec and Evelyn, who were hugging a tiny, dark-haired woman, heavy-set but still quite lovely. The little woman put her hand on Alec's chest; in truth, she thumped him.

"Did ye not think tae send word of yer arrival?" the woman said after she pounded on his chest. "We've had no time tae prepare!"

Alec could see his aunt, Lady Jordan, with Patrick's captive in-hand. He pointed to Jordan and Brighton. "Atty has a bit of an issue and he needs Uncle William's counsel," he said. "Mother, the woman with Aunt Jordan is Lady Brighton."

The tiny woman whirled around, amber eyes fixing on Brighton. In fact, Brighton was probably more intimidated by the little Scotswoman than she was of all of the men around her. Around the same age as Lady Jordan, she nonetheless looked younger than her years, but something in the woman's expression bespoke of fire and grit. She was tough, this one, and nothing to be trifled with. Brighton resisted the urge to shrink away from her.

"Is that Atty's lass, then?" the woman asked, incredulous. Then, her cheeks reddened and she began looking about. "Where is that mountain of a man? He brings a lass with him and we know nothin' about it? *Atty*!"

She was yelling and Brighton was cringing. Patrick, a head taller than nearly everyone else around him, pushed through the crowd of people, lifting up one of Katheryn's boys when the child got in his way. He held the boy as he came near the little Scotswoman.

"It is good to see you, too, Aunt Jemma," he said dryly, although he kept a distance from her. One did not enrage Lady Jemma Hage and live to tell the tale. "Did I hear you bellow?"

Jemma put one hand on her hip while the other pointed to Brighton. "Did ye take a wife and we are only now findin' out about it?"

Patrick looked at Brighton in shock. "Wife?" he repeated. "God, no. Who told you that?"

Before Jemma could work up a righteous outrage, another man stepped in. He had been over by Katheryn's other two boys, admiring their ponies, but now he stood beside Jemma, a massive hand on her shoulder. Sir Kieran Hage, Alec's father, made an appearance at just the right time. Hearing his wife's angry voice had forced his attention away from his grandchildren for the moment.

"I do not believe Atty has taken a wife," he said calmly, his voice soothing and deep. He looked at Patrick. "Mayhap you had better introduce the lady and explain why she is here before your aunt blows the top of her head off thinking that you have gone and married without telling anyone."

Leave it to Uncle Kieran to defuse a situation. Patrick grinned. "Aunt Jemma, I assure you, I have not married without your permission," he said somewhat mockingly, looking around to the group that had gathered in the bailey, a group that was now looking at Brighton. He cleared his throat softly, looking from his aunt to his uncle to his mother and finally to his father. "This is Lady Brighton de Favereux. Two nights ago, we received word that *reivers* had raided an English settlement and possibly had English captives with them. As it turned out, they had raided Coldingham Priory and took Lady Brighton as a prize. I rescued the woman, killed the *reivers,* and now Lady Brighton is my guest for a time. Lady Brighton, I am sure you have figured out that this is some of my family – you have met my mother, but the dark-haired spitfire is my Aunt Jemma and the man next to her is my Uncle Kieran. And this… this is my father, William de Wolfe."

He said it rather proudly as he turned to the man standing next to him. Brighton, who had been rather overwhelmed with everyone's attention suddenly on her, focused on the man beside Patrick.

The great William de Wolfe was an older man. Some might have even called him elderly. But he was still a very large man, powerful, and seemingly quite healthy. He stood a little shorter than his enormous son but they both had the same square jaw and big dimples in their cheeks, only in William's case, age had carved the dimples deeper. He wore an eyepatch over his left eye and he seemed to be scarred, in general, from what she could see. Only so great a knight could wear such battle wounds so well. Instead of giving the appearance of a beaten man, it gave the illusion of an invincible one. Brighton didn't even know the man but, already, she liked him.

"My lord," Brighton dipped her head to the man politely. "It is a great honor to meet you."

William regarded the stunning young woman for a moment; busty, pale-skinned, with luminous blue eyes and an angelic face, he was seriously wondering why Patrick had brought the woman with him. But his expression remained impassive, not revealing his confusion. He nodded his head in greeting.

"Welcome to Castle Questing, Lady Brighton," he said. Then, he looked at Patrick. "She is from Coldingham?"

Patrick nodded. "Aye," he said in a manner that suggested he didn't want to spill his business for all to hear. "May we speak inside, Da?"

William was very curious about this quandary. "Indeed," he said. "Alone? Or shall we invite Kieran?"

"I would like to have him there. The other men are welcome as well."

William nodded, sensing something rather serious. Patrick wouldn't have come all the way from Berwick, with a woman from Coldingham Priory no less, if it hadn't been a serious issue. William very much wondered what it was.

"Then go into my solar," he said. "I will meet you there. But first, I want to see my grandchildren for a moment. I promise I will not be long."

The group began to dissolve a little bit, with Katheryn and Evelyn and their children ganging up on grandfathers while their husbands went about disbanding the escort party. Jemma was already over with Jordan and Brighton and Patrick, too, was focused on the woman. He thought she looked rather natural standing with his mother and aunt, as a fellow Scots. He thought she looked rather natural as part of the family.

... as part of the family?

He couldn't believe that thought had just crossed his mind. *God, what in the hell are you thinking?* He scolded himself. *If you continue to think such thoughts, you are going to ruin everything you've worked for!* This woman was making him entertain ideas he'd never entertained before, thinking of things that weren't part of his plan. More than once, he'd found himself thinking of the woman in ways he shouldn't have been. He'd known other women before, so what made Brighton so special, other than her obvious beauty? He didn't even know that much about her, but therein was the problem.

What he knew of her, he liked.

Frustrated with himself, he yanked off his gloves and made his way over to where the women were standing. He thought not to look at Brighton, as maybe that would help his problem, but his eyes were drawn to her like a moth to flame. He couldn't seem to *not* look at her. Before he could reach her, however, a little figure with a toy sword intercepted him. Patrick came to a halt, finding himself facing off against his baby sister.

His frustrated mood fled.

Penelope de Wolfe was a little over three years of age, an extremely late baby for her parents, but the cutest little creature on the face of the earth. She had dark hair and hazel-gold eyes, and was so bright that she could carry on a fairly serious conversation with an adult. But she'd been coddled and catered to and indulged to the point where it was well-known that little Penelope ruled Castle Questing, not William as most were led to believe. The child opened her mouth and everyone ran right to her.

But Patrick didn't blame them, truthfully; he was one of those who ran right to her. He missed not seeing her day to day because of his appointment at Berwick. Other than his father, he'd been the first one to hold her after her birth and he was quite attached to her.

"Greeting, my lady," he said to her, bending down to pick her up and kiss her. "It is good to see you again."

But Penelope wanted none of his affection or greeting. She held the dull wooden sword out at him, tip pointing up at him.

"Halt," she barked. "You shall not pass!"

Patrick's face fell dramatically. "Why not?" he begged. "Aren't I your favorite brother?"

Penelope shook her head, her dark hair wagging in her face. "Nay," she said flatly. "Thomas gives me sweets. I love him best."

Patrick fought off a grin at his utterly adorable, but naughty, sister. "If I give you sweets, will you love me best?"

She cocked her head, looking very much like their father in that gesture. "What sweets will you give me?"

"What do you want?"

"Candied grapes!"

Patrick had no idea where he was going to get candied grapes but he nodded. He simply couldn't let Thomas be the favored brother. "I shall, I swear it," he said. "Am I your favorite brother again?"

"What else will you give me?"

He burst out laughing. "I'll give you my hand to your backside, you little thief," he said, watching her squeal with laughter. "Come here and give me a hug!"

He swooped down on her, hugging her, pretending to bite her arm, and she screamed in delight. Penelope beat on his arms, on his armored shoulders, swatting him with her wooden sword as he carried her towards the inner ward. He was bringing up the rear behind his mother, aunt, and Brighton, but his focus shifted from Penelope's antics to the sway of Brighton's backside in a hurry.

Soon, he was back to thinking of the lady as he watched that sensual sway. It was rather like he was in a fog where the only thing clear to him was that heart-shape of her bottom. Meanwhile, Penelope started hitting him on the helm with her sword so he flipped her upside-down and carried her so she was facing away from him and unable to hit him with her sword any longer. Penelope screamed in both glee and frustration, enough so that Jordan turned around to see what had her youngest daughter so upset. She came to a halt, and Jemma and Brighton with her.

"Penelope?" she asked, bending her head downward to look at her daughter in the face. "Why are ye screamin' so, lass?"

Penelope was swinging that sword around as Patrick flipped her upright and set her to her feet. She immediately charged him angrily, smacking her sword against his mailed legs.

"Bad Atty!" she said. "You are *bad*!"

He pushed her away by the head, gently, but it was enough to nearly send her onto her backside. "And you are a spoiled little goose," he said.

She charged him again and would have made contact had Jordan not grabbed her child. She yanked the sword away and handed it over to Jemma, who was more than happy to take it. Neither one of them approved of the lass' toy sword, so any chance to take it away from her was happily taken. Jordan scowled at her rambunctious daughter.

"What have I told ye about hitting with yer sword?" she scolded. "Now, ye've lost it. I'll not give it back tae ye for the rest of the day."

Penelope immediately broke down in tears. "It's mine!"

Jordan wouldn't have any of it. Grasping her daughter by the hand, she dragged the girl into the inner bailey as Penelope's wailing echoed off the walls. It was loud enough that her brothers, uncle, and father began to gravitate in her direction, all of them wondering why the baby was so unhappy. Jordan had to fight off William because he wanted to comfort his youngest and as Brighton watched, she saw Jordan give William a good scolding about spoiling his child. William simply grinned.

It was all quite humorous to watch but it was also very sweet. Brighton could see that the love and affection between Patrick and his knights and their wives wasn't simply limited to them. It was clear that, here at Castle Questing, there was much familial love and affection as well.

It was all quite astonishing, truly. More and more, Brighton was coming to see what her affectionless days at Coldingham had cost her. Outside of those austere walls, there was life and love. She'd had no idea how much. People cared for one another and they laughed together, and the de Wolfe group seemed to be the most loving and joyful of all. It was true that she had nothing to compare it to, but she couldn't imagine anyone, anywhere, had more joy than this family did.

Lord, did you send those reivers to free me from Coldingham to discover what I have been missing? Is this truly what life should be like?

She wondered.

"In case you did not realize it, that is my baby sister, Penelope," Patrick said, coming up beside her. "My mother will be stern for an hour or two and then my father will take over and ruin everything she has done. Penelope is his angel."

Brighton grinned. "S-she is terribly cute," she said. "She seems to want her sword back very badly."

"She willna get it," Jemma said sternly. "I should burn the thing."

Patrick shook his head. "If you do, Father will just have another one made for her," he told his aunt. "Let her have it. She will soon grow weary of it."

Jemma wasn't so sure. "She's attached tae it as yer father is attached tae his," she said with disapproval. "The lass has too much William de Wolfe in her."

"She *is* his daughter."

Jemma pursed her lips irritably at her mountainous nephew with the smart-aleck replies. "Go about yer business," she said, swishing her hands at him. "I will take Lady Brighton inside and find Moira and Rosie." She turned to Brighton. "Would ye like some other lasses tae talk tae?"

Brighton wasn't sure what to say to that. More new people? Did the parade of Patrick's relatives never end? She simply forced a smile and allowed Jemma to pull her through the inner ward, towards the buildings that housed the great hall and the family apartments, following the weeping Penelope and Jordan as they went.

Patrick simply stood there and stared, his gaze on Brighton's backside again, watching her until he could watch no more. In fact, when she disappeared into the building that housed the great hall, he was forced to look away only to realize that his father was standing next to him, studying him closely. Realizing he'd been caught staring at a woman, Patrick smiled weakly and tried to cover it up.

"Let us go inside and speak, Da," he said, grasping his father by the arm. "Much has happened since I rescued Lady Brighton from the *reivers*. You are going to want to hear this because I very much require your counsel on it."

William wasn't stupid. He knew that Patrick was trying to distract him from what he'd witnessed, which was his powerful, invincible son seemingly besotted with a woman. He could tell simply by the expression on Patrick's face. William had always hoped for a great marriage for his greatest son, but he wanted a marriage as befitting Patrick's destiny in life. The man needed a fine wife from a fine house, a marriage that would make his son wealthy and even more prestigious.

But the way Patrick had been looking at that woman he'd saved from the *reivers*… aye, William knew that look. He'd seen it before on other men but never on Patrick. It was the look of attraction. *The look of surrender.* Although William didn't know anything about Lady Brighton, he was fairly certain she wasn't the impressive marriage he was looking for when it came to Patrick.

Whatever was going on, he wanted to know about it.

And then he wanted to end it.

CHAPTER SEVEN

Later that evening

"WHAT IS SO important that you'd trek halfway across Northumberland with women and children, Atty?" William asked his son quietly. "What has happened? And who is this young woman you have brought with you?"

They were standing in his father's solar. Patrick had always loved the smell of the dark, cluttered chamber. Something between leather and steel. Still, it was difficult to describe but as a child, he'd always derived a great deal of comfort from the scent. To this day, the smell of leather reminded him of his father.

It was the smell of power.

The question William asked hung in the air, expectantly. There were others in the solar as well – Kieran, Alec, Hector, Kevin and Apollo. Thomas and Nathaniel and Adonis had not been invited because they were really little more than children themselves and William didn't want young men involved who hadn't yet learned to keep their mouths shut. He wasn't sure what troubles Patrick had brought with him and Patrick was well aware of his father's wariness; he could see it in the man's face.

And he was certain the man was in for a shock.

"Something quite unexpected has happened," he finally said, reaching for a pewter pitcher of wine he'd seen a servant bring in. He poured himself a cup. "As I told you, we received word two days ago that *reivers* had raided an English settlement along the border. At least, that was our initial information, but when we caught up to the raiding party, they had two women with them from Coldingham Priory. One was a nun and the other was Lady Brighton."

"I am listening," William said steadily.

Patrick took a long drink before turning to his father. "I managed to wrest Lady Brighton from the raiders. While she was in the company of Kevin and Apollo, I went in search of the second woman I was told was somewhere among the raiders. I found the old nun dying on the road but before she passed on, she told me a very interesting story about Lady Brighton."

"And what was that?"

Patrick fixed his father in his one good eye. "She told me that I must protect the lady with my life and when I asked why, she told me that the lady was the daughter of King Magnus of the Northmen and a Scottish mother of Clan Haye. Evidently, the lady had no idea of her true identity but I was told that the lady's mother was sent as a hostage to the Northmen and ended up with child by Magnus. She was sent home in shame and when the child was born, it was given over to the nuns at Coldingham under an assumed name."

By this time, William was sitting back in his chair, his hands folded in front of his mouth as he listened to his son's story. "The daughter of Magnus the Law-Mender?" he repeated, awe in his tone. "A bastard Norse princess?"

Patrick nodded confidently. "The nun swore to it," he said. "She also swore than it was a secret known only to her. When I informed the lady of what the old nun had told me, she clearly knew nothing about it. In fact, she was quite hysterical over the information. The old nun also told me that if anyone knew of Lady Brighton's true identity that it would bring war and strife such as we have never seen. But here is where it becomes interesting, Da; the *reivers* were from Clan Swinton and they had gone to Coldingham specifically asking for Brighton de

Favereux. They *knew* she was there. That begs the question – *how* did they know? If it was such a secret, who told them? I ask that you send a missive with a messenger to Coldingham asking the prioress what she knows. And as far as going to Coldingham specifically for the lady, I can only guess at the purpose– mayhap to ransom her back to Clan Haye, or to enemies of Clan Haye, or mayhap even ransom her back to Magnus. Had I known the turn the night was to take, I would have taken captives, but I did not. We left no man living so there is no one to interrogate and discover their purpose."

A heavy silence hung in the air as he finished his explanation, looking to his father for the man's reaction. He was positive his father would understand the situation and agree with him. But William remained much as he had since entering the room; seated in his chair, his hands folded in front of his lips, he appeared thoughtful. After several long moments, he drew in a deep and pensive breath.

"A Norse princess," he muttered. "A woman who knew nothing about her identity and was raised at Coldingham as a pledge, I am assuming."

Patrick nodded. "She calls herself a postulate."

"And you are certain that she knew absolutely nothing?"

"Aye."

William scratched his head. "I suppose I fail to see why you have brought her here," he said. "She is not our concern, lad. She is a pledge of Coldingham and we have no right to hold her in any capacity."

That wasn't the answer Patrick was looking for. Frankly, he was shocked. His brow furrowed.

"I swore to a dying nun that I would protect her," he said. "Da, if Clan Swinton is looking for her to ransom her and I return her to Coldingham, then they may once again raid the priory and abduct her. If I have sworn to protect her, then I cannot return her there."

William looked at him. "So this is a matter of honor? Because you swore you would protect her?"

"Of course it is. What else would it be?"

William cocked an eyebrow. "That is what I am attempting to discover," he said. He looked at his son, knowingly. "I understand you swore an oath to protect the girl, but that does not mean you should be burdened with her. Protecting her can mean many different things. In this case, I believe taking her to one of the big abbeys along the border would suffice in fulfilling your vow. Take her to Kelso or Jedburgh – if you are truly worried about her safety, she will be safe there."

Patrick was genuinely stumped at his father's lack of compassion in the case. He couldn't believe the man didn't understand his point of view. "How do you know?" he asked. "If the Swinton Clan breached Coldingham, there would be nothing to stop them from breaching Kelso or Jedburgh."

"And nothing to stop them from attacking Questing if they know she is here," William pointed out, his manner growing more forceful. "Patrick, you have brought a woman who is not your responsibility to my home. Clan Swinton notwithstanding, my biggest concern is that we will incur the wrath of the church by keeping her here against her will. Does she even want to be here? Did she ask you to bring her here to protect her?"

Patrick felt as if he'd been slapped. He stared at his father, feeling confused and disappointed and foolish. He was going to feel even more foolish when he answered his father's question truthfully.

"Nay," he muttered. It was a difficult admission. "She did not ask me to protect her."

"Then what does *she* want from you?"

Jaw ticking, Patrick looked away. "She wants me to return her to Coldingham."

William sighed heavily and stood up. "Then take her back," he said. "You have no right to hold her here. Your oath to the old woman was to protect her and you have done that. You saved her from the *reivers* and she is safe. Now, you will return the woman to her home where she belongs."

Patrick felt like an idiot. "But what about the fact that she is the daughter of Magnus?" he asked. "The Swinton already knows that. What if, by not protecting her, we are inviting the wrath of the Northmen to come down on the borders as they seek their lost princess. By keeping her safe and away from the clans who wish to use her, we keep peace for us all."

William could see that he was grasping at straws at this point; it was a weak argument he was giving. He put a big hand on Patrick's shoulder.

"I understand you feel strongly about your vow to protect the woman," he said. "But you have done your duty. And anything between the clans and the Northmen is not our fight. I will not get involved in it and neither will you. You have a noble and altruistic spirit, Patrick, but you must think logically about this. And I fear you are not."

Patrick tried not to appear hurt by his father's words. "I am thinking as I thought you would think," he said. "I always believed my father to be compassionate in matters such as this. Was I wrong?"

"You were not wrong. But I will not risk my family or my empire for the sake of something we do not need to be involved in. You are not that woman's last line of hope, Patrick. Let the church protect her. That is where she belongs."

Patrick couldn't even respond after that. He sank back against the windowsill, crossing his arms and hanging his head. He didn't have anything more to say. Out of the corner of his eye, he could see men leaving the solar, whispering among themselves and he knew it was about him. He'd made a fool of himself. And for the first time in his life, he didn't agree with his father in the least.

But doubt began to creep upon him. Was his father right? Was he not thinking logically about the situation? At least his father hadn't said what he was probably thinking – that Patrick had been swayed by a pretty face. At least his father had saved him that embarrassment, but the message was clear nonetheless.

The great Patrick de Wolfe had allowed a woman to get the better of him.

As Patrick stood next to the window and stewed in a situation of his own making, he felt a big hand on his shoulder.

"Do not let your father's words upset you so," Kieran said. He'd lingered back behind the others, waiting until everyone left the solar before returning. Big, gentle, wise Kieran adored his nephew a great deal. "William is trying to think of everyone, not simply one small lady. He fears what will happen if the Swinton Clan and their allies discover where the lady is. Your father has his family to protect and fighting another man's war is not something he relishes."

Patrick snorted softly. "I did not expect his condemnation," he said. "Had he been in my position, he would have done exactly the same thing. Now I see that coming to him for support was wrong."

Kieran shifted so that he was standing opposite Patrick and able to look him in the face. "Was it his counsel you sought?" he asked, watching Patrick nod. "He gave it to you. It simply was not what you wished to hear. That does not equate to a lack of support. If you want my opinion, it is reasonable."

Patrick looked over at the man he'd grown up idolizing. Kieran Hage, almost as much as his father, was a legend upon the borders. Patrick realized the man was right. His father had, indeed, given his counsel and it was sound.

Sighing heavily, Patrick turned his attention to the gentle night outside of the window. The sun had set and the torches were lit on the battlements of Questing, guarding the inhabitants against the night. There was peace in that vision but Patrick couldn't feel much of it over his own distress.

"I leave for London in a fortnight," he muttered. "I am to assume a new post and a new title. My life is spread out before me. But now…."

He shook his head, unable to find the words to continue, and Kieran's brow furrowed. "What, Atty?" he asked quietly. "Tell me truthfully – does this woman mean something to you? How can she possibly mean something to you when you have only known her for a few days at most?"

Patrick shook his head quickly, before Kieran could even get the words out of his mouth. "She means nothing to me," he said firmly; perhaps *too* firmly. "But my oath means something. I swore to keep her from harm and that does not mean returning her to Coldingham where she will only be abducted again. If they tried once, they will try again. I could not live with myself if I knew that somehow, someway, I contributed to that poor girl's misery."

"Then marry her and take her with you to London."

Patrick's eyes widened and he pushed himself away from the window. "I will *not* marry her," he said. "I am to assume the most important post in the court of Henry and that appointment does not include a wife. I do not want one; I do not *need* one."

Kieran watched his nephew stomp about. *Thou doth protest too much*, he thought. But he didn't voice his thoughts, not wanting to agitate Patrick further. But something told him that Patrick was in denial when it came to the lovely lady he'd caught a glimpse of in the bailey.

Denial of his attraction to her.

"I know," he said after a moment. "It was just a suggestion. Forgive me."

"It was a foolish suggestion."

"Agreed. Now, will you come with me to the hall? Sup should be served soon and it has been a while since I've sat at a table with you and heard of your adventures at Berwick. I want to hear about this raiding party and how you circumvented them. Will you tell me of your greatness, Nighthawk?"

Patrick glared at Kieran for a moment before breaking down into a reluctant grin. It was Kieran's way of easing his distress and he knew it. Moving to his uncle, he put a big arm around the man's neck and began to pull him from the chamber.

"I will tell you how great I am," he said. "And then I will drink you under the table, old man."

"Careful who you call an old man."

Patrick snorted. "Is it not true?"

"That depends on your point of view. I can still take you down if I need to."

"I would genuinely like to see that."

"Ply me with enough drink and I just might be stupid enough to attempt it."

Patrick laughed all the way to the great hall.

BECAUSE ALEC HAD a horse that was turning up lame, he ended up out in the stables after the meeting in William's solar. With the smell of hay and animals heavy in his nostrils, he wanted to check the horse before heading in to sup. But the truth was that he wanted to think about everything he'd just heard in the solar, Patrick's explanation of the situation and William's response.

Truth be told, it had been surprising.

He had been present when Patrick had rescued the lady captive from the *reivers*. He had seen the ferocity with which the Scots had fought. It had been a rather nasty battle and chaotic, and the explanation that Patrick had uncovered for the raid had ominous tidings for them all. *A Norse princess with ties to the Scots....* But Alec wasn't quite sure how he felt about any of it.

It was all rather exhausting.

"I thought I'd find you here," Hector said, interrupting his thoughts as he wandered into the stall. "How is the horse?"

Alec was bent over the horse's right front leg, feeling up the fetlock. "Hot," he said, "and swollen. With all of the riding and fighting we have done over the past couple of days, I am not surprised. 'Tis quite tender."

Hector moved around him, squatting down to get a look at the hairy leg. He touched it, gently, feeling the heat in the tendons. "Wrap it with a mustard and mint poultice," he said. "That should help."

"I know."

"You will have to rest him for a week or so. You'll have to ask Uncle William to loan you a steed to return to Berwick."

Alec simply nodded, still focused on the leg. "It sounds as if we are to be returning soon."

Hector stood up, stretching his long legs. "What did you think of the discussion in there?"

Now, the true crux of Hector's visit was out. Alec suspected that the man hadn't come to the stables simply to chew the fat, perhaps stewing about the conversation in the solar just as Alec was. It was something that concerned them both, as knights sworn to Patrick. Whatever was coming involving the lady, they would more than likely be involved. But Hector was a little more edgy about things while Alec, with his father's disposition, didn't particularly get worked up about things that he couldn't control.

"What do you mean?" he asked.

"Of Uncle William's reaction. What did you think of it?"

Alec didn't reply for a moment, still patting down the leg. "Do you really want to know?"

"I do."

"You will not tell Uncle William?"

"Nay."

Alec sighed heavily. "Then I think he was without compassion in the situation," he said honestly. "Now we are to return that terrified woman back where she came from? I agree with Patrick – if we return her to the priory, it will only be a matter of time before the Swinton Clan comes for her again. God only knows what they will do to her."

Hector leaned back against the wall of the stall, crossing his big arms. "Uncle William has a point, Alec," he said quietly. "She is not our problem."

"Patrick swore to protect her. Does his oath mean nothing?"

"Of course it means something. But Uncle William was right when he said that Patrick had fulfilled it. He had protected the girl, removed her from the battle, and now he must return her home. I cannot believe the old nun expected Patrick to protect the woman for the rest of his life. That is unreasonable."

Alec shook his head. "An oath is an oath," he said. "When we swore ours to the king and to God, did we give it a time limit? Of course not. Oaths do not expire."

"Then you believe Patrick should protect the girl indefinitely?"

Alec shrugged, confusion in his manner. "I am not certain," he said. Then, he looked up at Hector. "But I will tell you this – look at him when he watches her. It is my suspicion that he feels something for her and that is why he is so unwilling to forgive his oath. He is using it as an excuse."

Hector was intrigued. "An excuse for what?"

"To keep her with him."

Now, Hector was doubly intrigued. "Atty is interested in a woman?" he asked. Then, he shook his head. "It is not possible. He is only interested in his path as a knight. God's Bones, the man is heading to London to assume the position as Lord Protector to the king. That is all he cares about right now."

"Then why is he fighting so hard to keep the woman safe?"

Hector didn't have a swift answer for that. "Frankly, I do not know," he said, hinting at exasperation. "But I do not see anything bizarre in his behavior."

Alec returned his attention to the horse. "Then watch him tonight as sup. See how he behaves with her."

Hector didn't like the sound of that. "Uncle William will not be pleased," he muttered. "You know he expects great marriages from his sons, and Patrick most of all. I believe he is hoping the man will find the daughter of a duke or a niece of the king when he goes to London."

Alec snorted softly. "And the bastard daughter of a Norse king is not good enough? She's a pretty little thing, I will admit. Lovely, actually. But do not tell Katheryn I said that or she will box my ears."

Hector grinned. "Katheryn is much like her mother that way. That is why I chose Evelyn – a calmer, more sedate female."

"I like a woman with fire."

"You are very much like your father in that respect. He married a woman with enough fire in her to burn down half of Scotland."

Alec laughed softly, standing up from his horse and moving to gather the ingredients for the pack he would put on the horse's leg. "Then what do we do, Hector?" he asked. "If Patrick will not take the woman back to Coldingham, what shall we do?"

Hector shook his head. "Nothing," he replied. "We are sworn to Atty's command. His wishes are our wishes. If he wishes to keep the woman, then we will have nothing to say about it."

Alec shook his head slowly. "We are sworn to Uncle William as well," he reminded Hector. "I agree with Atty in that the woman should not go back to Coldingham, but if he disobeys his father, who is ultimately our liege, we will be complicit."

"We shall cross that bridge when we come to it, I suppose."

"I suppose."

"Are you coming into the hall soon?"

"Aye. Tell my wife so she does not fret."

Hector left the stall, heading back to the keep where his wife and children were. As his long strides made haste towards the great hall, Alec's words were beginning to weigh upon him.

Watch Patrick at sup tonight. See how he behaves with her.

It was an interesting prospect and one that surprised Hector, for Patrick had been the target of some very fine marriage offers that he had summarily refused. In fact, he had refused a marriage contract to Moira Hage that had nearly split the family in half. Now, of all the past situations, he found a woman he had interest in who was probably the most undesirable marriage prospect that Hector had ever heard of.

The bastard daughter of a Norse king? A woman that Clan Swinton was evidently after? Hector had to admit that the entire situation had him baffled. He would, indeed, watch Patrick tonight. If he saw even a hint of the man showing interest towards the woman, he was going to pull Patrick aside and slap some sense into him.

Trouble was, Patrick would slap back. Therefore, Hector shouldn't be the one to do it. But William, if he saw where his son's attention was focused, wouldn't hesitate to throw a slap that Patrick would have to accept.

Aye, it was going to be an interesting evening.

CHAPTER EIGHT

THE REGALIA OF the great hall of Castle Questing was something on an entirely new scale of splendor and pageantry. It was pure majesty.

Living in the ascetic world of Coldingham, Brighton had never seen anything like it. The enormous great hall was built against the family apartments, splayed across the inner wall with a pitched roof and long, slender lancet windows. One side of the hall had two levels of balconies, made of polished wood, and across the ceiling hung the banners of the House of de Wolfe, the House of Hage, and the House of de Longley, who was William's liege.

The floor, usually packed earth in great halls, was lined with stone, which was kept very clean in accordance with Lady Jordan's wishes. There were rushes about, but only on the edges of the room, and fresh straw was sprinkled liberally under the three enormous feasting tables in the room. The tables were now laden with great baskets of bread, tubs of butter, and bowls of fruits and cheeses.

It was to be a joyous meal with the unexpected arrival of Patrick and his sisters, and the tables were festively arranged accordingly. Brighton had never seen such festivity, as if she had traveled from earth and entered an entirely new world, one of warmth and excitement and prosperity. It was clear from everything she had witnessed that the House of de Wolfe was quite prosperous, down to the pewter salt cellars on the tables that were fashioned in the shape of a little castle with the de Wolfe crest on them, a stylized wolf's head.

After having spent a few hours in her very own chamber, assigned to her by Lady Jemma, Brighton was quite excited for the coming meal. She was supposed to have rested during her time in the chamber but she found that she could not. The window of the chamber faced towards the gatehouse and the noise from the bailey drew her attention, so she'd perched herself at the window, curiously watching the happenings as soldiers and servants went about their duties. It was a new place, a new experience, and she wanted to see everything.

The sun had set and the battlements of Questing were lit up by what seemed to be a thousand torches, giving off golden light into the dark night. From her window seat, she watched a soldier work with a young dog, training it to be a good guard dog, but the dog wasn't cooperating. It made her smile because the dog was no more than a puppy, long-limbed and shaggy, and it wanted to lick and play. More often than not, the soldier gave in to the joyful dog and let it kiss him.

In truth, she had been content to watch the activity of the castle forever but that time came to an end when a little servant appeared with warmed water and an offer to help her dress before sup. Brighton had been given a travel bag by Katheryn and Evelyn but she truthfully hadn't looked inside of it; it had been brought up to her chamber before she'd arrived with Lady Jemma. Between her and the little servant, they pulled out everything in the satchel and laid all the garments out over the bed.

The red silk and blue damask had made it into the satchel, carefully rolled up to minimize the wrinkles. The soft lamb's wool gown had also made it into the satchel, as had two linen shifts. There was a pair of hose and ribbons to tie them with, as well as a small bronze mirror, a hair comb, and pins for the hair. There was also a small piece of white soap that smelled of lemons. Upon closer inspection, Brighton could see yellow pieces of lemon rind in it.

In all, it was a very substantial collection and Brighton was touched by the generosity of Katheryn and Evelyn. The little servant helped her to change out of the green wool that she had worn on the journey and wash her limbs and face with the soap, before bundling her into the red silk gown. The dress was simple in construction, with long flaring sleeves and a flaring skirt, but the bodice was cinched up with a built-in corset that laced up her torso. The servant had to tie her into the thing, lacing her up so that her waist appeared very small and her full breasts fuller.

When the servant held up a small, polished bronze hand mirror for Brighton to see her reflection, she'd never been so shocked in her life. The only time she'd ever seen her reflection had been in water or another reflective service, so the first time seeing herself as a true reflection was something quite astonishing. While she gawked, the servant went on the hunt for the comb.

Brighton didn't pay much attention to the servant as the woman combed her hair out and began to braid it; she was still fascinated by her own reflection, seeing the defined lines of her face for the first time. But she soon began to watch the servant as the woman made many small braids on the top of her head before taking the smaller braids and winding them into a bigger one. The result was a gorgeously elaborate hair style that draped over her right shoulder.

As Brighton watched her transformation, it was somewhat overwhelming for her. She never knew she could look so lovely out of the coarse woolen robes prescribed by Coldingham. She'd always been cold, irritated, with dirty feet because of the inadequate shoes. Looking at herself now, she vowed at that very moment that she would never return to such a state. She liked being warm and clean and groomed, with soft clothing so her skin wouldn't itch.

She liked what the outside world had to offer. Perhaps she didn't want to return to Coldingham, after all.

Ever.

At the dinner hour, Evelyn and Lady Jemma returned for her, fussing over her in the red garment and telling her how beautiful she looked. Unused to compliments, Brighton had flushed furiously, which delighted the ladies. Evelyn darted out of the room and returned bearing a garnet necklace set in silver, which she placed on Brighton's neck because it had been the jewelry Hector had given her to match the dress that had formerly belonged to her. When Brighton took a look at herself in the mirror again, now with the lovely necklace gracing her throat, tears popped to her eyes. It was an emotional moment for the woman who had lived such a sequestered life.

Taking her tears as joyful ones, Jemma and Evelyn escorted her down a flight of spiral stairs to the level below which was where the family slept. Katheryn was there, with Lady Jordan, and a herd of small children including little Lady Penelope. Jordan and Katheryn were trying to dress the children for dinner, cleaning off little dirty faces and hands, but the children were running about like wild animals, playing and screaming.

Jemma jumped into the fray and began to swat naughty behinds, which made Evelyn leave Brighton's side to protect her children from her frustrated aunt. But she managed to summon a servant before she went and asked the woman to take Brighton down to the hall, so Brighton went down to the great hall alone.

And that was where she was as of this moment. The servant who had escorted her down to the hall had asked her to sit at the end of one of the feasting table and Brighton had obeyed. The servant then brought her warmed wine with bits of spice floating in it, which was delicious. She picked up a piece of tart white cheese from a platter on the table, chewing it as she drank her wine and inspected the banners along the ceiling. She was just coming to the end of the cheese when a body plopped onto the bench across the table from her.

"Greetings, my lady," Thomas de Wolfe said, his young face lighting up at the sight of her. "Are you really here all alone?"

Brighton nodded. "I-I am," she said. Then, she looked around to see if there weren't more de Wolfe brothers around – like Patrick – but she could only see two more young men lingering over near the hearth.

"Where is the rest of your family?"

Thomas shrugged, calling a servant for wine before answering. "My father is in his solar with Atty and the others," he said. "My sisters are upstairs, I think. Did you not see them?"

Brighton nodded. "I-I did."

Thomas greedily snatched the goblet of wine from the servant as it came near. He slurped at it. "I have five brothers, you know, but I am the only one who is left behind at Questing. My brothers all have command of outposts along the border. Someday I'll have command of an outpost, too."

Brighton thought that he sounded a little bitter about being the youngest de Wolfe male without any responsibility. "I-I am sure you will," she said. "Where are your other brothers?"

Thomas took another gulp of his wine. "Scott and Troy are my eldest brothers," he said. "They are twins. Have you met them?"

"I-I have not."

"Scott commands Rule Water Castle and Troy commands Kale Castle," he said, chattering on in a cross between pride and disdain. As if he could do a better job than his silly older brothers. "They are not too far from here, at least not far enough that they cannot summon help when they need it. My brother, James, also commands a small tower called Wark Castle. It is closer to Northwood Castle but it sits right near the river where the Scots like to cross."

Brighton was listening with some interest now. "A-am I to understand that all of your older brothers have a garrison to command?"

Thomas nodded. "All but Edward," he said. "He serves Scott at Rule Water. Did you know that the Scots call it Wolfe's Lair? Well, they do. All of the garrisons have names that the Scots have given them. Scott's castle is Wolfe's Lair, Troy's is Wolfe's Den, James has The Wolfe's Eye, and Atty commands Wolfe's Teeth. I am going to have my own outpost someday and call it Wolfe's Ass because I shall shite upon the enemy!"

He giggled hysterically at his own joke and Brighton couldn't help but grin at the naughty youngest brother. She was coming to see, more and more, that he was a young man who very much envied and admired his older brothers. It must have been difficult being the youngest of so many great knights. But something else he'd said caught her attention.

"A-Atty," she repeated. "I have heard others call Patrick by that name. What does it mean?"

Thomas snorted. "When he was a child, he could not say his name so he called himself Atty," he said, grinning. "My mother likes to tell that story. So the family calls him Atty. You can call him Atty, too."

Brighton wouldn't dream of doing that. Perhaps it was fine for the family, but not for a stranger. Somehow, she sensed that calling him that was something to be earned and she'd not yet done that, not in the least.

"H-he is Sir Patrick to me," she said, watching the young man shrug and down his wine. "Have… have you lived here all of your life, then?"

Thomas nodded, smacking his lips of the sweet wine. "I was born here," he said. "But I shall go to Northwood Castle in the autumn to train with my Uncle Paris. My father and Uncle Kieran have taught me a great deal, but Uncle Paris will teach me how to be a great knight. I will squire for him."

He seemed quite excited. Brighton smiled. "I am happy for you."

Thomas smiled because she was. In fact, he was gazing at her quite intently. "Why did my brother bring you here?" he asked in a complete change of subject. "I heard him say that he saved you from *reivers*. What happened? How did they get you?"

Brighton's smile quickly faded. She didn't really want to tell him the details of how she came to be in Patrick's company. It wasn't something she wanted to talk about at all, truthfully. She averted her gaze, turning to her wine.

"It is a long tale," she said. "Mayhap your brother will tell you. I do not remember most of what happened, in truth. Everything happened so quickly."

Thomas didn't let up. "But he brought you here," he said. "Why?"

"That is not a question you should be asking."

Both Brighton and Thomas turned to see William approaching the table. Behind him, men were filtering into the great hall, as were women and children, having descended from the upper floor. The entry to the hall, in fact, was now crowded with people drifting into the hall as servants began to emerge with plates of steaming food. But Thomas and Brighton were solely focused on William.

"Why?" Thomas wanted to know. "Is it a secret?"

William sighed faintly, looking down at his youngest, and most curious, son. The lad wanted to grow up very badly, made worse by a gaggle of big brothers who were doing the very things he wanted to do. He put a hand on Thomas' shoulder.

"It is none of your affair," he told his son. "You will not ask our guest such questions. It is impolite."

Rebuked, Thomas scooted down the table and lost himself in the bread and butter that were sitting further down. William's gaze lingered on his nosy son for a moment before turning his attention to Brighton only to see that she was gazing up at him. He smiled weakly.

"My lady," he said. "I hope not everyone at Questing has been so rude."

Brighton grinned. "H-he was not rude, my lord," she assured him. "He was pleasant and curious."

"You are kind."

"I-I promise I would tell you if he was rude, but I swear that he was not."

William flashed her a smile that suggested he didn't believe her but he let it go. Then, he extended his arm towards the other end of the table, nearer to the hearth.

"Will you not come down here and sit near the fire?" he asked. "It is our pleasure to have you as our honored guest tonight."

Brighton stood up, cup of wine in hand, and moved with the man down to the far end of the table where it was delightfully warm next to the enormous hearth, big enough for five men to stand inside of. It was the biggest hearth she had ever seen.

"T-thank you," she said, a bit giddy to be in such an important man's company. It made her run off at the mouth a bit. "I have never supped in such a grand place as this."

William indicated where she should sit and she did. "I can imagine the halls of Coldingham are not quite as elaborate."

"N-not at all, my lord."

He moved to take a seat across the table from her. "My son says you wish to return to Coldingham," he said. "I have instructed him to return you on the morrow. I apologize he brought you to Questing in the first place. I am sure it was a taxing journey after your harrowing experience with the Scots."

Brighton felt as if she'd been struck. Gone were the warm feelings and awe of being in such a grand place, and shock filled her expression as she absorbed his words.

"T-take me back to…?"

William reached out to grasp a large cup of wine brought him by a hovering servant. "Patrick meant well, you must understand," he said. "He felt he was doing what he needed to do for your safety, but he understands now that, as a ward of the church, you must be returned. I am sorry if he was not clear on that before."

Brighton's heart began to pound, a feeling of anxiety filling her. "B-but I do not wish to return," she said. "I-I cannot return. It will not be safe for me to return and it will put everyone else in danger."

William looked at her, hearing Patrick's words as she spoke and it did not please him. Was it possible his son had persuaded her with his own thoughts, convincing her that she did not want to return?

"If you do not wish to return to Coldingham, then we can take you to Kelso or Jedburgh," he said steadily. "You will be safe at either of them. They are big and fortified."

He sounded as if he'd already made the decision, as if this was something not open to debate. Brighton felt sick in the pit of her stomach.

"P-please, my lord," she said softly, urgently. "I do not wish to return to Coldingham. What Sir Patrick said was correct – the *reivers* came there looking for me. They asked for me and they killed the nun who had spent her life tending me. If I go back, they will only breach the abbey again and many will be in danger. Please… please do not make me go back."

William regarded her over his wine cup. "Patrick said you had asked to return."

She nodded her head, so hard that some of her careful hair style came loose. "A-at first, I did," she said. "That was before I understood how dangerous it was. The truth of my lineage is now known to me and… my lord, I asked Patrick if you would send word to the prioress at Coldingham and ask her what she knew of my heritage. Sister Acha said that I was the daughter of Juliana de la Haye and Magnus, king of the Northmen. If I could beseech you for help in discovering if this is true… in asking Mother Prioress if she knows this to be true… please, my lord. I beg for your help."

William's face was emotionless, but inside, he was starting to slip. Being begged by a frightened woman was weakening his resolve and, as he spoke to her, he began to see what had Patrick so enamored. She was exquisitely beautiful with her big blue eyes and rich brown hair. In spite of the slight stammer in her speech, she was well-spoken. She was also quite endearing, something soft and sweet that all men wanted to protect. He was starting to wonder if he wasn't about to fold over just as his son had, for certainly, the woman had that power about her. It was a struggle, but he summoned his strength for one last stand against her.

"You may ask her yourself when you return to Coldingham," he said quietly. "My lady, please do not think me unkind, but your troubles are your own. I cannot involve myself, especially where the church is concerned. I would assume you are a pledge?"

Tears were filling Brighton's eyes. "I-I am, my lord."

"And you are intending to take the veil?"

"A-aye, my lord."

"Then I truly have no business involving myself. You must return to Coldingham."

Brighton didn't argue with him, mostly because she was close to openly weeping. She dropped her head, her chin to her chest, trying desperately not to cry but not being successful at it. The tears trickled down her cheeks and she reached up, flicking them away quickly with shaking hands. William was coming to feel increasingly terrible about denying her when his wife approached the table with their young daughter and most of the grandchildren. Distracted from the weeping lady, he began lifting little bodies onto the bench beside him as Jordan lifted Penelope up to sit beside Brighton.

"I feel as if I've been herding ducklings for the past hour," Jordan grumbled. "Ye get most in line and two wander away. Ye find those two and another two wander away. Keep watch of them, English, while I see tae their meal. I've had the cook make a fowl stew for their little bellies."

William had Evelyn's youngest daughter on his lap, little flame-haired Lisbet. "Go ahead," he said. "I will try and keep them entertained."

Jordan blew out her cheeks, indicative of her level of frustration, but as she turned from the table, she caught sight of Brighton's lowered head and a glimmer of water on her face. She paused, putting her hand underneath Brighton's chin and forcing the woman to look at her. Immediately, she saw the tears and her eyes widened.

"What's this?" she demanded softly. "Why are ye weeping, lass?"

Brighton tried to swallow her tears and answer; she really did. But the moment she saw Jordan's concerned face, everything crumpled. She burst into quiet tears and Jordan dropped onto the seat beside her, putting her arms around the woman.

"There, there, lass," she said soothingly. "'Twill be all right, I promise. What has ye so upset?"

Brighton struggled; she didn't want to incriminate William but that would be difficult if she answered Jordan directly. She tried to stammer through it.

"I-I have been told that I-I will be returned to Coldingham," she sobbed softly. "I-I do not want to go."

Jordan hadn't heard the discussion in the solar with her husband and Patrick. All she knew was that the lady had been abducted from Coldingham Priory by *reivers* and that her son had saved the woman. But she also knew that there was something more to it, something Patrick would not tell her. There had been a great mystery about it. She was therefore confused in general.

"Then ye dunna have tae go," she assured Brighton. "We willna send ye back if ye dunna wish tae go. Will we, English?"

Across the table, William cleared his throat softly. "She must return."

Jordan looked at her husband, frowning. "Why?"

"Because she is a ward of the church and she must be returned."

"*Why?*"

He sighed with exasperation. "I will not discuss this with you," he said. "I am sorry that she does not wish to be returned, but she must go back."

Brighton wasn't a manipulative person by nature but she saw a chance to, perhaps, plead her case to a higher power than William de Wolfe himself – the man's wife.

"I-I am afraid that I will be in danger if I return, my lady," she wept. "The *reivers* that abducted me had gone to Coldingham to find me. I-I am afraid that if I am returned, they will simply abduct me again. They might hurt others in the process. I am afraid to go back."

Jordan was stricken with what she was hearing. She looked at her husband. "Do ye hear this, English?" she asked, incredulous. "The lass is a-feared tae return and ye'll make her go? I canna believe me ears!"

William rolled his one good eye, shaking his head because he was coming to sense there was a battle on the horizon – one between him and his wife. Rather than escalate it with a response, he knew his wife well enough that he knew he had to placate her, somehow. He held out a quelling hand.

"I do not wish to discuss it with you now," he said, "but I promise we will discuss it later. If you will just give me an evening of peace, I promise I will tell you everything tomorrow and you will know why I have decided upon this course. I think you will agree with me."

Jordan wasn't so easily pacified but she respected her husband enough not to fight with him in front of a stranger. Eyeing him for a moment, as if to silently convey that he had better keep his promise, she returned her focus to Brighton.

"Enough tears, lass," she said, wiping at the woman's chin. "I will discuss this with me husband and we will settle it. Ye'll not have tae do anything ye dunna want tae, I promise. Will ye stop yer tears now and enjoy yer food? I've had a few special dishes prepared that I hope ye'll like."

Brighton was very grateful for Lady Jordan and her fierce advocacy. She nodded, swallowing away the remainder of her tears and wiping off her face. "Y-you are very kind," she sniffled. "Thank you for your hospitality."

Jordan nodded, patted her on the cheek, and left the table. Brighton didn't dare look at William for fear of seeing disapproval in his eyes for pleading to his wife, so she kept her gaze averted. It wasn't long before she noticed the child sitting next to her, a doll-like little girl with big hazel eyes and dark hair who was looking up at her quite curiously. Brighton smiled weakly at the child.

"G-Greetings," she said.

The little girl looked her over. "Who are you?"

"I-I am Bridey. Who are you?"

"Penelope."

"'Tis a pleasure to meet you, Lady Penelope."

Penelope continued to look her over. "Why are you crying?"

Brighton cringed inwardly, knowing that William was listening. "I-I suppose I am sad," she simply said. "How many years have you seen, Penelope?"

Penelope cocked her head. "Three," she said. "I have a sword."

Brighton pretended to be impressed. "Y-you do?" she said. "Are you soon to fight alongside your father?"

Penelope nodded. "I will be a knight someday," she declared.

"Not if Mother has anything to say about it."

Patrick had come up behind them and Brighton turned at the sound of his voice, her heart swelling with joy as she gazed up at the man. But just as elation filled her, it was doused by the thought that Patrick must have agreed with his father if William was intent on sending her back to Coldingham. His reasoning with her the night they'd left Berwick must not have meant anything to him now – the danger she would face and his vow to protect her from it. Nay, she was certain it meant nothing to him now and she was starting to feel like a fool. A silly, burdensome fool. Just as quickly as she had looked at him, she lowered her head.

It was a gesture not lost on Patrick. Brighton sat there with her head down, refusing to look at him. With his father sitting at the table across from her, he could guess why. He knew his father had told her of her imminent return to Coldingham. As he went to sit beside her, Penelope jumped up and tried to climb on his lap even as he was sitting down.

"Atty!" Penelope said. "I want to fight! Will you fight with me?"

She meant with her wooden sword. Patrick shifted her so she was sitting on his thigh and not trying to climb up all over him.

"Mayhap after sup," he said. "You must ask Mother."

Penelope frowned. "She will not give me my sword back."

"Then how are we supposed to fight each other?"

Penelope grinned, a very big grin with a mouth full of big gleaming baby teeth. "You will give me another sword!"

Across the table, William chuckled; Patrick could hear him. "Alas, I do not have another sword for you," he told his little sister. "You must ask Mother to return your sword and then we shall fight."

Penelope didn't like that idea in the least. As she tried to argue with her brother in favor of him lending her another sword, a real sword, servants began to bring about trenchers of boiled beef and carrots. Next to Patrick, Brighton leaned over and whispered something to the servant that had just placed a trencher in front of her and the servant pointed towards the east side of the hall. Then, she suddenly stood up and quickly shuffled in that direction. Although Penelope was chatting in his ear, Patrick turned to watch her go, seeing her figure in the beautiful red silk. She looked positively stunning. Ignoring his sister, he turned to his father.

"You told her, didn't you?" he asked quietly. "About Coldingham, I mean. You told her."

William regarded his son over the top of his wine cup. "She asked," he said evenly. "I am not going to lie to her, Patrick."

Patrick sighed heavily and removed Penelope from his lap. "That news should have come from me," he said flatly. "I am the one who has been directing her life for the past two days. I am the one who told her that it would be dangerous for her to return to Coldingham. News of returning her to Coldingham should have come from me."

With that, he abruptly stood up. William watched him. "Where are you going now?" he asked.

Patrick was clearly displeased. "To talk to her," he said. "To apologize for the fact that my father will not help me protect her."

William could see the anger from his passionate son. "You came for my counsel. If you did not want it, then you should not have come."

Patrick looked at him with an expression William had never seen before. It was wrought with anger, with disgust, and, perhaps, a great deal of disappointment. "You are correct," he said, lowering his voice. "I should not have. I will not make the same mistake again."

With that, he stormed off, heading in the direction that Brighton had gone and nearly running his mother over in the process. She was carrying a bowl of something destined for her grandchildren. Patrick paused and apologized for nearly knocking the woman down but continued on before Jordan could reply. She stood there a moment, watching him walk off, before continuing to the table where her grandchildren and husband were sitting.

Setting the bowl down on the table, which the children swarmed on because it contained fried balls of dough, chicken, and carrots, Jordan looked at her husband most curiously.

"Where is Patrick going?" she asked.

William wasn't pleased about the entire situation and he was particularly upset about his son's words. Patrick adored him and he adored his son, so harsh words between them were very unusual. He downed the entire contents of his wine cup and slammed the vessel onto the table.

"He is unhappy with me," he said. "He has gone to speak with Lady Brighton."

Jordan turned to look off in the direction Patrick had taken again but he was gone by that time. She paused, perhaps thinking of her enormous son and the lovely lady he had brought with him. She'd seen the interaction between the two, the expression on her son's face when he looked at the woman. If she didn't know better….

She returned her focus to her husband.

"Careful, English," she murmured. "When it comes tae a woman, ye must be very careful."

William's jaw ticked. "He should have never brought her here in the first place," he said. "He was wrong and he does not want to admit it."

Jordan mulled over those words. "It is possible that is not the only thing he doesna want tae admit."

"What do you mean?"

Jordan shook her head, finding a seat amongst her grandchildren. "I am not sure," she said. "It 'tis possible that Atty brought the young woman here for other reasons than what he has told ye."

William didn't want to hear that. God, he didn't want to. He'd been wrestling with that fear for the past hour.

"Nay," he finally said, shaking his head. "I will not hear of it. Patrick is going to London to assume his post and there is no time for what… whatever it is you are suggesting."

Jordan could hear the distress in her husband's tone. "Something like this doesna have a time. It happens when it happens. She is a lovely lass and quite kind from what I've seen. And she's beautiful; surely he's noticed that."

William was becoming increasingly frustrated. "If she was English, would you be so supportive?"

"What do ye mean?"

"I mean that she is Scots. Is that who you see for Patrick? A Scots wife?"

Jordan lifted her eyebrows. "It was good enough for ye, English. Why not Atty?"

William sighed sharply, with frustration. "Not him," he mumbled, holding up his cup for a servant to fill. He remained silent until the cup was overflowing and the servant moved away. "Not for Patrick. He will have a great marriage, Jordan, and a wife that can bring him wealth and prestige. The daughter of a man who has a mighty army and lands to offer him. My son is destined for great things and needs a wife who can help him achieve them."

Jordan shook her head slowly. "I canna believe what I'm hearing," she said. "Ye were destined for great things and ye achieved them. Did I hold ye back?"

He rolled his eye, taking a huge drink from his cup. "It is not the same."

"Aye, it 'tis!"

He was perturbed that she was arguing with him. "You were the daughter of a clan chief. Marrying you secured an alliance. Lady Brighton – for all of her obvious beauty – offers nothing to him."

Jordan just looked at her husband, shaking her head sadly. "Is it true, then?" she asked softly. "Is it true ye've forgotten what is in a young man's heart? Atty will love who he loves, regardless of her station in life. I canna believe ye'd be so blind tae that. And so cruel."

"Cruel?"

"That's what I said – *cruel*. Are ye deaf?"

William didn't want to be lectured by his wife, and most assuredly not when she was actually making some sense. Taking his drink, he rose from the table and headed off into the crowd of men who were gathering over near the entrance. He could see Alec and Hector, Kevin and Apollo and Kieran. Men who would confirm that he was doing the right thing by sending Lady Brighton back to Coldingham where she belonged.

And she belonged away from Patrick.

Damn his wife for making sense. Damn her for explaining the situation as a matter of the heart and not of the head. Was she right? Was he so upswept in what he wanted for Patrick that he failed to see what Patrick wanted?

He wondered.

CHAPTER NINE

HE FOLLOWED THE sounds of the sniffling.

The eastern end of the hall had an alcove used by the servants to prepare trenchers and plates meant for the table, and it also had a door that led out to the kitchen yard and gardens. Once outside that door, off to the left, was a garderobe built into the thickness of the wall. A well-like trench below it then went under the outer bailey, under the outer wall, and dumped everything into the moat. It was a clever feat of engineering.

It was dark when Patrick emerged from the great hall and into the kitchen yard, and he immediately heard the sniffling. The part of the yard that he emerged into was actually a small grove of trees that grew inside the walled garden area, trees that bore apples and pears. On a warm day, they made wonderful shade and, therefore, there were several stone benches underneath the trees.

Patrick could see a lone figure on the perimeter of the trees and that was where the sniffling was coming from. Small and shrouded by the shadows, he could see the silhouette trembling as it sniffled. He headed in that direction.

Although Patrick really couldn't see who was weeping in the darkness, the size and general shape told him that it was Brighton. When he drew closer and could confirm his suspicions, with the distant light from the kitchen's fires casting just enough light to see by, he cleared his throat softly to announce his presence.

"I cannot believe you have already eaten your fill and have come out here to wallow in gluttonous misery," he said, trying to lighten the mood. "Or did Penelope chase you away from the table?"

Startled by his presence, Brighton very quickly wiped at her face, erasing the tears that had been so freely flowing. "N-nay," she said. "I… I simply came to have a breath of fresh air. I-I have never supped in a great hall before. It was quite warm and overwhelming… so many people…."

Patrick knew she was lying but he didn't contradict her. "I see," he said, moving closer to the stone bench she was sitting on. There was just enough room for him. "It is peaceful out here. May I sit with you?"

Brighton didn't say anything for a moment, nor did she look at him. "Y-you should be inside with your family."

"Yet I am not. May I sit?"

She shrugged and he took it as permission. Planting his large body beside her, he didn't look her in the face. At least, he tried not to. His attention was everywhere but her face because he knew the minute he looked at her, the situation would grow personal. Even just sitting with her, so close to her, he could feel it growing personal. As much as he had fought such a thing the night before, he didn't feel much like fighting it now. He'd run from her the night before, hiding in his chamber like a frightened squire. But the truth was that he wasn't a squire and he was attracted to her. God help him, he was. Perhaps that was why he was so upset with his father.

He was willing to admit he might have a personal stake in all of this.

Might….

"I spoke with my father this afternoon about your situation, just as I said I would," he said. "My father seems to think you will be better off returning to Coldingham. He is concerned that you are a ward of the church and therefore their property. He feels that mayhap the church is better suited to protect you from whatever trouble follows you."

That was fairly close to what William had told Brighton. She could hear, indeed, that the man had completely changed his son's mind from what Patrick had been telling her all along.

It will be dangerous to return to Coldingham.

So now she was to be sent back from where she came. Sent back to those cold halls, with no Sister Acha to guide her, wearing rough woolen underwear and working in the gardens until her hands bled. Well, she didn't want to do it. She didn't want to go back. This taste of the outside world had turned her head completely and she didn't want to return to a place where there was no love and no laughter.

No Patrick.

Her emotions were already running high and something inside of her suddenly snapped.

"T-then take me back," she hissed, standing up and moving away from him. "T-take me back and let me take my chances. Take these beautiful clothes away and do not let me become upswept in my reflection when I see how beautiful my hair has been braided or how lovely this dress is upon me. You should have never brought me here, Patrick de Wolfe. You should have left me on the road and let me escape back to Coldingham where I would have never known the joy and beauty of the outside world because now that I see it, I do not want to return to cold walls and even colder people!"

She was yanking out her beautiful braid, mussing her hair up, sobbing as she spoke. Quickly, Patrick stood up, genuinely concerned with her tears. "I did not say that I felt that way," he insisted, hoping she would calm and stop trying to ruin her lovely appearance. "I said that my father felt that way. I still feel the same way I have all along, Bridey. I will not take you back to Coldingham."

Brighton stopped pulling at her hair, her eyes wide with surprise as she gazed upon him. "Y-you will not?"

He gazed into those red, tear-filled eyes. "Nay," he said softly, his heart lurching at the intense emotion on her face. He could hardly breathe for the sight of it. "I am not exactly sure what I will do, but I will not return you. I swore to protect you and I intend to do that. My father… he is afraid. He is afraid that we are sticking our noses where they do not belong and we will incur the wrath of the church. I suspect we will return to Berwick on the morrow and then I will try to determine what will be best to do with you."

That wasn't what Brighton had expected to hear. She'd expected apologies, excuses. But to hear that Patrick had not changed his mind filled her with both astonishment and gratitude. With a gasp, she pitched forward, catching his big hands and holding them so tightly that she nearly cut off his circulation.

"T-then I shall not return?" she breathed. "Truly?"

His large fingers wrapped around hers, small and warm things. "Truly," he said quietly. "I am sorry my father upset you so. He should not have said anything to you until I had a chance to speak with you."

Brighton simply shook her head, at a loss for words for a moment. But she quickly recovered. "I-it is of no matter," she assured him as he led her by the hands over to the bench and practically forced her to sit. "But what will happen now? Will your father not be angry if you disobey him?"

Patrick was still holding her hands as he sat down beside her. In fact, he found himself caressing her flesh, loving the feel of it. Her small hands were calloused from work at the priory, but the flesh was nonetheless soft. He rather liked the feel of it, sending pinpricks of excitement racing through him.

"My father trusts my instincts," he said. "They have never failed me. He will trust that I will do what is best for all of us."

That was an answer without really giving her much information. Brighton's brow furrowed with some confusion. "W-what does that mean?" she asked. "Can I remain at Berwick?"

He shrugged. "I do not see why not," he said, realizing that she was starting to caress his fingers as well, mimicking his actions. "Do you want to?"

She nodded quickly, before the words were even out of his mouth. "I-I do," she said. "I know that your sisters are already chatelaines, but it is a very big place. Mayhap I could help with the children. There are so many of them and I know how to read and write. Mayhap I could teach them."

He smiled faintly, seeing the outline of her face in the weak light. There was such hope there. "That is a very good idea," he said. "I will speak to my sisters and see what they think. I am sure they would like to have your companionship."

Her face lit up. "D-do you really think so?" she asked. "They are so kind. I have never known such kindness. You have all been so very kind. No one has ever shown such regard for me."

Patrick wasn't entirely sure what to say to that. It seemed to him that the conversation was on the tipping point of him saying something incriminating, perhaps something to the effect of *you are easy to be kind to.* She could construe that all different ways and he would find himself with a lot of explaining to do. He didn't want her to think that there was anything in his manner other than pure duty, pure courtesy. But looking into that lovely, doe-eyed face, it was difficult to remain detached.

"Did the nuns at Coldingham beat you so severely, then?" he asked, trying to jest his way out of what could possibly become a tender moment. *Romantic.* "You make it sound as if no one has ever shown you an ounce of compassion."

She smiled and his heart began to beat faster, just as it always did when she smiled. He was becoming a slave to that smile.

"W-when I was young, they were quick with a switch or a slap," she admitted. "Fortunately, I learned quickly. I have not been switched or slapped in many years."

He grunted. "The Brides of Christ are brutes," he muttered. "You can get more out of a man with encouragement than with fear. That is a lesson those nuns need to learn."

Brighton giggled. "Y-you can tell them so," she said. "Then make sure you run away very quickly. Those switches are very fast when they swing them."

He grinned because she was. “They cannot catch me,” he insisted. “I take one stride for every three of theirs. They would have to run like the wind to catch me.”

“A-are you brave enough to test that theory?”

He shook his head without missing a beat. “Not me. I have no desire to be switched.”

Brighton was rather enjoying the jesting mood. For a woman who had never flirted in her life, it seemed that she had somewhat of an innate ability because she squeezed his big hands tightly as she gave him a rather impish grin.

“N-not to worry,” she said. “I will protect you from them. I will have my own switch and fight them off. Any man who would save me from *reivers,* I dare not permit the nuns at Coldingham to lash.”

All of that resistance he’d fronted against possible romantic feelings was being summarily crushed by her expression and warm hands. Here they were, in the dark, alone, with only a hint of moonlight through the trees, and he was being foolish enough to resist showing the woman any kind of tenderness. She frightened him but she also intrigued him; he was resistant yet she continued to lure him in.

He had no idea what to do.

God’s Bones, what are you thinking, you fool? You have a royal appointment you are leaving for soon! You do not need this complication!

Aye, his common sense screamed to him, that part of him that was professional and driven. He didn’t want to complicate something he’d worked very hard for. But as he looked at Brighton in the dim light, he began to realize that even if he were to leave her tomorrow, he would still think of her. He’d still have visions of a lady with enormous blue eyes and a rosebud mouth, a postulate who was half-Scots and half-Norse. A woman he’d sworn to protect yet a woman who had endeared herself to him very quickly. *Too* quickly, in fact. He had no idea how or why, but this woman was already under his skin and she didn’t even know it. She hadn’t even tried. Perhaps that’s *why* she was under his skin. It simply… happened.

... was it fate?

Patrick had always thought his fate was the halls of Westminster Palace, not a postulate from Coldingham. Everything he'd ever known, or ever expected, had been jolted by the lovely Lady Brighton.

Now, as he gazed at the woman, he realized that she had said something to him and expected something of an answer. The smile on her face was fading, turning into a grimace as he stared at her, lost in thought, and refused to answer. He could see that she was afraid she'd been too forward or too silly in her statement. Gently, he lifted her hands, still wrapped around his, and kissed them.

"I should be so fortunate to have such a protector, my lady," he said softly. "I am grateful, Bridey."

Patrick watched as Brighton's eyes widened at his kiss and she looked at her hands, where he'd kissed her, as if she could see his lip prints on her flesh. He rather liked the astonished look on her face. Before he could stop himself, his big head loomed over hers and he deposited the sweetest of kisses on her warm, soft cheek.

"Now," he said huskily, "shall we return inside to eat? I am famished."

Brighton was genuinely speechless. She stared at him, wide-eyed, her hand on her cheek where he had kissed her.

"Y-you... y-you...," she stammered. "Why did you do... that?"

Her mad stuttering amused him. It made him feel powerful and in control. "Because I wanted to."

Brighton stared at him a moment longer before grabbing his face between her two small hands and planting a kiss on his lips that literally knocked him backwards. She came at him so forcefully, so unexpectedly, that he hadn't been prepared for it and when she pulled back, looking at his now-astonished expression, she burst into gleeful giggles.

"B-because I wanted to!" she said.

Patrick couldn't help it; he broke down into soft, deep laughter, rubbing at his lips where she'd nearly bruised him. "I would say so," he said. "Are you always so impetuous?"

"I-I do not know!"

"Did you hurt your mouth?"

He reached out, touching her chin and lower lip as if to inspect where she'd roughly hit him, but she shook her head, unable to stop giggling. Giddiness swept her, as she'd never been giddy in her life. Yet another new experience in a few days that had been full of such things, only she liked this one better than all the rest.

"O-of course not," she said. Then, she abruptly sobered, looking at him with a worried expression. "Did I hurt *you?*"

He shook his head, giving her a half-grin because she was so excited about the kiss. "You could not hurt me if you tried," he said softly. "But we will have to work on your technique if you plan to do that again."

As the giddiness faded a bit, uncertainty came to the forefront with the reality of what she'd done. *Sweet Mary... she'd kissed a man!* "I-I did not plan to do it in the first place," she said. "D-did I offend you? I did not mean to. I do not know what came over me."

Patrick just chuckled, taking one of her hands and kissing it again. "You did not offend me."

"I-I have never done that before. Kissed anyone like that, I mean."

"I can tell."

Her eyebrows shot up. "Y-you *can?*" she gasped, now feeling mortified as the reality of what she'd done began to sink in. "I am so very sorry, Patrick. Please forgive me."

He shook his head, holding both of her hands tightly. "I kissed you first," he said. "If anyone should ask forgiveness, it should be me."

Brighton wasn't sure if that was an apology or an invitation for future kisses, but one thing was certain – she'd liked it. She'd liked it a great deal.

"Atty!"

A shout came from the alcove door, abrupt and loud, and Patrick stood up, taking a few steps to see who it was. He could see Alec in the doorway.

"I am here," he said. "What is –?"

"'Tis a night raid," Alec said quickly. "Your father is already moving to gather the men. You must come."

Patrick's brow furrowed but he was walking towards Alec with Brighton following close behind.

"A night raid?" he repeated. "Where? What has happened?"

Alec turned away from him and headed into the hall with Patrick on his heels. "It seems that the Scots have launched a night raid on Coldstream," he said. "Several of the villagers have come here, injured and terrified. They have large grain stores meant for market and it seems as if the Scots have gone after it. A soldier from Pelinom Castle is also at the gatehouse. Your father is going there now to speak with him."

Patrick was quickly shifting into battle mode. "Pelinom is north of Coldstream by a couple of miles," he said. "That is a fairly large castle, de Velt men. Why have they come to us for help?"

Alec shook his head. "I do not know," he said. "But your father wants us all mounted and ready to ride."

Patrick didn't hesitate. He charged after Alec on his way to gear up for battle but he hadn't taken five steps when he suddenly remembered Brighton. Swiftly, he turned to her and she nearly plowed into him from behind. He grasped her by the arms to steady her.

"You will remain here with my mother," he said steadily. "She will tend you until I return."

Brighton simply nodded, perhaps a bit stunned by what was happening. Up until three days ago, she'd never been around a battle in her life. Now, Patrick was heading off to another one. There was tension in the air; it was frightening. Perhaps this was something about the outside world that she didn't like at all. But before she could say anything to him, a word of blessing for his safety, he turned away from her and stormed from the great hall.

Brighton stood there and watched him until he faded from her sight. After he was gone, she turned away from the hall entry with a sick feeling in the pit of her stomach. Everything had happened so swiftly over the past few days, including this, that she was still trying to absorb everything.

Muddled, and perhaps a bit frightened on Patrick's behalf, she wandered back over to the table where Lady Jordan was sitting with her grandchildren, her daughters, and Lady Jemma. As she approached the table, little Penelope crawled off the bench and went to her, slipping her little hand into Brighton's. Big, innocent eyes gazed up at her.

"Will you sit with me?" Penelope asked. "Mama returned my sword to me. Come and see it."

The little girl was very excited about her sword, seemingly oblivious to the mood of depression that hung over the women of the table, the fear that seemed to carve into the very air around them. Fear for their men, fear for what was to come. Brighton sat down next to Penelope and was promptly shown a dull wooden sword with the lass' name carved into it. *Penelope*, it said. The little girl was very proud of it and proceeded to show Brighton how it was used.

Brighton watched her but without much enthusiasm. This was all very new to her, men leaving for battle and her confusion over her feelings for Patrick. But looking into the faces of Lady Jordan and Lady Jemma, she could see that whether it was the first time or the one hundredth time, the men leaving for battle never got any easier. The men were heading out to risk their lives and there was nothing anyone could do about it.

All they could do now was wait.

CHAPTER TEN

IT WAS A nasty skirmish from the start.

It wasn't just a few Scots raiding the border town of Coldstream for grain, it seemed like several clans. Patrick saw Nesbit tartan and he also thought he saw Armstrong, but it was difficult to tell because of the darkness. The entire town was in an uproar as homes burned and people fled for safety.

The army from Castle Questing charged in like avenging angels. William, who had handled raids like this many times in the past, had a system for these attacks – he split his group in half, with some men going to one side of the town while the rest went to the opposite side. One group of men would then plow through town and drive the Scots to the waiting contingent, which usually resulted in the end of the raid fairly quickly. This time, the plan was the same. William led the group that would wait for the Scots to be driven to them while Patrick led the group that would do the driving.

Given the fact that half of the village was in flames, it was easy to see who the enemy was. Patrick, Alec, Hector, and Kevin charged through town striking down anything that resembled a Scots, predictably driving raiders and townsfolk alike towards the other end of town where William, Kieran, and Apollo await. It seemed like a simple enough plan and Patrick drove his sword through more than one raider who tried to fight back.

While *reivers* seemed to be unorganized groups of men from many clans, these raiders seemed to be organized from one or two specific clans. He saw only two specific tartans but there were a lot of men, much more than the numbers that *reivers* usually carried. Still, it was of little consequence. Having been raised on the borders, Patrick knew how to handle them.

Or so he thought.

His first hint that something was wrong was when he made it towards the end of the town, with a clear field of vision to where his father and the others were waiting. Only they weren't alone. They seemed to be in a massive battle themselves and Patrick realized that the raiders must have also been split into two distinct groups, one of them lying in wait for the English who had their backs turned. Clearly, what he was seeing was far more than a skirmish.

It was a battle.

When Patrick and the other knights saw what was happening, they gave up herding the raiders through the town and made a break to go help his father and the others, who were seemingly overrun. Unfortunately, the men they'd been herding turned on them and the entire village deteriorated into two separate brawls. The raiders were going for the knights more than the men-at-arms, and Patrick found his skills being tested again and again. Men with short swords were trying to undercut him as he sat upon his horse, but he kept his shield low. With his sword, he managed to slice more than a few heads. He emerged the victor with confidence, but it was clear that this was no ordinary raid. The English had been drawn into something planned. Now, it occurred to him why the men from Pelinom were asking for help.

It was an English death raid on the borders this night.

With that knowledge, Patrick switched strategies. It was kill or be killed. Turning, he watched his fellow knights to make sure they weren't in any particular danger. He easily held his own, especially astride his big war horse, who was biting and snapping and kicking. The horse injured or killed as many men as Patrick did. Off to his right, several dozen yards away, Patrick could see his father fighting off hordes of men trying to bring him down. They were swarming, really. He could also see Kieran fighting off men intending to do him harm.

Old knights who had done this too many times to count, still fighting off the Scots even in their advancing years. Patrick respected and admired them greatly, but he was also very concerned for them. His father was aging and he would hate to see the man get hurt, or worse, in what was supposed to be a simple raid.

And then, he couldn't see his father anymore.

Panic seized him and he spurred his horse through and over men who were trying to block his way. The horse stomped and snapped, and Patrick was able to drive the horse through the roiling horde until he reached the spot he had last seen his father. He could see his father's horse off to his left, struggling against many hands that were trying to subdue him, but William was nowhere to been seen.

More panic seized him. Patrick spurred his horse towards his father's steed, getting close enough to the horse to remove his bridle, which gave the raiders the inability to control the animal. Patrick kicked the horse in the side, startling it, sending it bucking and kicking and running away, heading back to Questing. At least the horse would be safe that way and not fall into the hands of the raiders, but that meant William was without a mount. Patrick tried not to become hysterical as he searched the sea of fighting men for his father. Too many men, men on the ground dying, men on their feet fighting. But still, no William.

Then, he saw his father.

William was on his knees, being set upon by several men who were beating him more than they were actually trying to kill him, although one man had a short sword that he was trying to shove through William's neck. The old knight was too seasoned and too skilled to allow that to happen. The great Wolfe of the Border managed to disarm the man with the sword and turn it against him, killing the man even as others were trying to beat him.

That was all Patrick had to see. He charged through the men attacking his father, kicking them in the head or using his sword on them as he reached down to pick his father up. William grabbed hold of Patrick but was pulled down by more men who were trying to separate the father and son.

That was when Patrick went mad.

His sword was swinging ferociously, cutting off limbs and slicing through bodies. Men began screaming, falling away from him, as he reached down a second time to pick his father up from the ground. William, weakened by his fight, grabbed hold of Patrick a second time. This time, Patrick managed to lift his father up onto his saddle, which was no easy feat considering how much William weighed. He was not a small man and the fact that Patrick was able to lift him up onto his horse was a testament to Patrick's sheer strength. William ended up behind his son, on the back of the horse, holding on as Patrick drove his war horse through the fight and away from the battle for the most part. When they were outside of the perimeter of the burning town, Patrick pulled his frothing horse to a halt.

"Are you injured?" he asked his father, panic still in his voice. "Did they get to you?"

Behind him, William grunted. It sounded as if he was in pain. "Where is my horse?"

"Safe. He is running for home."

"Your mother will be worried if the horse returns without me."

"Do you want to return home as well?"

A bloodied hand suddenly appeared in Patrick's line of sight.

"I think I'd better."

That was all Patrick needed to hear. As the battle raged on behind them, he took his father back to Castle Questing as fast as the horse would carry them.

"I AM FINE, love. You do not need to weep any longer."

In the lavish bower suite of Questing, William was upon the massive bed as his wife and Jemma, as well as Katheryn and Evelyn, hovered over him. Everyone was hovering over him, fearful he was about to disappear.

The long gash in his left side had been stitched by his wife, twelve stitches in all, and his torso was bound with boiled linen to stop any leakage or bleeding. It wasn't a deep gash but mail had been shoved into it, meaning it was a dirty gash. Jordan had spent an hour picking mail out of her husband's side before stitching it.

Once the job was done, the delayed tears of fright and relief came. Jordan had been through this kind of thing with her husband for over thirty years and it never got any easier. In fact, every time, it grew worse.

"If it wasna for yer son, I would have lost ye." Jordan wiped her nose with a big linen kerchief, torn between tears and anger. "Have often have I told ye that yer too old tae fight? Ye dunna need tae prove yerself any longer, English."

William was propped up with some pillows while Penelope snuggled against his right side, sucking her thumb and half-asleep. He listened patiently to his wife's scolding, but it was something he'd heard before, many times. He pulled the covers up around his baby girl before answering.

"And I have told you that if there is action involving Questing, then I must attend it," he said quietly so he wouldn't wake Penelope. "We have had this argument too many times, love. I am a knight and…."

She cut him off, waving her hands angrily. "… and fighting is yer vocation," she finished his standard line. "I know that. I've heard it a thousand times and I hate it when ye say it. But the fact remains that ye're too old tae fight any longer. The only reason ye go these days is tae satisfy yer pride. I willna stand for it any longer, do ye hear? Do ye want Penelope tae grow up without her father? Is that what ye want?"

William sighed faintly, looking down at his little girl, sleeping contentedly against him. Nay, he didn't want her to grow up without him.

But he also didn't want to fight with his wife about it. She didn't want him to risk himself; he was doing the only thing he'd ever known.

It was a painful dilemma for them both.

A knock on the chamber door interrupted the argument and Jordan wandered away from the bed in an attempt to calm her tears. Katheryn, feeling a good deal of pity for her mother's side of things, pulled the panel open to see Patrick and Kieran standing there.

"Come in, Atty," Katheryn said. "Has everyone returned?"

"Aye."

"Where is my husband?"

"In the bailey disbanding the men."

"Is he injured?"

"Not a scratch," Patrick replied as his gaze drifted to their father. "How is he?"

"Papa is going to be fine, the old fool."

Patrick entered the chamber, dirty and splattered with blood, and Kieran followed him in. Kieran looked absolutely exhausted, pale to the point of being pasty, and his wife went to him immediately, putting her arms around him in concern. Patrick could hear them speaking softly, her great worry for her husband and Kieran's soft assurances that he was fine, but his focus was on his father.

"What is the damage?" Patrick asked William, trying to make light of the situation and the room full of worried women. "You look better than you did the last time I saw you."

William held up a hand for his son, who took it strongly. He squeezed his boy's hand. "I will survive, thanks to you," he said quietly. "You returned to the battle after you brought me home. What is the situation now?"

Patrick scratched his head wearily. "Half of the village has been burned down," he said. "I caught up with some of the Pelinom men and it seems that this was a fairly large and organized raid by Clan Nesbit. The soldiers at Pelinom were drawn out into a rather large battle which is why they sent for us. Then we were drawn into it as well. The best I can come up with is that it was a murder raid. The Scots never touched the wheat stores."

William listened to the news grimly. "I would not be surprised," he said. "They have tried that before. Pelinom sits in Nesbit territory and they want the fortress badly."

"Have they ever made any attempts on Questing like that?"

"Never. We are too big and hold too many men for them. They'd have to rouse half of the lowlands to overtake Questing and they do not have the support."

"But they keep trying."

"Aye, they do."

Patrick chewed his lip thoughtfully. "What about James?" he asked, speaking of his younger brother who was, in fact, Katheryn's twin. "Wark Castle sits closer to the border than Questing does and North-wood sits directly upon it. Do they have the same trouble with Nesbit?"

William shook his head. "Only Pelinom because it is actually in Scotland."

Patrick grunted. "The Scots left it alone for years, especially when Ajax de Velt was in command," he said. "No one would dare challenge the Dark Lord. Now his descendants have the castle, men who are fine knights. They've managed to hold off the Scots this long."

William leaned his head back against the wall, wearily. "Aye, they have, but it hasn't been for a lack of trying on the part of the Scots," he said. He fell quiet a moment, gazing up at his enormous son. "Had it not been for you tonight, I suspect I might not have made it out of there alive. I am very grateful, lad."

Patrick looked down at his father, seeing how exhausted the man was. He'd always seen his father as strong and young and powerful, not older and more easily tired. He was coming to realize that his father was no longer that young, powerful man, but an older man who more than likely shouldn't be fighting battles any longer. At least, not skirmishes like this. He squeezed his hand.

"Maybe you should let the younger men flight these little skirmishes, Da," he said quietly. "You are the greatest knight who has ever lived and it would be a fine prize for some foolish Scotsman to claim your life. I would have to go on a murder rampage myself if that were to happen. So on behalf of the Scots along the border, spare them my rage and do not go out on any more of these little skirmishes. They would be grateful and so would I."

William smiled weakly. "Your mother was just saying the same thing."

"Aye, I was," Jordan said, no longer able to stay out of the conversation. "Now ye've heard it from yer son. Ye're too old tae be fighting other men's wars like that. Ye've earned the right not tae fight every little battle that pops up."

Patrick eyed his father. "I must agree with what she says," he said. "Save yourself for the big things. Let others fight the smaller battles."

William sighed heavily as he turned his head, looking away. "I have never been very good at avoiding battles," he muttered. Then, he caught sight of Kieran over near the door where Jemma had pushed him down into a chair. "But Kieran… he has not been well lately. The physic says it is his heart. I worry for him."

Both Patrick and Jordan turned to look at Kieran in a chair as his wife wiped at his brow. The big man looked ready to collapse. Patrick's gaze lingered on the man for a moment before returning his focus to his father.

"He will never let you go to battle without him," he said quietly. "If only to spare Uncle Kieran's life, mayhap you should reconsider going to battle every time there is a little skirmish."

It was a reasonable way of putting it, as if being thoughtful of Kieran's health as an excuse to stay out of battle was easier to swallow. Still, William was reluctant.

"Mayhap," he said softly.

Patrick wouldn't let it go so easily for he was genuinely concerned. "Please, Da."

William sighed heavily, unhappy that he was now getting pressure from his son. "I said I will think on it and I shall," he said. "For now, please know I am very grateful for what you did, Patrick."

Patrick nodded, his gaze lingering on his father a moment. "There was nothing else I could do," he said. "When I saw that you were off your horse, there was only one thing on my mind – to find you. I am glad I was in time."

"So am I."

A brief pause followed. "Da," Patrick said slowly. "What I said earlier... about the fact it was a mistake to seek your counsel today. I did not mean it. You are the wisest man I know and I shall always require your counsel. I am sorry for my harsh words."

William looked at his son and thoughts of the day began running through his head; in particular, thoughts of Lady Brighton. William and Jordan had been speculating all day about Lady Brighton's relationship to Patrick and what the man could possibly feel for her. It seemed to William that now was the time to ask about it. They could speculate all they wanted but nothing would solve their dilemma more than seeking the truth from Patrick himself. Perhaps it was time for a bit of honesty, on all sides.

"There is no need to apologize," William said. "I suppose if my father was meddling in my affairs, I would be angry, too. But I would like to ask you a question."

"Anything."

"What does this woman mean to you?"

Patrick faltered; both William and Jordan could see it. He seemed to grow nervous very quickly and averted his gaze.

"I told you," he said. "I swore to protect her. I do not give my oath lightly."

"Is that all?"

"Aye."

"Ye dunna feel something for the lass, Atty?" Jordan pressed when her husband wouldn't. "Are ye... fond of her?"

Patrick refused to look at either parent. "I have only known her for a couple of days," he pointed out. "How could I be fond of her in so short a time?"

Jordan put a hand on his arms. "Stranger things have happened," she said softly. "Sometimes there is no timeframe for feeling something for someone. It happens when it happens. She is a lovely lass and I like her."

Patrick sighed heavily, looking vastly uncomfortable when he was trying hard not to. "I have only known her a short time," he said again. "But… well, if you must know, I feel a strong sense of protection for her. She is as vulnerable as a babe outside of the walls of Coldingham. She knows nothing of the outside world. Aye, I feel very protective over her for many reasons, not the least of which is the fact that she has a legacy that could very well destroy her."

"Being the bastard of Magnus?"

"Aye."

"Magnus?" Jordan repeated, confused. "Who is Magnus?"

William shook his head at his wife. "I will tell you later," he told her. Then, he returned his focus to Patrick. "Patrick, be honest with me, please. Do you feel something for this girl? Because I cannot understand why you would feel so strong a sense of protection over her if you do not."

Patrick thought back over the course of the past two days, the contact he had with Brighton, the conversations, the laughter. *The kiss*. Did he feel something for her? He did. He forced himself to admit it now that he'd been asked. But there was vast confusion beyond that. Confusion and embarrassment.

"I… I am not sure," he finally muttered. "All I know is that I feel very protective over her."

That wasn't much of an answer. They'd heard those things before. Jordan lowered her head, trying to look her embarrassed son in the eye. "Protective like a sister?" she asked.

Patrick didn't respond for a moment. He didn't move, then, slowly, he shook his head. "Nay," he whispered. "Not like a sister."

He didn't say any more than that and both William and Jordan could see how torn he was. There was confusion there. Their great son, a man who was born and bred to fight, was feeling something human towards another person. *A lady.* He was feeling something and he either couldn't admit it or had no idea what to say.

William remembered those days of his youth, when he was in love with a certain young Scotswoman, so it was easy to relate to Patrick in that sense. He felt pity for him. He still didn't want a match between his great son and a former postulate, a bastard daughter of a Norse king. But if Patrick felt something for the woman… well, William could understand that. It had happened to him once, too.

"Patrick," he said quietly. "You asked me to send a missive to the prioress at Coldingham to see if the woman knew anything about Lady Brighton's heritage, as did Lady Brighton. If you still want me to do that, I would be willing."

Patrick's head snapped up, his eyes fixed on his father. "Would you, Da?" he said, relief and gratitude in his tone. "That would be greatly appreciated. It was a request that the lady made to me, for her own clarification about her parentage, and I am grateful to you for your effort."

William could see the gratitude in his son's expression and that alone told him that Patrick was feeling more for the lady than he would admit. "And when she learns of it, what then?" he asked. "What will you do with her?"

Patrick was back to feeling confused. "I do not know," he said truthfully. "But she cannot return to Coldingham in any case. I told her that we could mayhap find her a position in a great house as a lady's companion or a nurse to children. There are useful things she could do."

"What about marriage?" Jordan said as her husband cringed. "Ye could marry her and take her tae London with ye. If ye're so concerned with protecting her, then why not marry the lass?"

Patrick turned a little pale; both parents could see it. But he came back strong. "I cannot," he said flatly. "The position with Henry will take all of my time. It would be unfair to her to marry her and take her to London where she would spend most of her time alone."

"But not all of her time," Jordan said softly. "She would be with ye and ye would see her when ye werena with the king."

Patrick was shaking his head. "It is impossible."

Jordan went for the jugular of her stubborn son. "If ye dunna marry her, then someone eventually will," she said. "Is that what ye want? For someone else tae have her?"

Patrick stopped shaking his head, now looking at his mother. He was clearly stressed. "I cannot think of something as serious as marriage right now, Mother," he said. "I have been waiting all of my life for this royal appointment and nothing is going to interfere – not you, not Father, not a young woman who fell into my lap two days ago. I cannot change my life so suddenly on nothing more than a whim. I will not marry her before I go."

Jordan's eyes flashed; she couldn't abide by stubborn men and her son had inherited a wealth of stubbornness from her. "Then take her back tae the priory and be done with her," she said. "Stop wasting her time and yers, for it seems tae me that everything ye're trying to do for her is a waste of time if ye have no intentions beyond simply protecting the lass. She needs a husband or she needs tae go back tae the priory."

Patrick could see that this was about to turn into an argument with his mother, something he had no desire to enter into. Few people entered into arguments with his mother and won. She may have been right in all things, but he wasn't going to let her push him around. He turned his attention to his father.

"If you could write that missive, I'll arrange for a messenger to take it," he said. "I will inform Lady Brighton of your change of heart. I am sure she will be very grateful."

With that, he turned and left the chamber, leaving his parents looking after him, each to their own thoughts. Jordan wondered why he was being so stubborn while William was thinking that his wife had been right all along; Patrick felt something for Lady Brighton. But rather than push his son into admitting it, William's strategy was a little different.

So it wasn't the great match that William had hoped for his greatest son; there wasn't a thing he could do about it. But perhaps if he helped his son and the lady, whatever Patrick was feeling for the woman might burn itself out. William suspected that if he continued to fight Patrick on the lady, it could very well have the opposite effect and drive him into the woman's arms.

Therefore, he was willing to help, to see if what Patrick was feeling was just an infatuation. Although he hoped it was, something told him that it wasn't.

It was just a feeling he had.

The next morning at dawn, a messenger was heading for Coldingham Priory with a missive from William de Wolfe, Baron Kilham, to the mother prioress.

CHAPTER ELEVEN

One week later
Coldingham Priory

It was a bright day in summer with puffy white clouds overhead being pushed around by the sea breeze. Days like this were rare on the coast and the residents of Coldingham were out in force, repairing the damage from the raid nearly two weeks before. Walls had been toppled, gardens trampled, and two rooms burned out entirely. Still, the determined clean-up effort went on. As both nuns and peasants busied themselves in the cloister, the mother prioress stood near the altar in the chapel.

The chapel was dim, even in the bright day, because the small windows allowed for little light and ventilation. It was a massive stone building, built for strength, and the center of a rather large and complex religious center.

In years past, Coldingham had been run by monks, headed by a prior, and there had been a good deal of commerce that brought wealth into the church. For decades, the priors had been financial geniuses with Coldingham's production of crops and ale, but back at the turn of the century, King John – Henry's father – had raided the priory and damaged it heavily. It was the beginning of the priory's decline.

Now, local clans were heavily invested in a priory that was struggling to stay solvent. Clan chiefs were taking the "buy your way into heaven" approach and tithing heavily to the church in exchange for the absolution of their sins against each other, even though there was never any attempt at actually paying reparation for those sins.

Moreover, Clans Douglas, Home, and Gordon had been vying for control of the priory, which now included women and had for the past forty years. There was a cloister for nuns headed by a mother prioress while the monks, kept separately, continued to manage the dwindling finances and production of the declining priory.

Twenty years ago, Lady Ysabella Gordon's father had purchased a position for his daughter in the priory. Young as she was, she took the veil quickly and worked her way up to Mother Prioress within a few years. The more her father would donate, the more she was promoted. The lure of money to the failing priory was great and, in truth, it was all her father could do for her, considering she had been sullied by one of the Clan Haye sons, a man who had raped her and beget her with child. The child had died, fortunately, but most knew of Ysabella's misfortune, so the church was her only option. She became Mother Prioress and the secret of the rape was buried.

But not to her.

Mother Prioress kept her hatred buried in her heart even as she sang God's praises and administered her sisters and postulates. Nineteen years ago, when Juliana de la Haye came to the abbey with an infant in her arms, an infant that needed protection, the mother prioress was more than happy to take the infant along with a sizable donation for her keep. But even as little Brighton grew up in the church, emotionally abused by most of the sisters except for Sister Acha, who was protective over her charge, Mother Prioress kept watch of the girl.

A Haye bastard.

And she brought her family into this hatred, so the offense against her had been an offense against them all. For many years, the mother prioress plotted with her family about what to do with the girl once she became of age. There was much need for revenge in the hearts of the

Gordon, and when Brighton saw her nineteenth birthday come and go, the plan that had been formulating most of her life was put into action.

The raid.

But it was a plan that had ultimately not been successful. The English had involved themselves in it and Lady Brighton was now missing, definitely not where she was supposed to be. Mother Prioress was fairly certain she knew where the girl was, as the massive garrison at Berwick had more than likely been the English who had confronted the *reivers* because of its close proximity. That suspicion was confirmed when the woman had received a missive from none other than William de Wolfe two days prior.

With that missive came serious problems and Mother Prioress had sent word to her brother, head of Clan Gordon, to come to her. He was to meet her on this day and peasants working the fields for the priory had spread word of his impending arrival. They'd seen him and his men upon the road and word had traveled fast.

The Gordon had finally come.

"What's this I hear?" Richard Gordon said as he charged into the church where his sister waited. "Those bastards failed, did they?"

Mother Prioress put up her hands. "Silence," she hissed. "Ye must be quiet!"

Richard was a big man with a head of brown, messy hair and small brown eyes. He had a few of his men with him, men who knew what he knew, including his distant cousin and best friend, a flame-haired man named Tommy Orry. Tommy and Ysabella had been childhood sweethearts, years ago, but that was long ended. Still, Tommy had come with him to ensure that Richard didn't do anything foolish to a sister he controlled as his father had controlled. Given Richard's rage at the moment, that wasn't going to be easy.

"The Swinton bastards failed?" Richard demanded, ignoring the request to keep the volume of his voice down. "Where is the lass?"

Mother Prioress sighed heavily. "Anger will not help the issue, Richard," she said. "Ye must be calm and I will tell ye what I know.

Certainly, there has been an added… complication."

Richard threw up his hands. "What complication?" he asked, exasperated. He pointed a finger in his sister's face. "We agreed on this, we did. The girl was tae be taken by the Swinton and brought tae me. I've paid them well for this!"

Mother Prioress nodded quickly, waving her hands at him to keep his voice down. "I know," she whispered loudly. "But the English intercepted the Swinton Clan before they could take her tae ye. They have her now."

That seemed to make Richard even angrier. "*Who* has her?"

Mother Prioress didn't want to tell him. "I…I…."

Richard lifted a hand to slap the answer from her but Tommy stopped him. "Nay, Richie," he muttered, looking at Ysabella and still seeing that girl he loved from long ago. "Strikin' yer sister willna help the situation. Ysabella, who has the Haye lass? Do ye know?"

It had been years since Ysabella had been called by her birth name. God bless Tommy for being rational. She still adored him; she always had. "Aye," she replied. "I received a missive from the Wolfe of the Border himself, William de Wolfe. He has the lass. He has asked me what I know of her parentage and if it 'tis true that she's the daughter of Magnus, King of the Northmen. Richard, as far as I knew, the lass had never been told this. Sister Acha must have told her the truth."

At the mention of William de Wolfe, Richard seemed to calm drastically, but it was in sheer disbelief. "She is with William de Wolfe?" he gasped. "Saints preserve us… the man himself has her now?"

Mother Prioress nodded. "Aye," she said. "I suspect 'tis the English from Berwick who intercepted the Swinton. 'Tis the closest garrison."

"Then the lass is at Berwick?"

"I think so," she said. Then, she sighed with great emotion. "I told Sister Acha never tae tell the girl of her parentage, for there was no need for her tae know. She is the daughter of Magnus, King of the Norse, but even knowin' such a thing wouldna mattered. 'Tis not as if the man knows or cares about her. But somethin' must have happened that

Sister Acha felt the need tae tell her."

"Did the Swinton take Sister Acha also?"

Mother Prioress nodded. "I… I told them to," she said, hoping her brother wouldn't lash out and try to strike her again. "I didna want the Swinton tae compromise the lass before they delivered her to ye. I thought a chaperone would deter their hot blood."

Richard wasn't thinking about striking his sister again but he was thinking about the mess that had been made out of their plans. "Compromise her?" he repeated, aghast. "Ye take no issue with what is tae become of the lass, but ye dunna want men tae *sully* her first?"

Mother Prioress nodded hesitantly, embarrassed at her twisted sense of protection towards her charge. "Aye."

Richard's eyes narrowed. "So ye send an old nun with the lass who told her about her true self," he said with disgust. "And the lass has now told de Wolfe. The man has what is rightfully mine. *I* paid for her. Ye write tae him and tell him that he must return her tae ye. She is a ward of the church and she must be returned immediately."

Mother Prioress nodded quickly, eager to do her brother's bidding and keep a lid on his temper. "I will tell him," she said. "That was my intention all along. But if he knows about the girl and her parentage now… ye canna send the Swinton after her again. I know ye didna want tae have a direct connection between the abduction and ye, and ye hired the Swinton tae make her abduction look like a raid, but if ye do that again and de Wolfe hears of it… it may not go so well in our favor. He speaks kindly of the lass in his missive which leads me tae believe he may be friendly with her."

Richard looked at her, stricken. "*Friendly* with her?" he said in outrage. "That Sassenach bastard has what belongs tae me! I want her back and I dunna care how ye do it, but do it. That lass means our revenge agin' Clan Haye. Are we tae go back on those plans after all of these years?"

Mother Prioress shook her head, her features pale with strain, glancing at Tommy as she spoke, hating that he was hearing of her complicity in the plan. As if he would think less of her. He already thought her a damaged creature for the Haye rape those years ago, the very thing that prevented their marriage. But now with her complicity in the murder of an innocent girl… she'd fallen very low, indeed.

"Nay," she finally said. "This is my revenge more than it 'tis yers."

Richard's eyes narrowed. "They shamed our clan when a son of Haye touched ye. It isna only yer revenge, Ysabella. It belongs tae us all. Ye canna take it away from us."

Mother Prioress could see the bloodlust in her brother's eyes and the sorrow in Tommy's. The problem was that these days, she wasn't completely cold-hearted towards Brighton, a lovely young woman she had seen grow up right before her eyes. But old hatreds die hard and there was still a good deal of hatred in her heart for Clan Haye.

Still, the plans her brother had for Brighton were shocking, even to those seeking revenge for a horrible wrong. She cleared her throat softly.

"Do ye still plan tae crucify her, then?" she asked softly.

Richard lifted an eyebrow. "Nothin' has changed," he said coldly. "I hired the Swinton tae bring her tae me. I plan tae take the girl to the lands of her mother, to the family who shamed us, and put her up on a cross for all tae see. That lass has been raised by the cross; she shall die by it. And we will have evened the score with Clan Haye."

This time, Tommy spoke up. He couldn't help it. Like the others, he'd known of this plan for years but hearing it spoken of with such venom was giving him fits of conscience. Now that the time for their plan was actually upon them, he wasn't so sure it was a good idea to punish an innocent for crimes of her kin. Unlike the others, Tommy simply wasn't that cruel. But he was a bit of flotsam in the crashing waves of Richard Gordon's world. If he went against the man entirely, he would be crushed and he knew it.

So would Ysabella.

"Do ye still believe this is the right thing tae do, Richie?" he asked. "Killin' an innocent lass?"

Richard turned to look at him, his eyes flickered in the dim light, a deadly glimmer. "She's a bastard," he said. "Much like the bastard the Haye beget my sister with, this lass should have never been born. One bastard for another, I'd say. There is no great loss."

Tommy didn't have an answer to that and neither did Mother Prioress. She, too, had known the plan all along so this was of no great shock. But these days, there was reluctance in her heart to follow that scheme. She knew Brighton and the thought of seeing the lass crucified… it simply didn't sit well with her any longer.

Perhaps the years had mellowed her rabid sense of vengeance or perhaps her years as a nun, and in serving God, had taken their toll. All she knew was that once this plan was in action, she wasn't eager to see it through. But she was terrified to tell her brother that, terrified he would take his vengeance out on her.

"Then I shall tell de Wolfe tae return the lass," she said, averting her gaze from her furious brother because she was afraid he would see her cowardice. "She belongs back at Coldingham. The man canna go agin' the church."

Richard's gaze lingered on his sister, who seemed weakened now that their plan had gone into action. She tried to hide it from him but he knew. He could see it.

"See that ye tell him," he said. "When the lass is back wit' ye, you will send me word. Then I will do what needs tae be done."

Mother Prioress nodded, although she wasn't looking at him. She found that she couldn't. "I will," she said quietly. "Ye must go now. I will send the missive tae de Wolfe before the day is out."

Richard didn't say anything right away but, after a moment, he reached out to grab her around the neck before Tommy could stop him. Mother Prioress gasped as his flushed faced appeared in her line of sight.

"See that ye do," he snarled. "If ye've become a coward after all of these years, I'll cut yer heart out."

Tommy yanked him away at that point and she stumbled back, her hand on her neck, as Tommy practically pushed Richard from the church. She could hear them scuffling and hissing as they went.

Even after they were gone, Mother Prioress stood there and rubbed her neck, wondering if there was any way to salvage the situation. Certainly, she couldn't go against her brother. He meant what he said; he *would* cut her heart out. Therefore, if she had any hope of helping Brighton, it would have to come from another source. De Wolfe – the man who wrested her from the Swinton – would be able to resist Richard and protect the girl, but de Wolfe had no real stake in the situation. There was no reason why he should risk himself to try.

But there was someone else who had a stake, indeed.

Along with the missive Mother Prioress sent to de Wolfe, another missive meant for Magnus of the Northmen was sent by way of a monk traveling with papal immunity. No one would dare rob or kill a man of God, and he was instructed to take a cog from Berwick, the biggest nearby port, across the sea to the land of the Danes and then find his way to Magnus to deliver his message. He was told to go with all due haste.

Although Mother Prioress wasn't sure how long it would take to reach Magnus, if it ever would, she prayed daily that it would reach him sooner rather than later, for her missive contained twelve simple words…

Your daughter with Juliana is at Berwick Castle. She is in danger.

Perhaps Magnus' paternal instinct would cause him to come. But it was equally as likely that he wouldn't give a thought to a bastard child.

Mother Prioress could only pray it wasn't the latter.

CHAPTER TWELVE

Castle Questing

EVEN FROM THE stables, Patrick could hear the screaming and it made him grin, for he knew exactly what was going on. He'd been hearing it, daily, for the past week. Nine days, to be exact. He'd been watching Brighton play with the de Wolfe grandchildren, and in particular, with Penelope.

The youngest and insanely spoiled de Wolfe child had found a best friend in Brighton de Favereux, so much so that she'd taken to crawling out of her own bed at night and seeking out Brighton. She would then climb into Brighton's bed and sleep soundly until morning. Then she would follow Brighton around most of the day. Brighton had shown an inordinate amount of patience and sweetness with Penelope, playing with the child but also reciting stories to her and generally entertaining her. As the days passed and the routine continued, something wonderful unfolded.

There was an innocence about Brighton that was apparent from her years of living at the priory. She hadn't been tainted by fostering in other households, learning to gossip, perhaps learning to be petty or vain. She was the most beautiful woman Patrick had ever seen, both inside and out, and she wasn't even aware of it. Her beauty was in her actions, every day. And every, day Patrick watched her, more and more enamored with her to the point where he actually held her hand in public once, in front of his family, who had been wide-eyed about it but said nothing. None of them could blame him, after all, if he'd fallen in love with the girl.

They'd fallen in love with her a little bit, too.

Therefore, Patrick grinned as he listened to the screaming and finished cleaning the hooves of his war horse, a duty he had to attend to personally because the horse wouldn't let anyone else around him. Penelope and her nieces and nephews, many of them older than she was, were playing a game of chase in the kitchen yard with Brighton. One of them had a rock which, according to what he'd been hearing, was really a valuable ruby and must be kept safe. Hence, the chasing going on. Everyone wanted the ruby. He could hear giggling along with the screaming.

"There ye are."

Patrick was distracted him from his thoughts as Jordan entered the stables, her hair wound upon her head and wrapped in that faded yellow shawl she always bound herself up in. It was an old shawl and something William teased her about, telling her they would probably bury her in it because she loved it so well, but Patrick saw the shawl as something innately his mother. It reminded him very much of her. He stood up from his task, smiling at her as she came in.

"Aye, here I am," he said. "Were you looking for me?"

Jordan nodded, distracted by the screaming going on. She shook her head reproachfully. "God bless Bridey for keeping the children occupied as she has," she said. "I dunna know what I did before she came. The lass has the patience of Job."

Patrick's grin broadened. "They are my kin and I do not even have such patience for them," he said. "But she seems to love being with them and they love her in return, so I believe everyone is happy with the arrangement."

Jordan nodded. "I suppose," she said. "I will miss her when she is… well, I willna speak of it, not now. I came tae ask ye a favor."

Patrick nodded. "Of course. What is it?"

Jordan pulled out a couple of spools of thread, one a faded white color and the other a deep blue. There wasn't much left of the thread. She held the spools out to her son.

"I need ye tae go tae Wooler," she said. "The town is south along the road, about ten miles away, but there is a merchant there who has all manner of fabric and threads. His stall is near the town's well and there is a sign above it with a spinning wheel etched upon it. I need these spools. Will ye go for me?"

Patrick nodded, eyeing the spools just the same. "Since when do you purchase thread?" he asked. "I have seen you and Aunt Jemma spin for hours and hours."

Jordan cocked a well-shaped brow. "'Tis true, but I canna seem tae dye me thread that exact shade of blue," she replied. "And the other thread is a linen thread that is difficult tae come by. I canna make it. I need at least two spools of each. In fact, while ye're there, ye can pick up other colors as well – brown, red, yellow. Make the trip worth it."

Patrick shrugged and took the spools from her, tucking them into the pocket of his tunic. "Is there anything else you need?"

Jordan cocked her head thoughtfully but more screaming caught her attention. "Aye," she said, pointing to the kitchen yard. "Take Bridey with ye. That poor woman deserves some peace away from those screaming children. Take her with ye and buy her something pretty, Atty. Tell her it is a gift from all of us for tending the bairns as she has. I think she would like that."

The thought of spending time alone with Brighton did not displease him. In fact, he liked the idea very much. The past several days had seen him spend very little time alone with a woman he was growing quite fond of and he tried not to sound too eager.

"I will," he said. "Make sure you tell Da that I have gone so he knows."

"I will."

Jordan stood back as he reached onto the half-wall of the stall and collected his saddle blanket, shaking it out. There was something more on her mind other than spools of thread but she was careful how she approached it.

As he swung the blanket onto his horse's back, Jordan's thoughts turned to Brighton and Patrick as a whole. There was much swirling around them, much that the family could see, but nothing that anyone would mention. Patrick was clearly attracted to the woman and she to him, but no one would say anything for fear of breaking the spell.

They were all quite aware that Patrick was due to leave for London at the end of the coming week and there was still much unresolved about Brighton. As much as Jordan was hoping that Patrick would simply forget about London and return to Berwick with Brighton as his wife, she knew that was more than likely not going to happen. William had told her to remain silent about it but, being Patrick's mother, she simply couldn't.

She had to know.

"Have ye heard nothing from Coldingham, then?" she asked as her son settled his saddle on the horse's back. "I've not heard if a message was received. Yer father hasna said anything."

Patrick shook his head. "Nothing has come from them," he said. "I find that strange, actually. I would have thought they would be very quick to respond considering Bridey was abducted from the priory. I would think, at the very least, they would send word of their joy at her safety."

Jordan watched him strap on the saddle, a piece of equipment that more than likely weighed as much as she did. "As would I," she said. She paused a moment before continuing. "Ye're soon tae leave us for London, are ye not? Yer da said it 'twas at the end of the month."

Patrick's movements slowed somewhat, lethargy in his actions. Perhaps even some reluctance. "Aye," he said. "I am to depart in six days. At least, that was the plan."

"Has the plan changed?"

Patrick stopped completely, looking at his mother over the top of the saddle. "I do not know," he said honestly. "I cannot leave with

Bridey's future in limbo. I cannot simply leave her here at Questing and allow you to assume her problems. That would not be fair."

Jordan pulled the shawl more tightly around her shoulders. "Will Henry wait for ye, then?"

Patrick shrugged and resumed tightening the saddle. "I do not know," he said. "That has never come up. There was no reason to ask him to wait for me until…."

He trailed off. Jordan helpfully supplied the end of the sentence. "Until Bridey came about?" she said softly.

"Aye."

"I told ye that ye could marry the lass and take her with ye, but ye'd have tae get permission from Coldingham, I would imagine."

Patrick put up a hand to stop his mother from saying anything further about marriage when Brighton suddenly dashed into the stable and pressed herself against the wall right next to the door. It was clear that she was hiding from someone.

As Jordan and Patrick looked at her with some surprise and amusement, Penelope came charging through the stable door. Brighton grabbed the girl from behind in a sneak attack. Penelope screamed in both delight and frustration as Brighton squeezed her hard and gave her a big kiss on the cheek.

"No kisses!" Penelope screamed. "No kisses! I don't want any kisses!"

Jordan, grinning, came up to her trapped daughter and began kissing her little face. "Just for that, I will kiss every bit of ye" she said as Penelope howled. "How can ye not want kisses, lass? Ye're a cruel and terrible child, ye are."

Laughing softly, Brighton set Penelope to her feet. The girl ran off, back into the kitchen yard. Brighton moved to follow but Jordan stopped her.

"Wait," she said. "I'll tend tae the children. Ye've earned a few hours of peace from that mob. I need tae send ye and Patrick on an errand."

Surprised, Brighton watched Jordan head out into the kitchen yard, herding the children together to take them back inside. Puzzled, she looked at Patrick.

"W-where are we going?" she asked.

With a smile, Patrick dug into his pocket and pulled out the two spools. "Shopping," he said, holding the thread up for her to see. "There is a town a few miles south and a merchant there has what she needs."

Brighton fought off a smile. "A-am I to escort you while you shop or is it the other way around?"

"I believe it may be the other way around. My mother wants thread and I know nothing about it."

"I-I do."

"I was hoping you did."

"B-but I have never been to shop. Not once. Anything we needed at Coldingham, we made or purchased from travelers."

He put the spools back into his pocket, his eyes glimmering at her. "Then let us not delay," he said. "There is much to do and we are wasting daylight."

Brighton was more than ready. Her day had taken an unexpected twist but she was thrilled with the turn of events. It was difficult to play with children and try to watch Patrick at the same time. She'd been doing it for nine days now, endearing herself to the youngsters at Questing simply to give herself something to do while all the time trying to keep track of Patrick and his comings and goings. She thought she'd been fairly clever about it but something told her that Patrick was well aware of what she'd been doing.

Staying close to him while pretending not to.

She watched him finish putting tack on his horse, thinking that the past nine days with him and his family had been the best days of her life. The love and affection she'd seen with the families the first time she'd been around them wasn't a rarity; it was constant and delightful, as if they'd all known and loved one another in countless lives and in countless forms. There was something that went beyond normal camaraderie with this group, something inherent and deep. More than ever, she wanted to be part of it. It was a rarity she admired greatly.

But she admired none more greatly than Patrick himself. He was the biggest man in the room and with that size came innate intimidation. But Patrick had such an easy rapport with his family that the intimidation factor was nonexistent. He adored his parents, and his sisters and brother. One night, he and Alec and Hector had gotten in to a wrestling match that had seen men rolling all over the floor of the great hall, onto the tables, and back down again as their fathers shouted encouragement. The children, unable to contain themselves, eventually ran into the fray and jumped onto the men who were wrestling.

Once the children got involved, the match was over and Patrick had lain on the ground, laughing, as his nephews sat on top of him and were convinced they'd brought him down. At that moment, Brighton knew that she was in love with the man even though she'd never been in love before. Still, for what she was feeling towards him, it could only be love – something bright and clear and true, feelings that set her head to swimming and her heart to lurching. Surely only love came with such delightful giddiness like that. It was the most wonderful feeling in the world.

It was a giddiness she felt as she watched him lead his horse out of the stall, a scarred war horse he had muzzled for safety. The man was as big as a mountain. Instead of his size frightening her as it first had, now she found immense beauty in the enormity of the man that was difficult to describe. All she knew was that she wanted to be close to him, all of the time, in every way.

"I must collect my weapons and armor," he told her as he led the horse out into the stable yard. There was a gentle breeze, warm with summer air. "I would suggest you bring a cloak in case the weather turns cool upon our return. Did my sisters give you a cloak back at Berwick?"

"N-nay," she said, shaking her head, "but your mother loaned me one the other evening when I was cold. I have since given it back to her."

He tipped his head in the direction of the keep as he tied the horse to the post. "Go and ask to borrow it from her," he said. "I will meet you back here. Be quick, now."

Brighton nodded, dashing for the keep on the hunt for Jordan, who was last seen herding her gaggle of grandchildren back into the keep. Brighton went to the great hall first, thinking she might find them all there, but the hall was empty with the exception of a few servants.

She did, however, run into Jemma, When she told the woman what she needed, Jemma was more than happy to loan her a very nice blue cloak with rabbit lining. It was the loveliest thing Brighton had ever seen and she tried to give it back, twice, fearful that she would damage it, but Jemma insisted. Wrapped in the rabbit fur on a day too warm for such a thing, Brighton headed back out to the stables.

Patrick was waiting. He was bringing the horse out from the stable yard when Brighton emerged from the keep, bundled up in the heavy cloak. Right after her came Jemma, the little Scotswoman walking briskly. Patrick waited patiently as both Brighton and Jemma reached him. He pointed to Brighton when he noticed the furs.

"That cloak is made for freezing temperatures," he said. "Are you sure you will not be too warm in it?"

Brighton wasn't sure what to say to him. "Y-your aunt has been gracious enough to loan this to me," she said, making it sound as if Patrick should be very grateful, too. "I think it will be just fine for the journey."

Patrick's gaze lingered on her as she nodded her head at him, encouragingly. Before he could reply, Jemma spoke.

"The nights are cold when the sun goes down, Atty," she said. "So ye're goin' tae Wooler, are ye? There is a fine huntsman there and his wife makes all manner of cloaks and gloves and shoes. Go and see the man and see about getting' Bridey her own cloak and gloves and shoes. She's a-wearin' Evelyn's old things and Evelyn had nearly worn them through. The lass needs somethin' of her own."

Brighton shook her head. "T-the things that Evelyn gave me are more than serviceable," she insisted to both Jemma and Patrick. "I do not need anything more, truly."

"Pah," Jemma said. She pointed a finger at Patrick. "Get the lass what she needs. The merchants in town know us; tell them we'll pay for the things when next we come tae town."

Patrick nodded, taking his orders from Jemma and not from Brighton, who was mortified that the de Wolfe family should spend money on her. As Jemma walked away, she turned to Patrick.

"P-please, nay," she begged quietly. "There is no need to purchase anything for me. I would be terribly ashamed because I cannot pay you back."

Patrick smiled at her as he mounted his horse, holding down his hand to help her up. With a heavy sigh, because he seemed to be ignoring her concerns, she put her hand in his and he lifted her up onto the back of his saddle. She shifted around to find a comfortable spot, gripping his trim torso as he spurred his war horse onward.

"D-did you hear me?" she said as they passed through the enormous gatehouse. "You do not need to purchase anything for me. I am perfectly content with what I have."

Patrick gaze moved over the landscape as he began to make his trek down the hill to the road below. "I heard you," he said. "But you have been overruled."

"W-what does that mean?"

"It means that my mother already told me to buy you a few things, as a gift for having spent so much time entertaining the wild animals that pose as children. She is very grateful for all you've done."

Brighton wasn't convinced. "B-but that was nothing," she said. "It was great fun to play with them. I love children."

"And they love you. Penelope insists you are her best friend in the world, which means that you have superseded me in that position. I may have to challenge you at some point for the honor."

Brighton laughed softly. "S-she is strong willed and brilliant, that one," she said. "Your parents are in for trouble when she comes of age and they want to seek a husband for her. She has told me she will never have a husband and that she will fight for your father as a knight."

Patrick grinned. "That is because my father tells her she is the best knight at Questing," he said. "My mother tries to temper that with proper things for little girls to do, but my father ruins it when he sword fights with her. He purchased a pony for her six months ago and keeps the animal hidden away with the war horses, where my mother has not seen it, because he wants to give it to Penelope and is afraid of what my mother will say."

Brighton continued to giggle. "H-he is going to have to tell your mother sometime," she said. "Mayhap she will be understanding."

"You do not know my mother."

"B-but I am sure many young girls have ponies… don't they?"

"Not a pony that has been fitted for miniature armor."

"O-oh, goodness…."

"Exactly."

Brighton simply grinned and the conversation trailed off after that, but it wasn't an uncomfortable silence. They spoke now and again, about the weather, the road, or anything else that popped to mind. Moreover, Brighton had her arms around Patrick, something that was quite thrilling. As they made their way to the road south, she carefully laid her cheek against his armored back, closing her eyes and wallowing in the closeness between them. The last time she had ridden with him like this had been after the raid, when everything had been frightening and disorienting and cold. But today, the mood was different – everything was different.

It was heavenly.

It was mid-morning on this mild summer day as they headed south along a well-traveled road. The road was also relatively flat, strung along in flatlands between mountains to the west and rolling hills to the east. Everything was green and the lack of rain over the past few weeks had left the land dry and lovely. The road was a little dusty, in fact, kicking dirt up on the ends of the rabbit fur cloak. But Brighton didn't notice; she still had her cheek against Patrick's back as the horse plodded along, her arms around his torso and feeling him breathe.

She could have stayed like that forever.

Ten miles went very fast when one was hoping it would last a lifetime. That's what Brighton thought when the outskirts of Wooler began to come in to view. There were farms dotted across the landscape and people out working the land. She saw small homes all bunched up around the edges of the town as they drew closer.

As they passed into the town, Brighton lifted her head, watching her surroundings most curiously. She'd never seen anything like this, not ever, so this was a new experience and a very interesting one. Her life since leaving Coldingham had revealed to her so much about how others lived, those who weren't pledged to the cloister. Now, they were entering a small town that seemed quite busy and prosperous for the most part. Life seemed to be rich here.

Brighton found it fascinating how the beautifully-colored fields of greens and yellows and golds transformed into the rather colorless huts that were clustered around the edge of Wooler. The homes seemed to look the same, slapped together with waddle and daub, with pitched roofs, sitting on avenues that were uneven and full of ruts. Women in dirty caps stood in the doorways, yelling at children who ran about the streets with dogs barking after them. She saw a little girl with a stick poppet and a little boy with a boat he'd made from a leaf. It was a wondrous world before her and she drank in every single drop of it.

"My mother said that the thread merchant is near the town's well," Patrick said, breaking into her thoughts. "When we are finished with him, I will have to find the huntsman that Aunt Jemma spoke of."

Brighton leaned sideways so she could see around him, seeing that the road headed up a hill to the town square up ahead. "T-truly," she said. "You do not have to purchase a cloak for me, or shoes or gloves. I am very uncomfortable accepting such things when your sisters have given me perfectly serviceable clothing."

"Quiet, woman," Patrick said softly, but with jest. "Do you not know when people are trying to do something nice for you? If you are not careful, you will offend my entire family and then we'll be in the soup. Just you see."

Brighton grinned, looking up at him. But she could only see the side of his helmed head. "I-in the soup?" she repeated. "What does that mean?"

He turned his head, which was difficult with the helm he wore. "Have you never heard that term?"

"N-never."

"It means we shall be in a bind. In trouble. In a stew, as it were. Now do you understand?"

She laughed softly. "T-thank you for being so kind and explaining it to me."

"My pleasure, my lady."

His free hand ended up resting on her right arm, his fingers seeking hers. Thrilled, Brighton held his hand tightly as they headed into the heart of the town.

Up ahead, they could see that the village's center was rather crowded. The buildings here were of better construction in this main part of town, with a few stone shops that had both a first and second floor.

As the horse plodded into the crowded part of town, Brighton found fascination in the people they passed – merchants, visitors, travelers, and some armed men as well. There were several hanging out front of a stone building called the Angel Inn, drinking and generally being loud even at midday. They stopped their drinking and chatting to eyeball Patrick as he rode by, but no one moved against him. It was a professional assessment and nothing more. Once Patrick moved past, they resumed their conversation.

But their attention to Patrick had concerned Brighton. She was nervous that armed men should pay such attention to him and also to her. She was glad when they rode past the group in relative peace. But her attention was soon diverted as they passed by one of those stone buildings and Brighton could see that it was a food vendor. She could smell fresh bread and there were people inside the business, emerging with food in their hands. Being that she hadn't eaten since the morning meal, her stomach was rumbling.

"A-are you hungry?" she asked, hoping for an affirmative answer.

It wasn't long in coming. Patrick turned to look at the food vendor as well. He deeply inhaled the culinary scents.

"Aye," he said. "There is a livery around the corner. Let us leave the horse off and then we can go about our business."

Brighton was quite agreeable with that. Patrick spurred the big war horse down the road and turned down an offshoot, a small alley, where there was a big stone livery there complete with two separate yards. Patrick took the horse straight to the livery owner, muzzled the beast, and paid well for the man to tend the animal. Then, he removed Brighton from the horse, tucked her hand into the crook of his elbow, and headed back out to the street with its gastronomic delights.

Brighton held tight to Patrick as they made their way to the main avenue and headed back towards the food vendor. All the while, she was looking around at the new sights, her head was on a swivel, with enough enthusiasm so that Patrick noticed. He watched her as she investigated every sight and every sound.

"You are swinging your head around so much that it is going to fly off at any moment," he told her with a smile. "Surely not everything is so interesting."

Brighton grinned sheepishly. "I-if you have never been outside of the walls of your home, then everything *is* interesting," she said. "There are so many people here. Where are they all going?

Patrick looked around. "I do not know," he said. "Farmers, merchants, women going about their shopping. This is a busy market town. I can remember as a child that there was a merchant who imported sweets from all over the world. He had marzipan, candied fruits, honeycomb, and cakes made with sweet salt. Have you ever had such a thing?"

Brighton shook her head with wonder. "S-sweet salt? What is it?"

Patrick could see their destination up ahead. "Men brought it back with them upon returning from pilgrimage to the Holy Land," he said. "It is from the Far East. Sweet granules that are white and look like salt."

Brighton was intrigued. "I-I have never had it but it sounds delicious."

"It is. I will see if we cannot find you some to sample while we are here."

Brighton thought that was an astonishingly good idea. The food vendor was looming close now and there were people coming in and out of it. Brighton got a good look at the steaming food in their hands – roasted meat with carrots and peas all packaged up in neat little trenchers. People were eating it with gusto, which only made her more hungry. Just as Patrick ducked his head down to enter the door of the shop, a shout stopped him.

"De Wolfe! I thought that was you!"

Patrick calmly turned towards the shouting and Brighton watched as the man's face suddenly split into a smile. When she looked to see what had him smiling, all she could see was a very big knight in well-used armor and a dirty tunic crossing the road towards them.

"Bloody Christ," the knight said as he approached. "The Nighthawk himself. There is no man in all of England as enormous as you are. Has anyone tried to put a saddle on you and ride you yet, you big stallion?"

Patrick laughed softly as he reached out to take the man's offered hand. "Le Sander," he muttered with satisfaction. "Has anyone tried to cut that glib tongue from your mouth yet?"

The knight laughed. "I am too fast and too powerful," he said. "Mayhap they have a dirk with my name on it, but it would do no good. They cannot catch me or kill me."

Patrick slapped him affectionately on the cheek. "That is true," he said. "You have survived battle when it should not have been survivable, my friend. And it has been a long time since I have seen you."

"It has," the knight agreed, his expression suggesting he was quite fond of Patrick. But his gaze inevitably trailed to Brighton, standing next to Patrick with her hand still on his arm. "But it looks as if life has been very good to you. Lady de Wolfe, I presume?"

Brighton's cheeks flushed a bright red and as she shook her head, Patrick answered. "Nay," he said. "She is not my wife. My lady, this is an old friend, Sir Kerk le Sander. The last I heard, he served Sir Henry Grey of Chillingham Castle. Is that still true, Kerk?"

Kerk nodded. "It 'tis. I am his captain, in fact. I am in town on an errand for my lord."

Patrick nodded before finishing the introduction. "I see," he said. "Kerk, this lovely creature is Lady Brighton de Favereux."

Kerk, a devilishly handsome man with eyes the color of the sea and hair so blonde that it was nearly white, displayed his best alluring smile. He took Brighton's free hand, bringing to his lips for a chaste kiss.

"My lady," he greeted in a deep, sweet voice. "It is an honor to meet you. May I ask if there is a chance that I may steal you away from my enormous friend?"

Brighton was so red in the face that she thought she might ignite into flames at any moment. "I-I do not know," she said, gazing up at Patrick as he smiled down at her. "D-do you mean to have me for a servant?"

Patrick laughed loudly as Kerk shook his head. "Nay, lady," he said patiently. "Not as a servant. I should like a beautiful woman on my arm today."

"Why today?" Patrick asked, not entirely sure he liked Kerk's attention towards Brighton. "What are you doing in town, anyway?"

Kerk threw a thumb back over his shoulder, in a westerly direction. "Did you not see the banners for the games?" he said. "Lord Horsden of Highburn House is sponsoring contests today. Tugging rope, archery, that kind of thing. I have no lovely lady to cheer me on so I thought you might sell me yours."

Patrick was interested in the games. "I will not," he said flatly. "She stays with me. But these games – are you competing?"

"I am."

"Have you already entered?"

"I have."

Patrick looked at Brighton a moment, perhaps to see her reaction to the mention of entertainment, before replying. It occurred to him that having her watch him compete in a game of skill might make her proud of him, if only just a little. He'd never had a woman's attention like that, at least not attention that he really wanted.

And he very much wanted hers.

"It has been a long time since I have competed in any games," he said to Kerk. "Where are the marshals so that I might see the areas of contest?"

Kerk's gaze lingered on Brighton, too, realizing that Patrick had no intention of parting with the woman. *His betrothed*, he thought to himself. Certainly, from the way Patrick looked at the woman, it was an easy deduction.

Lucky bastard!

"They are up by the competition field," he said. "Come along; I will show you."

Patrick was eager to see where the games would be held. But the moment he took a step to follow Kerk, he remembered the food he'd promised Brighton. He quickly turned for the shop again.

"A moment, please," he said to Kerk. "I promised my lady some food. I will be just a moment."

Kerk dipped his head politely in Brighton's direction. "By all means, feed the lady," he said. "In fact, I will join you."

Patrick was more than happy to have his old friend attend them but he found himself having to fend Kerk off of Brighton. He wanted to talk to her but Patrick would not permit it. He actually put himself between Kerk and Brighton at one point, a very large guard dog protecting a flower of a lady. Kerk had no choice but to take the hint.

Oddly enough, Patrick knew he had nothing to worry over, because

Kerk was a noble knight and a man of good character, so his reaction to his friend underscored just how protective he felt over Brighton. It also showed how attached he was becoming to her. The past nine days at Questing had only sealed those feelings.

Your wife? Kerk had asked. Patrick realized he had wanted to tell him that she was. God, he'd been afraid of such thoughts before. Terrified of her *and* thoughts of her. That first night at Berwick, he'd literally run from her when he realized he was attracted to her. He'd put off his mother's questions, or any questions about his feelings for Brighton, because he was afraid. But looking at her now, he wasn't afraid of those feelings anymore. Intentions of assuming his post with Henry as a married man were fading further and further away.

God help him, they were.

It was a stunning realization and one he was finally ready to accept. It had taken Kerk's unwanted attention towards Brighton to force him to make a decision. He couldn't, and wouldn't, stand for Brighton being with another man. He couldn't stand the thought of leaving her behind when he went to London. But with that decision came peace he'd never experienced in his life. Something settling and warm. Something that seemed to soothe his soul.

He'd never felt such confidence in something that was right.

She belonged to him.

He was distracted from his thoughts once they entered the food shop, a rather large space within the stone building that smelled heavily of fresh bread and roasted meat. Straw was scattered over the hard-packed earthen floor, something to keep the dust from getting into the food. There was an open door at the rear of the building and beyond, a yard that had two great fires going. Over those fires were a pig and half a cow on a spit. Glendale beef, the vendor was telling everyone. People, lured by the smell of the roasting meat, were standing around waiting to pay for their food just as Brighton and Patrick were.

But Patrick had the advantage – being very big and armed, he was able to procure food for himself and Brighton because people naturally moved to get out of his way. Kerk came in behind him and demanded food as well, so the three of them were sent away with stale bread bowls of beef, carrots and peas in gravy. It was delicious and filling, and the gravy soaked the bread so that they ate that up at the very end. By the time they were finished, Brighton was miserably full but she didn't complain in the least. Many times at Coldingham, she had gone to bed hungry. So to have a full belly was the best feeling she could imagine.

Another thing about the outside world that was far better than what she'd known.

It was a day of days after that. Drunk on beef and bread, Brighton and Patrick and Kerk headed up to the contest field where, already, some of the contests were underway. The contest field was literally that – a meadow that had some hastily-constructed lists on the south side for spectators – and there were several contests going on at once.

On one side of the field, they had started the hammer throw. On the other side, they were playing a game that had men with sticks batting a ball all over the grass. Patrick explained to Brighton that there were two teams and the object was for one team to hit the ball through the other team to the opposite side of the field. The problem was that some of the men had grown frustrated and ended up hitting each other over the head with the sticks, resulting in some bloodied scalps. Brighton thought it very strange that the men were laughing with blood running down their faces, thinking it was all great fun.

As the games went on, she followed Patrick and Kerk as they wandered along the edge of the field, watching the activity, until Kerk pointed out the marshals and Patrick went to speak to them about competing. He was too late for the hammer throw but just in time for the quarter-staff, archery, and wrestling games. He entered them with relish and Brighton, who'd never seen such games before, soon found out why.

He dominated them.

Between Kerk and Patrick, they easily wiped through a field of men in the quarter-staff competition, including some of the drunken soldiers they'd first seen when they'd come into town. Patrick plowed through them as easily as if he were fighting with children. After the first couple of bouts, Brighton began to feel a very odd pride in the man. Watching him knock over his enemies was very exciting and, soon enough, she was cheering loudly for him as he shamed man after man. But then she began to hear whispers in the crowd, people murmuring of the enormous knight and pointing.

De Wolfe, they said.

Nighthawk.

The realization that the son of the great border Wolfe was in their midst seemed to have two influences on people – either it greatly excited the men and they demanded to compete in all of the games that Patrick was entered in, or some men actually withdrew when they found out who Patrick really was. Brighton simply sat in the corner of the lists, cheering Patrick and, on occasion, cheering Kerk. But she paid no attention to those who were whispering about Patrick. She couldn't have been prouder of the man.

When the quarter-staff competition finally came down to Patrick and Kerk, it turned into a great battle of both skill and strength. Kerk, as it turned out, was an excellent knight and quite talented with the staff, but Patrick had him on two accounts – size and strength. The battle went on for quite some time, each man refusing to give in to the other, until Kerk took a bad step and went down on his back. Once a man was down he wasn't allowed to rise again and Patrick was declared the winner.

Brighton cheered for him, delighted, but what she wasn't prepared for was the awarding of the prize for the winner of the contest. Lord Horsden's daughter, a young woman resplendent with her red hair and yellow silks, presented Patrick with a small golden staff as a prize. She fawned all over Patrick, hanging on his arm and laughing.

Brighton watched the spectacle, increasingly dismayed by the woman's behavior. Lord Horsden came out to meet Patrick because it seemed as if the daughter had no intention of leaving him. More laughing and more conversation went on, and Brighton was feeling increasingly insecure.

Of course, Patrick was an eligible and handsome man. Brighton didn't blame the girl in the least for being enchanted by him. But Patrick didn't seem to be doing anything to discourage her… and why should he? He wasn't married. He didn't have a special woman, a betrothed, who held his loyalties. He was free to accept any woman's attention, including a lord's daughter who was clearly quite wealthy. Surely that was the kind of lady Patrick would consider marrying. A lady with everything to offer.

Not a former postulate with only borrowed clothing to her name.

Depression swept Brighton. She hadn't truly realized how inadequate she was to Patrick's greatness until now. There had never been any competition for her to be marked against. Now that she realized just how lacking she was, she felt sick to her stomach. Sweet Mary, how horrible it was to be in love with a man who was as attainable to her as the moon.

He was utterly out of her reach.

As she watched the lord's daughter loop her hands through Patrick's big left arm, her thoughts went back to the night she had kissed Patrick in the kitchen yard. It had been such a gleeful, wonderful night and she had been fairly certain at that time that he was as interested in her as she was in him. The nine days following that encounter only cemented her belief. She'd been even more sure that the man was interested her as more than just a ward, a damsel in distress. Brighton had foolishly allowed herself to believe there could be more between them, a hope that was fragile but difficult to kill. It lingered, this hope, but as she watched Patrick standing in the middle of the field, tall and strong, the more she realized it had been a stupid hope. She'd been stupid to believe it.

The man was destined for greater things than her.

Deeply grieved, Brighton simply couldn't watch anymore. She would go back to the livery and wait for him to finish his games and then he would take her back to Questing. But, oh, the pain of going back to that place. She loved it so. But she could not stay there, nor could she go back to Berwick and become a tutor for Katheryn and Evelyn's children as she'd once suggested. It would keep her too close to Patrick, too close to something that was a part of him. She didn't know what she wanted to do or where she wanted to go – all she knew was that she had been a fool to believe there was hope between her and Patrick.

Her grief was of her own doing.

Tears threatened and she made her way from the lists, almost in a panic, not wanting to see Patrick interact with the wealthy lord's daughter anymore. She simply couldn't watch. She climbed down from the lists and lost herself in the crowd of spectators, groups of women and children and men who had come to be entertained. There was a small, dusty road that led back down to the town center, the same road that she and Patrick and Kerk had used to come up to the contest field, and she quickly made her way down it. She was nearly to the main street that went through the town center when someone grabbed her arm.

"Bridey," Patrick said, breathing heavily from having run after her. "Where are you going? Why did you leave?"

Brighton looked up into that handsome, worried face and it was all she could do to keep from bursting into tears and running away. Completely unused to speaking on her feelings or experiencing feelings towards the opposite sex, she tried to pull away from him.

"B-back to the livery," she said, averting her gaze even as she tried to yank her arm from his grip. "I will go back to the livery and wait."

Patrick frowned. "Why would you do that?" he asked, genuinely confused. "What is the matter?"

Brighton shook her head. "I-I do not wish to watch the contests any longer," she lied. "I will go wait for you at the livery."

Patrick was coming to sense that something was very wrong but he couldn't figure out what it could be. She had been happy and cheering minutes before and now… now, she was running from him and she wouldn't tell him why. Had he not been keeping an eye on her in the lists from the field, even in the midst of speaking to Lord Horsden, she would have run off and he wouldn't have even been aware. He had no idea what had happened.

"Nay, you will not," he said, his voice low and calm. "You will tell me why you are upset, Bridey. What has happened? Has someone frightened you?"

Brighton shook her head but she was still trying to pull her arm from his grip. "N-nay," she said. "I… I simply do not want to watch any longer. Please let me go."

He didn't like that she was being evasive with him. It made him feel rather desperate because if something was wrong, he wanted to make it right.

"Stop pulling," he commanded softly. "Bridey, if something has happened, please tell me. I only wish to help."

She stopped trying to dislodge his grip but she wouldn't look at him. "Y-you cannot help," she said, her voice trembling. "You have already been too kind to me. Please… please let me go back to the livery."

There were people walking around them up and down the road, either heading to the field or away from it. There were too many ears hearing what was going on between them. Grasping Brighton by both arms, Patrick pulled her over to the side of the road, into an alley that led down between small homes clinging to the side of the hill. There wasn't anyone around that he could see so he gently pushed her up against the wall, keeping his grip on her for fear she would try to run off. He was both greatly puzzled by her behavior and greatly concerned.

"Now," he said quietly. "I am not going to release you until you tell me what is wrong. Not a few moments ago, you were cheering happily from the lists. I could hear you. Why do you think I won? Your support fortified me. And now you are near tears, wanting to go back to the livery. Tell me what has happened."

Brighton was miserable. She hung her head, looking at her feet. *How can I tell him what I am thinking? How can I confide in him? I will only sound foolish!*

"P-please," she whispered. "There… there is nothing wrong. I…."

He shook her, gently. "No lies," he snapped softly. "Tell me now or we shall spend the rest of our lives here because I will not let you leave until you tell me. We will become quite hungry and our feet might actually grow into the ground like tree roots, but it does not matter. I am not leaving until you tell me why you are distressed. Do you not trust me enough to tell me?"

Her head came up, then, drawn to him by his attempted humor. "O-of course I trust you," she insisted softly. "It has nothing to do with trust."

"Aye, it does, because you will not tell me what has distressed you. I can only assume you do not trust me."

Brighton shook her head. "I-I do, I swear it," she said, but it occurred to her that he meant what he said; they weren't leaving until she told him… something. But what to say? Her stomach was in knots and her breathing was coming in labored gasps. She was going to sound foolish but she had little choice. "I-I… I was thinking that you and Lord Horsden's daughter made a handsome couple. When you do marry, your wife should be a woman of culture and wealth, for that is what you deserve. I…I suppose I was upset because of my circumstances. I never had the opportunity for culture and wealth but it wasn't anything I thought of until I came to know something of the world outside of Coldingham. Does that make any sense? It probably sounds foolish. Sister Acha said that my real father is a king, but I do not feel that is true. I will live like a pauper my entire life and seeing you with that wealthy lord's daughter, it made me realize how different you and I are. And I was simply being foolish in thinking such things; forgive me for running off."

Patrick let her go. "Is that the truth?"

She nodded, embarrassed, and hung her head again. "Aye."

Patrick sighed heavily and leaned back against the wall, his gaze fixed on Brighton's lowered head even though she couldn't see it. Had she looked up, she would have seen a glimmer of warmth in his eyes that was a glimpse of what he was feeling in his heart. Aye, she made sense to him. More than she realized. Since she was being brave and speaking what was in her heart, he thought that, perhaps, he should, too.

It was time.

"It is strange you should say that, for I was thinking nearly the same thing," he said softly. "You see, I happen to believe you are the daughter of a king, for only a princess would be so beautiful and so bright as you are. Here I am, the son of a mere war lord, and I was thinking that I was quite beneath you. It is a fear I have had."

Brighton's head snapped up, her eyes wide on him. "*Y-you*? Beneath *me*?"

He nodded. Then, he folded his enormous arms across his chest, cocking his head as he spoke. "Imagine how men would look up to me with a wife who was a Norse princess," he said. "Lord Horsden's daughter doesn't have a splinter of your beauty or sweetness. I would sooner throw myself on my sword than marry someone like her. But you… I cannot imagine anything finer in this life than being able to tell men that you are my wife. It would make me greatly envied."

Brighton couldn't believe what she was hearing. She was looking at him with such shock that she almost had a horrified expression. "D-do you mean that?"

"Of course."

"Are you *mad*?"

He laughed softly, nodding his head. "I am," he said, sobering. His features suddenly took on an intensity that was difficult to describe. "Exceedingly mad for you. Marry me, Bridey. Marry me and make me the envy of every man."

Her jaw fell open. "B-but… but you cannot mean that!"

"Of course I do."

"B-but… your parents…what would your father and mother say?"

A smile tugged at the corners of his mouth. "My mother adores you," he said. "My father… well, he will approve. I believe he likes you a great deal."

Brighton just stood there, staring at him with her mouth open. "H-he does?"

"He does."

"Truly?"

"Truly."

Brighton exhaled sharply, coming out like something of a choke. But the expression on her face now was nothing short of wondrous. A hand flew to her mouth as if to hold back the burst of emotion that was sure to come.

"O-oh… Patrick…."

The tone of her voice speared him, ripping into him and embedding itself deep into his heart. One moment he was standing across the alley from her and in the next, he was sweeping her into his arms, lifting her off of the ground as his mouth slanted over hers. Brighton wrapped her arms around his neck, blocking out the world around them as he suckled on her lips. But it wasn't enough and Patrick licked her lips, her teeth, snaking his tongue into her mouth and tasting her deliciousness as she gasped and whimpered in his arms. The kiss in the garden had been nothing like this.

This was heaven. The realization of dreams neither one of them ever realized they'd had.

"Patrick… my sweet Patrick," Brighton breathed as he tore his mouth away from hers and devoured her cheeks, her jaw, her neck. "Never did I believe… Sweet Mary, how I hoped for this moment!"

That sweet, breathy gasp filled his veins with fire and he set her on her feet, backing her up against the wall and cupping her face between his two enormous hands. He kissed her soft mouth again, lingering over her tender lips, feeling such elation in his soul that he was giddy with it. He'd never felt like this in his entire life.

"I do not know if I hoped for it," he whispered against her. "To be truthful, you terrified me. But your allure… it was impossible to resist. I cannot tell you when I realized I loved you, only that I did. I do. I am leaving for London next week and you are coming with me. It would destroy me to leave you behind."

Brighton was weeping quiet and happy tears. "Atty," she murmured as he kissed her wet cheeks. "My sweet, Atty. I love you, too. I have never known love before but I cannot imagine this joy is anything else. It embraces me and fills me until I cannot feel or think of anything but you. And I will love you until I die, I swear it."

Atty. The nickname given to him as a child never sounded so wonderful, so endearing coming from her lips. He continued to hold her face in his hands, his lips on her forehead reverently.

"And I, you," he whispered. "You and no other."

Brighton sighed faintly, with great satisfaction. Her eyes closed as his lips moved over her face and down her temple. His hands left her face at that moment and he wrapped her up in his big arms, holding her tightly. He squeezed her until she grunted, but he didn't stop squeezing and she didn't seem to care. She was finally his and he would never, ever let her go.

Ever!

"I shall marry you before I depart for London," he said quietly. "In fact, I shall marry you this very day so there will be no delays or complications. I will not wait to call you my wife."

Brighton thought it all sounded too good to be true. But somewhere in her haze of delirium, images of Jordan and William came to mind. She pulled her face out of his chest to look up at him.

"But what of your mother and father?" she asked. "Will they not be angry if we marry without them?"

He shrugged. "It is not as if I need their permission," he said. "And you… you became mine when I promised Sister Acha that I would protect you, always. No priory is going to dictate to me whether or not I can or cannot marry you. Once we are married, they cannot do anything about it."

Brighton was showing signs of hesitation. "Are you certain?"

He nodded. "Are you of age?"

"I am."

"Do you wish to marry me?"

She softened. "More than anything."

"Then you have given your consent. That is all I need."

He sounded so confident, a man with the world at his feet who would give control of his life to no man save his father or the king. Because he was confident, Brighton was confident. She would have let him take her to hell and back if he wished it. She was more than willing to abide by his wishes.

"Then where shall we be married?" she asked. "Is there a church in town?"

Patrick kissed her one last time, sweetly, before taking her by the hand and leading her from the alley and onto the busy road again. There were more games going on now and, from what he could see, the wrestling had started. He knew Kerk was somewhere in the middle of it but he couldn't take the time to seek the man out. He had a mission to accomplish this day and would waste no more time in accomplishing it. Marriage, that very thing he had shied from all of these years, had come astonishingly easy when it pertained to Brighton.

Perhaps he was being impetuous or perhaps he was simply a man who knew what he wanted, finally, and would wait no more. He really didn't know which best described him. But in any case, he and Brighton headed back toward the town center to purchase the thread his mother wanted before collecting his steed and heading to the edge of town where St. Mary's Church was situated.

The old church was grand with a tall spire and moss-covered stone walls, the interior smelling of dirt and fatted tapers. With a few coins to the priests, generous enough so that there weren't any questions, Patrick and Brighton were married at the entrance to the church with two priests, four acolytes, and a few of the townsfolk as witnesses. It was a bit surreal for him and for Brighton, too. She had a rather dazed look about her, but nothing in the world had ever felt so right.

When the priest said the wedding mass and wrapped their joined hands with holy silk borrowed from the second priest, Patrick knew that marrying Brighton was the most certain thing he'd ever done in his life. That beautiful postulate, that divine and sweet guest of the de Wolfe family, was now his wife and when the priest gave the final blessing, it wasn't Brighton who shed a tear. It was Patrick.

It was done.

CHAPTER THIRTEEN

Angel Inn
Wooler

"ARE WE NOT returning to Castle Questing tonight?"

Patrick shook his head as he escorted Brighton into the biggest and best room that the Angel Inn had to offer. He had his saddlebags in one hand, bags that contained various possessions including his coin purse, and he tossed them onto the end of the bed.

"Nay," he said. "We are going to stay here tonight."

Brighton wasn't particularly seeing his logic. "But why?" she asked. "Castle Questing is not so far away. The sun has not even set."

Patrick shut the door to the chamber, throwing the bolt. The walls were thin and noise from the common room below could be heard, loud laughter and an occasional woman's scream. It was all quite chaotic and the door didn't do much to shut out the commotion as Patrick crossed the floor towards Brighton, who was confused by the fact that they weren't returning home for the night.

"I realize it is still light outside and we could easily travel back to Questing, but I will be honest when I say that I do not want to," he said. He smiled thinly. "We must make sure this marriage cannot be dissolved."

She still had no idea what he was talking about. "It cannot be dissolved at all," she said. "We were just married."

He could see she was clueless. Sitting on the bed, he pulled her onto his lap, relishing the feel of her in his arms. God, she felt good. He propped his chin on her shoulder.

"Has no one ever told you of the ways between men and women?" he asked. "The ways between a husband and a wife?"

She eyed him as if only just coming to realize what he meant. Her cheeks turned pink. "Not much, I am afraid," she said, trying not to look too embarrassed. "We have goats and pigs at Coldingham and I have seen them couple. Sister Acha told me once about the way that a man plants his seed in a woman, but she said it was wicked and painful."

He lifted his dark eyebrows. "As a nun, I suppose she would see it that way. But I assure you it is not wicked, at least between a husband and wife."

"But is it painful?"

Now he was becoming a bit pink in the cheeks. "Not for me," he said, watching her eyes widen. He laughed softly and kissed her cheek. "Not to worry, Bridey. I will be very gentle with you. But we must consummate this marriage so it cannot be annulled or dissolved, by anyone."

A flicker of fear crossed her features. "Do you believe someone will try? Your father, mayhap?"

He shook his head. "Nay," he said. "I do not honestly believe he would. But it is better to be safe."

Brighton trusted him. He knew so much more than she did about the world in general so she didn't question him further. She simply wrapped her arms around his neck and hugged him.

"As you say," she murmured. "What would you have me do?"

That was a question with many answers as far as he was concerned. *Aye, lass, let me count the ways!* He almost laughed but managed to hold off any semblance of a smile because he knew she'd have no idea about the double entendre. So, he gave her a light squeeze and set her on her feet.

"I want you to remain here," he said. "I have something I must do, so you will remain here and rest. Take a bath if you wish. I will return shortly."

She looked surprised. "A bath in the middle of the day?"

He winked at her. "It is not the middle of the day," he said. "Dusk will soon be upon us. But if you do not wish to bathe, send for wine, sit in the window, and watch the street below. You have been fascinated with watching the people since our arrival."

She nodded, turning to look at the big window, shuttered. There was a bench seat directly below it.

"I have simply never seen so many people in one place," she said. "But I will wait for you, of course. Where are you going?"

He bent over, kissing her on the nose. "Do not ask any questions," he said. "If I wanted you to know, I would have already told you. But know I shall return as soon as I can."

He had effectively shut her down so she smiled timidly. "Please do."

"I promise."

With that, Patrick quit the chamber, hearing her bolt the door as soon as he shut it. A smile played on his lips as he headed down into the common room of the inn, a big room that was sunk down into the earth. Old straw covered the floor and the tables and benches appeared as if they had been repaired and repaired again. A few of them were even whitewashed. As far as inns went, it was one of the better-tended ones he'd seen, and he hailed the nearest serving wench and instructed her to take wine and cheese up to his wife.

His wife.

Even saying that made his heart leap, for when he stopped to think about it, he'd never been so happy about anything in his life. But that happiness was tempered by the reality of what he'd done. To be truthful, he didn't want to think about what his parents would say to the spur-of-the-moment marriage and he didn't want to think of the consequences. He knew his father would be worried about Coldingham, since the lady had been their charge. But the fact remained that he had married Brighton and no one could separate them, not even the church. He didn't give a hang about Coldingham. The only thing he cared about was marrying the only woman who had ever meant anything to him.

The Nighthawk had finally found his mate.

As he headed out onto the busy street, he had something in mind – gifts for his wife on the event of their wedding. So he was looking for any merchant who sold goods for women. He thought about looking for the huntsman Aunt Jemma had told him of, but he was more concerned with purchasing something other than leather.

Perhaps something pretty or even something that smelled good. He'd rushed Brighton into marriage and now he was about to dump a load of gifts upon her. He found that he wanted to, very much. She had spent her entire life with absolutely nothing by way of possessions and that was going to change. He was going to make sure of it. As the wife of Patrick de Wolfe, she would be well-dressed, well-respected, and adored.

Definitely adored.

"De Wolfe!"

Patrick heard the shout behind him, turning to see Kerk as the man rushed up. Kerk was filthy from having been rolling about in the field all afternoon, smudges of dirt on his face. But Patrick didn't stop to talk to the man; he just kept walking as Kerk pulled up beside him.

"Where did you go today?" Kerk asked. "I could have used your help in the wrestling matches."

Patrick smiled thinly. "Why?" he asked. "I would have only humiliated you. Has history taught you nothing, my friend?"

Kerk laughed softly. "Mayhap you are right," he said. Then, he seemed to look around, as if he had lost something. "Where is your lady?"

Patrick has his eyes focused ahead because he thought he saw a merchant with women's items posted outside of it. "Back at the inn," he told him. "And she is my wife."

Kerk looked at him curiously. "But you told me she wasn't."

"As of a half-hour ago, she is."

Kerk's eyebrows lifted in surprise. "I see," he said, peering strangely at Patrick. "That seemed rather… sudden. Was the marriage planned, then?"

"Nay."

Kerk sensed that either Patrick was being defensive or he really had nothing more to say on the matter. It was odd. But Kerk, a man of great communication and curiosity, wasn't satisfied with the answers he was receiving. He wanted clarification.

"Patrick, wait," he said, pulling the man to a stop in the middle of the street. "I suppose congratulations are in order but you do not seem happy about this. Why not?"

Patrick paused, looking at his friend and thinking that, perhaps, he was coming across as a bit hard and cold. He and Kerk had a long history of trust, having fought together over the past decade in what history would call the Second Barons Wars. They both fought at Evesham when Simon de Montfort was killed as well as the later and more decisive battle at Chesterfield. Therefore, he knew the man. He trusted him. He struggled to ease his harsh stance.

"I am extremely happy," he said after a moment. "But… if you must know, the lady is a ward of Coldingham Priory. I do not have their permission to marry her and I have a feeling my father is going to explode when I tell him. Strange what love does to a man, Kerk. All I know is that I had to marry her. Something in my soul required it."

Kerk sobered dramatically when he realized the seriousness of Patrick's situation. "I see," he said. "That is a bit of a quandary, my friend. Mayhap you should stay away from Questing for the time being and simply send your father a missive announcing the marriage."

Patrick resumed his walk at a much slower pace. "It is not a bad idea but that would be the cowardly way to do it," he said. "Nay, I must face my father with what I have done. I will worry about everything else when it is necessary."

Kerk didn't press him after that. He sensed that enough had been said, at least enough so that Kerk understood the situation. But one thing he said was correct; love had a strange effect on a man. Kerk had lived long enough to see too many instances of that and, therefore, had pledged never to fall in love if he could help it. But often there were circumstances beyond one's control and he understood that. Still, to see the great Nighthawk having put himself in a precarious position over love underscored to Kerk that all love was risky.

And foolish.

"Well," he said quietly as they approached a merchant who had all manner of pre-sewn garments hanging outside of his stall, "since you are happy with this marriage, I will congratulate you. But if you need to take the lady someplace safe, away from your father's wrath and away from Coldingham, bring her to Chillingham. No one would think to look for her there and I will tell Lord Grey that she is my cousin. We can hide her there if you need to."

They paused outside of the stall as Patrick turned to him, his expression softened. "Thank you," he said sincerely. "If the worst happens and I must send her away, then I will consider your offer. I am grateful."

Kerk forced a smile, hoping it didn't come to that. In spite of Patrick's demeanor, he could see fear in the man's eyes, something he'd never seen before. Patrick de Wolfe was invincible, a powerful knight the likes of which few men had seen, so to see genuine fear in the man's eyes was astonishing as well as depressing.

But he didn't want to point out that fear or expand on it. Instead, he caught sight of the hanging dresses and he grasped the one next to him. It was best to simply change the subject.

"So," he said, "you are here to buy your new wife a few things, are you? Ask me what I think of them. I am very good at giving advice on women's clothing. I know what I like."

Patrick was grateful for the shift of focus. He lifted a dark eyebrow at his friend. "So do I," he said, yanking the garment out of Kerk's hand to inspect it. He shook his head. "Too rough. The woman has spent her life as a postulate at Coldingham and has worn enough rough woolen clothing for a lifetime. Everything I get her must be terribly soft against her skin."

Kerk eagerly plunged into the merchant's stall, seeing a pile of fabric on a table and lifting it up, sifting through it to see that they were loosely basted surcoats that had not been hung on pegs for all to see. He began holding some of them up for Patrick's approval.

"Look at this," he said. "Linen. It is quite soft. What do you think?"

Patrick really didn't want the man's help while shopping for Brighton but he couldn't be cruel and send him away, either. He very much wanted to do this alone, as it was a personal mission for him, but Kerk was trying to be helpful and polite, so he let him. Kerk found many garments, most of which Patrick rejected, but a few of which he liked. A white silk with yellow panels, a dark blue brocade, and an orange brocade that was truly beautiful.

The merchant eventually emerged from his hut in the back of the shop and, seeing two big knights leafing through his goods, came forth to assist. When Patrick told him that he was essentially purchasing a trousseau for his wife, the merchant raced back into the shop and emerged a short time later with his wife and another older woman, all of them bearing things for Brighton. They were prepared for a very big sale.

Between Kerk, the merchant, his wife, and the old woman who was evidently a grandmother, Patrick found himself bombarded by many items that were brought forth for his approval. Very quickly, he became overwhelmed and sought to break up the onslaught. He told the merchant's women that his wife required things like soaps and combs, and as they flew into a frenzy gathering such things, Patrick sighed with relief that he had at least eliminated half of the offensive. They were off on a mission and he was left with just Kerk and the merchant to deal with.

It was less chaotic now. The merchant presented Patrick with more surcoats, shifts, and other undergarments than he had ever seen so he simply began pointing to things, which were then set aside. A large pile of clothing was soon reduced by half when he went through it again. All items that he wanted to purchase, but he had no satchel or capcase to carry any of it so the merchant brought forth two big trunks, dusty from having been in storage, with pretty painted panels.

Being that the merchant had nothing else to put the merchandise in, Patrick agreed to purchase the two trunks and they were very quickly stuffed with a myriad of items – surcoats, shifts, scarves, soaps and oils, combs, and even a tiny bejeweled dagger, everything a proper young woman would need. The only thing they didn't have were sturdy shoes although the merchant's wife had embroidered slippers imported from Italy and Patrick purchased a pair, just because they were so pretty. After paying the merchant handsomely for the haul, he and Kerk lifted the trunks and carried them back to the inn.

The sun was setting now, ribbons of pink and purple clouds strewn across the sky. Patrick tried not to think of how worried his mother would be when they didn't return from town. He was certain his father wouldn't be worried, trusting that Patrick would have a good reason for not returning home that night, but he knew his mother would fret. He was very sorry that he would have to upset the woman but he knew she would understand when she discovered why they had stayed the night in Wooler. At least, he hoped she would.

The inn was crowded now that the sun was setting and people were seeking shelter for the night. Patrick and Kerk came through the door, pushing men aside in order to enter the smoky, smelly room. It reeked of a poorly-functioning hearth and meat that was being boiled in the kitchens. Men and women were eating and drinking, some of them singing, others simply huddled at their tables, ignoring what was going on around them. Patrick pushed into the room, heading for the stairs that led to the upper floor, but he came to a halt just shy of the staircase and turned to Kerk.

"This is where you leave me," he said, a twinkle in his eye. "I do not need or want your presence for what I am to do tonight."

Kerk grinned and slung the trunk off his big shoulder, setting it down next to Patrick so the man could get a grip on it. "Understood," he said. "I can find my entertainment elsewhere."

"I am sure you can."

Kerk laughed softly before sobering, his gaze on Patrick. The mood between them was warm now that farewells were to be said. "It was good to see you today, old friend," he said. "If you ever need me, you know where I am."

"Chillingham."

"Aye."

"And if you ever need me, send word to Berwick. I can bring two thousand men to your doorstep in less than two days."

"I appreciate it very much." Kerk reached out a hand, which Patrick took. Bonds and friendships were reaffirmed. "God speed you, Patrick."

"And you, Kerk."

Kerk gave his hand a squeeze and dropped it, turning to find an empty chair in the crowded inn. Patrick, meanwhile, took hold of the second trunk and hauled both of them up the stairs and down the small walkway to his rented chamber at the far end. He used his booted foot to knock on the door, which was swiftly opened.

Brighton stood in the doorway, her face alight when she saw who it was. Patrick frowned. "You should never open a door until you know who is doing the knocking," he said as he came into the room. "What if I had been a murderer or a thief?"

Brighton stood back as he made his way in with the trunks. "Then I would either be dead or robbed by now."

He set the trunks down against the wall and looked at her, displeased with her answer. "I am serious."

She grinned. "So am I," she said. Then, she pointed to the window. "I saw you and Kerk coming across the road so I knew it was you."

He stared at her a moment before breaking down into a grin. "Saucy wench," he muttered. Then, he noticed the table behind her, full of food and drink, with a fat, drippy taper to light the meal. "What do you have for my supper, wife?"

Wife. It was the first time he had called her by her new station in life. Brighton was eyeing the prettily painted trunks but turned to see what had his attention. She smiled, bashfully.

"I asked a serving wench to bring food to us," she said, moving to the table to point things out. "There is a capon pie, boiled carrots and beans, cabbage potage, and bread. I will admit that I did not wait for you and have tasted everything. It is delicious."

He laughed softly, moving to the table and putting his arm around her shoulders as he looked over the feast. "I do not blame you," he said. "I am rather hungry. Shall we eat before it grows too cold?"

Brighton was more than eager to sit down and eat, considering the food had been brought up nearly an hour ago. She sat down on a three-legged stool, leaving the only chair in the room for Patrick and his big bulk. He removed his tunic and mail coat, tossing both onto the bed, before planting himself in the chair.

Patrick began pulling the bread apart, giving Brighton the soft cream-colored innards as he took the crust. It was a polite thing to do, the gentlemanly thing to do, and Brighton was very appreciative. Taking the big knife on the table, she buttered her bread with the soft white spread.

"Did you find what you were looking for when you went out?" she asked innocently, thinking of the trunks he'd brought in.

Patrick wasn't unaware that she was fishing for information. He fought off a grin. "Mayhap I did," he said evasively. "Mayhap I did not."

Brighton looked at him, her lips twisted wryly. "You brought something back so you clearly must have found what you were looking for."

Patrick took the nearest spoon and shoveled some of the capon pie into his mouth. "It is possible," he said, his eyes glimmering at her. "I have noticed something about you."

He was trying to change the subject and Brighton wasn't entirely unaware but she was growing frustrated. "What have you noticed?" she asked.

He shoveled more food into his mouth. "That you no longer have a stammer in your speech," he said. "Do you realize you have been speaking to me ever since we were married with perfect speech?"

She hadn't. Her eyes widened and she instinctively put her fingers to her lips. "I have?" she said, astonished. "But I have always had a catch in my speech. Sometimes worse than others."

Patrick watched her as she struggled with her confusion and surprise. "I have not heard it since the church."

Brighton was truly at a loss. "But... how can that be?" Then, she looked more astonished than before. "Is it a *miracle*?"

He smiled faintly, taking her free hand with his big fingers. "Possibly," he said softly. "But it could also be because the Bridey before today was an uncertain, nervous creature. Nervous of her future, fearful of everything. But the moment I asked you to marry me... that Bridey ceased to exist. With me by your side, what do you have to fear? There is no need for you to be nervous or uncertain. Mayhap your heart understood that even if your mind did not."

Brighton continued to run her fingers over her lips, still puzzled by the entire situation. "I have not even realized," she said, awed. "But... but mayhap it is true. What has happened today... what has been said... I still feel as if I am living a dream, Atty. Do you?"

He nodded, noting that he had again called him Atty. "I do," he said, his smile returning. "And I see that you are officially one of the family in that you now call me Atty. The name never sounded so sweet."

She laughed softly. "Your brother, Thomas, told me that I should call you that on the day I arrived from Berwick," she said. "I refused to do it because it did not seem appropriate. But now... now, it does."

"Now you are one of the family. The most important one to me."

She beamed, returning to her food and eating with gusto. Patrick watched her, pouring her wine and still more wine when she drank the entire first cup. In truth, he was feeding her wine with a purpose – so she would not be so nervous with what was to come. The more she would drink, the more he would pour.

All the while she ate heartily, including almost all of the cabbage potage and a good deal of the bread and butter. But after her second bowl of potage, and on her third cup of wine, she finally came to a halt. Patrick watched her over the rim of his cup as she wiped her forehead, seemingly exhausted and sick from too much food.

"Have you eaten your fill, my lady?" he asked.

She nodded. "Indeed," she said. "Truthfully, I do not think I have eaten so much in one day, ever. First it was the beef in the bread bowls and now it is potage and capon pie. I feel as if I am about to burst."

He smiled as he set his cup down. "I know how you feel."

She looked at his trencher, which was picked clean. So was everything else on the table. She looked up at him with surprise. "All of the food is gone."

"It is. You ate it all. Or do you not remember?"

Her expression suggested horror until she realized he was teasing her. The wine in her veins caused her to burst out in silly giggles.

"I did not," she insisted. "*You* did."

"You cannot prove that."

She pointed at the table. "I sat here and watched you," she said. "Would you truly dare to tell everyone that I am a glutton? Do I *look* like I could eat all of that food?"

Truth was, Patrick had a good deal of wine in his veins, too, and there was another one of those suggestive questions. His gaze drifted down her body, wearing one of the dresses his sister, Evelyn, had given her. Evelyn had never looked so good in that dress, clinging to every curve. Or perhaps he'd never noticed. In any case, the dress looked incredibly seductive on Brighton.

"I am not entirely sure," he said. "Stand up. I want to see where it is you pack away all of this food."

He only wanted to see her body, but Brighton was oblivious to his desire. Naïve in such suggestive games, she stood up and opened her arms, spinning a circle before him and throwing herself off balance because of the wine. "Look," she said. "I have no place to put it."

"Are you sure?"

"I am."

"Come here."

She did, standing in front of him but weaving rather drunkenly. Patrick reached up and put his hands on her waist, completely encircling it. When she saw his hands go around her torso, his fingers touching each other, she giggled uncontrollably and he grinned. He was rather swept up in her silly giggles. The woman had an overabundance of charm that she was only just discovering and, fortunately for him, he was the recipient. He could have listened to her giggle all night, but that wasn't what they were going to be doing all night.

He had something else in mind.

Pulling her to him, his lips captured hers, hungrily and forcefully. He put his arms around her, pulling her in between his legs. Brighton gasped at first, startled by what was probably a rather demanding action, but she quickly succumbed to his kiss. He could tell because her entire body went limp and her arms, soft and warm, looped around his neck. Feeling the rush of lust flow through his veins at her reaction, he stood up from his chair and picked her up all in the same motion.

Brighton wasn't a tiny woman but in his arms, she was as light as a feather. He carried her over to the bed, which was far from the table and in the shadows because of the only lit taper in the room was over where their meal had been. There was a fire in the hearth, but not a big one because of the warmth of the day, so as he laid her on the mattress, they were essentially in darkness. Still, he could see enough of her.

But he wanted to see all of her.

His mail and tunic were lying on the end of the bed and he swept them off as he placed her upon the bed. He was still wearing a padded tunic and then yet another lightweight linen tunic under that. He quickly ripped them off and cast them aside. Clad only in his breeches, which were essentially drop-front and cinched up with leather ties, he came down on top of her, his mouth claiming hers once more and hearing her grunt as his weight pressed upon her. But she didn't complain so he didn't move.

His onslaught grew. The wine he had imbibed was heating his loins, something that always happened when he had too much to drink, and he quickly unfastened the side of Brighton's surcoat. He was rather good at undressing women and proud of the fact that he was. So his fingers deftly navigated the ties and he pulled at the dress to get it off of her even as she awkwardly tried to help him.

But he didn't want her help. He wanted to show her what it was for a man to make love to a woman, for a husband to bed a wife, and he wanted to do all of the work so she could understand what it meant to physically please another person. He knew she had no concept of such things.

Also, he was being the slightest bit impatient because he didn't want to stop and explain things to her. There; he'd admitted it. He didn't want to talk his way through this. He simply wanted her to be silent while he had his way with her.

His plans were working quite well until he came to her shift and Patrick considered it a barrier to his wants. He was frustrated because it was rather snug and he wasn't able to yank it over her head in one movement. He actually struggled with the thing, trying to pull it off and being denied more than once. He was coming to think that it was like the damnable walls around a fortress – the shift was the walls and the keep was Brighton's naked body. He had to breach those walls and make way to the keep. Another couple of tugs and the shift finally came up over her head. He heard her shriek softly, perhaps embarrassed by her nakedness, but he didn't pay much attention. He was more concerned with unfastening his breeches.

Once they were open, Patrick fell upon her, once more, coming into contact with her soft, warm skin. His mouth found her neck while a hand went straight to her breast. Victory! He'd breached the walls and now he was beginning his assault of the keep! As he suckled the tender skin of her neck, he could feel her nipple hardening beneath his palm and he squeezed gently, feeling her jump with surprise. And probably some fear. But that was to be expected considering she'd never had anyone breach her keep before.

Oh, God, was that what it had come down to? The wine was making him think most foolishly, equating bedding his virgin wife to laying siege. But that's essentially what he was doing – assaulting the woman he had married. In order to consummate the marriage, that was exactly what he had to do – breach her. She wasn't fighting him but she was probably somewhat terrified.

Therefore, he slowed his onslaught. He truly didn't want to frighten her. Taking a deep breath, Patrick lifted his head from her neck and saw that she was laying there with her eyes tightly closed. He tapped her gently on the cheek.

"Are you well?" he asked huskily.

Brighton's eyes popped open. When she looked at him, he could see the fear. "Aye," she breathed.

"Are you sure?"

She simply nodded her head and he kissed her mouth, gently. "I am sorry if I frightened you," he murmured. "Lie still and you will enjoy this. If you do not, tell me. I will do all I can to make you comfortable."

Hesitantly, she nodded and he kissed her mouth again and stroked her cheek before continuing onward in his tender offensive. His kisses slowed and he shifted his body weight off of her, the hand on her breast moving gently now, tenderly, acquainting her with his touch. But she was full-breasted, with both nipples hard, and his vow to slow his pace was in danger of breaking. He very much wanted to sate his lust but, for once, he pushed that primal need aside.

This time, it was different.

"Relax," he murmured against the swell of her breast. "It will make everything easier."

He could feel her take a deep breath as she struggled to calm her racing heart; he could hear it when he lay his head upon her chest. His tongue snaking out to toy with a nipple and she shuddered. *He* shuddered. The wine was giving him very little control in spite of the fact that he had vowed to go slowly with her. His lust for her was so great that he evidently wasn't capable of moving slowly. Shifting his big body, he wedged himself between her supple legs.

Unused to the vulnerable position, Brighton kept trying to close her legs as Patrick kept trying to keep them open. He got into a wrestling match with her knees until he was finally able to overtake them and keep them pinned, one on either side of his body. Then, and only then, did he resume his gentle kisses on her belly while a big hand moved down to the junction between her legs.

There was a soft matting of dark curls there and he touched her very carefully at first, allowing her to become acquainted with his touch, before moving forward with his fingers gently probing her. The pink flower was quivering and wet. He put his fingers into her body, listening to her gasp. Something between ecstasy and alarm. Patrick could hardly hold himself back as he lowered his breeches around his thighs and slowly, firmly, entered her body.

Even if Brighton was utterly naïve to the ways of men and women, her body was innately sensitive to the primal mating ritual, something that men and women had been doing for thousands of years. It was in her blood even if it wasn't in her mind. She was hot and wet, but Patrick could feel her tensing up beneath him even as he slipped into her body. When he could slip no more, he drew back, coiled his buttocks, and drove into her.

Beneath him, Brighton gasped at the sting of possession but she didn't cry out and she didn't try to pull away. Patrick's gentle kisses eased her as he worked his way in, making way for a manhood that was proportionate to his large body. In truth, Patrick was glad she hadn't seen his engorged manroot before he made an attempt to bed her. He'd had women cry at the sight, fearful of the size, but with Brighton, he seemed to fit her easily.

As if she was made for him.

Surely, she was.

She was slick and Patrick used that to his advantage, thrusting into her repeatedly until he was fully seated. Her virginal walls gave way to accommodate him. The knees that had given him such trouble were now rubbing up against his legs, growing more curious about his position within her as her hands began to move over his back. Her soft hands, warm and calloused, threw him over the edge and he began to move in and out of her, his hips doing the work, as his mouth lingered on her forehead, her ear, her neck. There was nothing about her that wasn't sweet and delectable, and he told her so. Soft whispers filled her ear, telling her how beautiful she was and how sweet she tasted. He'd never meant anything so much in his entire life.

His pace quickened but his release wasn't close. Wine gave him the ability to last a very long time before releasing himself and he had no real concept of just how long he thrust into her. All he knew was that it was an emotional experience as well as a physical one. He'd never made love to anyone he truly cared about, at least not like this, and at one point he stopped his movements, withdrew, and flipped her over onto her belly. Lifting her hips slightly, he entered her from behind.

Beneath him, Brighton groaned and he propped himself up on his hands so he could look down at her body. The weak firelight illuminated her and his hungry eyes devoured her slender shoulders, the curve of her perfect back, and, finally, her heart-shaped buttocks. The sight of her perfectly rounded arse fueled his desire to epic proportions and he could finally feel his release approach. His entire body was tense with it, like pins and needles in his belly, spreading outwards. A few more thrusts and he released his seed deep into her body, feeling satisfaction as he'd never felt before. Even after he climaxed, he continued to move for the pure joy of it and, soon enough, he could feel Brighton's body tighten around him with her first release.

The still air of the chamber was filled with her gasps as Brighton was swept up in something she'd never experienced before. Patrick lay down next to her pulling her into his arms as she convulsed with pleasure. It was incredibly arousing but, more than that, he felt whole and content as he'd never felt in his life. He never known such utter fulfillment and, even after her tremors had calmed, he continued to hold her against him, his body still embedded in hers, listening to the faint roar of the common room and thinking that the decision to marry Brighton had been the best decision he'd ever made.

Perhaps not the most popular decision, or even the most reasonable given the circumstances, but he didn't regret anything. He belonged to her, body and soul, and nothing on earth could change that. He'd go to his grave before he let her go.

He honestly hoped it didn't come to that.

CHAPTER FOURTEEN

Castle Questing
The Next Day

"I HAVE NEVER known you to behave foolishly or irrationally, but in this case, you have. You have gotten yourself into a load of trouble, Patrick. Do you have any idea what you've done?"

Patrick stood calmly in his father's solar as the man, having been informed that his third son had married Lady Brighton the day before, let loose on him. Between his parents, William tended to be the calm one of the pair, but at this moment, he was positively livid. Patrick had never seen him so angry. But before Patrick could reply to William's statement, his father reached over onto the big, scarred table where he kept his maps and writing implements and grabbed an unrolled piece of vellum. Patrick could see that it had writing on it as William thrust it at him.

"Read this," William demanded.

Patrick eyed his father before taking the vellum. He made sure to keep a distance from the man in case William decided to physically demonstrate his anger, but so far, William had kept his head. Not his tongue, but his head. Patrick moved away from his father and over to the hearth for more light as he held the vellum up and read the carefully scribed words.

He read it twice. When he was finished, he simply lowered the vellum.

"So the missive from Coldingham came yesterday after I had left," he said softly.

William nodded. "Aye," he said. "Did you read all of it?"

"I did."

"And?"

Patrick cocked a dark eyebrow. "None of this matters now," he said frankly. "I have married her and the marriage has been consummated. Not even the church can dissolve the marriage so I will simply write to the mother prioress and inform her that Bridey is now my wife. There is nothing she can do about it."

The veins on William's temples were flaring unnaturally. "Aye, there is," he said. "If the mother prioress calls on the Bishopric of Durham, which controls most of the borders, the church can take sanctions against us. Did you ever think about that? We support the church with manpower as well as coinage and your mother is a patron of Kelso. They can ban all of us from participating in communion and they can lean on Henry to punish us. You essentially stole from them, Patrick. Do you not understand that?"

Patrick knew that butting heads with his father would get him nowhere. He'd tried before and it had never worked. William was more stubborn than his mother at times. But Patrick had returned to Questing staunchly determined to show absolutely no remorse in what he'd done yet he could see that being unmovable wasn't going to force his father to see his side of things. In fact, it was doing the opposite. The more he resisted, the more furious William became. Therefore, he switched tactics.

Averting his gaze from his father, he moved away from the hearth, vellum still in-hand. As he moved to one of the lancet windows overlooking the stables and kitchen yard in the distance, Kieran opened the door to the solar. Concern was written all over the man's face, but William held up a hand to the big knight, silently telling him to keep quiet. Obeying, Kieran slipped into the solar unnoticed by Patrick, who had made it to the window and was gazing away from him. He leaned against the sill as a warm summer breeze lifted his hair.

"I think I knew I loved her from the start," he mumbled. "It is not a matter of defying the church or disobeying you. I had to answer my heart, Da. You of all people should understand that. You fell in love with Mother when she was pledged to your liege and you carried out a clandestine relationship with her until it was discovered. Is there anything about that you would change? Knowing what you know now, would you not have engaged in that relationship with her?"

William took a deep breath and cleared his throat softly. He turned away from Patrick. "We are not speaking of me," he said. "We are speaking of you."

Patrick looked at him. "You defied the king to be with mother," he pointed out. "I am only defying the church. Why can you not understand that this has to do with love and nothing else? I love the woman and she is now my wife. I refuse to believe that what I did was wrong."

William was losing ground. He had been young and in love once, as Patrick pointed out, and there was nothing he would have done differently. In that respect, he couldn't take the moral high ground with Patrick. Sitting heavily, he leaned on his table.

"I am not saying it was wrong, lad, but you should have sought permission from Coldingham," he said. "Did you read that missive? They want her back. She is meant for the veil."

Patrick moved away from the window. "Then I will ride to Coldingham and offer them everything I have," he said. "If paying them will ease whatever anger they may have that I married her, then that is what I will do."

William shook his head as Kieran, who had been standing back in the shadows, came forward. "Coldingham used to be a rich priory," he said to William. "They have fallen on hard times over the past few decades so I am sure a generous donation would go a long way, William."

William looked at his longtime friend. "Now you side with Patrick?"

Kieran shook his head. "I am not siding with anyone," he said. "But given the situation, it's not as if he can take the lady back. She is his wife now. Did you consummate the marriage, Patrick?"

"I did," Patrick replied.

Kieran turned back to William. "Then Coldingham is going to want compensation at the very least."

William knew that. God help him, he did. He knew that Patrick couldn't take the woman back now, which meant her problems had just become his problems. Everything that was happening with the woman – her Norse father, her Scots mother – had now become a de Wolfe problem. He was so furious and distressed he could hardly see straight.

"Damnation," he hissed. "Patrick, do you realize what you've done to *all* of us? Now we are all targets because you married her. Now she is a de Wolfe and, as our kin, we are honor-bound to protect her. Is that why you really did this? To circumvent me when it came to taking the woman back to Coldingham?"

Patrick shook his head. "I told you I married her because I love her," he said steadily. "I will not apologize for that. I will not apologize for any of this. In fact, I will take her back to Berwick and deal with this myself. I do not ask for your help, your pity, or your money. I will deal with this myself so that if the church is going to sanction the family, then let it only be me. You needn't worry that I would jeopardize everyone else since that is what you seem to think I set out to do. You are not thinking of me at all, only of yourself. That is clear."

He started to head for the door but Kieran stopped him, putting his hands on the man's arms. "Atty, that is *not* it at all," he said softly. "You know we would never allow you to go this alone. You married the woman and she is part of us now, just as you are. 'Tis simply that this complicates things a bit."

Patrick's jaw ticked angrily. He wasn't going to be lectured by men who, in their youths, had done the same thing he'd done – defied authority to marry a woman. Their pious attitude infuriated him.

"You were there when my father fell in love with my mother," he said. "You saw everything. You saw how he lied to his liege, how he defied the king. And *I* am the one who has done something wrong by loving a woman who is in a complex situation? If I did, it is because of the example he set. He led me to believe that love was the most important thing in the world. Did he lie to me about that, too?"

Kieran did something at that moment that he would have never done under normal circumstances. He reached up and slapped Patrick across the face, open-palmed. "You will never speak of your father that way again," he said, his dark eyes flashing. "I will never hear those words from your lips again. Do you understand me?"

Patrick wouldn't answer him. In fact, he had to back away from Kieran, moving around the old knight for fear of what he might do. Any man who would strike him as Kieran did would, under normal circumstances, end up with a sword in his belly. Therefore, Patrick would not be humiliated by the man, even if he did love and respect him. He didn't think he'd said anything wrong in the least.

With a lingering glance at Kieran, Patrick walked around the man and quit the solar in tense silence. When the door shut behind him, Kieran turned to William.

"He speaks his mind much as you do," Kieran said. "But I will not let him show disrespect to you. I am sorry that I hit your son, William, but that is the way I feel."

William was weary of the contention with his favored son; he and Patrick had such a beautiful bond that he was deeply grieved at the anger between them. He sighed heavily. "Am I wrong, Kieran?" he asked. "Am I wrong to scold him for this?"

Kieran moved towards the desk where William was sitting. "What does your heart tell you?"

"That I should not have lost my temper with him."

Kieran snorted softly. "I should not have, either."

William leaned forward on the table, pondering his next move in the battle with Patrick. Perhaps there was no next move. "I wanted such a great marriage for him," he muttered after a moment. "I had great dreams of a duke's daughter or even a royal niece. I wanted to see him marry well. It never occurred to me that he would have different ideas on the matter."

Kieran lifted his eyebrows in agreement. "Much like you, he fell in love with a woman he wasn't supposed to have," he said. "But he is right… love is the most important thing in the world, William. I would much rather see my sons married to women they love even if it meant living a simple life than see them married well with unlimited wealth to a woman they were miserable with. And Patrick loves Bridey, William. You should be happy for him because you, of all people, understand what it means to love a woman. He needs you now, more than he ever has. He is in trouble. Do not fail him."

William knew that. Now he was starting to feel uncertain and sad; sad that he'd argued with his son and uncertain for the future. But one thing was for certain; he had to stand behind Patrick and not against him, just as Kieran had said. He would not fail him. Wearily, he stood up from his chair.

"I will go and find him," he said as he moved to the door. "Hopefully he will not be too angry that you hit him and try to take it out on me."

Kieran watched him walk to the door. "Do you want me to come with you?"

William shook his head. "Nay," he replied. "He left this chamber so he would not strike you in return. If I were you, I would stay out of his way for the rest of the day."

"I can still hold my own against him."

William cracked a smile. "You are dreaming if you think so."

He left the chamber, leaving Kieran standing by the cluttered table, smiling. Kieran knew he was dreaming, too, but he had to show a good front. But staying out of Patrick's way for the rest of the day wasn't a bad idea.

The missive from the mother prioress was still over by the windowsill where Patrick had left it so Kieran went to retrieve it and bring it back over to put it on William's table so the man wouldn't lose it. There was so much clutter on the table that Kieran wasn't entirely convinced it was a good place for the vellum but he dropped it there nonetheless. He was just heading for the door when the panel shifted open and in came his wife along with his son, Kevin, and Apollo de Norville. The young knights had a rather curious but restrained look about them but Jemma didn't hold back. She went right to her husband.

"Well?" she demanded. "Did William banish Atty? I saw Atty leave the solar and head tae the upper floors, but when William came out, he headed tae the hall. What has happened?"

Kieran frowned. "Were you watching the solar door?"

As Jemma prepared a staunch retort, Kevin spoke. "Mother was coming down the stairs and Apollo and I were just entering from the bailey. I didn't see Patrick go upstairs, but I saw Uncle William head to the great hall. What happened, Papa? What did Uncle William say about Patrick's marriage?"

Kieran sighed. "I am sure you can imagine that he is not happy," he said. "Especially after we received the missive from the mother prioress yesterday. Patrick may have gotten himself into trouble by marrying a woman he did not have permission to marry."

"Pah," Jemma said. "A big enough donation tae Coldingham and he can buy permission. The lass told Jordy that she wanted tae marry Atty, and she's of age. It wasna as if he forced her."

Kieran shook his head. "It does not matter. Patrick should have asked for permission before marrying her."

Jemma still didn't see the issue. "And so he didna," she said, hands on her hips. "Bridey is a lovely lass and Atty did well enough tae marry her. Ye can see that they love each other and the church canna separate them now. It is finished."

Kieran wasn't so sure. "If they are angry enough, they can demand his arrest," he said. "They can have Patrick locked up for what he has done. That would separate them."

Jemma faltered at the realization. "Oh… Kieran," she breathed. "Ye dunna think they would do that, do ye?"

Kieran lifted his big shoulders as his son and Apollo stepped forward. "We will not let them get their hands on Patrick," Kevin said firmly. "I suggest we return to Berwick immediately so the church does not move against Questing. We will seal Berwick up and wait out Coldingham's anger. They'll not get Patrick while there is breath left in my body."

Kieran put his hand on his son's cheek affectionately. "You are a true and loyal friend," he said. "But Patrick will not go this alone. His father will not let the church arrest him, even if he has to defy Henry himself. And since Patrick is going to London to assume his post as Lord Protector, it is my thought that mayhap he should go now and take his wife with him. The further away from Coldingham for them both, the better."

"We have more men on the border than the church could summon in all of Northumberland," Apollo said, arrogant in his youth. "My father carries thousands as the captain of Northwood Castle and between all of Uncle William's garrisons, there has to be ten thousand men. The church would be foolish to take on the whole of de Wolfe and his allies for one small postulate."

Apollo was an astute young man and enthusiastic, much as Kevin was. Those two were usually the ones to charge headlong into any conflict before anyone else had the chance. Looking at the pair, Kieran could see that they were more than willing to draw a sword on Patrick's behalf. But he didn't need them cutting nuns in half in order to prove a point. He sought to soothe the savage young blood.

"William will do what needs to be done, I am sure," he assured the eager pair. "Meanwhile, the best thing you two can do is ride to Paris at Northwood Castle and inform him of the situation. He is very close to Berwick and if there is some kind of military undertaking, he must be informed."

Kevin and Apollo were more than ready to ride with that message. "Aye," Apollo replied. "Shall I tell him anything else?"

Kieran shook his head. "Nay," he said. "If anything else occurs, I will send him a missive right away."

With their orders, Kevin and Apollo left the solar, preparing for the short ride to Northwood Castle, a massive bastion where Apollo's father served the Earl of Teviot. With the two hotheads out of the room, Kieran turned to his wife, who was now seemingly quite worried about the situation. When she saw her husband's attention on her, she shook her head sadly.

"Poor Atty," she mumbled. "When the man finds happiness, it isna without a great price. And she is such a dear lass, Kieran. Even now, she is upstairs with the children, playing with them as if she doesna have a care in the world."

Kieran went to her, pulling her into his big arms, holding her snuggly. It was something that he drew strength from and had for almost thirty years. For all of Jemma's spit and fire, she was a woman with a heart of gold and Kieran adored her. He was whole when she was with him.

"I do not want you worrying her," he said. "When you see her next, do not mention this conversation. Everything she hears, she should hear from Patrick."

Jemma's head was against Kieran's chest, hearing his heart beating in her ear. "I know," she said. "I willna be the one tae tell the lass anything."

"Thank you." He kissed the top of her head and let her go. "I think I will go upstairs and play with the children, too. I must stay away from Patrick for the rest of the day."

Jemma looked at him, confused. "But why?"

"Because he accused William of lying to him so I slapped him."

Jemma's eyes widened. "Ye slapped that mountain of a man?" she gasped. "Saints help us; what were ye thinkin'?"

Kieran took her by the elbow and headed for the solar door. "I was thinking that he insulted his father."

"So ye hit him?"

"Slapped him."

"'Tis the same thing!"

Kieran shook his head. "Had I hit him, I would have knocked him cold."

Jemma scowled. "Atty? I doubt it. Did he hit ye back?"

Kieran opened the solar door. "Do I look like he hit me back?"

Jemma peered at his face. "Open yer mouth," she said. "Are ye missin' teeth?"

He frowned at her and urged her through the door. "I am *not* missing teeth."

Jemma only shook her head, a worried expression on her face. "For now," she muttered. "I think I will stay with ye the rest of the day. Atty wouldna dare strike ye in front of me."

Kieran had to roll his eyes; it wasn't as if he was a weakling. He was an enormous man of great power, but from the way people were reacting when it came to him and Patrick in a showdown, he was either dreaming he could win or, like now, his wife wanted to protect him. If people weren't careful, he was going to start feeling emasculated.

True to her word, Jemma stuck by his side for the rest of the day.

WILLIAM SAW THE back of Patrick's head as he entered the stable.

It was cool and somewhat dark in the stable, with beams of light steaming in from the ventilation windows. Patrick was saddling a small palfrey, evidently trying to repair a buckle on a lady's saddle, and he didn't see William when the man entered the stable. Not wanting to startle his son, who was probably in no mood to be surprised, he knocked quietly on the stable entrance as he entered, simply to alert Patrick that someone was coming up behind him.

Patrick turned to see his father and promptly turned back to what he was doing. William's gaze lingered on the man, thinking on how to start the conversation when Patrick was clearly still upset with him. He cleared his throat quietly.

"Patrick, you do not need to leave," he said. "I have had my tantrum. I've said what I needed to say. Now we must figure out how to solve this problem together, just as we have always done. When did you become so thin-skinned to my rantings?"

Patrick paused. "I have just been told that I am an utter idiot by the man I love most in this world," he said. "How thick-skinned would *you* be?"

William leaned against the stable wall as Patrick went back to fixing the buckle. "I did not say you were an idiot," he clarified. "I said that you were irrational. But you would not run from me if I was in trouble and I will not run from you. Now that I am calm, I gather that returning Bridey to Coldingham is out of the question?"

"It is."

"Then you and I will have to go to the priory and explain the situation."

Patrick paused again, looking up at his father. "You need not go," he said. "I got myself into this. It is my peril to face."

William shook his head. "Nay, lad," he said quietly. "It is *our* peril. You are my son and I will not let you face this without me. In fact, I will insist on going. I've yet to speak with your mother about this but there is the possibility that she may want to go as well. Remember she deals with Kelso Abbey on a regular basis and she is very involved in feeding the poor and tending the sick. Therefore, she understands the way these institutions work. And she may be able to express to the mother prioress what men cannot."

Patrick sighed, long and slow. "Now Mother is coming with us?" he said. "I am not entirely sure it is a good idea."

William lifted his eyebrows. "You cannot stop her if she wants to," he said. "If she wants to go and we deny her, then she will follow. Trust me, lad – your mother will not be denied."

Patrick finished fiddling with the strap on the saddle and cinched it up. "I know," he muttered unhappily, but his manner was softening. "Neither will you. I am sorry if I was rude to you, Da. I was… hurt. Hurt that you did not trust me."

This was the Patrick that William knew – soft-hearted when it came to his parents, loving and kind. He felt some relief at the man's apology. "And I am sorry that I became so angry with you," he said. "You were right – I do understand what it is to love a woman that I cannot have. Obviously, I did not let it stop me. My love for your mother has pulled me through time and space, and continues to do so. Not even death will end it. Therefore, I do understand what you are feeling. I understand it all too well."

"Then tell me what to do," Patrick said, his stony expression breaking. There was worry there now. "I fear that I may have lost my perspective. I speak of taking money to Coldingham to buy my bride, but is that the best thing to do? I am due to leave for London in a few days. Mayhap I should seek Henry's counsel on the matter. He has the power to make it so that the church has to listen."

William shrugged. "In any case, you must confess to him what has happened so he is not surprised by a missive from Coldingham or, worse, the Bishop of Durham demanding your head," he said. "I have a feeling that Henry will support you, whatever the case, but it would be much better if we could solve this ourselves. If you are agreeable, then we will ride to Coldingham tomorrow and offer the mother prioress a goodly sum of money in exchange for Bridey. The price of a bride, as it were."

"Then you believe that is the best course of action?"

"I do."

Patrick felt better about the situation now. This is the advice and support he had been seeking from the first but his father, who had many people to worry over, had reacted as had been his right – with concern and anger over something that could jeopardize them all.

Now, the situation was far calmer and he was able to think more clearly. Leaving the palfrey standing there half-saddled, Patrick leaned back against the wall next to his father. As the tension of their argument faded, the reality of what was to come settled in. Patrick was going to have to pay for Brighton, and pay handsomely. Not that he minded in the least but he began to tally up what money he had available.

"As for the money," he said, "I am mostly paid by you, as your garrison commander, and also by Lord de Longley, as your liege, for my *servitium debitum.* You pay me too much, you know."

William smiled weakly. "I pay you five pounds a year."

"De Longley pays me five pounds a year. That is ten pounds every year, an incredible sum."

"Are you complaining?"

Patrick shook his head. "Nay," he said. "Because I have saved my money over the past several years. Henry paid me well in the battles against de Montfort, as did his son, Edward. In coinage alone I have over two hundred pounds stashed away, and that is not including what I have been paid in plate or other valuables. Do you think Coldingham would take twenty pounds for the lady? That is more than they could make in ten years."

William nodded. "It is a very generous offer," he said. "If the mother prioress refuses, I will double it. Surely she would be foolish to refuse that."

Patrick felt much better than he had in some time. He and his father were speaking reasonably and rationally, and a plan was now set. He could only pray that the mother prioress would accept the money for Brighton, because truly, only a fool would refuse such a sum. Aye, he was feeling much better – he knew what he had to do and his father was with him.

All was right in the world again.

"Then I suppose we shall leave for Coldingham on the morrow," he said. "I do not have much time before I must leave for London so there is no time to waste. How long will it take us to reach it? I know approximately where it is but I have never been there."

William shook his head. "Nor have I," he said. "But I know it is north of Eyemouth. That is not far from Berwick."

Patrick agreed. "We must pass through Berwick to travel the road along the ocean north," he said. "And, Da… I think I should take Bridey back to Berwick. The place is impenetrable and she would be away from Questing. I know you are concerned for Mother and the others with her here, as a target. So if I return her to Berwick, that would alleviate your fear somewhat."

William heard his own words reflected in his son's statement, now feeling guilty that he'd said such a thing. It wasn't as if Coldingham would attack them, although they could raise an army at some point if they wanted to. As part of the Bishopric of Durham, they could call on the bishop's army. William had only said such things to his son because he hadn't wanted his family to be put in harm's way, but it had been selfish of him. He could see that now.

"Leave her here if it makes you feel better," he said. "She would have your mother, if she chooses not to come with us, and Jemma and your sisters for company. She might feel more comfortable if she remained here."

"But Berwick is to be her new home. She will have to go back some time."

"Then I shall leave the decision to you."

A warm silence settled between the two of them now that the storm had passed and they were on pleasant terms again. Patrick was vastly relieved to have his father's support once again because the more he thought on it, the more daunting the task seemed. In fact, now that the rush of the impromptu wedding was over, he was coming to grips with what he'd done on a larger scale. In truth, he didn't much blame his father for becoming so furious with him. He *had* rather gotten himself into a bit of a situation.

But it was of no matter. He wouldn't have changed a thing.

"When I first realized I was feeling something for Bridey, I was truly furious at myself," he muttered. "The appointment with Henry is what I have strived for all of my life and I did not need or want any complications. I kept telling myself that. But now that I am facing what could quite possibly be a terrible complication with the event of my marriage… it is all I can think of. Bridey is all I can think of. Going to London to assume my new post seems secondary in comparison."

William watched his son as he spoke, the sincerity in the man's features. A smile crossed his lips. "When I met your mother, I was facing the same thing," he said quietly. "Henry wanted me in London and I did not want to leave your mother. How odd we find ourselves in such similar circumstances at nearly the same time in our lives. But, unlike you, I had no father to guide me and no massive military empire at my disposal. Certainly, I had the late John de Longley as my mentor and liege, but there were times I felt quite alone in it all."

Patrick cocked his head curiously. "Even with Uncle Kieran and Uncle Paris to help you?"

William shrugged. "They were mere knights," he said. "They did not have men sworn to them at the time, so it wasn't as if I had their armies at my disposal. Not like I do now. In that respect, you are in a much better position than I ever was. Have faith, Patrick. We shall overcome."

It was the first time Patrick had heard his father speak in support of his situation. It made him feel vastly better. "Thank you, Da," he said sincerely. "That means everything to me."

"Family above all."

"Indeed."

William patted his son on the cheek before pushing himself off of the wall, stretching his body out, as it tended to become stiff these days. His joints weren't like they used to be. But he paused before leaving.

"Before I forget," he said. "I know that Kieran struck you earlier. I would consider it a personal favor if you did not go after him to retaliate. You can survive a blow from him but I doubt he could easily survive one from you. Am I making myself clear?"

Patrick laughed softly. "I will not retaliate," he said, a mischievous twinkle to his eye. "When you see him, tell him I said that my mother slaps harder than he does."

William snorted. "Poor Kieran," he said. "We keep telling him that he is a weak old man. Someday, he is going to believe it. There was a time when Kieran was the strongest man I'd ever seen."

Patrick's laughing eased. "He still is," he said. "At least, in my eyes he still is. I always admired him greatly and I still do."

"Can I tell him that?"

"Nay. Let him think that my mother slaps harder than he does."

Chuckling, and shaking his head at his cruel son, William left the stable. He was heading for the keep and his wife, who would soon learn that her husband and son were about to leave Questing to head into Scotland.

Patrick, meanwhile, went to unsaddle the palfrey and put the saddle away, at least for the day. He still thought it was a good idea to drop Brighton off at Berwick on their way to Coldingham for the very reasons he gave his father. It was to be her home, after all, and the fortress was impenetrable. He felt very confident having her there, settling into her new life while he went on to Coldingham to buy his bride. Twenty pounds was a lot of money but it didn't matter; there was no price too high that he wouldn't pay for his wife.

His wife.

The thought of that lovely woman he married had him grinning like a fool all over again.

CHAPTER FIFTEEN

FORTUNATELY FOR PATRICK and William, Jordan did not want to go with them to the priory, feeling that she could not genuinely contribute to the solution for Patrick's situation. She chose, instead, to stay behind and pray for a positive outcome, much to the relief of her husband and son. Penelope, however, was another story. She didn't want to stay behind. She didn't want to part with anyone. The three-year-old girl who ruled Castle Questing was in a snit from the very start.

Leaving Castle Questing before sunrise had been difficult because of wailing, sleepy children. Penelope was devastated that Brighton, as well as her father and her playmates, were departing for home. Katheryn and Evelyn had their hands full with fussy children that they bundled up into the carriage. The carriage itself wasn't all that large – meant to hold four adults – but with the unhappy children, it had three women, an infant, three little boys and one little girl, all of them squirming and crying. The carriage was nearly overflowing.

The only children who weren't crying were Katheryn's older boys, who rode their ponies proudly from Questing, being escorted by their grandfather and father. Brighton, Katheryn, and Evelyn each sat with a child in their laps while the other two crowded in on the benches around them.

Jordan and Jemma, very sorry to see their grandchildren and children depart, followed the carriage across the bailey and to the great gatehouse where they were finally forced to stop, waving to the carriage and the knights as they passed through the big gates. Penelope was so distraught she wouldn't even wave farewell. Brighton could hear Penelope wailing all the way down the hill to the road below.

It was another glorious summer morning as the sun rose over the dew-kissed fields, advancing majestically over the land. The war horses were excited, feeding off of each other as the knights and the one hundred men Patrick had brought with him headed out on the road, eastward bound for Berwick. William was astride his big silver beast, hanging back by the carriage and his mounted grandsons, as Alec took point and Hector brought up the rear.

The de Wolfe pack was on the move.

With Kevin and Apollo having ridden on to Northwood Castle the day before, the group was down one knight and Patrick remained fluid, moving up and down the column, stopping on more than one occasion to check in on his wife as she sat with little Lisbet on her lap. Not normally distracted by a carriage carrying women, that had markedly changed. He was very distracted by the carriage and everyone knew it. He would wink at his wife in the carriage and she would wink back.

But it was a good distraction. There was such joy in Brighton's heart at the sight of him, winking at him and waving to him as he would stop by. To her, he seemed much happier today than he had yesterday, which had been a day of turmoil mostly. Their return from Wooler to Castle Questing had been wrought with tension. No matter how much Patrick tried to reassure Brighton that all would be well, she was still fretful, terrified of how William and Jordan would react. Her fear was well-founded, for Patrick and his father had argued most of the morning only to come to a fragile peace by the afternoon. Brighton had remained in the family's chambers upstairs, playing with Penelope and praying for a good outcome.

Fortunately, someone had listened to her prayers.

When the yelling and arguing was over, William and Patrick had come up with a plan to deal with Coldingham and now they were heading back to Berwick to drop off the women before Patrick and his father continued north to compensate the priory for a loss of a postulate. Brighton had been surprised to hear of the missive where Mother Prioress demanded her return but she was confident, much as Patrick and William were, that the woman would accept monetary compensation for the cost of a bride.

At least, that was her hope.

She truly didn't know why Mother Prioress would have demanded her return unless the woman felt fear for her young charge. She had asked to go with Patrick back to Coldingham because she wasn't entirely certain that Patrick alone could convince Mother Prioress that he'd not forced the lady into marriage, but Patrick had denied her, assuring her that between he and his father, the mother prioress would understand that this had not been a forced marriage. Still, the doubt lingered in Brighton's mind. She sincerely hoped she was wrong.

As she tried not to fret about it, the trip back to Berwick was uneventful and they reached Berwick in very good time. It was still daylight, with the sun laying low on the western horizon. The children inside the carriage were restless, having spent all day traveling. The women in the carriage were more than eager to release the throng so they could run off their pent-up energy.

Through the gatehouse, across the bridge that spanned the chasm, and into the vast bailey the carriage lurched, and Katheryn wasted no time in throwing open the door and exiting the cab. Her youngest, Christoph, was grumpy and whining as she pulled him out, followed by Evelyn carrying her infant, helping Atreus and Hermes from the carriage as Brighton climbed out last, carrying little Lisbet.

The men were being disbanded as the children began to run about, looking for their fathers, chasing each other and generally blowing off several hours of being cramped inside a carriage. Only the young girls seemed not to want to join their brothers as Evelyn and Brighton carried them towards the keep.

Even though Brighton had little Lisbet in her arms, she kept searching for Patrick, spying him in the midst of the men who were disbanding, dismounting his charger and handing him off to a soldier. William was with him, the two of them standing in the middle of the enormous bailey in conversation. But something must have told Patrick that Brighton was looking at him, some innate sense, because he turned to her, now on the steps of the keep, and waved at her. Satisfied that he had acknowledged her, Brighton followed Evelyn and Katheryn into the keep.

"This is now your castle, Bridey," Katheryn said as they entered the tall foyer and she began removing the leather gloves she had been wearing. "Evie and I will take our orders from you now. Preparations for the evening meal should already be underway but you may want to see to them; would you like Evie and I to do that for you?"

Brighton grinned; Katheryn was being most diplomatic about the fact that she was now replaced as chatelaine. She was being just as kind as she could possibly be about it.

"I-I would appreciate that," she said. "Mayhap you would even let me come along as you go about your tasks?"

Katheryn returned her smile. "Come and supervise us," she said. "See how we do things to ensure it is the way you want them done."

Brighton nodded eagerly. "I-in truth, I never learned how to run a house and hold," she confessed. "That was not something we were taught at Coldingham. This will all be very new to me."

Katheryn patted her on the shoulder. "It will be nothing at all," she said. "You will learn all of this very quickly and Evie and I will help you. In fact, it is good to have three of us to manage this monstrous place. It is too much for one or two people."

Brighton was relieved to hear that. She hadn't really considered the fact that she would now be expected to administer the household, as Patrick's wife. With everything else they'd had to deal with, it was down on her list of priorities but it was probably more intimidating to her than anything else about this new life she'd embarked upon. To be in charge of this vast fortress was daunting. She was grateful for the kindness of Patrick's sisters.

"M-mayhap we can divide the duties," she suggested. "That is what we did at Coldingham. As I told you, I tended the garden and worked in the kitchen. I know a great deal about kitchens and stores."

"Perfect!" Katheryn threw up her hands in glee. "If you will see to the kitchens, I will tend to the management of the great hall and Evie can manage the servants and the rooms in the keep to ensure everything is properly kept. It will be so much easier this way."

Brighton agreed wholeheartedly. "T-that is a wonderful idea," she said. "S-shall we settle the children and unpack our belongings first? Then, I would love to see to the kitchens."

The ladies were in complete agreement and as Brighton followed the women up the stairs to the family chambers, helping Evelyn to put her daughters to bed, she was coming to think that, already, she was happy here. She loved Patrick's sisters and she loved their children. She was as content and happy as she could possibly be at the moment. The question of Coldingham was still heavy in the air, but that would be dealt with. There was no use worrying over it until Patrick and his father met with success… or not.

She hoped it wasn't the latter.

Still, her new life seemed surreal in spite of everything. Leaving Katheryn and Evelyn with the children, she headed back down to the entry level with the intention of seeking out her trunks. They had come back with them on a provisions wagon, the same wagon some of the children had ridden in on their journey to Castle Questing, but on the trip back to Berwick it was full of trucks and other things. Stepping outside onto the top of the steps that led down into the bailey, she shielded her eyes from the sun as she surveyed the area. She could see that most of the men had been disbanded and trunks and satchels were being brought into the keep by servants.

Brighton could see her painted trunks plainly and she directed the servants, when they came up the steps, to take the trunks to the chamber next to Patrick's. That was where she had originally slept her first night at Berwick and, to be truthful, she wasn't exactly sure how happy Patrick would be if she simply moved into his chamber without him having time to move his own things around to give her space. She was the man's wife now but she didn't want to presume anything. Better let him tell her what he wanted before she acted.

Retreating into her chamber once her possessions were dropped off, Brighton busied herself by opening up her trunks and removing the clothing. All of it had been carefully rolled up, so as not to wrinkle, but it was better to get them aired out and hung up on a peg. So she carefully shook out everything, laying it upon the bed and smoothing it out. It was more beautiful clothing than she had ever seen and, coupled with what Evelyn had given her, she had a wardrobe fit for a queen. Or, the wife of a prestigious knight, as it were. These were more beautiful things than she ever knew to exist.

Meant for a life she never thought to have.

Somehow, Brighton ended up on the floor going through the combs and soaps and oils that Patrick had purchased for her. So many wonderful, glorious things. A servant entered her chamber at one point with some wood for her hearth, lighting the fire as the sun began to set and bringing her two fat tapers to give light to the chamber.

She truly had no idea how long she had been on the floor, inspecting combs and scarves and other things. The sun continued to set and the land outside grew dark. Soon enough, she heard Patrick's voice as he came up the stairs. He was speaking to someone and, as Brighton rose to her feet and went to her open chamber door, she could see that Evelyn had met Patrick and their father at the top of the stairs. Evelyn was now showing William where he was to sleep for the night.

William was soon surrounded by several of his grandsons who wanted to help him with his saddlebags. One wanted to carry his sword. Brighton smiled, watching as William was very patient with his demanding little grandsons. William and the gaggle of boys followed Evelyn down the corridor to his borrowed chamber as Patrick headed in Brighton's direction. Her smile broadened when their eyes met.

"Your father has many helpers," she commented.

Patrick gave her half-grin. "Ah, yes," he said. "They all want very much to squire for him, although they are so young I do not know if they really know what that means."

Brighton laughed softly. "I will squire for you if you will let me," she said. "I have already unpacked my bags. I would be more than happy to help you unpack yours."

Patrick's grin broadened as he went to her, taking her in his arms and kissing her gently on the lips. "That is most kind, wife," he murmured. "I have missed you today. I hardly had any time to see you or speak with you."

Brighton wrapped her arms around his neck. "I could see you most of the day through the window of the carriage," she said. "But, alas, even in the carriage with your lovely sisters, I was still lonely for you."

It was a sweet thing to say, warming his heart, and Patrick kissed her again, feeling a spark ignite in his belly, a spark he was coming to equate with his feelings for Brighton. He'd felt that spark most strongly the night he bedded her and also last night when he had bedded her again. It was a very lustful spark and one he was more than happy to answer the call for, but the moment he bent over to kiss her more lustily, he caught sight of her open trunks in the chamber next to his and everything came to a halt.

"What are your trunks doing in there?" he nearly demanded. "You do not think to sleep in there, do you?"

Brighton shook her head. "Nay," she said. "But I did not want to move my things into your chamber until you told me to. That would have been quite bold of me."

He scowled at her. "Bold?" he repeated, aghast. "You are my wife. You will sleep where I sleep. Start taking your things into my chamber immediately, you silly wench."

It sounded very much like a command and Brighton quickly turned for the chamber, yelping when Patrick swatted her on the behind with a trencher-sized hand as if to punish her for being so foolish. She giggled, and he grinned, as she went to collect her things.

Seeing that she was doing as he had commanded, Patrick went into his big, cluttered chamber and began removing his mail. As he hung his mail coat on a frame near the door, he began to look around the chamber and think that, perhaps, this didn't look much like an inviting chamber for a woman. It was dusty and had clutter in the corners. When Brighton scurried in with an armful of her new garments, he held out a hand.

"Wait," he said. "You may want to clean this room to your liking before you move your possessions in here. I do not spend much time here and the servants are not allowed to come in when I am not here, so it is a rather dirty room. You may wish to clean it up first."

Brighton looked around the chamber. It was very big, with an enormous bed and a huge wardrobe among other pieces of furniture, but it was also very dusty. There were no oil cloths covering the windows and no curtains around the bed. In all, it was a spartan chamber meant for a man. She turned to him.

"I will not clean it up if you do not want me to," she said. "If you are comfortable here, I see no reason to disturb it on my account."

He smiled faintly, putting an arm around her shoulders and kissing her on the forehead. "There is every reason to disturb it on your account," he said. "A man-pig lives here. Feel free to do anything you wish to the chamber to make it more comfortable for us both. I give you permission."

Brighton turned to the room again, thinking that it did, indeed, need some sweeping and cleaning. Oddly enough, she was very excited at the prospect. *Make it comfortable for us both.*

She would.

"Tonight?" she asked.

He gave her a squeeze and let her go as he prepared to remove his padded tunic. "Tonight," he said. "Right now if you wish. I have some business with my father now, so do your worst."

Brighton beamed at him. "I will," she said. "I have much to do."

He watched her scurry back into the other chamber where her items were laid out. "I will see you at supper."

She had her back to him as she dumped her garments back onto the bed. "Indeed, you will."

"Bridey?"

She paused and stood up, turning to look at him. "Aye, Atty?"

His gaze lingered on her a moment. "I am glad you are here. With me."

Her joyful expression softened, adoration filling her features. "As am I."

"I do love you. You know that."

She nodded. "And I love you, my husband. More than you can ever know."

They were words to fortify him, filling him with steel for a soul and granite for determination. Nothing on earth could crush him as long as he had her love. Hearing those words from her… he never knew anything could mean so much to him.

Leaving his happy wife cleaning up their chamber, Patrick headed back down the corridor in search of his father. All he had to do was follow the clamor of children and he soon came upon his father being set upon by five grandsons. The older boys were trying to convince him that they needed his daggers while the younger ones were simply rifling through his saddlebags, throwing things aside on the hunt for something useful or valuable. Patrick stood in the doorway and shook his head.

"You are being robbed and you do not even know it," he said, pointing to the lads pawing through the saddlebags. "Eddie and Axel have you occupied while the younger ones steal your things."

William grinned, turning to see Christoph, Atreus, and Hermes pulling everything they could out of his saddlebags. He, too, shook his head.

"They remind me very much of you and your brothers when you

were their age," he said. "As I recall, you stole many an item from me, not the least of which was my coin purse. Do you remember that? You were about three or four years of age. We searched for it for an entire week and only found it when your mother forced you to give it up. You had buried it in the stable beneath the feet of one of the chargers. It was very clever of you, actually."

Patrick laughed softly. "That is still where I keep my money," he said. "Only a madman would go into the stall of a man's war horse. In fact, that is why I came. I am preparing to pull forth my coin. Do you want to come with me?"

William shook his head. "I had better not lest this group rob me blind while I am gone," he said. "I will see you in the hall for sup."

"Very well."

Leaving his father to occupy the young boys, Patrick headed down to the stable where he had, indeed, buried his money in the ground of his war horse's stall. The horse was the best possible sentinel. Once he reached the barn, he removed the horse from the stall with no issue before sweeping aside the hay and dung to reveal a stone laid flush against the floor of the stall.

Beneath the panel lay a locked chest containing Patrick's coinage. He pulled the chest forth, unlocked it, and opened it. Inside, there was an entire horde of silver dinars and two leather purses full of gold crowns. He pulled forth twenty pounds in silver and one of the gold coin-filled purses just in case he needed to sweeten the deal. Although his father was already doubling his twenty pounds, still, Patrick didn't want to leave anything to chance.

Soon, the depression of what was to come hung over him. He'd avoided it most of the day, keeping himself occupied with other things. He thought of Brighton, now up in his chamber making it a place she would be comfortable to live in, and his heart swelled with happiness. Never had anything felt so right to him. He wanted this day to be normal, a glimpse of their life to come, with feelings of security and happiness in the life they'd chosen for one another. Thieving kids and all, this was the life he wanted, the life he adored, but none of it would be worth it without Brighton by his side.

Was he frightened of what would happen at Coldingham? Of course he was. For a man who knew no fear in battle, he most definitely feared one small prioress because she had the power to rob him of everything he held dear. But quickly, his fear turned to anger; he simply wasn't going to allow that to happen. If she wouldn't accept his money, he had no problem slitting her throat and burning down the priory to cover his tracks.

That was how strongly he felt for Brighton. No man, or woman, was going to deny him his wants and get away with it. He armed himself with that knowledge, that understanding, and it fortified his courage, for no matter what happened with the offer of compensation, he and Brighton would remain together as husband and wife until death did they part. The Nighthawk had found his mate for life and he wasn't going to lose her, not for anything.

Rather than going to Coldingham seeking permission, he was now going to Coldingham seeking prey.

The mother prioress' answer would determine just how much longer she would live.

CHAPTER SIXTEEN

THE NIGHT HAD seen a summer storm roll through and by morning, the sky was clear but there was a blanket of wet across the land as Patrick and William gathered in the bailey of Berwick to bid their family a farewell.

While William spoke quietly to his daughters and sons-in-law, Patrick and Brighton were off to the side on their own. Patrick held Brighton snugly, his forehead against hers, feeling angst like he'd never felt in his life. It was purely due to the separation with Brighton and had nothing to do with the objective of the coming trip. After yesterday's decision on what he would do if the prioress did not take his money, he was at peace with that. He *knew* what he had to do. Now, his anxiety had to do with leaving Brighton, if even only for a few days. He couldn't imagine that what he had to do would take any longer.

But even a few days was too long for him. He was wrought with the pain of leaving her, struggling to control it because Brighton had been verging on tears since they had awoken that morning. Lying in each other's arms, they'd spoken of little things, trivial things, but the sorrow of the mood filled the room. If she wept, Patrick wasn't at all sure he could even leave, so it was imperative to keep calm so Brighton would be calm.

But it was a struggle.

"Do you have everything you need?" Brighton asked, huddled

against him, her hands on his woolen de Wolfe tunic. "You did not leave anything behind, did you?"

Patrick grunted unhappily. "Aye, I did," he said. "*You.*"

She smiled wanly. "But I cannot go," she said. "I have thought about this, Atty. As much as I would like to go with you to tell Mother Prioress that I am agreeable to this marriage so she will not think I have been forced into it, I am afraid that if I set foot in the walls of Coldingham, they might not let me out."

He lifted an eyebrow. "If you think those puny nuns can hold you, then you are greatly mistaken," he said. "I can take on a nun or two if it comes to that."

He meant it in jest, mostly, but she turned very serious. "You must promise me that you will not move against the priory," she said. "You cannot harm them if they do not give you the answer you seek right away."

Because she was serious, he grew serious. "I will tell you now that I will do everything in my power to ensure I have their agreement," he said. "Do you think for one moment I am going to leave there without a settlement in the matter? The mother prioress will give her permission or she will be very sorry."

Brighton knew he was determined but his words still frightened her. "What does that mean?"

"What do you think it means?"

She wasn't in a mood to be teased or toyed with. She pushed out of his embrace, facing him with great concern on her features.

"Patrick, what are you going to do if Mother Prioress does not accept your money?" she asked. "I want to know."

His gaze lingered on her, debating just how much to tell her. He'd come to his decision last night, but it was his decision alone. He didn't want her to know anything about it or have any complicity in it. This was something he had to do, for his own sake. *For their sake.*

There was no remorse in his heart whatsoever.

"I will do whatever is necessary to convince her that you will never return to Coldingham, with or without her agreement on the subject," he said after a moment. "What did you think I was going to do if she refused the money, Bridey? Take you back to her? Of course not. She will never see you again. I will therefore do what is necessary in order to gain her cooperation."

He was being vague, essentially letting her know it was none of her affair how he conducted himself. Brighton sighed heavily, thinking that it was, perhaps, for the best. Perhaps, she really didn't want to know. Contrite that she had shown her temper to him, she fell back against him, wrapping her arms around his torso.

"I am sorry," she said. "I did not mean to sound impudent. 'Tis simply that I am afraid of what will happen once you speak with her. She is a stubborn woman."

Patrick wrapped his arms around her again, giving her a squeeze. "I understand," he said. "But you must trust me in this matter. Your trust and your love mean everything to me, Bridey. You must never lose either in me."

She shook her head, her eyes closed as she held him tightly. "I will not, I swear it."

He kissed the top of her head. "Good lass," he said. "Now, do you want to wish my father a farewell? He is going on your behalf, after all. It would be polite of you to thank him."

Brighton nodded eagerly as Patrick took her by the arm and escorted her over to where William was standing with his children. As soon as William saw them approaching, his attention was diverted and he smiled faintly.

"All is well, I hope," he said, looking between Patrick and Brighton. "Are we ready to depart?"

Patrick nodded. "We are," he replied, "but Bridey has something she would like to say to you."

All eyes turned to Brighton as she gazed up at William. Realizing that everyone was suddenly watching her, she was a bit hesitant but forced herself to speak.

"I-I wanted to thank you for all you have done for me, my lord," she said. "I have not had much opportunity to speak with you but I would like to say that you have my undying gratitude. Patrick holds you in great esteem and I do, as well."

William smiled at the woman with the nervous catch in her speech. "Thank you, Bridey," he said, "and if you do not call me William or Papa soon, I shall be very disappointed."

Brighton smiled, relief in her expression. "I-I would be pleased to call you either," she said. "Since I have never had a father, mayhap you will not mind if I call you Papa?"

William shook his head, putting a hand on her cheek and kissing her on the forehead. "I would be honored."

Brighton's smile broadened and she looked at Patrick to see the approval in his eyes. He was quite happy to see that Brighton and his father were coming to like one another, thrilled, in fact. But Patrick couldn't help but notice that she seemed to speak perfectly to him, yet that slight stammer returned when she spoke to anyone other than him. Not that he cared, for he loved her with a catch in her speech or not, but he felt rather special that he seemed to be the only one who heard her perfect speech.

Or did he…?

Was it imagined or not? Was it because he simply found her perfect in all ways that he didn't hear the stammer in her speech any longer? He didn't know and, frankly, he didn't care. He loved her and was proud of her, regardless.

"Papa and I must be going now," he said, tugging on his father's arm, calling him "Papa" in a teasing tone because that was what his sisters called him. "I would like to make it to the priory before the nooning meal and we have a ways to go this morning, so we must depart."

William began moving towards his silver steed as Patrick grasped Brighton's hand and pulled her along with him as he headed towards his great muzzled beast. The saddlebags were full of provisions and loaded onto the animals, as were an impressive array of weapons including broadswords. William and Patrick were prepared for any hazards or circumstances that might come their way, including marauding Scots. They were heading into Scotland, after all. It was best to be prepared.

Brighton paused next to the horse while Patrick made a final check on the saddle cinch. When he was satisfied, he looked up to see Brighton smiling at him. But it wasn't a natural smile; it was forced, as if she was only smiling because he expected it.

"God speed you on your journey, husband," she said softly. "I will pray for you every day."

Patrick cupped her face with his gloved hands and kissed her gently on the lips. It was a lingering kiss, of painful sweetness, enough to bring tears to his eyes.

"And I will see you in my dreams," he whispered. "I will return as soon as I can."

With that, he mounted his horse and prepared to move out. Everyone stood back as the war horses danced. Katheryn reached out to take Brighton's hand, pulling her away from the animals. Everything seemed set until shouts from the inner gatehouse caught their attention. The group looked over to see Anson and Colm coming towards them.

Patrick's knights had been in command of Berwick ever since his journey to Castle Questing and it seemed as if they would continue to be in command for the time being, considering he was about to head into Scotland. But he was concerned with their shouts and the fact that the men at the main gatehouse seemed to be excited about something. He could see them shuffling around from where he sat.

Something was in the air.

"What is it?" he called to Anson.

"A rider," Anson replied. "Wearing braies and a leine and riding one of those stout Scottish ponies. Clan Gordon, he says."

Patrick didn't seem particularly interested. "I see," he said. "Well, I do not have time for him. My father and I shall return in a few days.

You can tell me then whatever the man wanted."

Anson and Colm crowded around the side of the horse that was opposite Brighton, who was over on the left side. "Nay, Patrick," Anson said, his dark eyes intense as he lowered his voice. "He told me that he wants to speak of the Coldingham lass. I think you should *make* time."

That information drew Patrick's attention immediately. His brow furrowed and he slid off the horse, rounding the beast to speak to his men. "He *what*?" he hissed. "What in the h-? When did this man arrive? I heard nothing about a rider entering the gatehouse!"

"It was only a few minutes ago," Colm said. "I was at the mouth of the gatehouse and saw him coming through the town. He came right up to the gate and said he wanted to know if this was a House of de Wolfe. When I told him it was and told him to be on his way, he said that he needed to speak with de Wolfe about the Coldingham lass."

Patrick was growing more and more curious and, if truth be told, more and more concerned. But Brighton came around the front of the war horse, at a goodly distance away from the ferocious animal. The moment he saw her face, he went to her and took her by the arm.

"Go back into the keep with my sisters," he said, trying to pretend as if nothing was amiss. "I have some business to attend to before I go. It will only take a few moments."

Brighton sensed he was rushing her away but said nothing about it. "Of course," she said. "Will you come to me before you leave?"

He shook his head. "Nay," he replied. "I am leaving now, in fact. I do not want my last vision of you to be out here in the cold dawn. I want you inside where it is safe and warm."

Brighton simply nodded her head and he kissed her swiftly, motioning to his sisters, who had just turned to head into the keep. At Patrick's beckon, they came to Brighton and huddled around her as they headed for the warm innards of Berwick's keep.

Patrick watched his sisters usher his wife back into the keep before turning to see Alec and Hector upon him. Even William had dismounted his horse by this time and was now speaking with Anson, hearing the same information that Patrick had just heard. He could tell by the odd expression on William's faced that he, too, was both confused and concerned.

"A rider is here. He wants to speak to de Wolfe about the Coldingham lass," Patrick said for the benefit of Alec and Hector. "Clan Gordon, so Colm says."

Alec and Hector looked at each other in confusion. "Why in the world would a Gordon be here to discuss Coldingham?" Alec asked, baffled. "This makes no sense."

Patrick didn't respond. But he could feel a spark of fear come to life. It burned low in his chest, twisting his stomach. None of this made any sense and he didn't like it at all. Without saying a word to his father, he walked past the man and headed towards the Douglas Tower entrance of Berwick. Everyone knew where he was going. William, Alec, Hector, Anson, and Colm followed.

Something was amiss and they could all feel it.

… but *what?*

The sun was starting to rise over the east, turning the sky shades of gold and pink. The River Tweed, off to his right, was reflecting those morning colors as it flowed gently to the sea. But for all of the tranquility of the morning, Patrick could only feel intense curiosity and intense concern. Marching across the bridge that spanned the chasm, he could see several men gathered at the gatehouse, including Damien. He could see his knight's blonde head over the mass of either dark-haired or helmed heads. When Damien saw him coming, he went out to meet him.

"I put the man in the guard's room," he told Patrick in his intrinsically calm manner. It did wonders to soothe Patrick. "He will say he is from Clan Gordon but that he will only talk to William de Wolfe. I told him that this was not William's home, but belonging to a son. Now, he seems to want to leave to find your father. He didn't know he was here, Patrick."

Patrick was even more confused than before. "Did he say anything about the Coldingham lass?" he asked. "Did he give a name?"

Damien shook his head. "Nay," he replied. "But be cautious; he has an odd look about him."

"Madness?"

"Mayhap."

That gave Patrick no comfort at all. He was starting to build up the man's purpose in his mind until it was starting to scare him, so he struggled to put aside fear of his own making. Still, it was difficult – he could only assume the Coldingham lass meant Brighton. No one knew she was here. He was just about to enter the guard's room when William caught up to him and grasped him by the arm.

"Nay, lad," he said quietly, pulling Patrick away from the door. "Breathe and calm yourself. I can see every vein in your head throbbing. Let me talk to this man since he has asked for me."

Patrick took a deep breath. "Is it that obvious?" he asked, watching his father nod. "I will admit that I am rattled. Mayhap it is best if you question the man. I am not sure I would be very good at it right now."

William patted his son on the shoulder before turning and heading into the guard's room of the Douglas Tower.

It was a nice room, spacious as far as guard rooms were concerned, with a table, two big benches, and a large hearth spewing out heat and smoke into the low-ceilinged chamber. Damien and Colm had already entered the room but the others hung back, waiting for William and Patrick. William entered, followed by his enormous son, who wandered over to the edges of the room, lingering in the shadows as William went straight to the table where a rather thin, pale man with curly dark hair sat, swathed in dirty woolens.

Alec, Hector, and Anson came in last, going to stand with Patrick in the darkness as William took the lead. If something happened and Patrick snapped, they needed to be near the man to stop him.

William came to a halt a few feet away from the Scotsman, studying him intently. He seemed like any normal Scots, clad in dirty clothing and pale-skinned. But the Scots were cunning as a whole. William knew that because he'd spent a good deal of his life battling against them. They were very smart and very deadly. With that in mind, he spoke.

"I hear that you seek a word with me," William said quietly, seriously.

The seated man eyed him without fear. Considering he was surrounded by English, it was an impressive show of bravery.

"Are ye William de Wolfe?" he finally asked.

William nodded. "I am. Tell me your name."

The Scotsman scratched his dirty head before replying. "I am Gordon."

"That is not your name."

The man nodded, giving William a rather quirky smirk. "'Tis true," he said. "I am called Tommy Orry."

"Why do you seek me, Tommy?"

Tommy puffed out his cheeks as if wondering where to start. Or, perhaps, he was wondering if coming here had been a wise decision in the first place. In any case, he shifted around nervously before replying.

"I've heard ye have the lass from Coldingham," he said. "The lass that the Swinton took. Do ye have her?"

William didn't reply right away. He could literally feel Patrick's apprehension as the man lingered over in the shadows, just out of his line of sight. But William kept his manner calm.

"If I do?"

Tommy leaned forward on his chair. "Then I have some information ye might want."

"Why would you think so?"

"Because Ysabella said ye sent a missive tae Coldingham about the lass. She said ye were friendly towards the lass."

William was trying to piece together what the man was saying without showing how confused he was. "Who is Ysabella?"

"Mother Prioress."

Now, William was growing about as apprehensive as Patrick undoubtedly was. "I am not sure what you are trying to tell me, but you had better come out with it," William said. "Make sense, man. Why have you come and what does this have to do with the lass from Coldingham?"

As if on cue, Damien slammed a cup down next to Tommy, half-full of old ale. It splashed onto the table. But it was wet, and Tommy was thirsty, so he took the cup and drank the entire thing. Damien had given it to the man to perhaps loosen his tongue and it worked. Tommy smacked his lips and began talking.

"Richard Gordon of Clan Gordon is Ysabella's brother," he said. "He took over as Clan chief when their father passed. But he also took over their need for vengeance agin' Clan Haye because, years ago, when Ysabella was a young lass, a son of Haye forced himself upon her and beget her with child. The child wasna born alive and Ysabella's father bought her way intae Coldingham since she wasna a marriage prospect any longer. There has been a sense of vengeance agin' the Haye ever since that time. When Juliana Haye brought her infant tae Coldingham, a bastard child of a Norse king, Ysabella took the baby in. But… she had a plan for the lass."

William could hardly believe what he was hearing; it was a great shock. But as great a surprise as it was to him, it was even greater for Patrick. He came out of the shadows at that point, his face pale with astonishment.

"A Norse king?" Patrick repeated. "The Mother Prioress told you that?"

Tommy nodded. "I heard her say so. The lass is his bastard."

Patrick looked at his father. All of the astonishment he was feeling was reflected in his eyes. *So it was true!* Now, the pieces of the puzzle were falling together a bit more; pieces that all seemed to fit together in odd and mysterious ways. But he didn't say anything more and Tommy, nervous of his presence, began to speak faster.

"I've come tae tell ye not tae send the lass home," he said, eyeing Patrick but mostly focused on William. "I know Ysabella told ye tae send the lass back tae Coldingham, but if ye do, they'll kill her. Richard

Gordon intends tae kill her in revenge for the wrongs committed agin' his sister by Clan Haye. He paid the Swinton tae take her from Coldingham tae make it look like *reivers* had taken the lass, but the truth is that he wanted her."

His rapid-fire delivery and sudden end left the room lingering in shocked silence. William looked at his son, who was looking at Tommy in mute revulsion. William finally reached out to touch the man on the arm.

"Atty…," he murmured. "Are you well?"

Patrick nodded, stiffly, his focus still on Tommy. "Why did you come here to tell us that?" he asked the man. William could hear a quiver in his voice. "Brighton means nothing to you and you certainly have no allegiance to the English, so why tell us? I do not understand why you are here?"

Tommy gazed steadily at the hulking *Sassenach*. "Because what Richie wants tae do tae the lass isna right," he said quietly. "Do ye know what he intended tae do? He wanted tae nail her tae a cross and post her on Haye lands. He wants tae crucify her. If ye return her tae Coldingham, that's exactly what he'll do. And it isna right tae kill an innocent lass like that. I came here tae tell de Wolfe tae keep her or send her somewhere else. Just dunna send her back tae Coldingham."

Crucify. Patrick looked at his father with such horror in his eyes that William was visibly moved by it. He reached out to touch his son, reassuringly, trying to give the man some comfort. But Patrick simply walked away from him, pacing the room as if in danger of losing his mind or his temper. No one was sure which. Patrick ended up pacing around with a hand over his mouth, struggling to come to terms with what he'd just heard. It was revulsion like nothing else they'd ever witnessed.

Crucify Brighton.

"You were brave to come here," William finally said to Tommy, although he was glancing at his son with worry. "I will make sure you are rewarded. That is why you really came, wasn't it?"

Tommy shrugged, wondering why the *Sassenach* around him seemed so disturbed by the news. As if there was something personal about it. "If ye have a mind tae," he said. "I just didna want the lass' death tae be on me conscience. I canna face God with that shadow on me heart."

"Are you telling me that Mother Prioress is in on this… this *travesty?*" Patrick finally spoke from across the room as he continued to process the information. "She is the one who arranged for Bridey to be abducted by the Swinton and make it look as if *reivers* had taken her?"

Tommy wasn't certain who Bridey was but he assumed the big knight meant Brighton. "Her brother did it," he said. "But she helped him arrange it. They'd been plannin' it for years, in truth, but they waited until the lass came of age. Killin' a small lass means little, but killin' a grown woman… it would mean somethin' to the Haye."

Patrick looked to William as if the man could help him process this terrible information. William felt a great deal of pity for his mighty son, a man who was usually so very in control of his emotions. But not when it came to his new wife, a woman he clearly adored. And the news coming from the Scotsman was enough to rattle all of them, men that weren't even in love with Brighton. They didn't have to be in love with her to see what a horrible plan had been centered around her. It was appalling in so many ways. William finally looked at Damien.

"See that Tommy is fed and given a bed," he said. "I'll reward the man before sending him home."

Damien nodded, pouring Tommy more ale now that the first round of questioning was over. William went straight to Patrick, taking the man by the arm and pulling him from the guard's room, out into the fresh morning air.

"Breathe, Atty," William said softly. "Just… breathe and be thankful this man came to us before we headed to Coldingham. God has been merciful."

Patrick simply nodded, laboring with every fiber of his being to do as his father instructed… *breathe. Just breathe.* He was trying, so very hard, to remain calm in the face of what he'd heard.

"My God," he finally muttered. "The brutality of it… the sheer brutality of it. How could they even think to crucify an innocent woman?"

William remained strong, if only for his son's sake. He could sense that Patrick was a hair's breadth away from snapping. "I do not know," he said. "I have never heard of such things and I have been fighting the Scots on the borders for nearly forty years. I have never in my life heard of anything like this."

"But… *crucifying* her? Nailing her to wood and posting her for all to see?"

William was trying not to imagine the mental image Patrick was painting. "As I said, I have never heard such things. The clan chiefs I know would never stoop to such brutality, not even in vengeance."

Patrick came to an abrupt halt, bent in half, and vomited the breakfast he had eaten with Brighton onto the dirt of the bailey. His emotions were twisting his guts to pieces. When he finally stood up, wiping the back of his pale lips with his hand, the pale green eyes flashed with fire.

"I am going to the Gordon stronghold and raze it," he hissed. "I will find Richard Gordon and I will draw and quarter him. Then I shall post *his* body for all to see."

William knew he meant every word, as passionately as he'd ever meant anything in his life. The man had every right to be furious, but William couldn't let him follow through on his threat, for many reasons. Calmer heads had to prevail.

"Unless you want to start a border war the likes of which we have never seen, I would suggest you think again about how to punish Richard Gordon," he said evenly, reaching out to grasp his son's arm with an impassioned plea. "Atty, I understand what is in your heart. There were times in the past when your mother had been in great danger, so I understand your pain very well. In fact, she had been kidnapped by rival clans when she was pregnant with you. It is a miracle you survived, but you did, and I refuse to believe it was because you would ultimately start a border war that would kill us all. Nay, lad – taking your army into Scotland to destroy Richard Gordon is not the answer."

Patrick's revulsion was being replaced by anger the likes of which he'd never known. Like a shooting star, the anger rose and flared within him faster than he could control it. He yanked his arm from his father's grasp.

"As long as Richard Gordon lives, Bridey will be in danger," he snarled. "If there was such a threat against Mother, would you so easily sit back and advise temperance? I do not think so. You would want to eliminate the threat just as I do. I will not stand for anyone who threatens the life of my wife."

William was coming to think that he may have a serious problem on his hands; he'd never seen Patrick so livid, which was not a good thing in a man as big, powerful, and capable as his son. Therefore, he labored to keep on an even keel if he had any hopes of defusing the situation.

"If someone was threatening the life of your mother, I would not stand for it," William said firmly. "But I also would not run off and possibly get myself killed in my quest to protect her. You are far more valuable to your wife alive than dead, Atty. You must keep a level head and we will calmly, and smartly, deal with this matter."

Patrick's chest was heaving with emotion as he faced off against his father. "If a man like Richard Gordon wants to crucify an innocent woman, I doubt the man thinks calmly or smartly," he snapped. "A man like that knows only brutality. If that is what he knows, then that is what he shall receive."

From the corner of his eye, William could see some of Patrick's men filtering in from the guard room and he was glad; it would take all of them to control Patrick should the man decide to physically demonstrate his fury. All he had to do was keep Patrick calm until his men drew closer and then they would be better able to stop Patrick from doing something foolish.

"Not now," William begged softly. "Listen to me, lad. We must think this through before you do anything. For the sake of the entire family, you must think this through."

"This has nothing to do with the family and everything to do with protecting my wife!"

By this time, Patrick's men had reached them and they heard the last few words spoken by Patrick. Because he was enraged, they were becoming rather enraged themselves. The entire situation had them on edge. Alec was the first one to speak.

"I am with you, Atty," he said. "What would you have me do?"

William threw up his hands. "You are not going to do anything," he said, loudly, emphasizing the fact that his word was law above all. "I am your liege and you will obey my command. We are not charging blindly into Gordon lands like animals. We will return to the hall, sit down, and discuss what needs to be done rationally as men do. Is that clear?"

The knights were looking at Patrick but nodded to William's question; a command from William de Wolfe was not meant to be disobeyed and they knew it.

"That is an excellent idea, my lord," Anson said, one of the calmer knights of the group. He began to push Colm towards the hall and reached out to tug on Hector. "Come along. We will solve nothing standing out here."

Hector wasn't so apt to be pushed around but he moved nonetheless, leaving Alec standing next to Patrick, staring at the man as if waiting for the command to go charging off into Scotland.

"Atty?" Alec asked. "I will do what you want me to do. What is your wish?"

William reached out and shoved Alec in the direction of the hall. "You will do what *I* want you to do," he said in a tone that left no room for doubt. "Get into the hall. I will not tell you again."

With a lingering glance at William, enough to show that he didn't like being pushed around but not enough to show disobedience, Alec began to follow the others. Patrick, however, was still looking at the ground, grinding his teeth.

"Where is Damien?" he asked hoarsely.

William looked around but didn't see the knight, the man who had been Patrick's best friend for many years. "He is probably still with the Scotsman," he said. "That is where I would be. I would guess he is trying to see if he can discover any more information before sending the man away."

"Do you intend to reward the Scot for the information?"

"I do."

Patrick merely nodded. William took him by the arm again, gently pulling him towards the hall as he began to walk. But Patrick wouldn't move.

"Da?"

"Aye?"

Patrick lifted his head and looked at his father. "I cannot go to London," he said quietly. "Not… not with everything that has happened. I cannot leave."

William was rather surprised with not only the change of subject, but the statement itself. "Why not?" he asked. "You can go to London and take Bridey with you. You can take her far away from the Gordons and the threat against her. In fact, I should think that would be the best place for her."

Patrick shook his head, now looking skyward as if to beseech God for wisdom and clarity in the matter. "I have looked forward to the royal appointment with Henry more than I have ever looked forward to anything in my entire life," he said, his tone strained with emotion. "But you know what it will be like if I take Bridey with me. I will never see the woman because my entire attention shall be with Henry. My time will belong to him. When he travels, I travel. If he decides he needs me by his side, then that is where I must be for as long as he wants me. Worse still, I am to be in command of his personal guard. That means his life is my life. I will never see my wife, ever. How could I take her to London and ask her to live alone for the rest of her life? Because that is what will happen. You know this to be true."

William did. He could see where Patrick was leading and he sighed heavily, feeling the weight of the man's decision and the intensity of his disappointment. Truth be told, he felt some disappointment of his own. Patrick was meant for such great things; he had always believed that. But, perhaps, they weren't the great things William has hoped for. Perhaps Patrick had to make his own great things happen, away from the crown. Perhaps the royal appointment was something that simply wasn't meant to be.

He struggled not to let Patrick see his disenchantment.

"Is that what you will decide, then?" he asked his son. "That you will decline Henry's appointment?"

Patrick looked at his father. "I must."

"Do you base this on your own wants or because you think it is best for your wife?"

Patrick faltered. "It is best for us both," he said. "Da, I know you do not agree with the fact that I married Bridey after knowing her so short a time. Now this marriage has put a stop to your great dream for me, the dream of a royal appointment. It was *my* dream, too, until I met my wife. Now, I find that my dreams have changed. *She* has become my dream. When I look at her, I see the joy of a life I never knew I would have. I see our future, our unborn sons, and a legacy as you have had. I see the continuation of de Wolfe greatness. I see all of these things but, more than that, I see my life and it belonging to me, not to Henry. If I go to London, my life will end and the king's life will take over. Does that make sense? Now that I have had a taste of my own life, I want it. I will not give it up. I have already made a name for myself. But in becoming Henry's Lord Protector… Nighthawk will cease to exist."

William listened to the impassioned speech with a good deal of pride and understanding. The disenchantment he'd been feeling was gone and a faint smile crossed his lips.

"So it has happened," he murmured.

Patrick had no idea what he meant. "What has happened?"

"My son has finally become a man."

Patrick looked at him for a moment before breaking out into an awkward grin. "And I was not before?"

William chuckled. "You were a warrior," he said. "You lived and breathed your profession, and I was proud. Very proud. But I have never been so proud of you as I am at this moment when you admit to me that living your life with the woman you love is better than living life in Henry's shadow. Aye, you've become a man. And there is nothing more powerful on the face of this earth."

"Then you understand what I am saying."

"I understand all too well. Long ago, I turned down a similar appointment to be with your mother."

Patrick sighed, perhaps with some relief. "Then I will write to Henry and explain the situation," he said. "He will not be happy about it, but...."

William cut him off. "Nay, you will not write him."

Patrick cocked his head. "What do you mean?"

William was shaking his head. "I mean that this is something you must tell Henry face to face," he said. "Do not hide behind a message. That is cowardly. You will personally decline his appointment and thank him profusely for his generosity. As my son, Henry will expect no less. Show the man the same respect he has shown you by offering such an appointment – be gracious in declining it."

Patrick understood what his father was saying but the thought of going to London, at least at this time, did not please him. "It will take me at least two weeks to reach London," he said, trying not to sound despondent. "I will be gone a long time. I do not wish to leave Bridey for that long and I also do not want to take her. It would be a difficult journey and I want to travel fast and light."

William agreed. "That is no journey for a woman," he said. "This must be your journey alone. Go quickly and return quickly. Bridey will be safe here, at Berwick. She will be well protected. Or, better still, send her to Questing to be with your mother."

Patrick thought on that. "Katheryn and Evie are here. They have become fast friends with Bridey. And this is her home now… she may not wish to leave it."

William put a hand on the man's shoulder. "Then leave it to her where she would like to stay for the duration of your absence," he said. "Meanwhile, there are men waiting in the hall for us. They are very worried about you, you know. Alec was ready to ride into Scotland this instant to avenge both you and Bridey. I fear we may have to calm the man."

"Alec is a good friend."

"He is a hotheaded banshee just like his mother."

Patrick smiled weakly; he couldn't disagree. He began to walk with his father towards the great hall, beneath a morning sun that was already increasing the temperature. He could also feel the humidity from the river rise. In all, however, it promised to be a beautiful day. Patrick glanced up at the sky, thinking that it had never looked so blue to him.

A new sky, a new wife, a new future.

And a man to kill.

But he didn't tell his father that, for no matter what William said, Patrick was going to make sure Richard Gordon did not live to a ripe old age. Perhaps not next week, next month, or even next year, but Patrick had no intention of overlooking the man's crime against Brighton.

The Nighthawk was coming for him.

CHAPTER SEVENTEEN

PATRICK HEARD THE soft knock on the chamber door. Lying down next to his wife, whom he believed was sleeping, he very carefully rose from the big bed, trying to navigate the new curtains that Bridey had hung, and made his way to the door. Carefully, he opened it to find his sisters standing outside, their features wrought with concern.

"Papa told us what happened," Katheryn whispered loudly. "How is Bridey?"

Patrick turned to look at his wife's sleeping form on the bed. "As well as can be expected, I suppose," he said quietly. "She is sleeping now."

Katheryn and Evelyn were very sad, indeed. "How did she react to it all, Atty?" Evelyn asked. "She must be positively terrified."

Patrick stepped out into the corridor, pulling the door shut behind him. "She was naturally very upset to learn that a woman she trusted had betrayed her," he said. "She was even more upset to learn of the plans Clan Gordon had for her. She cried herself to sleep, in fact."

Evelyn clucked her tongue sadly. "Poor Bridey," she said. "Who has ever heard of anyone wanting to crucify someone? The very idea is appalling!"

Patrick nodded, feeling limited patience. He knew his sisters were concerned for Brighton, and he was very appreciative, but he didn't want to answer a bunch of their questions. He wanted to return to the room with his wife in case she needed him.

"It is," he agreed. "She is quite upset about it. So when you see her next, please do not bring it up. I am not sure if it is something she wishes to discuss, but you will let her determine if it is or not. Agreed?"

Both Evelyn and Katheryn nodded solemnly. "I had Papa take the children over to the kitchen yard so there would not be so much noise," Katheryn said. "Is there anything we can bring Bridey? Wine? Mayhap a hot bath would make her feel better."

Patrick shook his head. "Not now," he said quietly. "Return in an hour or so and mayhap I will change my mind. For now, just let her sleep."

Evelyn and Katheryn nodded, turning for the stairs that led to the floors below. But Katheryn came to a halt and turned to her brother, once more.

"Papa told us that you are going to London to decline your royal appointment," she said, studying him seriously. "This is something you wanted so very much, Atty. I feel badly that you feel the need to decline it."

Patrick smiled weakly. "Do not feel badly for me," he said. "There will be other royal favors given. I want to remain here, with my wife, and I am very happy about that. This is a good thing, Katie, I promise."

Katheryn returned his smile. "Truthfully, I am happy about it, too," she said. "I was wondering if you were going to drag Bridey to London. I am thankful that you are not."

"So am I."

"But what about the titles Henry was going to bestow upon you? And the castle? Will you still receive them?"

Patrick shook his head. "More than likely not. But I have something better, instead."

He meant Brighton. He winked at his sister, turning for the chamber door and quietly opening it. With great stealth, he entered the room, making his way over to the bed as the faint noise from the bailey filtered into the chamber. It was very quiet outside so he was coming to think that maybe everyone had gone to the kitchen yard so that Lady de Wolfe could rest. He was just lowering himself onto the bed, very carefully, when Brighton suddenly rolled over and looked up at him.

"You do not have to be so quiet," she said softly. "I am not asleep."

He smiled at her and lowered himself down completely, propping his head upon his hand, elbow bent, as he gazed down into her lovely face.

"You can sleep all you want, you know," he said. "I will stay right by your side. I will never leave you, Bridey. Not ever."

She reached up, a gentle hand touching his cheek. "You will leave me when you depart for London," she said. "Patrick, I have been thinking. You do not have to refuse your royal appointment. It was nearly the first thing you ever told me about and I know how badly you want it. I will come to London with you. If we must spend time apart while you tend the king, then so be it. I am not troubled by it."

His expression turned serious. "But *I* am troubled by it," he said. "You do not seem to understand how much time I would have to spend away from you. Eventually, it would take its toll on you and on me. Nay, it is much better for us to remain here at Berwick where we will see each other with great frequency. I could not stand to be parted from you, Bridey. Not for an hour, a day, or a week. All the time I was with Henry, I would be thinking of you and would, therefore, be ineffective as his Lord Protector. It simply would not work."

Brighton considered his words. "But I do not want you to resent me someday. You wanted this appointment so badly… I could not stand it if you grew to hate me because you felt I had kept you from your destiny."

He sighed faintly, reaching up a hand to stroke her soft hair. "*You* are my destiny," he said. "When God led me to your captors those weeks ago, He put my destiny right in front of me. I can see that now."

Brighton was still unsure. She knew how much the royal appointment meant to him and that, coupled with the news from the Scots messenger, had her reeling. A crying jag followed by an hour or two of exhausted sleep had brought her to this point in her life. She still felt vastly uneasy and fearful, even more fearful now that Patrick was going to leave her to journey to London to inform the king that he would not accept his royal appointment. She didn't want him to leave her side but she understood his reasons.

She had to be brave.

"So you will leave me to go to London," she said, her hand still on his cheek. "How long will you be gone? London is very far away."

He kissed her hand when it came near his mouth. "Not so very far," he said. "It is summer and the weather is good. I can make thirty-five miles a day, which means that it will take me ten days, twelve at the most. I will seek Henry immediately. He will see me considering he believes I am there to assume my post. But I will tell him that I cannot accept and head for home as soon as I can."

Her expression was anxious. "But what if he makes you stay?"

"He will not make me stay if I do not want to. Lord Protector is an honored position, not a prison sentence. He will understand why I cannot accept it. The man is married to a woman he adores, by all reports, so he must understand my position."

Brighton accepted that. She very much wanted to have faith that everything would turn out just as he said it would. "And when you return, then what?" she asked. "You have spoken of your anger at Richard Gordon. Will you punish him?"

Patrick's hand moved from her hair to her nose, pinching it gently. "That is for me to decide," he said, not wanting to frighten her with just how badly he wanted to punish the man. "And that is not something I wish to discuss right now. You know what has happened and you know why your mother prioress betrayed you. I will thank God every night until the day I die that I did not return you to Coldingham when I had the chance. Fortunately, I listened to my instincts. I knew that you were not to return to the priory but I did not know that it was for a far worse reason than I could have ever suspected. Suffice it to say, that you are to remain here as my wife. I will go to London and return as quickly as I can. Then Richard Gordon will know his fate. His scheme against you will not go unpunished."

Brighton knew this was his general plan because, prior to her being informed about anything, she had heard her husband and his men in the great hall in an intense and loud conversation. It was such a lively discussion that it drew the woman simply from the volume of it. She had heard something said about a bastard paying for his sins, but she'd had no idea why until Patrick had taken her up to their chamber to inform her of a Scots visitor who had spoken of the corruption of Coldingham.

Then, and only then, did Brighton come to realize just how horrible the situation had been and how much her life had been in jeopardy. Just the thought of it made her grow frightened again and she threw her arms around his neck, holding him fast.

"Then it was truly God who sent you to save me that night," she said, her face pressed into his neck. "Had you not come when you had, I would be a victim to a terrible plot. People I do not even know want to seek vengeance upon me for something I had nothing to do with. Even as you thank God for your reluctance to return me to Coldingham, I will thank Him for sending you as my savior."

Patrick hugged her tightly, feeling her warmth and life against him, so incredibly grateful. She was healthy and safe, and that was all he cared about. Still, he hated to leave her. It was not something he was looking forward to.

"Then all is well, is it not?" he murmured, kissing the side of her head. "Everything is well, Bridey. You need not worry any longer. Now, we must speak of my journey to London. I have been speaking with my father and he wants to know if you would like to spend your time at Castle Questing while I am away."

Brighton pulled her face from his neck, looking at him thoughtfully. "Why?"

"He thought you might feel better with my mother and Penelope for companionship."

She smiled. "That is a kind offer, but I will stay here," she said. "This is my home, after all. *Our* home. I have Katheryn and Evie for companionship and I will tend your fortress while you are away. Truly, there is no place I would rather be."

He smiled, pleased at her words. They touched him deeply. "It is our home, isn't it?" he said. "But we could live in a cave on the coast and I would still call it home if you were there. Wherever you are, that is my home."

Brighton kissed him sweetly and hugged him tightly, feeling the pangs of separation already. Sweet Mary, she was going to miss him. Her heart hurt in ways she'd never known it could.

"When will you leave?" she asked.

"The sooner I leave, the sooner I return."

"Tomorrow?"

"I was thinking on it. I was due to leave in a few days, anyway."

She groaned softly. "As much as I hate to hear it, I know it is for the best."

"I believe it is."

Releasing him from her arms, Brighton crawled from the bed and stood up, going to a dressing table that she'd had the servants drag down from the storage room on the top floor. It was very old, having been some fine lady's table years ago, perhaps another wife of a commander of Berwick. It was heavy, made of oak, and had faded painted flowers on it. Katheryn had covered it with a white damask cloth, one with lace on the edges, and now the cloth was covered with all of the dressing items that Patrick had purchased for Brighton on their trip to Wooler.

There were combs, ribbons, oils, pins, and even a tiny dagger with a yellow jewel in the hilt. It was a lady's dagger, very pretty, and Brighton picked it up. Patrick caught the glint of the steel in her hand but before he could say a word, she took the dagger and sliced it through several strands of her hair, cutting it off. Patrick then sat up to watch what she was doing, curiously, and he could see her fussing with it on the dressing table.

"What are you doing?" he finally asked.

Brighton didn't reply right away. When she eventually turned around, she was holding up the locks of hair all tied up with a small piece of blue ribbon. She went over to the bed, extending it to him.

"Even if I cannot go with you, you can take something of me," she said, almost shyly. "I have heard that women sometimes do this so their lovers may have a keepsake of their hair. Will you take it with you?"

Patrick looked at the six-inch section of hair, reaching out to take it from her as if she were delivering pure gold into his hands. He held it up to his nostrils, smelling her in the silken strands. It was enough to melt his heart; a gesture that touched him more than words could express.

"I am deeply honored, my lady," he murmured, kissing the hair. "I could ask for no finer keepsake."

Brighton smiled, happy that he should be so touched. "Mayhap you will think of me when you touch it, just a little."

He reached out, pulling her against him, and planted a fairly delicious kiss on her lips. "I do not need a lock of your hair to think of you," he told her. "I will think of you endlessly while I am away, dreaming of the day I shall return to your arms."

Brighton quickly succumbed to his kiss, ending up on the bed beside him. He kissed her forehead, each eye, her nose, and finally her lips again. He was about to deliver a far more lusty kiss when there was a knock on the chamber door.

Making a face at Brighton to suggest he was quite perturbed with the interruption, he pushed himself off the bed, listening to her giggles, as he made his way to the door. He yanked it open.

"This had better be good!"

He ended up yelling those words into his father's face. William's head actually snapped back a bit at the force of the shout. Sitting on the bed, Brighton burst into laughter, covering her mouth with her hands as Patrick appeared sheepish.

"Sorry, Da," he said. "I thought it might be… oh, hell, it does not matter. How may I be of service?"

William cocked an eyebrow. "I am not quite over you yelling at me."

Patrick fought off a grin. "Do try," he said. "How can I help you?"

William could hear Brighton giggling and he peered into the room, smirking when he made eye contact with her. He refocused on his son, crooking a finger and pulling the man out into the hall. Patrick dutifully followed, shutting the door behind him.

"Are you going to beat me now?" he asked warily.

William turned to him. "I am not, although I should."

Patrick grinned, his mood good. It was always good when he spent time with Brighton. "Then I thank you for your mercy," he said, no longer wary of why his father called him into the corridor. "How can I help you?"

William looked at his son, seeing such joy in the man's face. The Patrick he'd known since birth had been a serious and somewhat intense individual, a man who was solely dedicated to the knighthood. But this Patrick was different… joyful, humorous, as if he found utter delight in life itself. William couldn't have been more thrilled to see the change; it did his heart good to finally see his shining star happy.

"Tommy Orry wants to leave," he said. "He seems to think that the longer he remains here, the more chance there is of it being discovered that he came. I have already given the man a few silver coins but I did not know if you intended to reward him as well."

Patrick shook his head. "If you have already paid him, then I do not see the need for me to pay him as well," he said, "but I will see him before he leaves. Where is he?"

"At the gatehouse."

"Then I will go and see him. I owe the man a debt of gratitude."

William waited while Patrick stuck his head back into his chamber to tell Brighton that he would return soon. He then followed his father down to the entry level and out into the bailey beyond, which was not particularly busy at this time of day. It was a very warm day and the flies were out in force, buzzing over people and animals, as William and Patrick made their way to the Douglas Tower.

On the way there, they caught sight of Alec upon the battlements, and Hector and Colm near the armory. Patrick didn't see Anson or Damien but he knew the men were busy, somewhere, seeing to their tasks. He took a moment to drink it all in, this empire he commanded, appreciating it as he'd never appreciated it before. There was such a wonderful, vast world here that he couldn't imagine being Henry's Lord Protector would be any greater or make him any happier. Nay, he quite enjoyed his life here at Berwick and his reputation as Nighthawk. The addition of Brighton only made him realize how very special it all was to him and how grateful he was.

Aye, it was a fine and good day.

The cool innards of the guard's room beckoned and he entered after his father. His eyes adjusted to the dim light. He saw Damien in the chamber near Tommy Orry, who was standing near the hearth with a bundle in his hand. When Damien saw William and Patrick enter, he went to the pair.

"The Scot is ready to depart," he said. "I have provided him with enough provisions to get him back to his home and his horse has been readied."

Patrick's gaze lingered on Tommy. The man was still a dozen feet or so away from him. "Did he tell you anything more?" he asked Damien, his voice low.

Damien shook his head, turning away from Tommy as he spoke. "He told you everything," he said. "I am fairly certain of that. But he did stress how volatile Richard Gordon is. He fears that man a great deal even though he seems to call him a friend."

"Oh?"

"And there is something else – he told me that he and the mother prioress were fond of each other as children. They were not betrothed, but they were evidently lovers when they were young. That was before she was raped by someone from Clan Haye. That ended everything."

That information confirmed to Patrick why the mother prioress would be so willing to see harm come to a bastard of the Haye Clan. But it didn't explain why Tommy, who was supposedly in love with the mother prioress as a child, had betrayed her. But he supposed it didn't really matter in the end. Putting a hand on Damien to silently thank him for the information, he took a few steps in Tommy Orry's direction.

Tommy, who had been watching the English knights warily as they whispered to each other, straightened when the big knight came close.

"I've given ye all of the information I can," he said to Patrick. "I must be a-leavin' lest it be discovered that I came here. That wouldna bode well for me."

Patrick could see that the man seemed nervous about it. "How would they even know?"

Tommy shrugged his thin shoulders. "Ye dunna know Richie," he said. "He has gangs of men who do nothin' but track others and spy upon them. I canna say for sure that I was followed, but 'tis possible. So I must leave."

Patrick didn't want to cause the man trouble since he had provided a very valuable piece of information for them, so he simply nodded his head.

"Then go," he said. "Your horse is prepared. Know that we are grateful for your information."

Tommy simply nodded, heading quickly from the guard's chamber and out to his pony. The horse was waiting for him outside.

Without a hind glance at the Sassenachs, Tommy fled the gatehouse. He lost himself in the streets of Berwick, heading for the town gate that would purge him from the city and into the great north beyond.

Home.

It was a very fine day for travel as far as Tommy was concerned. He was barely an hour out of Berwick but he'd made excellent time on his sturdy pony under clear skies and light winds. The land was warm and green, with brooks bubbling deep in their carved-out trenches. His pony had chased a few rabbits out of their dens and birds soared overhead, happy in the sunshine.

In all, it was a lovely day and he was feeling content with himself. Days of battling with his conscience before he decided to ride to Berwick because it was a known de Wolfe property had ended well enough. He'd cleared his conscience and gained a few coins in the process. Although his loyalty should have been to Richard, he simply couldn't support the man's idea of crucifying an innocent woman.

Somehow, that kind of brutality pulled them all down into the mud of inhumaneness, and Tommy wasn't that kind of a man. He had a soul and a heart, and he had compassion. Probably too much at times.

But he feared Richard; most of the men in the clan did. Richard's father had been only slightly more benevolent but from somewhere in the family lines, Richard inherited an evil streak. Ysabella was simply a pawn in his game.

In a sense, Tommy felt as if he'd scored a victory against Richard by telling the Sassenach of Richard's plan for the Coldingham lass. Although he never asked where the lass was, something told him she had been at Berwick from the way the knights were reacting to his information. Something told him that there was more to the lass' presence there than met the eye.

Something personal.

His thoughts were lingering on the mysterious lass that seemed to be so important to not only Richard and Ysabella, but also to the English, too. A postulate that would now need to find a new priory where she could serve. But those were Tommy's last peaceful thoughts as the foliage in front of him suddenly came alive with red grouse, all of them bursting out of the bushes and flying up to the sky. His pony startled a bit, as did Tommy, so he pulled the horse to a stop and watched the grouse fly off, wishing he had something to kill them with. They would have made a fine supper. But what came shooting out of the foliage next was not so fine.

Men were running out at him and someone knocked him on the back of the head. When Tommy came to, he was lying on his back staring up at Gordon men, men he recognized. But the face he recognized the most was that of Richard Gordon.

Dear God, it canna be!

His heart sank.

"Richie?" he said in disbelief. A hand went to the knot on the top of his head. "What's happened?"

Richard, swathed in filthy woolens that were dark in color, the type of woolens they wore when he was hunting or had a need for stealth, glared down at Tommy.

"I woulda never believed it had I not seen it with me own eyes," Richard said with disgust. "Not me Tommy, I would say. He wouldna betray me."

Tommy's heart began to pound against his ribs. He didn't try to sit up, fearful that Richard might take that as a challenge.

"And I wouldna," Tommy said, trying to sound firm and not frightened. "Why would ye say such things?"

Richard crouched down beside him. He wasn't wearing braies, simply his woolens, and his dirty, hairy balls were visible as he crouched. Tommy didn't like having the man so close to him, hairy balls and all.

"I will ask ye this and ye willna lie tae me," Richard said. "Why did ye go tae Berwick?"

Terror was swelling in Tommy's chest. "Who told ye I did?"

Richard's eyes narrowed. "I saw ye!" he snapped. "I was told ye left our village yesterday and ye said nothin' to me about leavin', so we followed ye. I couldna imagine where ye might go but we saw ye go intae Berwick. What business did ye have there?"

Tommy wasn't sure if they actually saw him go into Berwick Castle or simply into the city. The situation might yet be salvageable and he grasped at the hope that all was not lost. But there was a small problem; he never actually thought what to tell Richard or his men if they asked for an explanation. He struggled not to panic as he thought up a reasonable excuse, saying the first thing that came to mind.

"Can a man not go tae town for women he canna find in his own village?" he demanded, trying to make it sound as if he were doing something completely normal. "I went tae seek the comfort of a woman, if ye must know. Dunna tell me mother for she'll accuse me of lyin' in filth."

Richard was unmoved by his speech. In fact, he seemed to grow even more intense. "Men saw ye goin' tae the castle, Tommy," he said. "Were there whores in the castle a-waitin' for ye?"

So now Tommy knew what, exactly, they'd seen and he'd just perjured himself by stating he'd only gone whoring. Before he could open his mouth, a pair of Richard's men flipped him onto his belly, right on the rocky road, and bent his arms up behind his back. Tommy began to scream.

"Oooch!" he cried as someone pushed his face into the dirt. "Richie! Why, Richie, *why*?"

Richard stood over Tommy as his men bent his arms back, causing the man to scream in pain. But there was no remorse in Richard's heart, not in the least.

"Why did ye go tae the castle, Tommy?" he asked calmly.

Tommy didn't answer. He didn't answer while Richard's men bent his left arm back so far that they dislocated the elbow. As Tommy's screams of agony could be heard, the men then flipped him onto his back and extended the dislocated arm as far as it would go. Someone put a foot on Tommy's wrist, stomping down on it and breaking it when Tommy wouldn't clearly answer any of Richard's questions.

As Tommy writhed in agony, still more men frisked him, finding the silver coins that William had paid him. They turned the coins over to Richard, who looked at them in the palm of his hand as if they were the most telltale things he'd seen yet. Now, he was starting to grow angry.

"What did ye do for the Sassenachs that they would pay ye silver?" Richard asked, his temper starting to flare. "Paid ye silver like the Judas ye are, did they? What did ye tell them?"

Tommy lay on the road in utter anguish, knowing that if he didn't tell them the truth, worse things were yet to come. His left arm was broken and useless, but his right arm was still functional; he knew that wouldn't last if he didn't tell them what they wanted to know. But he also knew that telling Richard why he had gone to Berwick would sign his death warrant.

"Please, Richie," he breathed, spittle dripping from his lips. "I… I was lookin' for the Coldingham lass for ye. I thought I could find her for ye bein' that she is with de Wolfe."

That statement brought some interest to Richard. "Is she at Berwick?"

Tommy clutched his left arm against his chest. "I dinna see her," he said. "But I asked for the lass and they all acted… strangely. As if they had some bond with her. Berwick is close tae Swinton lands so I thought it would be the men from Berwick who would have taken the lass. 'Tis the Nighthawk's lair, ye know. He lives at Berwick."

"Did ye see him, then?"

"I… I think so."

"But he dinna tell ye if she was at Berwick?"

"There is no other place she *could* be. If the Nighthawk took the lass from the Swinton, then he would take her back tae Berwick. More than that, William de Wolfe, himself, was there – isna he the man who wrote tae Ysabella and asked about the lass?"

A light went on in Richard's eyes. "He was," he agreed. "Then the lass *must* be at Berwick since William de Wolfe is there! What did ye say tae them, Tommy? What did they tell ye?"

Tommy was in so much pain that he could hardly speak. "I told them that I… I had come on behalf of Coldingham and that they wanted the lass returned. I… I even offered tae escort the lass back tae the priory meself. They wanted tae know why. They… they wouldna tell me more than that. If ye've been followin' me, then ye know I wasna there for very long. I left quickly."

"And the money on ye?"

"I told them me mother was sick."

It was the only lie Tommy could come up with quickly enough and Richard knew it wasn't the truth. He wasn't clear why Tommy had gone to Berwick Castle but he didn't much care at that point; he'd gotten what he wanted out of the man, which was the very real possibility that Ysabella's postulate was there, guarded by the mighty Nighthawk and The Wolfe himself. But it didn't seem to matter to him; simply knowing the lass was at Berwick fed his bloodlust because he wanted nothing more in the world that to get his hands on that woman regardless of who was guarding her. She belonged to him, didn't she? He paid enough for her.

He wasn't going to fail in his second attempt to take her.

"We tell the allies that the *Sassenach* at Berwick have somethin' that belongs tae me," he said to the man standing nearest to him. In fact, he was speaking to the half-dozen men who were standing around Tommy. "We'll tell them that it was the *Sassenach* who raided Coldingham where my sister is the mother prioress. We'll tell them that they took a lass, a Scots lass, tae whore with them at Berwick. We will rally the allies with the promise of Berwick's riches if they help us save me sister's postulate. I want that lass! She is mine!"

The man standing next to him, with curly auburn hair and dirty as if he'd never taken a bath in his life, didn't seem convinced.

"Berwick is a big place, Richie," he said. "Big walls, two gatehouses, and the river on one side o' her. And she carries a big army."

Richard wouldn't be deterred. His face began to turn red. "Cowardly, ye are!" he snarled. "Berwick can be breached like any other castle if we get enough men. We build ladders and come in from the north, where there is only a wall between us and the keep. We can breach her,

I say! Purge de Wolfe from the castle once and for all! Do ye know how many Scotsmen would rise tae the call if they thought they could defeat William de Wolfe? De Wolfe shall be our battle cry!"

With that, he turned away from Tommy, shouting for his horse and shouting his intention to destroy Berwick. He wanted the girl within the walls and he was going to rally as many allies as he could to get to her. Once he had the lass, he would invite the allies to be part of his vengeance against Clan Haye. His allies weren't fond of Haye, in any case, so Richard knew he could reward them with riches from Berwick and the opportunity to see justice served.

Was it a mad dream? Probably. Even Richard was willing to admit that his battle plans smacked of madness. But he wanted the Haye lass badly enough that he didn't care. He had been planning for that girl for too many years to let her go so easily. Now, it was his pride that had him in its grip, a pride instilled in him from his father and something he couldn't let go. The more he shouted condemnation to those at Berwick, the more that pride got in his way.

He had set his own path, whether or not he truly believed it was the right one.

As Richard rode off towards the Gordon stronghold several miles away, the men that remained behind didn't forget about Tommy. They tied his ankles up with hemp rope, secured the rope to his pony's saddle, and smacked the pony on the behind so the animal spooked and took off down the road. Tommy took off right along with it.

And that was the end of Tommy Orry Gordon.

AN HOUR AFTER the departure of the Scots visitor, Anson and Colm entered the guard room to find Patrick, Damien, and William still inside, engaged in quiet conversation. Anson, who had been on the wall, went to a small table in the guard room to unload some of his heavy weaponry. On this warm day, wearing mail and leather was sticky on top of hot.

"So," he said as he pulled off his mail hood, "I saw our Scotsman depart and disappear to the north. He seemed to be in a hurry."

The group turned to look at him. "Why would you say that?" Patrick asked.

Anson went to the bucket of cool water near the door and poured a ladleful over his head, cooling himself. "Because he was moving at a clipped pace," he said, wiping the water from his eyes. "He seemed to be eager to leave."

Patrick shrugged. "We have been discussing the same thing," he said. "Tommy expressed fear that he'd been followed here. It would make sense he would want to return to his lands as soon as possible."

Anson shook the water from his hair and went on the hunt for the pitcher of watered wine that was always around for the men to drink. He found it over by the hearth and collected a cup. "I simply cannot believe he traveled all the way from Gordon lands to tell us about Richard Gordon's plans for Lady de Wolfe," he said. "It seems as if he went to great lengths for the enemy."

Patrick followed him, taking another cup as Anson poured him something to drink. "Whatever his motives, I am grateful," he said. "He must have had a serious attack of conscience to come. Or, mayhap, he simply needed the money."

"Mayhap it was all a lie," Colm said as he, too, unstrapped his sword and set it on the table next to Anson's. The others looked at him curiously because Colm only spoke when he truly had something to say. He wasn't one for idle chatter. "Mayhap, he came here to scout us out. Did you ever think of that? Mayhap, he told us that story as purely fiction simply to gain access to the castle."

Patrick took a chair at the end of the table, considering his words. "But for what purpose?" he asked. "To see our weaknesses? We have none. And if he did come here to see the interior of Berwick, then he can return to Richard Gordon and tell him that Berwick is impenetrable."

Colm sat at the table as well. "Mayhap," he said. "But I just found his appearance very odd."

"Odd, indeed," William said. He, too, went to take a seat. "Let us presume that most of what he said was true – that the mother prioress is the sister of the chief of Clan Gordon and that Clan Gordon has a score to settle with Clan Haye. There is no purpose to even tell us that because we have no bearing on Clan Gordon. At Questing, we rarely deal with them because they are far to the north."

Colm looked at William. "He came looking for you, my lord," he said. "He asked for you by name. He was not sure you were here, but your appearance confirmed to him that you were. Mayhap… mayhap he was seeking intelligence on your location but told us that story on Lady de Wolfe to throw us off the truth of his appearance."

Patrick looked at his father, seeing some evidence of believability in Colm's statement. "So he finds you here," Patrick said, "meaning you are away from Castle Questing."

William lifted his eyebrows. "That simply means that I am here and nothing more," he said, not wanting the men to start worrying when there was no reason to. "It is not as if Castle Questing is hugely vulnerable without me. Her army is still the largest one on the border."

Patrick shook his head. "Nay, that is not what I meant. I meant they were looking for *you*. At some point, you will have to travel back to Castle Questing. It would be a fine prize for the Gordon to be lying in wait as you traveled home."

It was an ominous thought. Now, no one was really certain about Tommy Orry's appearance or why he had really come. Being that they had to deal with life and death situations on a daily basis, no one was taking anything for granted. Patrick turned to Colm.

"Have some men follow Tommy's tracks to see if our suspicions hold any weight," he commanded quietly. "Send your best men to track him. Surely, he will return home. But I want to know if his presence here was for another reason than what he told us. Mayhap, the man will return to build an army against my father, or worse."

Colm nodded, rising from his seat and heading out of the guard room. While Patrick was nervous for his father's safety now, William wasn't concerned in the least.

"I do not think there is a horde of Scots waiting to ambush me as I return home," he insisted quietly. "In fact, I was thinking on leaving today since we are not traveling to Coldingham."

Patrick wasn't keen on that idea. "Can you at least wait until Colm's men return from following him? It would make me feel much better."

"I do not believe it is necessary."

"Please?"

William sighed sharply. "I think you are overreacting, Patrick. While I appreciate your caution, I do not believe there is any threat to me beyond the usual. Send me back to Questing with a few men-at-arms if it pleases you. But I would like to return today."

Patrick knew how to play the stubborn game with his father. He was ready and willing to counter the man. "If you insist on leaving, I will tell Katheryn and Evie what we suspect with Tommy Orry. They will not let you go. I will pull forth the women into this if I must, Da. You will not be able to leave."

William's eye narrowed. "You would not dare do that."

"Try me."

The game was up and Patrick had won. Frustrated, William took the pitcher on the table and poured himself more wine. "Then have it your way," he said. "It will give me more time to play with my grandchildren, I suppose. But Colm's spies had better return within a few days or I will simply leave and not tell anyone."

Patrick knew that wouldn't happen with his knights on the prowl, knowing and seeing everything that went on at Berwick, but he didn't comment. He simply nodded his head.

"Just a few days," he said. "Besides… I plan to leave tomorrow for London and I would like for you to remain with Bridey for a little while. I would feel better if you did."

Now, he was playing on his father's sympathies for Brighton and William knew it. He also knew he was sunk because he understood the situation with Patrick leaving his wife behind. It was a painful thing for them both. Resigned to the fact that he would stay at Berwick for a few days, he downed half of his cup.

"As you wish," he said. "How is she doing, by the way? Is she calmer now?"

Patrick nodded. "She is. But I can see the fear in her eyes and that disturbs me terribly. It makes me feel guilty, as if I am helpless to protect her."

Damien, seated at Patrick's right hand, spoke softly. "You are not helpless," he said. "Even though you go to London, you have all of us to protect your wife. I've not had much time to speak to the woman but I look forward to coming to know her. Any woman who could capture your heart is one worth knowing."

He was grinning, which caused Patrick to grin. He slapped an affectionate hand against the man's shoulder. "She is sweet and gentle, but there is strength in her," he said. "She is now in charge of the keep and you will obey her orders as if they are my own. Make sure the men understand that."

"I will. But I do not want you to worry while you are in London. We shall protect her with our lives."

Patrick sobered. "I know you will," he said. He looked between Anson and Damien, two men he trusted implicitly. "I will confess that I am not eager to leave but it is necessary. I told you earlier today in the great hall when we were discussing Richard Gordon and the threats against my wife that I will not be accepting Henry's royal appointment, so I must face the king when I explain my reasons. Although my body may be in London, my mind and spirit will be here, at Berwick. It gives me considerable peace knowing Bridey has you men to protect her. It means everything to me."

It was a surprisingly emotional statement from their usually emotionless commander. Damien lifted his cup to him in salute.

"We will take good care of her while you are away," he said. "And if I have not yet congratulated you on your sudden and surprising marriage, then allow me to do so. I wish you and your wife the best, Patrick, I truly do. You are most deserving of happiness."

Patrick smiled modestly, tapping his cup against Damien's and then Anson's when the man held his cup aloft as well. "Thank you, my friends," he said. "And I am truly happy, mayhap for the first time in my life. Your congratulations and support mean a great deal."

"You will always have it, Atty," Damien said quietly.

Patrick knew that. As the day progressed towards evening, Patrick sat with his men in the guard's room, drinking and reliving old memories and glories. It was a wonderful day, in truth, and something he very much needed, bonding with his men on a deeper and more meaningful level. Men that would be there for Brighton when he could not be.

As the sun began to wane, he left the guard's room and headed back to the keep where he had to hunt his wife down, eventually finding her in the kitchen with Evelyn. The kitchen of Berwick was part of the building complex, built in stone and sunk into the earth like a sublevel.

Patrick found his wife in the hot kitchen helping the cook sprinkle herbs on bread that was meant for the oven. He would never forget the look of joy on her face. Her red, hot little face was so very happy to be useful and to have found her place in the world, as the wife of a great knight. Patrick couldn't ever remember seeing the woman quite so thrilled and it did his heart tremendous good to see it. Like him, she was both content and delighted with what life had brought her.

But he didn't want to share her with the kitchen tonight. Patrick eventually convinced her to leave the cook to her tasks, alone, and they retreated to their chamber, at first to wash and change for the coming meal. But soon enough, it was simply to spend their last night together without having to share one another with anyone. Patrick made love to his wife slowly, gently, tasting her flesh, memorizing the curves of her body, so he could remember those things on the nights to come that would be particularly lonely.

On the nights when his longing for her was tearing him apart.

On into the darkness their lovemaking went until Brighton fell into an exhausted sleep a few hours before morning. Patrick lay there with her in his arms, watching her sleep, not wanting to relinquish one moment of it but he, too, eventually fell asleep, woken only when the guards changing shifts on the wall before dawn captured his attention. He arose then and dressed in silence as his wife slept peacefully a few feet away.

He didn't have the heart to wake her. He loved seeing her slumbering so sweetly and their farewells had already been said during the night, with every kiss and every touch. He gently kissed her cheek and slipped from the room, departing the gates of Berwick as the sun finally peeked over the eastern horizon.

His memories of Brighton were tucked deep into his heart and her lock of hair was tucked deep into his tunic, in a pocket right over the left side of his breast.

Close to his beating heart.

CHAPTER EIGHTEEN

⌖ The Conclusion of the Tale ⌖

Westminster Palace, London
Thirteen days later

"And that is my story, my lord," Patrick said to the king. "I realize it all sounds quite spectacular, unbelievable even, but I assure you it is the truth. It is why I cannot accept your appointment as Lord Protector. I must return to my wife and now you know my reasons."

Henry was looking at Patrick with a mixture of concern and surprise. So were de Lohr and the other advisors standing around the king. In fact, they all looked rather astonished by the wild tale coming forth from the de Wolfe son on his rescue of a woman that, as it turned out, was much more than met the eye.

An astonishing tale, indeed.

"So the mother prioress had planned from the start to turn Brighton over to her brother to crucify?" Henry asked with astonishment. He turned to the men around him, all trusted servants. "Has anyone ever heard of something like that? I find it incredibly appalling that he intended do to that to the lady. Barbaric. Only the Scots would do something so horrific."

Patrick nodded, feeling a huge amount of relief now that his story was told and the king understood about Brighton. To be truthful, he'd had his doubts.

"Indeed, my lord," he agreed. "Barbaric to say the least."

"And this Scotsman? Tommy Orry?" Henry asked. "Did your men follow him and determine if his visit to Berwick had been a ruse of some kind?"

Patrick shrugged. "I left before the men returned, but I am sure if it was some kind of ruse, my father has acted accordingly," he said. "You can understand that I am eager to return and find out for myself."

Henry did, in fact, understand. He understood everything Patrick had told him. Whether or not he was happy with it was another matter altogether. "So you want to go home," he said quietly, scratching his cheek in a thoughtful gesture. "I suppose I see your point. But you will not reconsider? If your wife truly is in danger from Clan Gordon, then bring her to London where she will be safe."

Patrick shook his head faintly. "As grateful as I am for your faith in me, I feel there are a variety of reason why that would not be suitable," he said. Then, he hesitated a moment before continuing. "My purpose in telling you this story was to not only explain why I must decline your generous appointment, but to also tell you that by marrying Bridey without permission, I may be in trouble with the church. I do not want to be a target for their anger but you can see why I had to marry Bridey and why I could not return her to Coldingham."

Henry didn't seem to think that was an issue. "The church is the least of your worries," he said. "I will have Boniface of Savoy, the Archbishop of Canterbury, give you written permission on the marriage. Given the circumstances, I am sure the man will agree, although he rarely agrees with anything I do these days. Better still, I will send you with a document demanding the arrest of the mother prioress who has sinned against God and Mankind with her collusion. Such a woman is the antithesis of a good and pious woman, and I am sure the archbishop will agree. When you return home, go into Coldingham and arrest her, Patrick. Take her to York. I will send word to the Archbishop of York to try the woman for her crimes. Her actions cannot go unpunished."

Patrick was deeply pleased to hear the declaration. Finally, some justice would be served and it was better than he could have hoped for. Already, the court scribes were writing furiously on their vellums at the edge of the room, preparing missives and documents at the king's command. He could see the men over near the western wall of the hall, monks from Westminster Abbey, scratching away with their swan quills.

"As you wish, my lord," Patrick said. "And… thank you. From the bottom of my heart, I thank you for punishing the mother prioress. But…"

He hesitated and Henry lifted his eyebrows. "But *what*?" he asked knowingly. "But what about Richard Gordon? I have not overlooked that detail but I rather thought you would like to take care of the man yourself. It is your wife's life he has threatened, after all. I would assume you want to punish the man personally."

A twinkle came to Patrick's eye. "It would not anger you if I did, my lord?"

Henry shook his head. "You have my blessing," he said. "And I will even provide you with men to assist. De Lohr, how many men can you provide your old friend and ally, de Wolfe?"

Daniel, who had been listening to Patrick's story with amazement and outrage, grinned. "I can have five hundred men here from Canterbury by early tomorrow morning," he said, his gaze lingering on Patrick. "Can you wait that long, Atty? Methinks you want to return home to your wife at this very moment."

Patrick smiled weakly. "I can wait until tomorrow morning," he said, "and I am very grateful, my lord. My father will be most grateful, too."

Henry sat back in his chair, waving a hand at Patrick. "For what your father has done for me all of these years, it is the very least I can do," he said. "I will match de Lohr's donation of five hundred men and send you back to Berwick with one thousand. That should be enough to march into Gordon lands and punish Richard Gordon however you see fit."

Patrick was extremely thankful. "It will be more than enough, my lord," he said. "Thank you again for your generosity and understanding in the matter."

Henry's gaze lingered on Patrick for a moment. "You know, a lesser man would have simply sent me a missive about the situation," he said. "You showed great honor by coming to London when I know you did not want to leave your wife. That also shows courage. Are you *sure* you will not reconsider my appointment?"

Patrick gave him a half-grin. "As honored as I am by it, I must again decline for now. But who is to say what the future will hold? Mayhap Bridey would like living in London."

Henry lifted his hands. "Why shouldn't she?" he said. "Fine shops, fine homes, the Street of the Jewelers… any woman would love to live here."

"Then give me a year or two and if you still wish to appoint me to your service, I would be willing to listen."

Henry seemed satisfied with that arrangement. He must have been in a generous mood because he was not demanding that Patrick reconsider his stance. In truth, he understood what it was like to love a woman, so he had empathy for Patrick's plight even if he was losing an excellent knight. *Losing another de Wolfe*, he thought with irony. When de Wolfe men fell for women, they fell hard. There was no turning back for any of them.

But Henry understood.

Rising from his heavily-cushioned chair, Henry made his way down the dais to Patrick as the man stood at the bottom of the steps. A tiny man when compared to Patrick's bulk, he put his hand on the Patrick's arm and began to walk.

"I want to know what this woman looks like who has taken you from me," Henry said. "And we must discuss her father as well. Does Magnus know of his daughter?"

Patrick walked beside the king at a leisurely pace. "I do not know, my lord," he said honestly. "The only person who would know that, I would assume, is the mother, Lady Juliana de la Haye."

Henry pondered that as they headed for the large, heavy doors of the audience hall. "Is the mother still alive?"

"I would not know, my lord. The old nun, when she confessed Bridey's true heritage, did not mention it."

Henry was thoughtful. "Surely you realize that by marrying Magnus' daughter, you have created an alliance with the Northmen. It might do well to inform Magnus that he has a bastard daughter married to an English knight. It might even bring about the grounds for a treaty with the Norse."

Patrick could see that Henry was looking at the political side of things, as he very well should. It was his business to see potential alliances. But Patrick, truthfully, wasn't so keen on it.

"He could also show up at Berwick and demand the return of his daughter, my lord," Patrick pointed out as they passed through the doors, heading into the corridor outside. "If I would not return her to the church, I surely would not return her to a Northman."

Henry rubbed his chin. "That could be quite a battle."

"One I would wish to avoid, my lord."

Henry pondered the idea a moment longer before lifting his shoulders. "It was a thought," he said. "But you are correct – telling Magnus he has a daughter married to an Englishman could do more harm than good. And I do not believe you need any more trouble than you already have so far north in the wilds. The Scots are trouble enough."

Patrick nodded fervently. "Indeed they are, my lord."

They came to another corridor at that point and Henry came to a stop, as did the dozen advisors who had been following him and Patrick from the audience hall. Henry happened to glance at the nearest window to see the angle of the sun to guess the time of day.

"I will return to my chamber now and rest," he said. "You will do the same and I will see you tonight at sup. I will have the missives from

Canterbury at that time regarding your marriage."

Patrick bowed his head in gratitude. "To thank you does not seem quite enough, my lord," he said. "Thank you for your understanding and your mercy. I am ever your loyal servant."

Henry began to walk away from him, his advisors closing in around him. "Remember that when I honor you with another royal appointment."

"I will, my lord."

"If you turn that one down, there may not be another."

"I understand, my lord."

"Do you still want to keep the lands and titles? I will give them to you as an incentive."

Patrick grinned. "And if I keep them and still decline the appointment, my lord?"

Henry's old eyes were shrewd. "Hopefully, you will not."

With that, Henry continued down the corridor surrounded by his advisors, following the man like loyal dogs. It took Patrick a moment to realize de Lohr was not among them; he was standing next to Patrick, watching the monarch walk away.

"That was quite a fantastic tale, Atty," Daniel said. "You were fortunate that you caught him in a good humor. I've seen men come to Henry with lesser tales only to be called a liar. He likes you."

Patrick emitted a heavy sigh, his relief evident now that Henry had gone. "That is well and good," he said. "I am very grateful. And thanks to you for providing me with men. Any chance your foolish son will be among them?"

Daniel laughed softly. "Chad?" he asked. "Nay, he will not. He is off with the de Shera brothers trying to help them rebuild their legacy after the defeat of de Montfort. He is a bit of a wanderer, like his father, but he married a lovely woman recently, a de Shera relation, in fact, and he is very happy. It does my heart good to see that."

Patrick thought of his own father and how the man had been proud to see that, in his words, his son had finally become a man after declaring his love for Brighton. It would seem that all fathers were happy to see their sons grow up, emotionally as well as physically.

"I am pleased to hear that he married," Patrick said. "Give him my congratulations when you see him, will you?"

Daniel nodded. "And I am sure he would congratulate you as well on your recent marriage." The conversation paused and he turned to look at the windows and the position of the sun, just as Henry had. "It seems as if there are a few hours before sup at the very least. Where will you go now?"

Patrick shrugged. "I was thinking on going to the Street of the Jewelers, as Henry mentioned, to purchase a wedding ring for my wife. She does not have one."

"I should like to purchase something fine for my wife as well. It is her day of birth soon. May I join you?"

"I would welcome it."

Together, the two of them headed out of Westminster, out into the wild world of London to purchase finery for the women they loved.

IT WAS DUSK by the time Patrick and Daniel returned from the Street of the Jewelers, which turned into a bigger trip because the Street of the Merchants was nearby and, somehow, they ended up there as well, hunting for delightful things to buy their wives.

Patrick had never had the opportunity to buy for a woman before so he was a bit of a slave to the merchants who were trying to coerce his money from him. The merchants figured out early on that Patrick was willing to drop money on pretty things, so they bombarded him with many. When all was said and done, Patrick had purchased three necklaces, several bejeweled hair combs, scarves, two cloaks, and a lovely silver and garnet ring because that was what all of the fashionable young wives were wearing. He hoped that it would fit her but the jeweler told him that any reputable jeweler would be able to make it the proper size for her.

It was a large and expensive haul that Patrick took back with him to Westminster that night, all of it tucked into a lovely embroidered satchel that he'd purchased for his wife. Most large families had townhomes in the city, like the House of de Lohr. But the House of de Wolfe kept no such residence, so Patrick had been assigned a room at Westminster since he had nowhere else to stay other than a tavern and Henry wanted him close by. Therefore, he dumped out the satchel when he returned, inspecting the treasures and hoping that Brighton would like them. The more he looked at the gifts meant for her, the more he missed her.

As he'd told Brighton, he thought of her every hour of every day. There wasn't a time when he wasn't thinking of her, wishing he had brought her with him but, in the same breath, knowing it was better that she had remained at Berwick. He'd left her thirteen days ago and he'd felt that pain of longing every one of those days. Sometimes he'd lay awake, thinking of her, missing her so badly that his stomach ached. What was it that he missed so badly? Everything. Her beauty, her silly giggle, her quiet wisdom. She had a strength about her that awed him. He missed it all. He still could hardly believe his good fortune in marrying a woman he was mad about. And that madness grew by the day.

So he packed her jewelry back into the pretty satchel and tucked it away into his saddlebags, making sure everything he owned was in those saddlebags so he could leave London as soon as the de Lohr troops and crown troops were assembled for him. He hoped those men were prepared for a hard march because he planned to make it back to Berwick in twelve days or less, a swift march, indeed. Those who couldn't keep up would be left behind.

He wasn't going to delay returning home again.

It was well after sunset and Westminster was alight with torch and candle light, giving the structure a rather ethereal glow. Sentries walked their rounds or manned their posts around the palace.

Patrick found himself standing at the window, watching the men at their posts, marveling at the size of the palace and the city beyond. London was growing steadily and it had since the last time he'd seen it, spreading out further and further into the surrounding countryside. Someday, it might take up the very length of the Thames, he thought. He found himself wondering what his children or his grandchildren would see.

Turning away from the window, he happened to catch a glimpse of himself in a polished bronze mirror that was near the bed. He peered at himself, thinking he looked rather slovenly with his overgrown hair and a beard that was growing in. He'd not taken much time to shave during the course of his trip south and his heavy beard was growing in quite nicely. He looked like a wild man. Grinning, he thought he might keep it and see if Brighton recognized him when he returned home.

A knock on the chamber door roused him from his thoughts of his dark beard. Thinking it was de Lohr, he casually made his way to the door and opened it only to find a familiar face gazing back at him. Patrick's eyes widened.

"Kevin!"

Kevin Hage looked as if he'd hadn't slept in days. He was haggard and pale, and Patrick was instantly seized with panic. Before he could say a word, however, Kevin pushed his way into the chamber.

"Thank God," Kevin breathed. "The sergeant at the gate said I could find you here. Gather your things, Patrick. We must return to Berwick immediately."

Stunned, Patrick realized he was shaking at Kevin's unexpected appearance. "Why?" he gasped. "What has happened?"

Kevin sighed heavily, clearly struggling to stay on his feet. The man was exhausted to the bone. "Scots," he said. "Hordes of them. Berwick is under siege. You must come home."

Patrick's heart was in his throat. For a split second, he simply stood there, staring at Kevin as he tried to process the information. Then, he was moving for the bedchamber in a rush, going to collect his saddle-bags because he had been told to. But he pulled Kevin along with him as he moved.

"What in the hell is going on?" he demanded. "Tell me everything."

Kevin couldn't make it much further. He saw the bed and ended up collapsing on it, staring at the ceiling as Patrick began to don his mail. Kevin couldn't even spare the strength to help the man.

"It started a few days after you left to come to London," he said, his voice without energy. "I am not for certain exactly when, but I was still at Northwood Castle when Uncle Paris received word that Berwick was being attacked. From what we could understand, Uncle William was still at Berwick when the siege started, so Uncle Paris sent word to your brothers and also to Castle Questing, requesting men. We marched on Berwick with nearly five thousand men but when we got there, the place was being overrun. That was when Uncle Paris sent me to London to find you."

Patrick had been listening to the tale with a myriad of emotions – initial disbelief, fear, then relief his father had been at Berwick when the battle started. But when Kevin mentioned that the castle had been overrun, he stopped in mid-motion.

"Dear God," he breathed. "Tell me that my castle was not breached."

Kevin rubbed his eyes wearily, too tired to be gentle in his delivery of the news. "When we arrived, the Scots had ladders on the walls but the ladders were not quite tall enough so they pulled them down and built extensions on them to try and reach the top," he said. Then, he angled his head back so he could see Patrick. "This was a well-planned operation with thousands of Scots, Atty. I have never seen so many Scots in my entire life, as if half of the lowlands had suddenly converged on Berwick. We believe there was a small breach on the northeast wall because we could see a good deal of fighting on the battlements, but when our armies arrived, we created a second front so we diverted the Scots and they turned on us. I cannot tell you what has happened inside of Berwick because we have not been able to get close enough to tell. All I know is that Berwick is surrounded by Scots, and we are surrounding the Scots, and it has been some of the most intense fighting I have ever seen. Uncle Paris sent me to bring you home."

Patrick was feeling oddly numb as he finished dressing, pulling on his mail cowl and adjusting his de Wolfe tunic. He was absolutely shocked to hear what was going on at Berwick because, in the years he had been in command, they'd never had a credible siege. The Scots had stayed away and, with the exception of a few minor skirmishes, they'd never seen a serious attack. But the moment he left, the Scots bastards converged on his garrison in a battle that had already been going on for almost two weeks. It was a struggle not to become completely overwhelmed with the news.

But then, it started to occur to Patrick… Colm had suggested that Tommy Orry had come to Berwick to scout it from the inside. He'd been looking for William and had spoken of the Coldingham lass. Perhaps Colm had been right all along and Tommy's presence had been the harbinger of things to come. The Scots, all along, had been focused on Berwick. Was it really true? Now, all of it was starting to make some sense and his stomach began to twist into knots of horror.

"Did you identify the Scots?" he asked Kevin. "What clans?"

Kevin was struggling to sit up because he was close to falling asleep. "Our scouts have told us they recognized MacKay and Gordon."

Patrick looked at him in utter horror. "*Gordon*?"

"Aye. Why?"

So much for trying to remain calm. Patrick stared at Kevin, hardly able to speak for the terror racing through his mind.

"You were not at Berwick when a man from Clan Gordon came to tell us…." He couldn't even finish. "They want Bridey. My God… they want my wife."

Kevin peered at him in confusion. "Why would they want her?"

Patrick struggled to bring forth the explanation. "Because the mother prioress of Coldingham was raped by a member of Clan Haye years ago," he said haltingly. "When Bridey was brought to Coldingham by her mother, who was a member of Clan Haye, the mother prioress and her brother came up with a plot to use my wife in vengeance against Clan Haye. Before I left for London, we had a visitor from Clan Gordon who came to Berwick to tell us of this plot. Colm thought the man was there to scout Berwick, to see our strengths and weaknesses, but I discounted that. And now… oh, Sweet God, now I see that I must have been wrong. They waited until I left to attack the fortress, hoping it would be easier to get to Brighton."

Kevin could see how distraught Patrick was, now coming to understand why the man was more distressed than he should have been. Something evil was centering around the woman he married, something unspeakable and dark.

"We haven't been able to speak with anyone inside of the fortress," he said. "We have been separated from the castle by a line of Scots. Are you telling me that they are there to target your wife?"

Patrick could only nod. Not having contact with anyone inside the fortress, Paris and Patrick's brothers, and anyone else, wouldn't know that the ultimate goal of the siege was to get to Brighton. They would think it was simply a nasty siege, like any number of sieges the Scots were so capable of. They wouldn't know that it was Patrick's wife who was in danger, the very woman who breathed life into his veins.

He had to get home.

"Listen to me," Patrick said, reaching out to pull Kevin off the bed. "I want you to find Daniel de Lohr. He is here, somewhere. I want you to tell him what has happened and tell him I am leaving for Berwick tonight. The man was supposed to supply me with troops to take with me to the north, but I cannot wait for them. You will stay here and bring the troops north, do you hear? I cannot wait, Kevin. I must go home."

Kevin lurched to his feet, weaving wearily. "I will find him and tell him," he said. "But I am going with you. You cannot go alone."

Patrick was in no mood to argue. "Do as I say," he snapped. "After you find de Lohr, find Henry and tell him also, for he will want to know. Tell Henry… tell him that the Gordon has attacked Berwick in an attempt to get my wife. Tell him I have already left for Berwick. He will understand."

Kevin wasn't happy with the command but he nodded his head. "As you wish," he said reluctantly. "Is there anything else?"

Patrick shook his head, grabbing his saddlebags and slinging them over one broad shoulder. "Nay," he replied. "Just do as I ask and come as quickly as you can."

With that, they fled the room. Kevin followed Patrick all the way down to the stable block, remaining with Patrick in case there were any last-minute orders. But none were forthcoming and Patrick eventually chased Kevin away to carry out his existing orders.

As Kevin headed off into the torch-lit grounds of Westminster, Patrick finished saddling his excitable beast. He was fairly excitable himself, hating that it would take so long to reach Berwick and wondering what he would find when he arrived. But above all of his fears, he was grateful for one thing – that his father and his knights were there to protect Brighton from men who wanted to kill her. They knew the grisly story of Gordon vengeance and they knew why the Scots had come. Patrick knew they would do everything in their power to keep his wife safe. It was, perhaps, the only thing keeping him sane at the moment.

He'd been gone from Berwick thirteen days. Kevin had said that the siege had been going on since a few days after he'd left, which meant it was almost a two-week siege at best. But he took comfort in his father being at Berwick and the great de Wolfe and de Longley armies there to engage the Scots and, hopefully, chase them away.

In fact, that could have already happened and he would return to a fortress that was picking up the pieces but mostly sound and whole. That was the best-case scenario. The worst-case scenario, he couldn't bring himself to entertain.

By the light of a three-quarter moon, Patrick set off for Berwick.

Have faith, Bridey, he prayed over and over. *I am coming!*

CHAPTER NINETEEN

Nine days later
Berwick Castle

BERWICK CASTLE, IF nothing else, was built to withstand anything. A bombardment from archangels notwithstanding, the walls had held off the Scots for nearly three weeks. The first few days of the siege had been somewhat sporadic and unorganized, but then a second wave of Scots appeared and the battle began to take some form. There were ladders, many of them, and the Scots were attempting to mount the walls with them but they weren't quite tall enough, so the ladders disappeared for a day or two only to reappear with extensions on the ends, making them very tall and very unstable.

Truthfully, William wasn't all that concerned. He'd fought Scots for more years than he cared to recall and he'd seen their tactics, including the unstable ladders. The walls of Berwick were enormous, more than twenty feet in height in some places, with some of the towers nearly sixty feet in height, so William knew that the Scots wouldn't be able to easily mount the walls much less breach them. They either had to go over them or under them, and either one of those choices was nearly impossible. Frankly, he was surprised they were making the attempt. Still, every time they drew close, William and the knights were ready for them.

Flaming arrows were launched by the archers in the center of the bailey at the Scots on the exterior of the castle, and more than one met its target. Being that the castle was now locked away from the world, William was careful with the ammunition, for arrows were valuable, so he conserved as much as he could. The men of Berwick spent most of their time on the walls, shoving away those unstable ladders and generally doing a good deal of damage that way. In fact, other than the arrows lost, the men of Berwick hadn't had all that difficult time of it with the Scots.

Then, the English armies arrived.

William had seen the massive army approaching from the west, lines of men in battle formation as they approached the castle, and he saw the standards of de Wolfe and de Longley and Teviot. Confidence filled him in knowing that his oldest and dearest friend, Paris de Norville, had made an appearance with the army from Northwood and also that Kieran had brought his own troops from Castle Questing. It was a prideful sight, indeed, to see the two armies merged and heading towards Berwick like a great steel tide.

The Scots, however, weren't so impressed. It was a sight that should have made them withdraw but, instead, they rushed out to attack the English army and as William and the knights of Berwick watched with some fascination, the Scots engaged the incoming English armies in hand-to-hand combat that grew nasty very quickly.

It went off and on for days, men fighting one another, killing each other, and soon the dead began to pile up. The armies had met to the north of Berwick on a great hilly, grassy plain, and the attack on the castle eased up because the Scots were diverted to the incoming English armies.

And William hardly slept because of it. He spent his time on the battlements watching the ebb and flow of the fighting, knowing that his dear friends, Paris and Kieran, were in the middle of it, older men who should be enjoying their advancing years but, instead, were in the midst of a battle because William was in need of them.

William also suspected that his sons, Scott and Troy and possibly even James, had come because the army of de Wolfe was quite vast and the banner they flew from garrison to garrison was always the same, so it was quite possible all of William's border garrisons had spared men to defend Berwick. It concerned William a great deal that his sons were in the midst of the battle, too, so he stayed awake, watching, trying to determine if the English were making headway against a particularly vitriolic band of Scots.

And then, it happened.

Because the garrison had been lured to watching the fighting on the northeastern side of the castle, clever Scots has used that distraction to bring their ladders up to the southeast corner of the fortress where the wall was the shortest. But the English were vigilant and only one ladder managed to get up, with a few Scots leaping over the parapet, only to be met by dozens of furious Englishmen swinging swords.

The clash on the battlements was great as more than one Scot was thrown back over the wall, and a few of the English soldiers injured, before Hector and Alec managed to dislodge the ladder and send it crashing. After that, there was even coverage over the entire wall walk to ensure they weren't caught off guard again. It was clear the Scots were looking for any advantage to mount the walls, so William vowed they would not be caught off guard again.

And so, the battle between the Scots and the incoming English armies went on for almost three weeks, although there was a definite ebb and flow to the battle. Sometimes it was greater, sometimes there was nothing at all. But through it all, the Scots refused to leave.

Exhausted from days upon days of fighting, the clans had dug in around the exterior walls of Berwick, no longer trying to breach the castle but remaining around the castle for the most part so the English army couldn't make their way inside and the inhabitants couldn't get out. The English army had backed off, too, watching the castle and the Scots from a rise to the north while the occupants of the castle remained relatively unscathed. At least, it had been that way for nineteen days.

On the morning of the twentieth day, William was on the walls, watching the encampments both below him and to the north, smelling the smoke from the cooking fires as it mingled with a seasonally-unusual fog bank that had rolled in during the night. It was cold and damp, strange weather for July, and it was also strangely silent. In fact, he didn't like it at all. There was a tangible stillness in the air, tense, as if there was a predator waiting to pounce somewhere in the mist that he couldn't see.

Something told him to be vigilant.

"Any movement this morning, Uncle William?" Alec came up beside him, his breath hanging in the cold early morning. "I will admit that I am curious to know what my father is waiting for. The English outnumber the Scots; they should simply drive them away."

William glanced at his son-in-law. "Paris and Kieran have attempted a few tactics to remove them," he said. "But these are Gordon men, Alec. They want something very badly inside this castle and they will not leave without it. They are stubborn that way."

Alec knew that the Scots beyond the wall were Gordon and MacKay; that had been established early on. He also knew that they had come for Patrick's wife, or at least that was what William believed based upon the whole confusing mess with the mother prioress and her need for vengeance against Clan Haye.

Colm and Anson were convinced that the visit by the Scotsman those weeks ago was merely a precursor to the siege. *Intelligence gathering*, they had presumed. But it seemed to Alec that the Scots had picked a very big hurdle to tackle in their quest for revenge against Clan Haye. Surely there was an easier way than attacking the biggest castle on the border.

"Those fools," Alec muttered. "They want Bridey so badly that they are going to tear themselves up against the walls of Berwick simply to get at her. What a stubborn bunch this is. Can they not see that taking the woman from these walls will be impossible? Yet they continue to try."

William nodded vaguely, his one good eye trying to penetrate the mist. "And they will continue to try until they simply give up and return home," he said. "It is my belief that they truly believe we hold something that belongs to them, as if we have somehow stolen Bridey from them. For there is truly no other reason for the Gordon to attack Berwick. I see no other logical explanation other than they all have a death wish."

As Alec leaned against the parapet, looking out into the mist just as William was, the other knights joined them. Hector followed by Damien, Colm, and, finally, Anson joined William and Alec as they gazed out over the wall into the fog. It was lifting slightly, but not enough. It made everything hazy and mysterious. Hector peered over the wall to see what was down below.

"They are dug in like moles," he said after a moment. "They have set up shelters even, crude as they are. Do they truly think to remain dug in like that?"

William shook his head. "I have never seen anything like this in all of my years fighting the Scots," he said. "I was telling Alec that I believe that the Gordon must sincerely believe we have something that belongs to them. There is no other reason why they would dig in like this."

Colm and Anson quickly glanced over the parapet as well, seeing the Scots huddled down below. "Do they truly think to wait us out?" Anson wondered. "And why haven't the English gone in after them. What are they waiting for?"

William shook his head. "They must have a reason," he said. "I can only imagine is it some kind of strategy. Either that, or Paris de Norville has gone mad."

Hector grinned at the mention of his father. "Many people have assumed that throughout his life," he said. His smile faded as he looked off towards the north as if to see his father through the fog. "I am sure Papa is working on something. He simply would not sit there and let us rot. But I am at a loss to imagine what it could be."

No one seemed to know. William leaned back against the stone, feeling the dampness to his bones. "If I could get a message to them, we could plan a joint offensive," he said. "Mayhap I can write a note and we can use an archer to shoot it over the heads of the Scots towards Paris' encampment. Mayhap a patrol would pick it up and take it to Paris."

The knights were interested. "What kind of joint offensive?" Hector asked.

William pondered that for a moment. "We have over a thousand men inside," he said. "We could separate five hundred and take them out of the bailey and then seal up the donjon. That leaves the men, and some knights, on the bridge that spans the chasm, trapped between the locked Douglas Tower and the donjon. With the donjon sealed, we open the gates of the Douglas Tower and charge out and into battle with the Scots. Have Paris and Kieran bring their men in at the same time and we can drive the Scots away from Berwick."

It seemed like a logical plan. "Who will go and chase the Scots away?" Hector asked hopefully. "And who will remain here at Berwick to man the walls?"

William turned to glance at the host of eager faces, all of whom wanted to charge out to fight the Scots. No knight worth his weight wanted to stand around and hope for an end to a conflict. They wanted to do something about it. William well remembered what it was like to be young and enthusiastic about battle.

"We have two choices," he said. "I can choose the men who will go and explain my reasons, or we can simply draw straws. What is your preference?"

The knights looked at each other for a moment, torn by his statement because no one wanted to be left behind. It was Alec who finally spoke. "You choose, Uncle William," he said quietly. "We trust your judgement in all things."

No one wanted to insult the integrity of the great William de Wolfe, so they all nodded as William considered his options.

"Hector, you will take Damien and Colm with you and lead the charge on the field," he said. "You are the senior knight and you can command the charge. You will need Damien and Colm's swords with you, as they are imposing men in hand-to-hand combat. I will remain here with Alec and Anson, because if the Scots somehow manage to enter the castle, as they did once before, then we must be here to fight them off. Alec has a powerful sword arm, like his father, and Anson can command the men easily because command is his strength. As for me – I will go to my son's wife and protect her personally. Those Scots will get her over my dead body."

He meant every word of it. It wouldn't have been a fitting ending for The Wolfe to die defending a woman in a corner of a castle, but it would have been an incredibly noble death. Still, no one wanted to see that happen. Alec and Anson knew they would be the last line of defense between William and the lady, and a gang of murderous Scots should the Scots breach Berwick. Suddenly, the misty day grew a bit more solemn. Plans had been made and roles defined.

It was time to act.

"Shall you write the missive to my father or would you like me to?" Hector asked quietly. "I will summon our best archer to land the note as close as he can to my father's encampment. We can only pray one of his patrols picks it up."

William waved him on. "You may write it," he said. "Tell him that at dawn tomorrow, as soon as the sun breaks the horizon, we charge from the castle to purge the Scots from our perimeter once and for all. Tell your father to make sure his men are ready to help us."

Hector nodded. With a lingering glance at the other knights with an expression suggesting that the worst was possibly yet to come, he headed down the wall walk on his way to a tower with stairs that would take him down to the bailey. The Baker's Tower was the nearest because it was near the kitchens. Just as he entered it, he could see a figure coming up the narrow spiral stairs towards him. Hector stepped back only to realize that it was Brighton.

Like the maid of the mist, she emerged from the tower, her skin as pale as the fog surrounding her. There was a little color in her lips and her eyes, big and bottomless. She almost looked surreal against the mists surrounding them. She was wearing a linen cloak with the hood partially covering her head and, in her hands, she carried a pewter pitcher and a few cups. She smiled timidly when she saw Hector.

"Good morn to you," she said politely. "I have brought warmed, watered wine if you would like some."

Hector returned her smile; he genuinely liked Brighton and his wife was extremely fond of her. A woman of good humor and a hard work ethic, there was nothing not to like about her and he could see why Patrick was so enamored with her. But here she was, on the battlements where she wasn't supposed to be, yet he hesitated to tell her so. It was difficult to be stern to that lovely face.

"No, thank you," he said. "I was just heading down. But I am sure there are others who will take you up on your thoughtful offer."

He slipped past her, down the stairs, and Brighton's gaze sought out the knights, standing down the wall. She could barely see them through the mist. Men who were sworn to protect her from the Scots trying to take her and she was terribly ashamed of the fact. Sometimes, she didn't even think she could look them in the eye.

All of this was her fault; she knew that. As soon as it had been determined that Gordon and MacKay were the Scots on the offensive against Berwick, she knew it was all because of her. The woman she had trusted all of her life had betrayed her and, after the failed abduction from Coldingham, Mother Prioress' brother had discovered where she had been taken and had come for her.

Brighton had been given twenty-three days since the day of Patrick's departure to come to grips with the fundamental flaw in everything she'd ever believed – a caring church, a mother prioress who had nurtured her, had all been lies. She could see that now. To say it was disorienting was putting it mildly because she felt as if her entire life had been turned upside-down. Perhaps her entire life had been one big lie, all of it aimed towards this moment in her adult life when

Mother Prioress' brother would steal her away and nail her to a cross for all to see.

More and more, Brighton was coming to realize that the English had been her saviors, angels sent by God to protect her from the mother prioress' evil. But she had also thought about Sister Acha, wondering if the old woman had been given any hint of the evil she was involved in. Perhaps Sister Acha was even part of the evil, but it was a blessing that Brighton would never know. She honestly didn't think she could accept the truth to learn that Sister Acha was part of this plot. It was her saving grace that the woman had died before she'd been questioned about it. For Brighton, it was better for her sanity not to believe ill of the dead.

But now, she was facing an even bigger dilemma. The Gordon wanted her badly enough to lay siege to Berwick and now men were fighting and dying, just because of her. It was enough to leave her sleepless at night, weeping over a situation beyond her control and feeling inherently guilty for it. But no one at Berwick had even hinted she was to blame. In fact, they seemed quite staunch about supporting her. Such good, good people believed in her. She wondered what she ever did to deserve it.

Now, she was on the wall where she wasn't supposed to be, bringing the exhausted knights a warm drink on this cold morning. She couldn't do much by way of helping them during the battle, but she could keep them fed and well-tended as much as possible. But all the while, she was praying that Patrick would hurry and return, for perhaps he could figure out a way to remove the Gordon from Berwick. He was the Nighthawk, after all.

God, she missed him so badly that it hurt.

But thoughts of her husband faded as she drew close to the knights and they turned to look at her, especially William with his patched left eye. She smiled hesitantly when their gazes locked.

"I-it is a cold morning and I have brought you something warm," she said, extending the stacked wooden cups to Alec, who took them and began distributing them. "Warmed, watered wine with spices. It should help fend off the cool of the mist."

The knights held out their cups gratefully as she began to pour the heated liquid. She came to William last and poured him the most, with bits of clove floating around in his cup. He sipped gingerly at it, for it was very hot and quite delicious.

"Thank you, Bridey," he said. "Now, you can remove your lovely and helpful self from this wall. This is no place for a woman and least of all you."

Brighton knew that. She was surprised it took him so long to say it, polite man that he was. But she didn't leave, at least not immediately. At the risk of angering William, she remained.

"I-I know," she said quietly, looking to the men standing around, sipping their hot wine. They were dressed for battle, with stubble on their faces, weary from weeks of a siege. "I simply wanted to say… I wanted to thank you all for what you are doing. A month ago you barely knew me, but now you are risking your lives for me. I have never seen a battle before, you must understand, and now to be in the middle of one is a sobering prospect at best."

William listened to her speak, this surreally lovely woman his son had married. Having come to know her over the past few weeks, he saw in her what the others saw – a woman of gentle humor and a kind manner, someone who wasn't afraid of hard work or afraid of learning what she needed to know outside of the walls of Coldingham. Brighton was, if nothing else, adaptable. In that respect, she reminded William very much of his own wife. The women were very similar and, perhaps, that made him just a wee bit more protective over the lass than normal.

"What you see is not unusual on the borders," he told her. "It is true that the Gordon and MacKay have been making trouble for us, but who is to say it is all for you? There are plenty of us they do not like, either, and I am probably at the top of that list."

Brighton couldn't help but smile at his attempt to make it seem as if this entire struggle wasn't about her when they all knew, clearly, that it was.

"Y-you are kind to say so but I think you are only being polite," she said, a hint of a scolding in her tone. "You do not need to coddle me, for I know why the clans are here. I know it is because they want me. I simply wanted to thank you all for everything you have done. Your sacrifice and your strength is something I shall never forget. You are all great and noble men in my mind."

William waved a hand at her, as if attempting to sweep her away. "You will make them all arrogant and difficult to live with if you continue to praise them like that," he said. "Go now and return to the keep. No more coming up here to feed men's pride."

He meant it half-serious and half in jest, but Brighton had said what she'd wanted to say so she took her pitcher and headed back to the tower. The mist was starting to lift somewhat near the river, or at least she could see the water to a certain extent, but it was still cold and wet and gray.

As she descended the stone steps of the tower, trying not to slip on them because they were wet from the weather, she thought on these people who had become her family. The de Wolfe family and their relatives had embraced her from nearly the beginning. She remembered how she had been so very awed at the love she saw amongst them, the devotion between husbands and wives, and how very much she wanted to know that same kind of love.

Now she had it with Patrick, something so beautiful and tender that she could hardly believe it belonged to her. She was part of this loving, wonderful group of people and all she had done was bring war and strife into their lives. She had repaid their kindness with heartache. When Patrick returned, he would find his castle besieged and his family trapped within it.

Although she didn't truly believe he would blame her for it, there was a part of her that wondered if she was brave enough to turn herself over to the Gordon simply to pull them away from Berwick and leave the de Wolfe family in peace. Perhaps if they had what they wanted, they would leave Berwick alone.

Leave Patrick alone.

She had suffered through twenty days of guilt, and of missing her husband. It was starting to take its toll. Would the Gordon go away if she turned herself over to them?

She wondered.

But to save these wonderful people that she'd come to love so well – *her family* – she was forced to consider it.

IF PATRICK HADN'T known the land so well, he might have actually gotten lost in this thick white soup that had rolled in from the sea. Berwick was foggy a good deal of the time so he was used to weather like this and he had learned to navigate it.

It was the ninth day since departing London and, truth be told, he was ready to collapse and so was his horse. He'd made at least forty miles every day, starting on his journey well before sunrise and then continuing well after sunset, making sure he went as far as he could before seeking shelter for the night.

His horse, a sturdy and durable animal, was showing signs of exhaustion so Patrick made sure his attention was on the horse every night. Plenty of food and water, and then he'd push the horse over in its stall to make sure it took some time off its feet. Not once during his trip had he sought an inn to bed down in. He'd slept with his horse, whose name was simply "Steed", in order to make sure the animal had a good rest and wanted for nothing. His entire journey north depended on the soundness of his animal.

On this ninth day, he was in range of Berwick; he could smell the sea and that distinctive rank odor of the River Tweed as it dumped into the ocean. The road was boxed in on both sides with wildly growing foliage like hemlock and ash trees, but there were gaps in the cover where he could see more fog off to the east but he knew the sea was there as well.

The smell of smoke from cooking fires made him aware that he was extremely close to Berwick even though he couldn't see it. His eagerness to rush to the castle, and to Brighton, was almost overwhelming and it was a struggle to remain calm. He was so desperate to get to her that it was nearly overriding his common sense.

But he fought the urge, knowing he had to get the lay of the land first and see where the Scots were, if they were even still here. Not wanting to draw close to the city for fear the Scots had overrun it, he decided to stay out of the town but ride parallel to it, heading towards the north side where there was a rise overlooking the town. Once the fog lifted, he could see for himself what was going on.

Coming to a fork in the road, he knew that the fork to the right would take him straight into Berwick while the other fork would run parallel to the town, cross the river, and then continue north. He took the left fork, spurring his horse into an easy canter as he traveled up the road, seeing patches of sun through the fog. He'd seen fog like this before and suspected, especially in the summer season, that it would lift by midday. When that happened, he wanted to be in a prime position to see Berwick. He pushed the horse a little faster.

He was fairly close to Berwick Castle as he crossed the wooden bridge across the River Tweed. On a clear day, he'd be able to see the castle plainly. But the heavy smell of smoke in the air told him that there were many cooking fires going, which bespoke of an army still present. That told him the Scots hadn't left and it made him extremely cautious as he finished crossing the bridge and spurred his horse onward in his quest to reach the rise to the north.

The mist was starting to lift a bit as he moved to a higher elevation and he could see the top of Berwick's keep poking through the clouds. *Home!* He found himself hoping he wouldn't run into any Scots because he really couldn't see where their lines were. For all he knew, he was heading into a nest of them. About a mile up the road, which swung east so it was above the town of Berwick now, he came to the rise that, on a clear day, would enable him to see the castle and surrounding land very clearly.

Pulling the horse to a stop, he debated on what to do next – wait out the fog or try to come in from the north for a look-see. Whatever decision he was about to come to was made for him when a pair of soldiers bearing bows and arrows, aimed right at him, burst forth from the heavily foliage.

"Halt!" one man shouted. "Who are you?"

It was an English soldier and Patrick felt a good deal of relief at the fact that the Northwood or Questing army must have still been in the vicinity. He held up his hands to show that he had nothing threatening in his grasp.

"What army are you with?" he asked the soldiers. "Is Northwood or Questing around here?"

The soldier, threatened by an English knight who had knowledge of the nearby armies, held the bow and arrow up in a very threatening manner.

"Who are you?" he barked again.

Patrick could see he was about to be shot. "I am Patrick de Wolfe, commander of Berwick Castle and newly returned from London," he said calmly. "Where is Paris de Norville?"

The second soldier rushed up to the first soldier. "Nighthawk!" he gasped. Noting that his comrade still had the arrow pointed at the knight, he slapped the man's hands down and the bow and arrow fell. "Do you not recognize a de Wolfe when you see one?"

Patrick lowered his hands. "You have every right to be vigilant," he said. "Am I to understand the Scots are still around here, somewhere?"

Both of the soldiers nodded eagerly. "Aye, my lord," the second soldier said. "They are dug in around Berwick. Our encampment is on the other side of that hill."

He was pointing to the north, to the very rise that Patrick was ultimately heading towards. Thanking the two soldiers for the information and congratulating them on their vigilance, he spurred his steed up the hill through the heavy, wet grass.

Just as he'd been told, a vast English encampment was on the other side of the rise. The fog was much lighter here and Patrick could see a camp spread out before him. There were temporary shelters and a few tents, trees stripped of wood and branches, and the ground was muddy from the grass having been trampled down by thousands of booted feet. Smoke filled the air from the dotting of fires all over the place. Patrick focused in on the large cluster of tents over near the northeast side of the encampment.

But he had to pass by two more rounds of sentries before they let him completely enter the encampment. Once he was in, he found the area where the horses were corralled and sought out a groom. His horse was hungry and tired, and he turned the beast over to the man, thinking the horse looked too tired at this point to really bite anyone. Leaving his possessions with the horse, he watched the groom lead his animal over to an area near the corral so they could feed him without the other horses trying to steal the food. Satisfied his steed was being properly tended, Patrick headed towards the big cluster of tents.

"Atty!"

Patrick knew that shout. He'd been hearing it since childhood. Turning in the direction of the call, he saw his older brother, Troy, heading in his direction. Tall and dark like their father, Troy had inherited Saracen blood from their grandmother and had an olive-skinned look about him. Had he not had their father's hazel eyes, one would have mistaken him for a savage from The Levant. A grin spread across Patrick's face as he opened his arms for his brother.

"Atty, you beast!" Troy said happily as he hugged the man. "God's Bones, let me look at you. Aye, you're as ugly as I remember."

Patrick laughed softly. "Flattery will get you nowhere," he said, drinking in the sight of a brother he hadn't seen in months. "It has been a long time, Brother. How is the wife?"

"Well enough. We are expecting another child in the winter."

"Congratulations. How is everything else at Kale Castle?"

Troy shrugged. "Quiet," he said. "I have the Scots so terrified that they dare not breathe for fear of upsetting me. But I notice that you have not been able to do the same with this gang. They have your castle surrounded, Atty."

Patrick sobered. "I know," he said. "Kevin found me in London and told me what had happened. Where is Uncle Paris? I have much to tell him."

Troy began walking towards the bigger tents, pulling Patrick along. "In truth, we have been waiting for you," he said. "Uncle Paris did not want to completely destroy your castle without your input. He's moving in siege engines from Northwood. We sent for them several days ago and they should be arriving shortly."

Siege engines. Patrick wasn't particularly thrilled to hear that but he understood the logic. Big trebuchets could hurl stones and other projectiles at the Scots, causing them to disburse. But they could also badly damage his walls. He found that he was desperate to know the situation over the past three weeks and whether Berwick had been breached by those seeking to harm his wife. Nearing a larger tent, he was suddenly confronted by another brother who had just emerged from one of the smaller ones.

"Atty!" Scott de Wolfe exclaimed with a mixture of surprise and joy. "God's Blood, 'tis good to see you. Give me a kiss, you fool."

Scott, the gregarious blonde brother who was Troy's twin and the eldest of the pair, grabbed Patrick's face and kissed him loudly on the cheek. Patrick made a face, pulling back to wipe the saliva off his face.

"Ah, my beloved eldest brother," he said, somewhat sarcastically. "Now I remember why I stay away from Wolfe's Lair."

Scott slapped him on the shoulder. "Why?"

"Because you kiss too much."

Scott and Troy chuckled, deeply pleased to see their brother. Patrick was fourteen months younger than they were and, throughout their lives, they had enjoyed a close relationship. He adored them and they adored him, and the teasing that went on between them had always been the way they had communicated their affections. Even as adults, their mode of communication was no different. They were brothers until the end.

"And you always hated it," Scott said, his hazel eyes twinkling. Then, he suddenly sobered. "I think Atty took all of the handsome traits away from you, Troy. The man must be making women swoon all over Berwick."

Troy cocked an eyebrow. "And he took all of the brains away from you," he said to his twin. He turned to Patrick. "Come along, you gorgeous stud. Uncle Paris will want a word with you."

Patrick had to grin as he followed his brothers towards the larger tent. Scott walked beside him, his hand on Patrick's shoulder, and Patrick felt as if he'd never been away from the pair. Times like this made him realize how much he missed them.

"There is much to tell," he said to his brothers. "Much has happened over the past several weeks. If you behave yourselves, I just might tell you of my new wife."

Both Scott and Troy came to a halt, looking at Patrick as if the man had just announced he was in league with the devil. Before they could bombard him with a flurry of question, Patrick flashed them a saucy grin and pushed into the tent.

It was dark inside the tent even with a big bank of lit tapers and a glowing brazier, but Patrick's gaze fell on the two figures in the tent almost immediately. Kieran and another man were bent over a well-used map that was spread out on a collapsible table, but when Patrick, Scott, and Troy entered the tent, the heads came up and surprise registered. As Kieran grinned like a fool, his relief evident, the other man charged towards Patrick.

"My God," the man breathed, throwing his arms around Patrick and nearly knocking him over. "Is it true? Has the Nighthawk finally arrived?"

Patrick laughed softly as Paris de Norville greeted him as one would a long-lost son. In truth, Paris had helped deliver Patrick as an infant, so there was a special bond between Patrick and the man who was his father's best friend. Arrogant, brilliant, and compassionate, Paris was a man with more life in him that most men could exhibit in three lifetimes. Everything about him was bright and exuberant, humorous and kind. Paris finally pulled back to look Patrick in the eye, his big hands on Patrick's bearded face as he inspected him.

"Tell me how you are," he said, "and leave nothing out."

Patrick sighed heavily, wondering where to start. "I am well," he said. "I am exhausted. I have ridden from London in nine days to make it back to Berwick. Kevin found me. He told me there has been a siege, which I see is still going on."

Paris dropped his hands from Patrick's face. "Indeed, it is," he said. "Is that all Kevin told you?"

Patrick nodded. "It is. Is there more?"

Paris suddenly looked quite weary as he turned back to the table with the map, as it turned out, of the city of Berwick. "I am not entirely sure how much more," he said. "All I know is that the Scots are dug in around your garrison and they will not move. I am bringing siege engines from Northwood to dislodge them but I may damage your walls in the process. Thank God you have come when you have because I did not want to do this without your permission. Patrick, why are the Gordon and their allies so determined to dig themselves in around Berwick? Do you know?"

Patrick began to feel his fatigue. Scott shoved a cup of wine at him and he drank the entire thing before speaking. "I do," he said as he smacked his lips. "It all has to do with my wife. It is quite a story, actually."

Kieran was the only one who had known Patrick had taken a wife and he hadn't told the others because he didn't think it was his right to do so. Therefore, everyone but Kieran reacted sharply to the announcement. Paris' eyes bulged.

"Wife?" he repeated. "You have married and I did not know?"

Patrick could hear the hurt and outrage in the man's voice. He held up a quelling hand. "It happened rather suddenly," he said. "Do not be offended that you were not invited to the wedding. No one was. I married her without my father's permission."

Scott and Troy still had rather surprised looks on their faces but Paris seemed to be rather keen on the idea. "Is this true?" he asked, astonished. "You married and William did not approve? I would say that I am shocked but I am not. You always did as you pleased, regardless of what anyone else thought. In fact, I am proud of you for following your head and not listening to your father on the matter."

Patrick had to grin; Paris and William adored one another, without question, but Paris loved it when William was frustrated by his children. It gave him something to laugh about.

"I listened to my heart, Uncle Paris," Patrick clarified. "You see, several weeks ago, we received word that a band of *reivers* had raided an English settlement. We rode out to route the *reivers* and it turned out that they had a female captive. They had taken her from Coldingham. I fell in love with the woman I saved and I married her."

It was a simple, concise story, but there were many things he had left out. Paris wasn't satisfied. "Why did your father not give permission for the marriage?" he wanted to know.

Patrick held out his cup for more wine and Scott poured it for him. Then, he looked around, seeing a chair over near the bed, and went to sit down upon it. He was utterly exhausted.

"I must tell you the entire tale because that is why the Scots are here," he said. "My wife is the bastard of Juliana de la Haye of Clan Haye and Magnus, King of the Norse. When Juliana gave birth to the child, she took her to Coldingham Priory to be raised by the nuns. As it turned out, the mother prioress, before she became a nun, was raped by a man from Clan Haye. She is also a sister to the chief of Clan Gordon. When my wife was brought to the priory as an infant, the mother prioress and her brother came up with a scheme to use my wife in vengeance against Clan Haye for the rape. In fact, the *reivers* that abducted my wife from Coldingham were paid by Clan Gordon. They were to bring her to the clan chief but we intercepted them and destroyed their plans. Now, they believe my wife is here at Berwick and they are here to take her."

By the time he was finished, jaws were dropping. Scott and Troy were genuinely shocked and even Kieran had a bit of an astonished look about him. He'd known most of the story but not all of it; he knew nothing about the scheme by Clan Gordon against Lady Brighton because all of that had come to light after they'd left Questing. Paris simply stood there with his eyebrows lifted, shocked by the news.

"Is *that* why they have dug in?" he asked, aghast. "Because they believe your wife is in Berwick and they will not leave without her?"

"Aye."

"*Is* she there?"

"She is."

Paris started at him a moment longer before turning away, blowing out his cheeks in disbelief. "I must say that is not a story I expected to hear," he said. "I thought this was a simple siege but it seems that there is far more to it."

Patrick nodded. "Right before I left, a Scotsman came to Berwick and asked for my father," he said. "He said he had information on the Coldingham lass, my wife, and he proceeded to tell us about the Clan Gordon plan. Evidently, their plan was to crucify my wife on Haye lands in vengeance for the rape. To tell you the truth, I was so swept up in the horror of what I prevented when I took her from the *reivers* that I did not stop to think about the Scotsman's visit beyond the information he provided. Colm de Lara seemed to think that the Scotsman had come to assess Berwick and determine whether or not Bridey was actually there. An advance scout, as it were. He must have thought she was at Berwick because the Scots came shortly after I departed for London."

Paris was listening intently to him. "Bridey?"

"My wife. Her name is Brighton but she is called Bridey."

Paris understood. He also understood everything of what he'd been told, a harrowing tale, indeed. Scratching his head, he glanced at Kieran.

"That sheds more light on this, wouldn't you say?" he said. "This is not a random siege. They want something."

Kieran nodded, his manner grim. "Which means they will be more difficult to remove. That is why they have fought so ferociously."

"Kevin said the combat had been brutal," Patrick said, looking between the two old knights. "How many Scots are there?"

Kieran shrugged. "I would say a thousand, at the very least. They are dug in around most of the castle at this point."

"How many English?"

"About fifteen hundred."

Patrick sat forward in his chair. "Kevin is bringing another thousand from London," he said. "He should have left with the men shortly after I departed. I did not want to wait for them; I wanted to return to Berwick and see for myself what had happened. But I would think that Kevin and the army are close behind me."

Paris thought on that bit of information. "We could certainly remove the Scots with that number," he said. "I was going to send to Questing and Northwood for more men but if Kevin is bringing a thousand men from London, then there is no need to risk more of our men than we already have. Besides… if Kevin is right behind you then I am not for certain we could get Northwood and Questing men here any faster."

"Most impressive, Atty," Scott said, standing over near the tent flap. "As Henry's Lord Protector, you have command of more men than we can imagine. It was generous of Henry to permit you to bring some of them north."

Patrick shook his head, preparing to deal the group another shock. "I am not Henry's Lord Protector," he said quietly. "I declined the position. It was more important to me to remain here at Berwick with Bridey than spend my time in London shadowing a dying king. I would have had no life of my own; you know that. My days and nights would have been spent at Henry's side. While I was unmarried, I saw no issue with that. In fact, you all know how eager I was to assume my post. But once I took a wife… I would rather spend my life with her here in Berwick than enjoy the prestige in London of being Henry's Lord Protector. I made a choice of the heart and I do not regret it."

No one said anything for a moment; it was more surprising information in a day that had been full of such revelations. They had all known of his royal appointment and they had also known how proud he had been to receive it. As Henry's Lord Protector, Patrick would have enjoyed immense distinction. To hear that he declined it because of a wife told them all just how deeply in love he was with the woman. It spoke volumes.

"So you have become one of us," Paris finally said, his voice soft with humor. "One of the men who would do anything for the happiness of their women."

Patrick gave him a half-grin; there was some embarrassment there. "Did you ever think you would hear such things from me?"

"Never."

"I assure you, it is true."

"It is," Kieran confirmed. "I have met Bridey. She is a stunningly beautiful woman who has a sweet way about her. You will see what I mean when you meet her. It would not be difficult to fall for her charms."

Paris looked at Patrick as if still in disbelief that the man had not only married, but had declined his royal appointment. But, truth be told, he understood… and he was very glad to see it.

"Then I congratulate you, Patrick," Paris finally said. "I congratulate you on your marriage and on your happiness, and I look forward to meeting the woman who finally stole your heart. I never thought it would happen. If you recall, I tried to marry you off to a daughter but you refused. You also refused Kieran's attempts. We thought that you would go through life without a wife so I am very glad to see that we were wrong."

Patrick grinned. "I hope you have forgiven me for refusing Helene and Rose."

Paris pointed at Troy. "Helene got a better husband than you in Troy," he said firmly, but he didn't mean a word of it. "And Rose married your brother, James. So in spite of you, the women married well. We did not need you, after all."

Patrick was still grinning as he drained his cup. "It all worked out for the best," he said. "Now, can we discuss the siege? I would like to see my wife at some point soon but I cannot do that if the Gordons are surrounding Berwick, so what is the plan to remove them?"

With the subject veered away from Patrick's personal life and his declination of the royal appointment, they returned to the situation at hand. Paris turned for the map on the table.

"We were just discussing that, in fact, when you came in," he said. "I had my scouts draw a map of the castle and try to map out where the Scots are dug in. This shows where they all are, at least to the best of our knowledge. We could try to purge them now with the men we have, but our men have been fighting for nearly three weeks. They are exhausted, which is why I was sending for fresh men. But if Kevin is bringing fresh troops from London, then I suggest we wait for them. The more men we have, the easier this will be."

It wasn't what Patrick wanted to hear but he understood. He stood up from the chair, wearily, making his way to the map to see what Paris and Kieran were looking at. Scott and Troy joined them and, together, the five of them looked over the map that had the Scots positions on it. Patrick could see that they were literally all around the castle with the exception of the chasm between the Douglas Tower and the donjon. But the city in front of the Douglas Tower was marked with Scots. He sighed.

"So they made it into the city," he muttered.

Paris nodded. "They did, but only so far as the main gatehouse. They are dug in there, waiting for that gatehouse to open."

"Have they tried to ram the portcullis?"

Paris nodded. "They have, but it held as far as we know. They've not managed to get inside the castle at all."

As they continued to discuss the situation at the Douglas Tower, from outside of the tent, they could hear a commotion rising. Men were shouting and it seemed as if something was happening. Curious, the knights left the map and proceeded to venture outside of the tent to see what the uproar was about. They were no sooner out of the tent than several soldiers came running up to them.

"What is happening?" Paris demanded.

The soldiers began pointing towards the west. "The Scots are fleeing!" the man said excitedly. "They have pulled from their position and are fleeing Berwick!"

Startled, the knights tried to see what the men were talking about but so many of their own men were running to the west side of the encampment that it was difficult to see anything at all. But there was a huge sense of excitement in camp, something quite electric, and Patrick grabbed Troy.

"Come on," he said. "Get to the horses. We must see what is happening."

The knights broke for the corral where the horses were kept. None of the war horses were saddled, except for Patrick's because they had not removed all of the tack yet, so the knights and grooms began putting bridles on the horses very quickly. Scott and Troy mounted their beasts without a saddle at all and Patrick leapt onto the back of his horse, gathering the reins and spurring the animal southward. Paris and Kieran followed and, soon, all five of them were charging southward, watching the Scots flee as they came up from the river and continued onward towards the west.

It was like watching a flock of migratory birds; wave after wave of Scots were rushing off and it seemed as if the Scots had no interest in the English who were now thundering in their direction. Astonished, the knights pulled their horses to a halt on a rise that gave them a vast vista of the land beyond only to see that the fog, so heavy that morning, had finally lifted. That was the first thing they saw. The second thing they saw was a shocking vision none of them ever thought they would see. Certainly, Patrick had never seen it in his lifetime.

Longships were approaching.

In all of his years by the sea, manning the garrison of Berwick, Patrick had never seen longships heading up the river towards the castle. The vessels had been concealed by the fog. But as soon as the mist lifted sufficiently, massive boats bearing the carved dragon prow of the Northmen were revealed to be moving slowly up the river, bearing down on the city of Berwick.

And that had been enough to scare the Scots away from the castle, for no one wanted to be caught outside of the walls when the Northmen attacked. Now, the fleeing Scots began to make sense. What over a thousand Englishmen couldn't do in three weeks, longships in the river had managed to accomplish in three minutes once the fog lifted.

The Scots were on the run.

"My God," Paris hissed. "Do you see them?"

Beside him, Kieran nodded. "I see four of them," he said, although there was no fear in his voice, only awe. "I have never seen such a sight, not ever. How many men does one of those ships hold?"

Patrick, much like Kieran, was genuinely in awe of what he was seeing. "I have heard they can hold upwards of one hundred men," he said. "But I do not know for certain."

Scott, who had been slightly in front of the group watching the longships row their way up the river, happened to look over at the castle. He pointed.

"Look," he said. "There is no longer a line of Scots around the castle. They are completely gone."

The rest of the knights looked to see what he was gesturing towards and they, too, could see that Scots had mostly fled. There were a few lingering, but they, too, were running off, terrified by the sight of the Northmen. It made the way clear for the English to head to Berwick without a line of Scots to stop them and Paris turned his horse around.

"We must make it to the castle," he said, a sense of urgency in his tone. "The Scots had a good reason for fleeing and I will not be caught on open ground with Norsemen invaders on our doorstep. Scott, Troy; get the men moving *now*."

It was a command and Scott and Troy whirled their war horses around, charging back towards an encampment that was generally in turmoil. Evidently, a few of the men had also seen the longships and now the whispers of Northmen warriors were spreading through the encampment like wildfire. They could hear the frightened shouts of the men.

Run for Berwick!

With Scott, Troy, and Paris racing back to camp to begin moving the men out, Patrick lingered on the rise, watching the longships as they made slow progress against the river current. Kieran, who also hadn't returned to the encampment yet, couldn't help but notice that Patrick seemed unusually preoccupied by the sight. There was something in his expression that suggested… confusion?

"Atty?" Kieran asked. "What is it?

Patrick had an odd look on his face. "I am not sure," he said hesitantly, "but it occurred to me that my wife's father is a Northman, and now there are suddenly Northmen in the river where there have never been any before. Could this be some kind of bizarre coincidence, Uncle Kieran?"

Kieran's gaze lingered on the ships in the distance. "Has Bridey ever had any contact with her father?"

Patrick shook his head. "Never," he said. "She never even knew of her true heritage until the *reivers* abducted her from Coldingham. So how… *how* would Magnus even know of her? And even if he did, *why* would he come to Berwick?"

Kieran shook his head. "Who is to say those ships belong to Magnus? There are any number of lesser princes or Norse lords who could have come. It may have nothing to do with your wife at all."

Patrick's eyes never left the longships in the distance. "Possibly," he said. Then, he turned to Kieran with something of an ominous expression. "I suppose we will find out soon enough."

Kieran didn't think that sounded like a very desirable option, but it was one that would very well come forth once the Northmen docked their longships. Now, it was a race against time to move the Northwood and Questing armies inside the walls of Berwick before the Northmen launched their attack, if that was, indeed, their plan.

As Kieran ran for the encampment, Patrick spurred his war horse straight to Berwick. Nothing in the world, short of the hand of God, could have stopped him at that moment. His only thought was of Brighton and it was a struggle to fight down the panic he felt. Panic for her safety, panic for protecting her from what was to come.

He had to get to his wife.

CHAPTER TWENTY

"*PATRICK!*"

Brighton was lifted up in his arms before she realized it. She'd heard the shouts of the sentries from her chamber window and she'd seen the gates on both the donjon and the Douglas Tower opening, allowing in men who seemed to be entering the castle grounds quite quickly. Soldiers were rushing in on horseback or in wagons, rushing in droves. As she watched curiously from the window, a man who looked very much like her husband came charging into the bailey on a horse that, coincidentally, looked very much like his. Curiosity turned to shock and shock to realization. Racing from the chamber, she met Patrick as he was just entering the keep.

And now she was aloft in his arms.

"God's Bones," Patrick hissed, his face pressed into the side of her head. "Are you well, sweetheart? Are you well and whole?"

Brighton nodded her head even though he couldn't see it. Surely he could feel it, the way she had him wrapped up in a death grip. "I am well," she assured him. "I am even better now that you are here."

Patrick couldn't even put her down to reply. All he wanted to do was hold her, to reaffirm that she was truly safe. His sisters and their children were coming down the stairs, clamoring around him, as their fathers came in from the bailey. Everyone was gathering in the entry of the keep as the commander of Berwick returned, triumphant. After twenty days of a siege, there was much joy to be had.

"Patrick," Alec said, trying to look the man in the face with his wife all wrapped up around him. "How is my father? Is he here with you?"

Patrick turned slightly so he could look at the man. "He is well and whole," he assured Alec. "He and Uncle Paris should be a few minutes behind me. They went to rally their armies to run for the castle."

"Run?" Brighton pulled her face from the crook of his neck. "We heard that the Scots have left. Why should they run now?"

Patrick lowered her gently to the ground. It occurred to him from her question that she had no idea what was in the river. Perhaps she had been kept away from the windows of the keep, bottled up where no enemy could get to her. If that was the case, then she was totally oblivious to the fact that death had just arrived in longships.

His focus shifted to Alec and Hector, having just come in from outside.

"Did you see the longships?" he asked them.

The knights nodded grimly. "We could see them from the wall," Alec said, nodding his head in the direction of the women. "We noticed them just after we saw the Scots begin to flee. But we have not told the women yet. We had only just come down from the wall when the army started entering."

Patrick understood, but now he found himself facing his wife and sisters, who heard the mention of a longship but truly had no idea what anyone was speaking of. Still, he could see the fear beginning to creep onto their features and he sought to clarify before it took over completely.

"The Scots fled not because of the brilliance of the English armies, but because of something else," he said calmly to the women. "When the fog lifted, it revealed four longships rowing upriver. They were just south of the city when I saw them so they should be fairly close to the castle by now."

Because he was calm, the women remained moderately calm. Still, they were clearly worried and that was natural. But the fact that the men didn't seem overly agitated about the situation kept them from growing hysterical.

"I have not sent men to the jetty," Hector said, referring to the walled and protected jetty on the river that was meant for boats on the river to dock at the castle in safety. "I assume it would be better to keep everyone inside. Until we know their motives, we should keep the castle locked up tightly."

Patrick nodded. "Agreed," he said. "Where is my –?"

He was cut off as William entered the keep and the grandchildren began to squeal, running towards him. William bent over to embrace his excited grandchildren and then stood straight, with children still clinging to his legs, to embrace Patrick.

Patrick threw his arms around his father. It was, perhaps, one of the most satisfying embraces of his life, feeling his father alive and warm and well in his arms. It was a huge relief.

"Da," he breathed. "I am very glad to see that you are well. After I heard that the castle might have been breached, I had my doubts."

William squeezed his son, finally letting the man go. "It was a very small breach and hardly worthy of note," he assured him. "In fact, there were so few Scots we had to take turns throwing them off the wall. Very unsatisfying."

Patrick grinned. "I am glad to hear that," he said, reaching out to pull Brighton against him. He didn't want the woman away from him, not even an arm's length. "It took me nine days to return from London and every second of those days was filled with fear for my family, wondering what I would find when I arrived. I cannot tell you how relieved I am."

William lifted a dark eyebrow. "Save that relief, lad," he said. "The Northmen are at our door. We may yet have a bit of trouble today."

Brighton, who hadn't quite overcome her great surprise and joy at her husband's return, was now distracted with talk of longships and Northmen. Patrick had been unruffled about it but William's comment set doubt in her heart. "Have they truly come?" she asked, looking between Patrick and William. "But I do not understand – why are they here? What do they want?"

Patrick looked down at her, cradled against his torso. He shook his head. "I have not seen Northmen here, ever," he said. "In fact, I cannot remember hearing of them along these shores during my lifetime. Do you, Da?"

William also shook his head. "Not in my entire life here on the border," he said. "I have heard of them much further north and I know that some of the outlying islands of Scotland are ruled by Norse princes, but they have not been this far south since I have been alive."

Patrick thought on the longships that, as he had mentioned, were undoubtedly close to the castle now. "Then mayhap we should go and see what they want," he said. "It would be the prudent thing to do."

William agreed. "Indeed," he said. "But I would have the women and children locked in the keep as a safety measure, not to open the door to anyone but the men they know."

Patrick looked around at his sisters, his wife. Katheryn was in Alec's arms and Evelyn was in Hector's. He could see the fear in the women, the comfort in the men. Then he looked down at Brighton, thinking of the longships and reverting back to the thought he'd had earlier – *Magnus.*

What *if* Magnus had come for his daughter? With all of the years that the Norse had stayed away from Berwick, he couldn't help but feel that all of this was connected. He didn't know how, or why, but he wasn't willing to believe this was a coincidence. If it was, indeed, Magnus, and the man had come to collect his daughter, then there was about to be one hell of a fight, worse than anything the Scots could ever throw at them.

Patrick wasn't about to relinquish his wife, not for anything in the world.

"You will be safe here," he said, kissing Brighton on the top of the head before letting her go. "We must go and see why our new visitors have come. Listen to what my father said; bolt this door and shutter all of the windows. Do not open anything for anyone you do not know."

Brighton nodded solemnly, but she was still clinging to his hands. "What will you do?"

He couldn't help but notice that she still had him in a death grip and he lifted her hands to kiss them. "Whatever I have to do in order to keep you safe."

Brighton was growing increasingly worried, no matter what he said. "Atty," she said softly, "do… do you think that this might be Magnus? Would he not come in longships?"

"Possibly."

"Do you think he was told about me?"

Patrick kissed her hands again and then peeled her fingers off of him. "Even if he was, how would he know where you were?" he said. "I have thought the same thing but there are too many questions and not enough answers. I will go and find out who our visitors are and what they want. Meanwhile, you will stay here. You will not come out of the keep no matter what. Promise?"

Brighton nodded reluctantly. "I promise."

He winked at her, kissed her, and headed for the door, grabbing at his father as he went. "Come along," he said to Hector and Alec, still with their wives. "We have an army to greet."

The men filtered out of the keep, with Hector pausing to ensure the keep entry was shut and properly bolted by the women. When he was satisfied, he ran after the others, who had joined up with the incoming knights at this point. Kieran, Paris, Scott, Troy, and Apollo had entered the vast bailey of Berwick and they met William and Patrick and the others in the middle of the bailey, with hugs and handshakes going all around.

It was a moment of bonding, of reaffirming ties and friendships as one battle passed but another one possibly loomed. These were the actions of men who had faced death and lived to tell the tale, and seeing an unharmed colleague was a welcome sight, indeed. As initial small talk bounced around, Patrick sent a soldier running for his knights. He wanted his men in on any discussions that would take place. Shortly thereafter, he could see his knights heading towards them from different directions – Anson from the Douglas Tower, Colm and Damien from the wall. Now, all of the men were gathered and Patrick held up his hands, emitting a sharp whistle between his teeth to quiet down the throng.

"Gentle knights," he said, loud enough for all to hear. "There is a great deal to do and little time to accomplish it. It seems that unexpected visitors have arrived and we must ensure that the castle is fortified against them. Anson, you will man the Douglas Tower with as many men as it will hold. I think we have had upwards of three hundred men in it before, so you may take as many men as you need from the incoming army to hold it. Uncle Paris, is that acceptable?"

Paris, standing next to William and listening to Patrick rather proudly, nodded. "It is. Take what you need."

Patrick continued. "Damien, do the same with the donjon. Fill it with men so that anyone attempting to breach it will not have a chance to enter." He looked at Colm, Hector, and Apollo, pointing at them. "You three man the walls. Hector, you have command. Fill the battlements with archers and men with long spears. I want projectiles on the walls."

"Can we use Northwood archers, Papa?" Hector asked his father.

Paris waved him on. "Take them."

With that matter settled, Patrick turned to the remaining men – Alec, Kieran, Paris, Scott, Troy, and his father. "Alec, I want you and my brothers in command of the bailey. See that the men are organized and prepared for anything that might come." Then, he turned to the three older knights. "You three will come with me. I intend to head down to the jetty where the Northmen are docking. I will greet them personally and I would like you with me."

Alec spoke out. "Why would you go down to the jetty?" he wanted to know. "We do not know why they are here, Atty. Any minute, screaming barbarians could be streaming from their ships and onto our shores. You would chance being caught in that rush?"

Patrick held up a hand to beg the man's patience. "I have been thinking about this," he said. "Truthfully, if they were going to attack us right away, they could have already done it. They could have used the fog to their advantage, docked downriver, and rushed Berwick. But… they did not. No hint of attack at all, which leads me to believe they may not be here simply to fight. It seems to me that their actions have been peaceful until now."

There was truth to his statement but it was clear some of the other knights didn't agree. "They could be attempting to lure us out," Troy suggested, unhappy with his brother risking himself. "I would not go down to the river if I were you."

Patrick lifted his big shoulders at the man. "So we simply sit here and make no attempt at contact?" he asked. "That makes no sense, Troy. We must discover why they are here. The wall to the jetty is fortified, as are the towers. Unless they want to scale a twenty-foot wall, they cannot climb up to where I am going to be. I will speak to them from the safety of the Water Tower."

"Patrick is right," William said, eyeing the dubious collection of knights. "Contact must be made. Moreover, they could have attacked the moment they entered the mouth of the river but they did not. It, therefore, stands to reason that their purpose might not be violence. The only way to find out is to engage in dialogue."

The great Wolfe had spoken, so the younger knights seemed to lose some of their doubt. Still, there was some lingering concern. "Do they even speak our language, Uncle William?" Apollo asked. "How will they know what is said?"

William shrugged. "A good deal can be said with smiles and gestures."

"Or swords and fists," Alec muttered, disgruntled at the whole situation.

Some of the knights chuckled at Alec's response, including Patrick. "Not to worry, Alec," Patrick said. "If it seems as if they are aggressive, then I will retreat to the castle and we will lock it up tight. Have faith that I will not do anything foolish."

There wasn't much more to say to that. Alec still wasn't in full agreement with Patrick's actions but he had the respect not to say so. Damien and Anson began to turn away, to head to the towers they were tasked with protecting, but Patrick stopped them.

"Wait," he said. He hesitated a moment. "There is something else. As many of you may or may not know, my wife is the bastard of Magnus, King of the Norse. It has occurred to me that somehow, someway, these longships could be related to that. I have no idea how they would even know to come to Berwick or how Magnus even knows he has a bastard daughter, but I must consider the possibility that these Northmen are related to that. I would be remiss if I did not tell you my thoughts on the matter."

That seemed to put an entirely new light on the situation. It was clear that no one, save Patrick, had really considered that. Standing next to his son, William scratched his chin.

"Not knowing the circumstances of her conception, I cannot comment," he said. "But as a father myself, I cannot imagine not knowing that I had a child somewhere in this world."

"Then you believe he knows?" Patrick asked.

William shrugged. "As I said, I do not know the circumstances surrounding her conception," he said, "but I suppose we shall soon find out what this is all about."

There was no more reason to speculate now. The time for answers had come. As the knights disbursed to go about their duties, Patrick headed for the Western Tower and its fortified gate that led down a long and protected staircase on top of the wall, which ended up in the Water Tower down next to the river. It was a steep staircase, slippery at times, and Patrick had more than a few men injured on it. Just as they reached the fortified gate, Patrick came to a halt.

"You can see what is happening from here," he said to his father, Paris, and Kieran. "I will go down alone to see if I can determine why they are here. You three will wait here."

The three older knights didn't even respond. Suddenly, they were shoving past Patrick, nearly bowling him out of the way as they began taking the stairs down to the jetty. Patrick was left bringing up the rear, frustrated that the old men would not do as he asked. Truth be told, he had a bit of Alec's concern in him. What if this was all a trap? If it was, he wanted to be the only one affected by it. He didn't want his father and uncles involved.

But the old knights had other ideas. They were not about to let him go at it alone.

As the group descended the stairs to the Water Tower, the top of which sat nearly twenty feet above the riverbank, they could see all four longships now neatly arranged along the shore. Men were out of the ships, making sure they were grounded enough so they would not float away on the rise of the tide. It was a very curious sight to see the Northmen walking the shore of the river, shouting to one another in their strange language.

It was also a bit concerning.

When they were about halfway down the stairs, the Northmen began noticing the knights and the shouts grew in earnest. They began pointing at the men upon the wall, and more men came up on the decks of the ships, looking to see what was going on. By the time the knights reached the bottom of the stairs, they paused to simply watch the activity. It seemed as if there was a good deal going on but they couldn't figure out if it was delight or anger.

"What do you suppose has them so excited?" Paris muttered, leaning in to William. "They are either thrilled to see us or eager to cut our heads off."

William was baffled by the behavior as well. "They have not produced any weapons," he said. "As long as they do not, I will assume they are happy to make new friends."

Paris rolled his eyes, completely in doubt of what William was saying, but he kept his mouth shut. Meanwhile, Patrick pushed through to the front of the group and made his way to the edge of the Water Tower where he could clearly see the shore below. Protected by the parapet, he peered between the crenellations.

"It does not look as if they have brought hundreds of men with them," he said, scrutinizing the men, the ships, and searching for any concealed weapons. "In fact, it does not look as if there are more than one hundred."

William, Paris, and Kieran were watching as well. "They could have more men below decks," Kieran said. "Or there could be more longships coming."

That was a distinct possibility. They continued watching as several Northmen came towards the Water Tower, a group of them in fact, and William suddenly pointed.

"Look, there," he said, trying to point but not wanting the Northmen to see it. "See the man in the ecclesiastical robes? They have a monk with them."

Patrick, Paris, and Kieran all jockeyed for better positions to see what William was talking about and they quite clearly saw a very small man with his hair cut in the *tonsure* style, wearing rough woolen robes. He was surrounded by Northmen but one man in particular had him by the arm, pulling him towards the tower. As Patrick and the older knights watched curiously, the man thrust the monk to the forefront.

The monk was a tiny and slender man, not particularly old, but frail looking from poor nutrition and, perhaps, a sickening trip across the sea. He seemed to be asking questions of the men around him, evidently quite nervous, until one man thumped him on the shoulder and pointed to the Water Tower where the English were huddled. It was a hint and the monk took it.

"I am Able," he said, his thin voice quivering as he yelled. "I have been brought to translate for these men who do not speak your language."

Patrick looked at his father with great surprise and curiosity before calling back. "Who are they?" he boomed. "Why have they come?"

Overhead, gulls screamed, flying over the riverbanks in search of a meal now that the fog had lifted. But their cries startled the monk. He cringed as the birds flew over before answering.

"I was sent from Coldingham to find the king of the Northmen," the monk said, wringing his hands and clearly in distress. "I had a missive for Magnus. It took me weeks to travel to the land of the Danes, and many water crossings, but I came to him and gave him the missive from Mother Prioress of Coldingham Priory. But Magnus would not permit me to leave. He said that I must come with him to Berwick to seek his child, a daughter. He has come in search of her. Do you know where I may find her?"

Patrick felt as if he'd been hit by a load of stones, thousands of pounds bearing down on him, crushing his chest, rendering him unable to breathe. He actually stumbled back, against the wall, turning to his father with a look of utter astonishment. He was as pale as the mist that had so recently lifted.

"It *is* him!" he gasped. "God's Bones… my suspicions were correct!"

William was only mildly less astonished, his years and experience giving him the ability to be more logical about the situation. Still, he was having difficulty grasping it as well.

Magnus had come!

"Jesus," he hissed. "'Tis true. My God, how astonishing. The mother prioress sent him word? Why, in God's name, would she do that if she was in collusion with her brother to murder your wife?"

Patrick didn't have an answer. Taking a deep breath, he struggled for calm, feeling Paris' hand on his back in a comforting gesture as he turned to the monk once again.

"Let me understand this plainly," he called back. "The mother prioress of Coldingham Priory sent you with a missive for Magnus?"

The monk nodded. "It was a missive that told Magnus his daughter was at Berwick and in danger," he said. "He seeks his daughter and is prepared to pay for her freedom. If you will not accept his money, then he will burn your city and destroy your castle. He has told me to tell you this."

Patrick wasn't any less confused than he had initially been but his shock had cooled into great bewilderment. He shook his head, baffled, as he turned to his father.

"The mother prioress sent word to Magnus that his daughter was in *danger*?" he repeated, hoping his father could help him make some sense of it. "Why would she do that?"

William couldn't even begin to guess. "I do not know," he said. "But, clearly, she knew that Bridey had been taken to Berwick. That must be how Richard Gordon came into the information."

It made some sense but Patrick was still greatly confused. "So she sends Magnus word of the situation? Possibly to have her returned?"

"You will have to ask him."

Patrick knew that. He turned his attention back to the monk. "Why did Mother Prioress send Magnus the missive?" he asked. "And what made her think Magnus' daughter was here?"

The monk shook his head. "I do not know, my lord," he said. "Is the daughter here at Berwick?"

Patrick stared at the monk for a moment. Then, he turned away and headed towards the stairs that led down to the entry level of the Water Tower. William, Paris, and Kieran followed.

"Where are you going?" William demanded.

Patrick paused at the top of the stairs, reaching for the set of keys that was always kept in a small niche at the top. "I am going to speak to Magnus face to face," he said. "This is not something I wish to shout for all men to hear. Magnus will hear the situation from my own lips, face to face."

William grabbed him when he was halfway down the stairs. "Nay, Patrick," he said sternly. "It is not safe for you to do this. They may take you hostage."

Patrick pulled away from his father, gently but firmly. "If they take me hostage, then I have you to negotiate my release."

He was already to the first gate, unlocking the enormous bolt. From behind, Paris grabbed his arm again. "Patrick, listen to your father," he said. "This is not a good idea. You do not know what these men will do."

Patrick pulled his arm from Paris' grip, pushed open the gate, and then suddenly shoved all three men back onto the stairs. Paris actually fell backwards and into Kieran, and the action was enough to send all of them off balance. Quickly, while they were stumbling around, Patrick locked the gate so that the men couldn't follow him further.

"I am sorry," he said sincerely, looking at the panicked faces of his father and uncles, "but this is something I must do myself. They have come for my wife and they will not have her. I must explain that to them as a man would. Isn't that what you told me when you instructed me to speak to Henry face to face on an important matter, Da? You were correct. It was the right thing to do. I showed Henry my respect and now I intend to do the same to Magnus. He will understand I am honorable and that I do not fear him. He will also understand that I have married his daughter and she will not be returned to him."

William heard his words echoed in Patrick's statement, a statement of honor that had now come back to haunt him. But he couldn't stand the fact that his brave, beautiful son was now heading out to meet with Northmen alone, a herd of them who could quite easily take him hostage. Imploringly, he reached through the iron bars, trying to grasp at Patrick.

"Atty, nay," he breathed. "Come back in here and we shall handle this together, rationally. I cannot return to your mother and tell her that I let you go to your death!"

Patrick smiled faintly. "You will not have to," he assured him softly. But his smile quickly faded. "Listen to me and listen well; no matter what happens to me, you will not give them Bridey. Not under any circumstances."

There was panic in William's eyes. "Patrick, I cannot –!"

"Promise me!"

William was beside himself. "I swear it," he swallowed hard. "They shall never have her. But, please… please let me come with you."

Patrick's smile was back. His pale green eyes glimmered at his father, at his Uncle Paris and Uncle Kieran. Men he loved too deeply for words.

"You have taught me well, all of you," he said softly. "Do not worry for me. Everything you have taught me in my life has brought me to this moment and I love you all dearly. I take the best of you with me. I will not fail, I swear it."

With that, he turned to the second gate and unlocked it as William watched with his heart in his throat.

"Atty…."

William didn't finish his sentence as Patrick threw open the second gate and marched forth into the bright sunlight beyond.

CHAPTER TWENTY-ONE

THE NORTHMEN WERE surprised to see him.

Patrick could tell by the looks on their faces, staring at him in shock as he came through the Water Tower gate, moving towards the collection of Northmen fearlessly. He intended to show them what English courage was made of. A few of them backed away but several stood their ground, watching him suspiciously as he walked steadily towards them.

Patrick knew he gave off an incredibly imposing vision, as tall as he was, and he used that to his advantage. He liked to see the wariness in their eyes as they gazed upon a massive English knight. His focus moved to the monk.

"Where is Magnus?" he asked. "I would speak with him."

The monk was visibly cowering from him. After a moment, he turned back to a man behind him and spoke to the man in Latin; Patrick recognized it. He'd spent enough time in church and in mass that he could understand the language. *Magnus enim qui petit…*

He asks for Magnus.

The man the monk had spoken to turned to still other men behind him and began speaking in their language. Men were shaking their head, pointing, clearly in some kind of disagreement. While that was going on, Patrick spoke to the monk once more.

"You," he said. "Are you from Coldingham?"

The monk nodded. "I am, my lord."

Patrick's eyes flicked to the whispering, hissing Northmen standing behind him. "You delivered the missive to Magnus personally?"

"I did, my lord."

"Did you see the missive Mother Prioress gave you?"

"I saw the missive because I had to translate it for them, my lord."

Patrick's gaze was still on the Northmen, making sure someone didn't do something stupid like try to rush him. They seemed to be very agitated and he was cautious.

"I do not understand why Mother Prioress sent the missive in the first place," he said. "Did she tell you?"

"She did not, my lord."

Patrick pondered that for a moment. It seemed that the monk didn't know much more than what he'd already told him. He took a step closer to the tiny man.

"Is Magnus standing behind you in that group of men?" he asked quietly.

The monk closed his eyes, tightly, as if Patrick had just asked him something horrible. But he nodded sharply, once, and that was it. Patrick didn't press him further because he could see how terrified the man was, but he needed to get a message across to Magnus. If the man wasn't going to be brave enough to show himself, then Patrick would just have to tell everyone what he needed to say and hope that Magnus had the courage to step forward. Reaching out, he grasped the monk by the shoulder.

"I have something to say to Magnus and you will translate for me," he said. "Does Magnus understand Latin?"

The monk was clearly frightened. "Nay, he does not," he said. Then, he pointed to the group of men who had now noticed that Patrick had pulled the monk away from them. "That man, in the red robes, is a holy man from the land of the Danes. He understands Latin, so I translate into Latin and then he translates it into their language."

Patrick could see the system they had going, clever if not entirely efficient. "Then you tell that holy man that he is to translate what I say. Do it now."

The monk spoke in his trembling voice. "Quod est loqui Anglorum Magnus."

The Englishman must speak to Magnus.

The red-robed holy man looked confused but, prompted by the monk, he relayed the words in their language. That seemed to have everyone's attention and Patrick didn't delay. He had a great deal he needed to say and he wasn't going to waste any time.

"You will tell Magnus this," he said. "Tell him that the danger his daughter was in was from the mother prioress herself. She plotted to have his daughter murdered and I saved her from that plot. His daughter is in excellent health and she is now my wife. I married her. Tell him that this is my castle and I am an honorable warrior. He needn't fear for his daughter or her safety."

The monk's eyes widened at the shocking information and hesitated to translate, but Patrick squeezed his shoulder with a trencher-sized hand. "Also know that I understand Latin," he rumbled. "If you do not tell him exactly what I told you, they will have to drag the river for your body. No Northman is going to save you from my wrath."

The monk went ashen. Turning to the group, he relayed what Patrick had told him, verbatim, and then Patrick could see the reaction on their faces when the holy man in the red robes related it in their language. More hissing and whispering went on when the man in the red robes said something to the monk, who turned to Patrick.

"Magnus says that a woman of God would never do such a thing," he said. "My lord, I cannot believe it myself. Mother Prioress is beyond reproach."

Patrick lifted a dark eyebrow. "Did you see the Scots surrounding my castle when you came upriver?"

The monk's brow furrowed with both thought and confusion. "I heard the men say that there was a battle at the castle," he said. "They saw something but, alas, I did not."

Patrick pointed a finger to the Northmen. "Tell them that the men they saw around the castle were Scots from Clan Gordon, led by a man named Richard Gordon. He is the brother of the mother prioress. They had come to take Magnus' daughter because they wanted to kill her. I believe that is proof enough. Tell them this."

He snapped the last three words and the monk jumped, relaying that to the red-robed holy man who then, in turn, relayed it to the Northmen. More disbelief, more hissing, but there wasn't the suspicion in their expressions that there had been before. Suspicion was transforming into something else; Patrick hoped it was understanding. The monk, huddled and trembling and still in Patrick's grip, shook his head.

"It does not seem possible," he said. "But… but I did see Richard Gordon at Coldingham before I was sent to deliver the missive to Magnus."

Now it was Patrick's turn to be surprised. "You did?" he asked, trying not to show so much astonishment in front of the Northmen. "Was it *after* Magnus' daughter had been abducted?"

"Aye, my lord."

"Do you know why Richard was there?"

"I do not know, my lord, but they came to see the mother prioress."

"Was that an unusual event? What I mean to ask is if Richard Gordon was a frequent visitor."

"Not too frequent, my lord. We did not see him often."

Then it was a visit, in Patrick's mind, that was not a coincidence and he felt more relief at that moment than he ever thought possible. Richard Gordon's presence at Coldingham, witnessed by the monk no less, was confirmation of everything he'd been speculating all along, everything that Tommy Orry had told them – Richard Gordon and Mother Prioress were in collusion. In fact, Patrick felt a good deal of validation in that moment.

"Then you have your proof," he said. "Richard Gordon came to Coldingham to plot with Mother Prioress to kill Magnus' daughter. Go on and tell them."

The monk did. From what Patrick could understand, he told the Northmen, in Latin, of his own experience seeing Richard Gordon at Coldingham right before he'd left to deliver the missive to Magnus and that, combined with what Patrick was telling them, seemed to convince them that Patrick wasn't lying. At least, they weren't looking at him so guardedly any longer.

Now, there was a basis for an understanding.

But Patrick wasn't satisfied with this level of communication. Understanding or no, he had come to speak with Magnus and that was what he intended to do. It was time to bring the man out.

His fingers dug into the monk's shoulder again.

"Tell Magnus that he shows a lack of respect to hide from me behind his men," he said, knowing full well that he could possibly be stirring a hornet's nest. "I came to speak to him and that is what I will do. Tell him that I consider his actions cowardly."

The monk's eyes widened but he dutifully relayed the message to the holy man, who relayed it to the Northmen. Just as Patrick had hoped, the group became indignant and the hissing was now directed at him. But Patrick stood his ground, bracing his legs apart and folding his enormous arms across his chest. At the moment, he did not regret saying such a thing but that might change if the group charged him. He hoped he was prepared but he wanted to give the illusion that he didn't much care what they tried to do. He was ready for them.

At least, he hoped so.

Patrick wasn't really sure how long he stood there. Men were whispering loudly, pointing to him, and arguing with each other. Just when he was certain he'd have to make an even more offensive statement about Magnus' bravery, a man pushed through the crowd and walked towards him.

Patrick studied the man closely. He was moderately tall, older, with a crown of graying hair and a handsome, if not weathered, face. But the eyes… the moment Patrick looked the man in the face, he recognized those eyes.

Brighton's eyes.

The man smiled broadly.

"You speak bravely, *Engelsk,*" he said. "You understand that I had to judge you first. I had to hear what you were to say to me."

Patrick's eyes narrowed in surprise. "You speak my language."

The man nodded. "I do," he said, although it was with a heavy Nordic accent. "I learned, years ago, when a young woman came to my village as a hostage for peace. A young woman I loved very much. She taught me her language so that I could communicate with her."

The flame of recognition burned brightly in Patrick's mind. "Juliana."

The man nodded, as if the mere mention of the name was pure music to his ears. "Juliana de la Haye," he said reverently. "What did you mean when you said the mother prioress meant to murder my daughter?"

Magnus. Even though the man hadn't formally introduced himself, there was no doubt who Patrick was speaking with and he unfolded his arms to make his body language less hostile.

"Exactly that, my lord," he said. "Years ago, the mother prioress was raped by a man from Clan Haye. When Juliana brought your daughter to the priory as an infant, the mother prioress plotted with her brother, Richard Gordon, to murder her in vengeance against the Haye when she came of age. They were just carrying out that plan when I rescued your daughter and brought her here to Berwick. I do not know why the mother prioress sent you a missive telling you that your daughter was in danger, but I can assure you that she is not. She is my wife and she is well-loved."

Magnus' gaze lingered on Patrick. His eyes were even the same color as Brighton's. He was actually rather young, younger than Patrick imagined him to be, but he also remembered that Magnus had been a young prince when Brighton had been conceived. Patrick gazed steadily at the man, wondering what was going through his mind about the entire situation.

He was soon to find out.

"I was well aware that Juliana was pregnant with my child those years ago," he said. "Juliana was sent back to Scotland because of it. It was unfortunate, truly, because I adored her. I was devastated when she was sent home, but before she left we agreed that if our child was a boy, she would name him Eric. If it was a female, she would be named Kristiana."

Patrick had heard the name Kristiana from Sister Acha. "She has gone by the name Brighton de Favereux all of these years," he said. "I do not know how she came about with that name, considering she is from Clan Haye, but that is what she has been called. Everyone calls her Bridey."

Magnus was back to smiling as he listened to the naming of his child. "De Favereux was Juliana's grandmother's family name," he said. "She told me that once. A great Norman family. But Brighton? That I do not know. I am sure whatever the reason, it was to protect my daughter from those who might seek to harm her. I see that in the case of the mother prioress, it did not do enough."

Patrick shook his head. "It did not," he agreed. "In fact, I have been ordered by King Henry to arrest the woman for her crimes and bring her to justice in York. I also plan to take an army into Scotland and punish Richard Gordon for his part in the murder scheme. I will not rest until all threats against my wife have been eliminated. If you came here because you were concerned for your daughter's safety, then I assure you I will do everything possible to ensure she is always safe."

Magnus simply nodded, his gaze still moving over Patrick as if dissecting the man. It was more than curiosity; it was scrutiny with no end. In fact, Patrick couldn't feel completely comfortable with the conversation because of the way Magnus was looking at him. He was about to invite Magnus into Berwick to feast simply because it seemed like the thing to do, considering the man was Brighton's father, when Magnus finally spoke.

"It took the monk from Coldingham weeks to find me but only a few days to sail here," he said. "I came to take my daughter back to my home. She is a princess, you know."

"I know."

"I have even selected a husband for her."

"But she is already married."

Magnus shrugged. "I know that now," he said. "But I did not choose you."

Patrick was starting to think the conversation was not turning in his favor. It was simply the way Magnus said it – *I did not choose you.* Something told Patrick that the situation was about to turn sour and he braced himself.

"I realize that, my lord, but considering the circumstances, I did what I had to do," he said. "My own father did not even give me permission. I married Bridey because I loved her. Being that you loved her mother, I am sure you can understand."

The warmth was fading from Magnus' face. "I understand," he said. "But you must understand that I must have the very best husband for my daughter. I must know that the man she is married to is the best warrior in all the land. As the daughter of a king, that is what she deserves."

Patrick could see that he was going to have to list his credentials, something he rarely did. But in this case, he did it without hesitation. "My father is William de Wolfe, otherwise known as The Wolfe of the Border. He is Baron Kilham and his lands include Castle Questing, the largest castle on the border," he said. "I, too, have earned a reputation. I am called Nighthawk for my prowess in battle and I was recently offered the position of Lord Protector to King Henry. With that offer, I was given Penton Castle as well as the title Lord Westdale. I assure you that I am a worthy man, my lord."

Magnus didn't reply immediately but Patrick knew he would; he could see the thoughts rolling around in the man's head, reflected in his glittering eyes.

"Are you willing to prove it?" he asked after a moment.

Patrick didn't hesitate. "Aye."

"You will fight for the woman you love?"

"Aye."

The humor was back in Magnus' expression. "Good," he said. "Because you will have to. I brought the man with me that I have selected for my daughter. So if you want to keep her, you will have to kill him. He has been looking forward to marrying her so you have no choice in the matter."

Now, the situation became quite serious. Patrick hadn't expected anything like this but he wasn't about to back down. So Magnus wanted proof of his love for Brighton, did he? He wanted to know if the best man had, indeed, married his daughter? Patrick was more than willing to prove it, to do what he had to do in order to show Magnus, and the world, that he loved Brighton enough to fight for her. He would kill any threat against her and any man who wanted to marry her.

Aye, he was more than willing. And the more he thought about it, the more furious he became. His eyes narrowed as he looked at Magnus.

"Then bring the victim to me," he hissed. "I will show you what an English knight can do. And I will show you that I am the best man for your daughter."

Magnus' smile broadened. He rather liked the massive knight with the limitless confidence. But the knight was going to have a fight on his hands; as big as he was, Magnus hoped the Englishman had enough strength to live through what he was about to face.

Magnus took a few steps towards the men still gathered behind him, saying something to them in their language. Based on the orders Magnus had evidently relayed, a few men ran for the first longship, the one that seemed to be the biggest, and a couple of them disappeared down into the lower deck.

Patrick, meanwhile, stormed back over to the Water Tower where his father and Paris and Kieran were now looking down at him from the top of the tower. When they saw Patrick heading in their direction, they ran down the steps to the locked gates below, waiting impatiently for Patrick to unlock them both. When Patrick finally opened the second gate, the older knights pushed through and surrounded him.

"What happened?" William demanded.

Patrick could see the fear in his father's eyes. "The man I was speaking with was Magnus," he said. "I explained the situation to him. We spoke of Bridey and of her mother, Juliana."

It sounded harmless enough and William breathed a sigh of relief. "Was that all?"

Patrick shook his head. "That is *not* all," he said. "Although Magnus seems like a reasonable man, he did not realize his daughter was married and I completely understand that. However, not knowing she was married, he brought a man along with him to be her husband. His plan was to take Bridey back to his kingdom."

A look of concern spread across the older knights. "But he knows you have married her?" Paris asked.

"He knows."

"And what did he say?"

Patrick made sure he was looking at his father when he answered. "He told me that if I love her, I have to fight for her. A battle to the death."

William wasn't pleased. "Christ," he hissed. "I cannot imagine this is a good thing, Patrick. You will end up killing the man Magnus selected to marry his daughter. He is more than likely a young lord, or even an old lord, surely someone with some status who cannot compete with you in combat. What will you do if you are faced with a frightened young lord or, worse, a frightened old man?"

Patrick shrugged. "It was Magnus who demanded the fight," he said. "I am simply following his command. Come with me; let me introduce you to him. As I said, he seems like a reasonable man. Mayhap you can talk him out of having me slay one of his lords."

William was more than willing to meet Magnus and evaluate the situation. Therefore, Patrick headed back to the riverbank followed by his father, Paris, and Kieran. The old knights felt much better now that they weren't locked away as Patrick dealt with the Northmen alone. Now, it was the four of them. Much better odds.

As the group drew close to the collection of men and boats, Magnus noticed the three older knights with interest. When Patrick came close enough, he began the introductions.

"My lord, this is my father, Sir William de Wolfe," he said. Then, he indicated the other two. "These men are his brothers-in-arms, Sir Paris de Norville and Sir Kieran Hage. Good men, this is Magnus, King of the Norse."

William bowed his head politely to the king. "It is an honor, my lord."

He wasn't really expecting a reply, unaware that Magnus spoke his language, but was surprised when Magnus answered. "Are you the man called The Wolfe?"

"I am, my lord."

Magnus looked at him a moment longer before gesturing to Patrick. "I like your son," he said. "What is it about my daughter that you found so offensive that you could not give the man permission to marry her?"

William remained calm but he was secretly ready to punch Patrick in the mouth for telling the Northman such things. Now he found that he had to defend himself.

"Your daughter is a lovely, bright, and delightful woman, my lord," he replied. "I only had reservations in the very beginning because she was a ward of the church and we did not have permission for the marriage."

"Was permission ever given?"

"Nay, my lord."

Magnus looked at Patrick and grinned. "Then you must have wanted to marry her very badly."

Patrick simply nodded. Still grinning, Magnus' only reply was to shake his head as if in complete understanding of the impetuousness of youth. He had been young and in love, once, himself. There was almost a frivolity in his manner as he gestured to the group of men behind him, with the longships beyond.

"Then you can prove how much you wish to keep her," he said, turning to the men behind him. "Elof!"

Patrick, William, Paris, and Kieran watched as the group of men behind Magnus shuffled around and then finally parted, revealing the longship behind them. Something was moving below deck; they could all hear it. Like great footsteps or the beat of a drum, it was something rhythmic and menacing. It was quite strange, really, and the English knights watched with interest as men began to appear from the lower deck of the ship. Two men emerged, carrying shields and swords, followed by a man.

But it wasn't *any* man.

A warrior easily the size of Patrick emerged from the bowels of the ship, carrying a wooden shield and a short, broad sword with him. The banging noises they had been hearing had been the warrior beating his shield with his sword as he walked. He was grunting, too, working himself up into a fighting frenzy. When he finally came out onto the deck, the English knights got a good look at just how big the man really was; he was taller than Patrick. And heavier.

And meaner.

"Christ," William hissed, standing next to Patrick. "Is *this* the man you must fight?"

Patrick didn't have a ready answer because he was fairly shocked himself. Truthfully, he found something ironically hilarious about the situation. At seven inches over six feet, he had always been the tallest, broadest man in the room. He'd intimidated, squashed, and even sometimes bullied lesser men when the mood struck him. He'd never run into anyone as big as he was or as tough. But the half-naked warrior making his way off the ship had to be the biggest bastard he'd ever seen. He could hardly believe his eyes.

"Evidently," he finally muttered.

William was genuinely trying not to react at the sight of the gargantuan warrior but, beside him, he could hear groaning and he knew it was coming from Paris. The man had never been very good at concealing his emotions.

"William," he whispered. "Create a diversion. Give Atty a chance to run for his life!"

William glanced at him. "*You* create a diversion," he countered. "Throw yourself at the man. Sacrifice yourself so that Patrick may live."

Paris shook his head. "He would turn me into pulp," he said. "Kieran, you still fancy yourself the most powerful warrior in the north. Do something!"

Kieran was watching the colossal Norse warrior as the man came onto the riverbank. "Not me," he said. "You keep telling me I am an old man and no longer able to best the younger men. For once, I am going to listen to you."

The words were softly uttered between the three older knights, the same camaraderie and levity they had always had when facing a serious situation. It was simply the way they dealt with such things. But the more William got a look at the muscular warrior dressed in skins and breeches, as barbaric as he had ever seen a man, the more fear he began to feel for his son.

But he couldn't let Patrick know it. That was the main reason he was willing to jest in the face of such terror. Patrick had to believe he could beat this man and William would not take that away from him. To say anything negative, or fearful, would be to cast doubt on Patrick's skills as a warrior, and William wouldn't dream of doing anything like that. Therefore, he turned to his son, turning his head slightly so his voice couldn't be heard by the Northmen.

"This should be a simple thing," he muttered. "I would suggest you simply let the man wear himself out. Let him chase you if he must; fight him but do not fight hard. Then, when he has exhausted himself, strike and strike hard. Let this be a battle of wit, Patrick, and not brawn. You are smarter than he is; prove it."

Patrick could hear the confidence in his father's voice but he knew, deep down, that William was frightened for him. Truth be told, Patrick was a bit wary about what he had to face. But he knew his love for Brighton would keep him going, feeding his strength in a way it had never been fed before. All he had to do was think of his wife at the mercy of this animal and he was seized with rage and determination. He was the only thing that stood between Brighton and this monster.

He had to win, no matter what the cost.

"This is the man I have selected to marry my daughter," Magnus said, cutting into Patrick's thoughts. He gestured to the enormous warrior. "This is Elof Red Beard, Slayer of Beasts. He has killed many an enemy and has earned his place at my table. By gifting him my daughter, I honor him for his devotion to me. He is a man of honor but also a man of anger, and he wants what you have. If you do not want him to have it, then you will have to kill him."

Patrick was more than ready to do what he needed to do. "As you say, my lord," he said, his eyes never leaving Elof as the man stood there and glared at him. "What are the rules of this combat?"

Magnus gestured to the men who had brought the swords and shields from the lower deck of the longship. The men swiftly ran forward and dumped the weaponry at Magnus' feet.

"Each of you will be given three shields and a sword," he said. "When a shield is broken or smashed, the fight will cease and you will retrieve another shield. When all shields are smashed, the battle will continue on until one of you is dead. All combat must take place right here in front of the ship, so you may not run. You must face your opponent. Those are the only rules, Sir Patrick. Do you agree?"

Patrick nodded. "I do."

"When you are prepared, we will begin."

Patrick stepped back, eyeing Elof and seeing that the man wore no armor while he had his mail on and his heavy tunics. Quickly, he turned to his father.

"Help me remove my mail," he said.

William looked at him with concern. "But why?" he asked. "Patrick, you were trained to fight with protection on. If you remove it, then you are removing your chance of emerging from this unscathed."

Patrick began pulling his cowl off and Kieran, standing behind him, began to help. "I am handicapped by the weight of it," he said. "Look at Elof; he is wearing no protection at all. That means he will be more agile than I am. If I wear all of this protection, I will be more vulnerable to his attacks because I will not be able to move swiftly enough."

As he began to untie his tunic with Kieran's assistance, Paris stepped in to help as well. "He is correct, William," he said quietly. "In order to fight that beast on his own terms, he will have to level the playing field. A knight on foot is a lethargic creature and you know it. He cannot go in fighting as an armored man if his opponent has none. It will not make this a fair fight."

William reluctantly understood. As knights, they were trained to use all of the protection available to them but the Northmen didn't fight that way. Their weapons were cruder, their tactics barbaric, but they were still just as effective and terrifying. If Patrick was going to fight on the Northman's terms, and win, then he had to fight like a Northman. With that in mind, William began helping his son strip down.

The tunic came off followed by the mail coat, a padded under tunic and another tunic beneath that. When Patrick was finally stripped to the waist, left only in his breeches and boots, William went over to where the weapons and shields were laid out and selected a weapon for his son. Then he picked up a shield and carried it over to him.

"Since you are going to be in close quarters fighting, your broadsword will do you no good," he said. "This sword is well-made and the style of the pommel will provide some protection for your hand. If you do not like this sword, you may choose another. There are a few others they have brought forth."

With his broad chest and muscled arms gleaming beneath the midsummer sun, Patrick took hold of the sword, getting a feel for the weight of it. It was fairly lightweight and not anything like his enormous broadsword, but he would be able to move faster with it and strike faster with it.

"The craftsmanship is excellent," he said, inspecting it. "You have chosen wisely, Da."

William smiled weakly as he handed him the shield. "Remember what I told you," he said. "Let your opponent exhaust himself and then strike when he is too weak to fight back. Brains over brawn, Atty."

Patrick looked over his shoulder at Elof, who was huffing and puffing, working himself up into a sweat. "I doubt he will exhaust himself," he said casually, turning back to give his sword one last look-over. "He looks as if he eats small children for breakfast."

The humor was still there. That was good; it showed that Patrick wasn't feeling any real fear. Concern, perhaps, but not fear. It was time to begin.

"May God be with you," William muttered. "I will see you at the end."

Patrick looked at his father and, for the second time that day, felt inordinately sentimental towards the man. He knew his father was frightened for him and commended the man for not showing it. In the same situation, Patrick was quite sure he wouldn't have been so calm. Leaning forward, he kissed him on the forehead.

"Not to worry, Da," he said. "We will be roasting a Norse beast by sup tonight. But remember your promise to me."

"What was that?"

Patrick's humor left him and, for a split second, a flash of fear was in his eyes. But not for him; it was for his wife.

"You promised me that you will not let them take Bridey," he murmured. "If anything happens to me, you must hold true to that promise. If you do not, I will never forgive you."

With that, he turned and headed over to the riverbank where Magnus himself was overseeing the start of the battle. As William, Paris, and Kieran watched Patrick take position against his opponent, Kieran leaned in to William.

"You will not stand by while your son is killed, will you?" he asked quietly.

William, his eyes riveted on Patrick, shook his head. "Never," he murmured. "If it looks as if it is coming to that, I will intervene and I will kill anyone who gets in my way."

Kieran breathed a sigh of relief. "I was hoping you would say that," he said. "I will return to the castle and tell Bridey what is happening. It is her right to know."

"While you are at it, arm the knights and tell them to be ready. If I must intervene, I have a feeling the Norse will not take it well."

"We will be ready."

"Good."

As Kieran headed back to the castle, William found himself praying that this day wouldn't bring any death to him or to his family. Scared to death, he struggled not to show it.

CHAPTER TWENTY-TWO

"I-I WILL NOT let this happen!" Brighton was in tears. "Why did he agree to this? Why did *you* allow it?"

Kieran was trying very hard to keep the woman calm but he wasn't doing a good job of it. In fact, no one in the castle was calm about what was transpiring with Patrick, including Hector and Alec, who had converged on Kieran when the man had come back up from the Water Tower.

Kieran had been forced to tell them what was happening and that turned them into mad men, sending soldiers to call the knights away from their posts, bringing Scott and Troy on the run when they were told that Patrick was in a fight to the death against the man that Magnus had chosen to marry his daughter. The de Wolfe twins were in a fury over it, understanding it one minute and lamenting it the next.

But the worst reaction was yet to come. Brighton, informed that her husband was in the fight for his life, had no intention of remaining in the keep. Worse still, Katheryn and Evelyne agreed with her. The two sisters were weeping over Patrick's situation while Brighton, a usually congenial and sweet woman, had turned into a tempest. The trouble was, no one blamed her, least of all Kieran.

"It was his choice, Bridey," Kieran said, understanding a thing or two about agitated women because he had married one. "Those longships were, indeed, Magnus, your father, who had come to Berwick because he had received a missive from the mother prioress at Coldingham that his daughter – *you* – were in danger. He came here in good faith to save you, lass. What he did not expect was a happy daughter who was already married. He brought a husband he has chosen for you and, given the situation, Patrick chose to fight for you. He chose to prove to Magnus that he is the best husband for you."

Brighton was beside herself. It was too much confusing and terrifying information, leaving her struggling to process it all. The more she built it up in her mind, the more frightened she became.

"B-but I do not understand," she pleaded. "Mother Prioress sent a missive to my father? Why would she do such a thing?"

Kieran shook his head. "This we cannot know, lass. We have been trying to find an answer for the very same question."

Not only was Brighton alarmed, now she was baffled. Nothing about this situation made any sense to her. "A-and now Patrick must fight to keep me? This is madness!"

"Madness or not, it is his choice."

"B-but… *fight* for me? I am already his!"

Kieran sighed faintly, seeing that she didn't fully understand the situation. "And he intends to keep it that way," he said patiently. "You must understand something about men, Bridey. When something they love is threatened – a home, a wife, a king – they are compelled to protect it. To fight for it. This is no different from doing battle against Richard Gordon because the man wants to kill you. In this case, another man wishes to marry you. And Patrick will not permit that to happen."

Brighton was trying to understand; she truly was. But this manner of thinking was incredibly foreign to her. All she could see was that she was already Patrick's wife and for him to risk his life fighting off another man was lunacy.

She hated it.

"N-nay," she finally said, shaking her head. "I cannot allow this to happen!"

She started running for the keep entry but Kieran grabbed her before she could get away. "You cannot stop it," he insisted quietly, forcing her to stand still and listen. "It has already begun. If you go running down to the riverbank, you will distract Patrick and get him killed. Do you understand me? Seeing you or hearing your voice will distract him from defending his life in battle and that distraction will be deadly. Do you want to kill him?"

Brighton was looking at him fearfully, tears swimming in her big eyes now. "N-nay. Of course not."

"Then do not distract him. If you want to watch what is happening, I will not stop you. But keep silent." He paused, looking around him at the knights, the sisters, of Patrick. They were all in turmoil. "That goes for all of you. Watch if you will but if you utter a sound, you will kill him. Patrick cannot hear a sound from any of you."

While Katheryn and Evelyn were gazing at Kieran much as Brighton was, with tears in their eyes, the knights were far more somber. They understood exactly what Kieran was saying; they understood that distraction was deadly when it came to a battle. As the seriousness of Patrick's situation settled, Hector turned to his wife.

"You can watch from the keep if you have a notion to," he told her quietly. "You will be able to see from the top level. But I do not want the children to watch. They are too young to understand it."

Alec heard Hector and he, too, turned to his wife. "The boys are not to watch," he said. "In fact, I would prefer you remain with them. I will come to you when it is over."

Katheryn didn't like the sound of that at all. She clapped a hand over her mouth to keep from sobbing openly. "Please do not let anything happen to my brother," she whispered between her fingers. "Please, Alec."

Alec nodded solemnly, kissing her on the head and gently shooing her back up the stairs, back up to the sleeping chambers where the children were. Evelyn followed and, together, the pair made their way up the stairs, disappearing into the upper levels.

Hector and Alec stood at the bottom of the steps, watching until the women were gone. Then, they made their way over to Kieran and Brighton.

"I am going down to the Water Tower to watch," Hector said, his jaw ticking. "I will be fully armed. If it seems as if Patrick is in trouble, I will not hesitate to assist him, Uncle Kieran. I want to make sure we are clear on that."

Kieran nodded. "I know," he said. "William feels the same way. He asked me to tell the knights to arm themselves and await his command. He is not about to watch his son fight to his death, so we must be ready to help him."

Scott and Troy were standing behind Kieran and heard his command. Truth be told, they hadn't even formally met Brighton yet but now was not the time. There would be plenty of opportunity to get to know Patrick's wife later, but now, they were on a mission. They immediately headed to the armory to arm themselves even more than they already were, sending word to Colm and Damien, Anson and Apollo of what was transpiring. They were assembling a force for Patrick, a needed force to step in and save the man if necessary. Brighton watched the speed with which they were moving, impressing to her just how serious the situation was and the fact that they were as concerned about it as she was.

Understanding that there were men to intervene in Patrick's fight, Brighton was far calmer than she had been only seconds earlier. As long as men were willing to help her husband, then she was willing to believe that Patrick would make it out of this alive. But she had to go to him; she had to see what was happening. Even if she kept silent and he didn't know she was there, perhaps he would feel her spirit around him.

Her love.

She refused to believe that God had given her a taste of such happiness only to take it away.

"W-will you take me to watch?" she asked Kieran. "I swear to you that I will be silent."

Kieran was reluctant but, as he'd told William, he felt it was Brighton's right to know what was happening to her husband and to witness it. This was for her, after all. He had to admit that he felt terribly sorry for her. Gently, he took her hand.

"Come along, then," he said softly. "I will take you."

Brighton followed Kieran out into the sunlight; a glorious day revealed behind the lifting of the fog. He took her over to the gated portal that led out to the stairs down to the jetty. The Water Tower was at the end of those stairs and the moment she began to descend, she could see the longships and a large gathering of men on the riverbank. She could also hear the distinct sounds of a fight, steel against steel and men grunting with exertion.

Patrick fighting for his life.

Halfway down the steps, the sounds of a battle were having an effect upon her. She began to tremble, her stomach in knots because she knew the sounds were of Patrick trying not to be killed. Having been raised at a priory, praying was all Brighton knew. God listened, she was certain of it, but she prayed that He would never listened more so than right now. As she reached the bottom of the steps and began to head to the edge of the Water Tower to view the spectacle below, she found herself repeating a prayer for Patrick's protection over and over.

O My God, I adore Thee and I love Thee with all my heart. I thank Thee for having created me and for having watched over me this day. Pardon me for the evil I have done this day; and if I have done any good, deign to accept it. God, watch over my husband and deliver him from danger. May Thy grace be always with him and Your strength be within his sword. Protect him, O God, and let him live.

Amen.

WITH THE FIRST blow from Elof's sword across his wooden shield, Patrick knew he had met his match.

It wasn't just any blow; it was as if he'd been kicked by a horse. He thought that he'd been prepared for such a blow but the truth was that no amount of preparation could have prepared him for that. Elof went on the offensive first and the blow to Patrick's shield sent the man staggering backwards. And with that blow, the fight began in earnest.

It was evident early on that Elof had a tremendous amount of strength and Patrick was starting to hope that what his father said might actually be true; *let the man tire himself.* Considering the ferocity of Elof's attack, Patrick could see that the man was going full-force in the first few moments of the battle. Surely he couldn't keep it up forever. Perhaps Elof would, indeed, tire himself out, after all.

It was a hope Patrick clung to.

The first round was vicious because Patrick, unable to simply stand back and let a man beat on him, came back with equal force and hammered Elof so steadily that not only did his shield break, but Elof fell back into the crowd of Northman watching the fight. Victorious in the first bout, Patrick tried not to become arrogant about it. He made his way back to his corner of the battle area and stood there, shield and sword in hand, as Elof righted himself, tossed aside the broken shield, and picked up a second shield. When Elof was fully armed, he and Patrick charged at each other again.

The second clash of titans wasn't a simple thing. Elof pounded on Patrick's shield and then Patrick would return the favor. Patrick was coming to see that Elof really didn't have any tactics in a fight; he simply rushed him and tried to beat his brains out by smashing Patrick's shield repeatedly with his sword. For Patrick, that meant Elof wasn't thinking beyond the initial battle. So at that point, Patrick began to throw in some tactics of his own.

As William had said, wits would win the war.

After a particularly tough barrage from Elof, one that cracked Patrick's shield but didn't break it, Patrick charged Elof with a vengeance, forcing the man backwards. Patrick was close enough that he was able to get a foot in behind Elof and trip the man. Elof went down on his back, hard, and Patrick swiped the corner of his shield into Elof's face, clipping his nose. He then proceeded to use his feet on Elof, kicking the man brutally, but Elof was somehow able to roll to his knees and lurch to his feet. Bleeding from the nose and mouth, Elof attacked Patrick in a fury and ended up breaking his own shield.

Now, Elof was down to his last shield while Patrick still had his original shield in his hand. It was cracked but not broken. As the Northmen, and William and Paris, stood in a wide ring around the combatants, Elof once again went after Patrick, who dodged the man and tripped him once again. Elof went down, on his face this time, and Patrick threw aside his shield and sword and jumped on Elof's back, pinning him to the riverbank and putting both hands on back of the man's head, pushing his face into the dirt in an attempt to smother him.

Elof may not have been a particularly smart fighter, but he knew how to survive. As soon as he realized that Patrick was trying to suffocate him, he took a handful of sand and tossed it back into Patrick's face, getting it into Patrick's eyes. It was enough to stun Patrick so he loosened his grip and Elof was able to turn slightly and throw a big elbow into Patrick's belly. With sand in his eyes and the wind knocked out of him, Patrick staggered to his feet as Elof launched an offensive.

Blinded by the sand, Patrick didn't see Elof throw himself at him, but he certainly felt it. Elof hit him so hard that both men flew through the air, with Patrick landing on his backside and Elof landing on top of him. Then, the punches started to fly and, blinded by sand or not, Patrick wasn't going to let this beast get the upper hand. He grabbed his own handful of dirt and tossed it into Elof's face, causing the same type of reaction that Elof had caused in him. It was enough of a distraction for Patrick to throw a devastating blow into Elof's already-damaged nose. Elof toppled off of him and into the dirt. After that, it was an all-out brawl.

Patrick was perfectly at home using his fists and feet instead of a sword. Unfortunately, so was Elof. The punches flew furiously, each man landing some fairly seriously blows on the other. Patrick had been hit, hard, in the eye and in the jaw, and his lips were bleeding where his teeth had been forced into his lips. Elof, too, was bleeding fairly seriously from the nose and mouth and, soon enough, blood began to splatter the more they punched. It was turning into a bloodbath as red droplets sprayed on the spectators.

On and on it went, blow after blow, and soon Patrick had to admit that he was growing weary. The punch to his jaw had almost knocked him out so his ears were ringing badly and his balance was off. But he wasn't going to surrender, not in the least, and at one point, he threw his arms round Elof's neck, enough to force the man to the ground and nearly cause him to lose consciousness. Elof, however, threw a thumb into Patrick's eye and Patrick was forced to retreat.

Unfortunately for Patrick, being blinded in one eye caused him to miss a devastating left-handed blow from Elof that sent him right to the ground. The darkness of unconsciousness beckoned him but he fought it. He simply wasn't going to permit that to happen. If he did, he knew he'd be dead.

And then… he saw it.

The short sword he'd tossed away was just a few inches from his hand. He could see a way to end this confrontation, once and for all, because he didn't honestly think he could stand much more of the brutal pummeling. One of Elof's blows was like being kicked in the head by a horse. Any more of those and he wouldn't be able to fight off the unconsciousness. Therefore, he had to take his chance now to end this fight for good. Elof wasn't going to win.

He was.

So, he feigned unconsciousness. He could hear his father calling to him, telling him to get up, but he ignored the man. He also prayed that William would stay out of it because he had a feeling that if his father thought he was truly in danger of being killed, he would intervene. And he knew for a fact that William couldn't handle a blow from Elof. Therefore, he couldn't delay too long to act because the timing had to be just right.

He waited.

Patrick could hear Elof coming behind him, presumably with a sword or something else to kill him with. He could hear his father's pleas growing louder and he knew he had to take this chance because it would be his last. When he felt Elof at his feet, he suddenly grabbed the sword and rolled on to his back, lifting the sword just as Elof was lifting his own. But Elof's sword was over his head, preparing to deliver a deadly down stroke, while Patrick's sword had been lifted right into Elof's gut.

Patrick's sword made contact first.

Patrick struck and struck hard, driving his sword into Elof's belly as the man looked down at him with an oddly confused expression. It was as if he could hardly believe he had lost. Once the sword was in Elof's belly, Patrick lurched to his feet and removed it. Wielding it with both hands, he then swung it with all of his might straight at Elof's neck. The short sword was very sharp and, in one stroke, Elof's head went rolling off into the shallow waters of the river as the man's big body remained upright for a moment longer before collapsing into the dirt.

Winded, half-blinded, and badly beaten, Patrick turned to Magnus, who had a somewhat surprised look on his face at the swift turn of events. Patrick pointed the sword at Elof's collapsed body.

"He was the finest warrior I have ever faced," he panted. "Make sure he receives a funeral fit for his greatness."

With that, he took the sword in his hand and threw it as hard as he could, sailing it into the middle of the river. He then turned to his father, staggering in the man's direction and barely making it to him before collapsing in his arms. Between William and Paris, they lowered Patrick to a sitting position.

From the grunting sounds of battle, of men in a life or death struggle, to the sudden sounds of silence, the battle was finally over. The stunned Northmen were crowded around the body of Elof, unconcerned with the English knight who had just killed him. It had been a fair battle and an entertainingly brutal one. They had great respect for the Englishman who had bested their finest warrior.

But William wasn't concerned with any of that; he was more concerned with the son in his arms. Patrick might have been seriously beaten, but he was alive. He would recover. And that was all William cared about.

"Well done, Atty," he murmured soothingly, fighting off the tears of relief. "You did very well. You did what you had to do. Let us take you back to the castle now where your wife can tend your wounds."

"Patrick!"

They all heard the scream, turning to see Brighton rushing from the gates of the Water Tower, her skirt hiked up around her knees as she bolted. Scott, Troy, Kieran, Hector, and Alec were running behind her, all of them heading for Patrick, while still more men were rushing down the stairs from the castle, all of them rushing in Patrick's direction.

But Patrick didn't see anything other than Brighton. He was focused on her. Right now, she was the only thing in the world. She dropped to her knees beside him, her hands going to his face because she was too afraid to hug him, too afraid to cause him pain. Her face was flushed and her eyes were bright with unshed tears.

"My sweet, sweet husband," she breathed, unable to stop herself from kissing his swollen lips. "You are alive. Thank God, you are alive!"

Patrick nodded, a big, bloodied hand moving up to cup her face. "I am," he assured her softly. "Where did you come from?"

Brighton kissed him again, getting blood on her mouth. But she hardly cared. "From the tower above," she told him. "I saw the battle and prayed as hard as I could for God to defend you. He must have listened to me because He knew I could not live without you."

As Patrick and William and Paris watched, she hesitantly removed a tiny bejeweled dagger that had been tucked into her shift, holding it up so Patrick could see it. He recognized it as the one he'd purchased for her in Wooler. When Brighton saw his questioning expression, she explained.

"I have been carrying it with me ever since the Scots attacked Berwick," she said softly. "If I was to fall into their hands, I vowed that they would not take me alive. But now… now with your fight against the Northman, I kept it close to my heart because that is where it would end up had you not survived this fight. You and I belong to one another, Atty, in this life or in the next. Mayhap it is wrong to feel so, but I cannot help it. You are my life and my love. You are my everything."

Patrick was looking at the dagger, thinking several things at that moment, not the least of which was Brighton's determination not to live without him. As he stared at the dagger, a single tear fell from his red, damaged eyes and trickled down his cheek. Reaching out, he took the dagger from her.

"I would fight a thousand men as I did today if only to keep you safe and happy," he muttered. "The bond you and I share is too great to feel any other way. You are the heart that beats within me, Bridey. That will never change, in this life or in any other."

Brighton smiled tremulously as he stroked her cheek with his bloodied hand, a tender moment between them that was more powerful than a thousand suns. Two hearts that beat as one, two souls that were irrevocably entwined. Now, it was understood between them that their love went deeper than anything mortal.

It was ageless.

And it was a proud thing for William to witness. His greatest son, the man who was the embodiment of his legacy, had finally found the love that William had always wished for him. As Patrick leaned forward to capture Brighton in his embrace, William caught a glimpse of a shadow coming up behind them. He turned to see Magnus approach.

"I hope this means you feel my son is worthy of marrying your daughter, my lord," William said, rising to his feet. "He beat your man fairly. I hope you honor that."

Magnus nodded but his gaze was on Brighton, clearly quite curious about the woman. "I will, indeed, honor it," he said. "I know now that she is married to the best warrior in all of England. Possibly in the entire world."

Patrick and Brighton heard Magnus speak, both of them turning to look at him. For Brighton, it was a surreal moment gazing into eyes that looked much like hers. She stood up, facing the man who had given her life and inspecting him just as he was inspecting her. There was great curiosity and great emotion there; the air was full of it.

"M-my lord," she finally greeted. "It is an honor to meet you."

Magnus' face creased with the most joyful smile. "To hear your voice for the first time is like hearing the angels sing," he whispered, his throat tight with emotion. "You look so much like your mother. I can see her in everything about you."

Brighton smiled timidly. "I-I never knew her," she said. "I wish I had."

Magnus laughed softly, brushing away the tears that were starting to fall. "You speak as she did, too," he said. "She had the same catch in her words as you do."

Brighton's smile broadened. "I-I did not know."

"It was what made her so beautiful to me."

Truly sweet words that touched Brighton's heart. "Y-you loved her, then?"

"I did. Very much."

"I-I am very happy to know that."

Magnus' gaze lingered on her for a moment longer before looking to Patrick, who was still seated on the ground. Magnus couldn't help but notice that the man had hold of Brighton's skirt as if fearful that Magnus would still somehow try to take her away, even now. After so brutal a fight, the man was still only concerned with his wife. He wasn't even concerned for himself. Magnus crouched down beside him.

"Today, I witnessed greatness," he said to Patrick. "I witnessed *you*. My daughter is very fortunate to have you as her husband and you have my blessing for this marriage. I hope… I hope you will allow me to return some day to ensure that life has been prosperous to you both."

Patrick looked at the man, not an easy feat considering how painful his eyes were at the moment. "You are welcome at Berwick, always," he said. "In fact, we would be honored if you would stay this night and feast with us. Bridey and I never did have a wedding feast and it would be particularly appropriate if you were here to celebrate with us."

Magnus liked that idea a great deal. "You honor me," he said. "We will drink, you and I, and speak of our countries and our women. And I would like to speak to your father of his land and his women."

Patrick grinned as he turned to look at his father. "Do you hear that? He wants to speak of women."

William laughed softly, standing up as many hands moved to help Patrick to his feet. "There is only one woman for me, my lord, as there is only one woman for my son," he said. "A Norse princess he was fortunate enough to marry."

Patrick was on his feet, but barely. He leaned heavily on Scott and Troy, beloved brothers who rushed up to brace him. In fact, all of his men had flooded out of the castle and he was swarmed by his knights who had seen the battle, men that were vastly proud of their commander and concerned for his health. There was also great curiosity with the Northmen, who seemed to be more relaxed now that the battle for Magnus' daughter had finished. Even though they had lost one of their own, still, there didn't seem to be any bitterness.

It was the way of their world, after all.

Through the crowds of men, Brighton stayed by Patrick's side as he walked, gingerly, to the gates of the Water Tower. At that point, she had to stand aside while Scott, Troy, and Kieran helped Patrick navigate the stairs. As she stood and watched her husband make his way slowly up the steps, she felt a presence beside her and she turned to see Magnus standing next to her. He was with William but when their eyes met, he smiled at her. She smiled in return. When Magnus extended a hand to her, she placed hers in his warm, rough palm.

It was a gentle touch, father to daughter, for the very first time.

"Did you know that hawks have one mate for life?" he asked.

Brighton shook her head. "N-nay. I did not know that."

"It is true. It would seem your Nighthawk has found his mate for life in you."

Brighton's smile grew. Impulsively, she kissed him on the cheek and fled up the stairs, after her husband and the men who were helping him. Magnus remained at the bottom of the steps with William, watching her go. When he finally turned away, he caught William staring at him. Embarrassed, he smiled.

"She looks so much like her mother," he said. "I have difficulty taking my eyes from her."

William smiled in return. "Then her mother must have been an exquisite woman."

Magnus' expression grew wistful. "I still long for those days when Juliana and I were very much in love," he said. Then, he shook himself. "But it was not to be. I am glad our daughter found the love that we were denied."

William couldn't help but feel pity for the man who had loved and lost. "She is in very good hands with my son," he said. "You needn't worry about her, ever."

Magnus nodded, his expression warm with gratitude. But then, his smile faded and he held up a finger. "That is not entirely true," he said. "Who is this Richard Gordon that means to kill my daughter and where may I find him?"

William hesitated. "It is not only Richard Gordon, but the mother prioress as well."

"Both of them are still a danger to Brighton."

"Indeed, they are."

Magnus leaned his head in to William as if to whisper to the man, lowering his voice as he spoke. "I'll tend to Richard Gordon if you tend to the prioress."

To protect his beloved son and his beloved daughter-in-law, William couldn't refuse the offer. Patrick and Brighton had been through enough, in his opinion, and now it was time for him to help. He couldn't help Patrick as he faced against Elof, nor could he do anything else for the man. Patrick was too stubborn to allow it. But with the man badly wounded, too wounded to do for himself, William took the opportunity to take care of business. He was The Wolfe, after all. And this was de Wolfe business.

"Agreed."

Magnus discovered, through William, that the Gordon stronghold was north of Kelso. The River Tweed, in fact, ran through Kelso, and the river was wide enough to handle the longships. Magnus thanked William for the information and then shifted the subject to the barrels of mead and beer that he had in his hold, drink he wanted to bring to his daughter's wedding feast. It sounded like a wonderful idea and, soon enough, both Englishmen and Norsemen were hauling up barrels of drink to the great hall in preparation of what turned out to be a four-day feast.

It was a celebration like nothing any of the English had ever seen. As Paris put it, the Norsemen had come to merrymake like no other. As injured as he was, Patrick could only stay for just an hour or two of the celebration, but he could hear the revelry from his bedchamber as he slept on and off for the next several days. As Brighton sweetly tended to her wounded husband, she could hear the merriment, too.

Lost in their own loving little world, they hardly seemed to care about the noise in the great hall. The only thing that mattered to them was that, for the moment, all was right in their world again.

But there were still outstanding issues, things that Patrick vowed to tend to once he was well enough. Yet, he never had the chance. When Kevin arrived from London the next day with the fresh army, bearing missives from Henry that included the arrest order for Mother Prioress, William took the arrest warrant and departed Berwick at dawn the next day. Even though he told Patrick he was departing for home, that wasn't the truth. He left for Coldingham where he, Scott, Troy, Paris, and Kieran, along with about one hundred men-at-arms, arrested Ysabella Gordon and secured her for transport to York for her trial.

At the same time, Magnus departed his English hosts and traveled upriver, heading into the heart of England. It wasn't until a few weeks later that Patrick heard that the entire Gordon stronghold had been burned out and Richard Gordon killed. Everything the Gordons held dear had been wiped clean in a stunning attack. *Northman raiders*, some said, but it was a rumor. No one ever saw Northman raiders so far inland. Still, those at Berwick suspected the truth.

At least, Patrick and Brighton knew the truth.

If the King of the Northmen and The Wolfe of the Border had anything to say about it, the Nighthawk and his mate would know peace, forever more.

... and they did.

EPILOGUE

Haye Stronghold of Garvale
East Lothian
September 1270 A.D.

"JULIANA DE LA Haye, did ye say?"

Brighton nodded. "A-aye," she said. "My husband and son and I have traveled all the way from Berwick to see her. Can you tell me if she lives here?"

The man, older and bearing a big leather apron suggesting he was a servant, looked at Brighton rather dumbly. But he had answered the door of the large if not slightly run-down manor house of Garvale. It wasn't too far away from Berwick, a little over thirty miles, but travel had been a little slower with the carriage carrying Brighton and her infant son. That, and the fact that about four hundred men had accompanied them considering they were heading into Scotland.

Patrick hadn't wanted to take any chances with his wife and son on the journey even though he hadn't wanted to bring them on this journey at all. But Brighton had insisted. She had been insisting for the past year. Having come to know her father, she wanted to know her mother. She wanted her mother to meet their son.

So off to Scotland they went.

Garvale. According to the register at Coldingham, Juliana de la Haye had lived at Garvale Manor in East Lothian. It was the seat of the

Haye Clan in the lowlands of Scotland, so that was where Patrick had decided to start with the hunt for Brighton's mother. Garvale Manor was more of a castle because it had a wall around it and two enormous towers on one side of the manse, the entire structure built with red sandstone that had worn to a dirty yellowish-gray over the years.

As Brighton spoke to the servant at the door, Patrick stood back behind his wife, in the yard of the manse, holding their son in his enormous arms as Brighton tried to find out anything she could about her mother. He would have been irritated with the situation had he not been preoccupied making faces at his six-month-old son, Markus, who had the most delightful grin. A happy baby, he smiled at everyone and was quite possibly the most adorable baby ever born with his dark hair and blue eyes. At least, Brighton and Patrick thought so. Markus' grandparents, William and Jordan, were simply wild about the lad.

So were Patrick's knights. A little heir among them turned most of them into doting fools. They had all come with the family on the journey to Scotland, all except Anson, who had remained in command at Berwick. But Kevin and Apollo had come, as had Damien and Colm. Surprisingly, it was the serious-minded Colm who was the most enamored over the baby.

Even now, he stood next to Patrick, making faces at the child and then pretending to be serious if he thought anyone was watching. He and Patrick kept the baby entertained as Brighton tried to uncover information with a man who seemed to be very confused with her questions. In fact, Patrick had finally had enough of the man's idiocy so he handed the baby over to Colm, who took him happily, and went to stand with his wife.

"I am Patrick de Wolfe, commander of Berwick Castle," he said, butting into the conversation that was going on. "This is my wife, Lady de Wolfe. Her mother is Juliana de la Haye and we were led to believe that Lady Juliana lived here at some point. Where is your master? Bring him to me so that I may speak with him."

Orders from an enormous knight were not meant to be disobeyed and the man in the leather apron scampered off. As he ran, Brighton looked at her husband with irritation.

"I was handling the situation just fine," she said.

He peered down his nose at her. "I could see that from the way he was rushing to do your bidding."

Her eyes narrowed at him. "He would have if you had only been patient."

Folding his enormous arms across his chest, he bent down so he could look her in the face. "I *have* been patient," he whispered loudly. "I have been patient about this entire affair. I was patient when you demanded to come to Scotland and…"

"Demanded?"

"Aye, *demanded.* And I was patient when you wanted to bring my son because you could not leave him behind."

"I am still feeding him! He is too young to be left behind!"

"You did not have to come now. You could have waited."

Brighton's entire face was a one big scowl that was now bordering on hurt. Too upset to argue with him, she simply turned away. He could see that he'd injured her feelings. Forcing himself to relent, which was difficult considering he knew he was in the right, he put his arm around her and pulled her to him.

"I am sorry," he said, pretending to be contrite when he wasn't in the least. "I did not mean to upset you. But you know I did not want you to come in the first place. This is something that could have easily been settled with a missive."

Now Brighton was bordering on tears. "But I want to see her," she whispered tightly. "I could not see her if I sent a missive."

Patrick was feeling the least bit guilty now. He didn't understand her drive to see a woman who had abandoned her at birth but perhaps that was because his own mother hadn't. He still had her, and his father, and was secure in his relationship with them. Kissing the top of her head as an apology, he tried to hug her but she didn't want to be hugged. In fact, she pulled away from him and now he was the one feeling badly. But the interplay between them was interrupted when a man suddenly appeared at the door.

"Who are ye?" he demanded in a throaty, ill-sounding voice. "What do ye want here?"

Both Patrick and Brighton looked at the man, seeing an individual who was an ashen gray color, with long, dirty hair and dressed in woolen clothing that looked as if he had been rolling around in the mud in it. He coughed again, spraying something out of his mouth. Patrick immediately pulled Brighton well back from the man. If he was sick, Patrick didn't want either of them to contract it.

"My name is Patrick de Wolfe," Patrick said steadily. "I am the commander of Berwick Castle and this is my wife, Brighton. My wife has come seeking Juliana de la Haye. Do you know her?"

The man's eyes narrowed at them both, suspiciously. "Why do ye want her?" he rasped. "Why have ye come?"

Patrick wasn't sure he should divulge everything. After all, telling someone that he had come seeking a woman who had borne a bastard child was a rather touchy piece of information. As he thought on a way to tactfully explain their presence, Brighton spoke up.

"I-I am her daughter," she said simply. "She left me at Coldingham Priory twenty years ago and the nuns raised me, but I have come to meet my mother. Is she here?"

The man in the doorway suddenly lost all of his annoyance. He stared at Brighton, his expression going slack, and Patrick could feel himself tensing for what was to come. If the man tried to verbally abuse his wife in any way, he was going to get his neck snapped. So, he waited; they both waited, until the man in the doorway seemed to overcome his shock.

"Ye… ye lived at Coldingham?" he finally asked, his voice considerably less hostile.

Brighton nodded. "Aye."

The man seemed to stare at her an inordinately long time. "Juliana's lass?"

"Aye!"

"Ye look like her."

Brighton's heart soared with hope. "P-please… do you know her, then?"

He nodded. Then, he lowered his gaze and pulled out a filthy kerchief from the top of his tunic, wiping his nose and eyes with it. When he finally spoke, he was looking at the kerchief.

"Lass," he said, "ye dunna know what ye're askin'."

Brighton looked at Patrick in confusion before responding. "W-what do you mean?" she asked. "You *do* know her, don't you?"

The man continued to wipe at his nose as if pondering the question, which put Brighton increasingly on edge. The hope so recently in her heart was fading quickly.

"I havena heard that name in a long time," he muttered. "A very long time. *Juliana.*"

Even Patrick was becoming anxious. "Answer my wife. Do you know Juliana?"

The man stopped wiping his nose and looked up at them both. "Aye, I do," he said. "She's me sister."

"Is she here?"

"She's dead."

Brighton's heart sank and her hope was completely dashed. She sighed heavily, looking up at Patrick with such sad eyes that he immediately felt very sorry for her. He put his arm around her, comfortingly, feeling sadness that their quest for her mother had come to an abrupt end. Not that he was surprised, but it was still sad.

"Then I thank you for your time," he said quietly, pulling his reluctant wife away from the door. "We are sorry to have disturbed you."

"Dunna ye want tae know what happened?"

Brighton wouldn't be so easily led away when the old man asked that question. She paused. "I-I do," she said eagerly. "Would you please tell me?"

From the way the old man asked the question, Patrick wasn't so sure it was a good idea for Brighton to know what had become of her mother. But he wouldn't pull her away. He feared she would resent him if he did. She had been eager to know of her mother for well over a year, ever since her separation from Coldingham, so Patrick thought she'd better hear all of it. They'd come this far. Therefore, he paused right along with her, standing next to her as they waited for the old man to tell them.

It wasn't long in coming.

"I'm Gilbert, Juliana's brother," he said. "I was here when Juliana returned from the land of the Northmen, pregnant with a bastard child. With *ye*. Before ye were born, she tried tae run away because she knew our da wouldna let her keep the bairn. But me da… he was a devil, he was. He brought her back and locked her away until she had her child."

Brighton was listening to the tale with great distress. She could feel Patrick's hand on her back, comfortingly. "A-and then… then he forced her to give me to Coldingham?"

Gilbert nodded. "Right after ye were born," he said. "He made her go. She was so weak; too weak tae travel but he made her go. I went with her. I was there when she handed ye tae the mother prioress."

A mother prioress who was now locked away at York, doing a lifetime of penitence for her crime. Brighton actually found it both interesting and validating to finally hear of her delivery to Coldingham from someone who had been there, but she had no intention of telling Gilbert what they had actually delivered her into – into a plot of vengeance. Nay, she wouldn't tell him that. There was no reason to. It was all in the past now.

"A-and then what?" she asked.

Gilbert leaned against the stone door jamb, weary in his recollection of a distant memory. "She came back here and me da locked her away again," he said. "She was kept in the room as punishment for her sins, never leavin'. But me da… he was still seekin' tae make an alliance with her, with someone who wouldna know of her shame. He finally found an alliance with the MacNaughton Clan far tae the north, where no one would know of me sister's sin and of her bearin' a bastard. But me sister had a mind o' her own… she refused tae marry the man and the day before she was tae leave for the north, threw herself from the north tower. Killed herself, she did, and sometimes on moonless nights, ye can hear her screams as she plummets to the earth."

Brighton gasped, a hand flying to her mouth in horror as Patrick simply closed his eyes with regret. Deep-seated regret that he permitted Brighton to hear the fate of her mother. He silently cursed the old man, knowing that those words would be the last and only memory Brighton had of her mother. In fact, he resisted the urge to strangle that foolish old man.

"O-oh… no," Brighton gasped. "That is a horrible tale. My poor mother!"

Tears filled her eyes and Patrick came up behind her, putting his arms around her to comfort her. Brighton pressed her face into his tunic, turning her head away from the old man so he wouldn't see her weep.

But Patrick wasn't so subtle; he looked at Gilbert pointedly. "You did not have to be so blunt," he said, his voice low and threatening. "My wife has come here to know of her mother's fate, not of her grisly end."

Gilbert wasn't intimidated by the big English knight; he simply shrugged. "If she dinna want tae know all of it, then she shouldna have come."

There was truth to that but Patrick was too angry to comment. His concern now was to remove Brighton and head for home. Now that she knew the truth, hopefully, her curiosity would be satisfied.

But Brighton wouldn't be led away quite so easily. When she realized Patrick was trying to turn her away, she gently pushed from his embrace, wiping at her eyes as she looked at Gilbert again.

"C-can you really hear her screams?" she asked. "From the tower, I mean. Is it true?"

Gilbert had to admit that he was feeling some pity for the young woman. He thought he'd lost that ability long ago, but looking at the daughter of his sister and seeing the resemblance, he began to feel compassion for Juliana again. Compassion for a young woman he had been so fond of.

"Aye," he told her. "I've heard them meself. Juliana was me sister and I… I loved her. She was a good lass but she fell in love with a Dane. She loved him tae the end. That was why she wouldna marry the MacNaughton. Dyin'… it was her only way out."

That news tore out Brighton's heart; her mother had loved Magnus until the end, just as Magnus had repeatedly spoke of his love for Juliana. Two lovers who could never be together, who had produced a daughter with that love. Brighton was coming to understand that she was the product of a love that would never die, something powerful that still lived on. It lived in her and now in little Markus. In that thought, she gave herself comfort.

True love never dies.

"I-I know Magnus," she said. "The Dane you speak of, the one that Juliana loved… I know him. He is a good man and we have been able to establish our family bonds. But it was tragic that he and Juliana could not marry. He never stopped loving her, either."

Gilbert's sympathy was in his features. The kerchief came out again and he began wiping his nose. "Then I will tell her that," he said quietly. "On the next moonless night, I will tell her that the Dane still loves her. Mayhap that will give her spirit some rest."

"I-is she buried close by that I might visit her grave?"

That question seemed to hit Gilbert particularly hard. "The priests wouldna allow her tae be buried in the church yard," he said. "We buried her outside the yard beneath an oak tree. The grave was meant tae be unmarked but I went back later and put a big rock atop her grave. If ye turn the rock over, ye'll see a cross I carved intae it. Even if me da and the priests were willin' tae forget her, I couldna. She deserved better."

Brighton was touched at the length Juliana's brother went to for her. She could also see how it pained the man to speak on her. Truth was, it was painful for her, too. She wasn't entirely sure how she was going to tell Magnus what had become of the woman he loved but she would have to think of something. Politely, she thanked Gilbert for the information.

"Y-you have been kind and gracious to tell me what became of my mother," she said. "May I ask you one final question?"

"Aye."

"M-my name...," she began hesitantly. "She told the nuns at Coldingham that my name was Brighton de Favereux. Do you know why she decided upon that name?"

Gilbert smiled faintly. "Yer birthname was a Northman name and she knew she couldna send ye tae the priory with that name, so she changed it," he said. "De Favereux is from our Norman grandmother, our mum's mother. And Brighton... when we were young, our da took us tae the south. He was a bit of a wanderer and felt that we should see somethin' of the world, so he took us all the way south tae a place called Brighton. It was by the sea. Juliana said it was the most beautiful place she'd ever seen, just like heaven. I suppose that's why she called ye that – because ye were the most beautiful thing she'd ever seen, just like heaven."

It was a sweetly poignant explanation of her name and Brighton couldn't help but smile. Patrick had heard it, too, and he smiled at her, glad to see that something in all of this had given her a small measure of joy. For all of its sorrow, perhaps this trip hadn't been without a tiny measure of happiness, after all.

"Thank you again for your time," Patrick said, reaching out to take his wife's hand. "Since you are my wife's uncle, should you ever need anything, do not hesitate to send word to Berwick Castle. We are family, after all."

That thought hadn't really occurred to Gilbert. His eyebrows lifted in shock. "Me?" he asked. "A kin tae a Sassenach? They'll run me out of Scotland!"

He said it in jest and Patrick grinned at the man, gently pulling

Brighton away from the entry and back out to the yard where their escort waited. Gilbert was still snorting with laughter as he closed the door. Patrick and Brighton made their way towards little Markus, who quickly recognized his parents. He began to crow in delight and kick his little feet as Brighton reached out to take her son from Colm.

"Well?" Colm said. "Did you find out what you wanted to know?"

Patrick eyed Brighton, unsure how to respond, but she was kissing the baby, wiping the drool from his chin. Then, her attention moved inevitably to the manse and the massive towers on one side of it.

"Atty?" she asked. "Which tower would be the north tower?"

Patrick looked at the towers, glancing up at the sun and then to the landscape around them. Rolling green hills and bright skies greeted him as he determined their orientation.

"That one," he said. "The one closest to us."

Brighton craned her neck back to look at the tower, which was at least four stories high and possibly more. She really couldn't tell. After a split-second of indecision, she began walking towards the tower with the baby still in her arms. Patrick watched her go.

"Where is she going?" Colm asked. "Did she discover anything about her mother?"

Patrick nodded, his gaze never leaving his wife. "She did," he said. "I will tell you about it later. Gather the men, now. We must be ready to leave."

As Colm went off to prepare the escort, Patrick continued to stand there and watch Brighton as she walked all the way to the tower and just stood there, looking up at it. He knew why and thought that it would be best if she dealt with this aspect of it alone. In reconciling herself to her mother's tragic death, that was something she had to do on her own. But he would be here if she needed him.

He would always be here for her if she needed him.

And Brighton knew that. She knew Patrick had not come with her to the tower out of respect and she appreciated it. She was intensely curious about the tower her mother threw herself from, even going so far as to inspect the ground at the base of the tower where her mother had undoubtedly landed in a heap. It was intensely heartbreaking to think that she had been cursed to repeat her tragic death every time there was a moonless night, condemned to throw herself from the top of the tower for eternity. Perhaps that was her penitence for her crime. As the baby cooed and chewed on his fingers, Brighton found herself gazing up at the top of the tower.

"M-Mother?" she said quietly. "'Tis me. 'Tis Brighton. I came here looking for you but was told of your tragic circumstances. I simply wanted to tell you that I forgive you everything. I know you took me to Coldingham because you had no choice. It was not your fault. I did not have a bad life there, in fact. The nuns took care of me. They educated me. Although I did not expect to marry, I have been fortunate enough to have married a man I love deeply. He is the most wonderful man in the entire world and we are very happy together. And look – we have a son. His name is Markus. We let Magnus choose the name. Did you hear me? Magnus, the man you love and my father, chose our son's name. I hope you can hear me because I want you to know that he never stopped loving you. Even though he has a wife and children, you are his first love. He comes to visit us regularly and he is a truly remarkable man. I thought you would like to know. We are all happy, Mother. I wish you could be part of this joy but my prayer for you is that you find some peace."

The only response was the sound of the wind as it whistled through the stones of the tower. No ghostly motherly appearance, no voice from beyond. Simply silence. But Brighton didn't mind; she actually found a great deal of comfort in speaking to the last place her mother ever saw alive. Somehow, it was cathartic to her soul.

"P-please, Mother, find peace," she said again, more softly now. "I do not want you to be sad or lonely any longer. Although I did not know you, I love you and will only speak fondly of you. My son will grow up knowing the story of his grandmother who loved very deeply. Be happy, my sweet mother, wherever you are."

There were tears in her eyes as she turned from the tower, carrying the baby back to the escort that was waiting for her. But the tears weren't completely those of sadness; there were some tears of joy, as well. Joy for a mother who understood what it was to love deeply and completely. Brighton hoped that wherever her mother's spirit happened to be, that she had heard her.

That was her prayer.

And it was a prayer answered. Beginning with the next moonless night, the screams were never heard from again.

ꕥ THE END ꕥ

About Kathryn Le Veque

Medieval Just Got Real.

KATHRYN LE VEQUE is a USA TODAY Bestselling author, an Amazon All-Star author, and a #1 bestselling, award-winning, multi-published author in Medieval Historical Romance and Historical Fiction. She has been featured in the NEW YORK TIMES and on USA TODAY's HEA blog. In March 2015, Kathryn was the featured cover story for the March issue of InD'Tale Magazine, the premier Indie author magazine. She was also a quadruple nominee (a record!) for the prestigious RONE awards for 2015.

Kathryn's Medieval Romance novels have been called 'detailed', 'highly romantic', and 'character-rich'. She crafts great adventures of love, battles, passion, and romance in the High Middle Ages. More than that, she writes for both women AND men – an unusual crossover for a romance author – and Kathryn has many male readers who enjoy her stories because of the male perspective, the action, and the adventure.

On October 29, 2015, Amazon launched Kathryn's Kindle Worlds Fan Fiction site WORLD OF DE WOLFE PACK. Please visit Kindle Worlds for Kathryn Le Veque's World of de Wolfe Pack and find many action-packed adventures written by some of the top authors in their genre using Kathryn's characters from the de Wolfe Pack series. As Kindle World's FIRST Historical Romance fan fiction world, Kathryn Le Veque's World of de Wolfe Pack will contain all of the great storytelling you have come to expect.

Kathryn loves to hear from her readers. Please find Kathryn on Facebook at Kathryn Le Veque, Author, or join her on Twitter @kathrynleveque, and don't forget to visit her website at www.kathrynleveque.com.

Made in the USA
Columbia, SC
05 August 2019